THE SORCERESS OF
LYCASTER

For all the lionesses finding their roar,
And all the bulls who dreamed of more.

Author's Note

This story contains dark fantasy themes and is not recommended for readers under age 18. Although the content is written to uplift and empower survivors of mental illnesses and abuse, reader discretion is advised.

Content Warning: alcohol abuse; anxiety; blood; conquest of nations; death of a parent; depression; disordered eating; emotional manipulation; enslavement; familial abuse; fantasy violence; generational trauma; memories of child abuse; grief; memories of childbirth; memories of intimate partner violence involving strangulation; mention of prior pregnancy loss; misogyny; murder; non-fatal overdose; non-graphic depiction of sexual assault; nudity; profanity; post-traumatic stress disorder; public execution; realistic depiction of the cycle of abuse; sexual assault by proxy; sexual content; substance abuse; violence; and war.

Dukedom of Lycaster
N
W   E
S
Fraleigh's Palace
Nordingaard Mountain
Bloodstone Fortress
Ravenwood
Hyton Palace
Bloodstone
Ravenwood Manor
Meadowshyre
Hyton
Odeneye Lake
Elvar
Amberfield
Western Sea
Mydina
Pebblebrooke
Thornebow

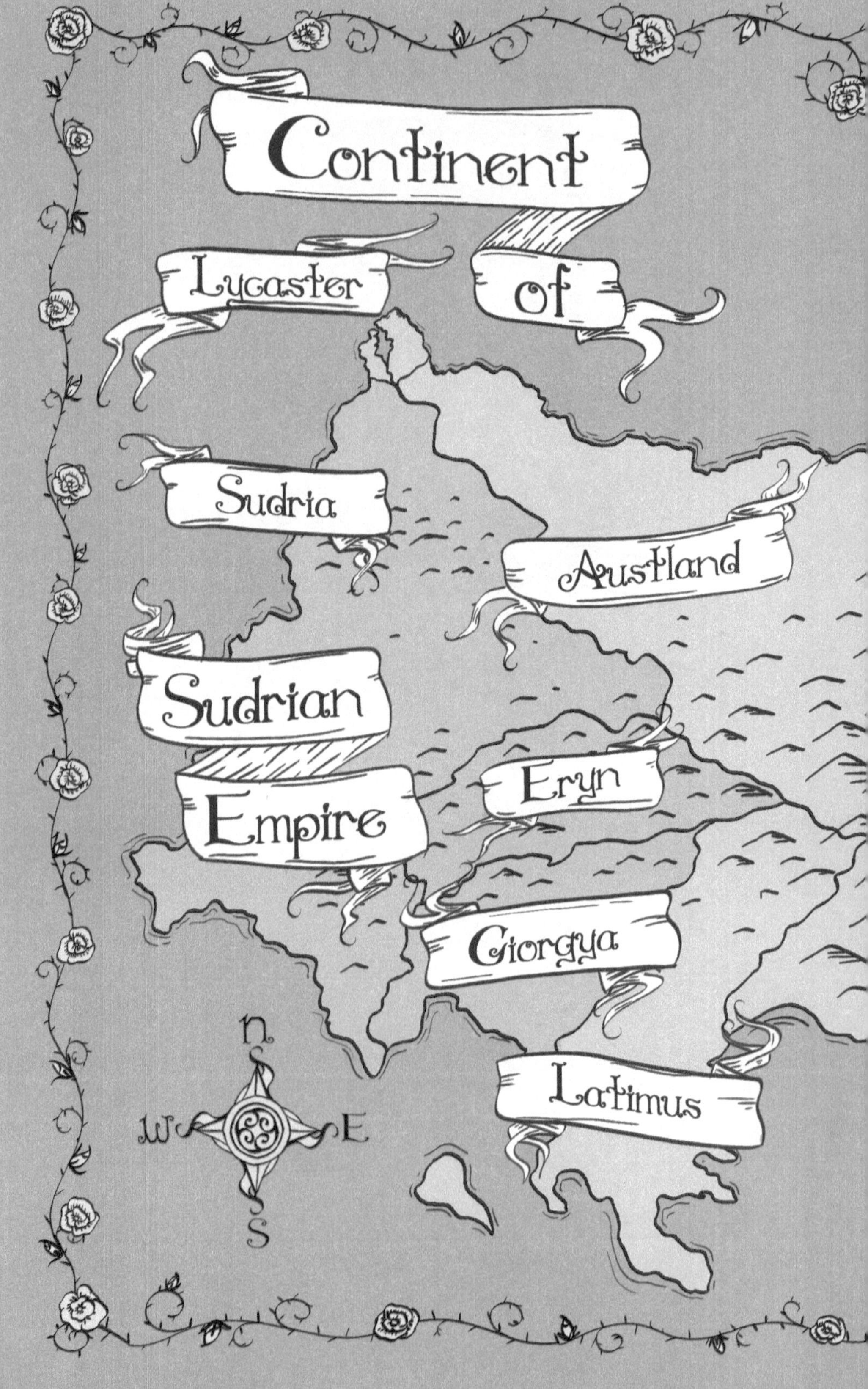

Continent
of
Lycaster
Sudria
Austland
Sudrian
Empire
Eryn
Giorgya
Latimus
N
W
E
S

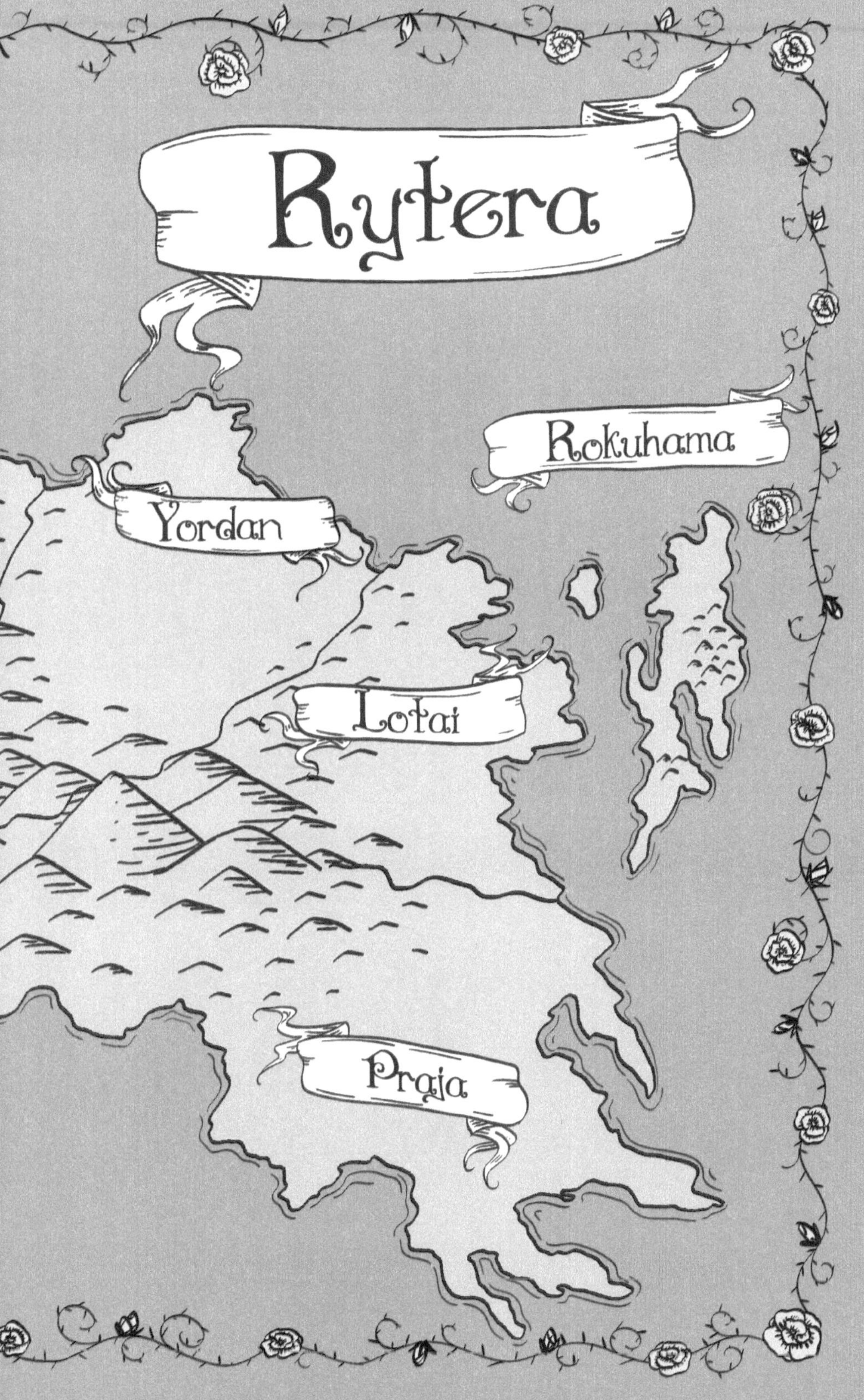

Rytera
Rokuhama
Yordan
Lotai
Praja

Prologue

I could not breathe until the Hytons disappeared.

As the golden carriage pulled away, ribbons of sunlight broke through the clouds over Ravenwood Manor.

I basked in the sunlight as the memory of Derrick's sweet words from mere minutes ago filled my mind. *"Seven years is a long time, Serafina, but I am counting down the days until I see you again."*

Warmth filled my chest like a flickering hearth and I smiled. The heir to the Dukedom of Lycaster was mine.

Before Derrick and his father had visited the manor, I was trapped in a cage of circumstance. My older brothers were dead and Ravenwood province was doomed to desolation and poverty.

But Derrick was my key out of the cage. If he married me, I would be the next Duchess of Lycaster. If I had that power, I could save the province. All I had to do was make him love me.

If he loved me, he would free me.

I ran back into the manor to tell my parents the good news. I was a mere fourteen years old, but I was going to save the House of Ravenwood.

My footsteps echoed through the dark halls as I rushed to Father's study. I pushed open the cracked door to find Father at his desk with his head buried in his folded arms. A thick black ledger was open in front of him.

Just as I was about to cheer up Father with the promising future I had crafted, the weight of the darkened study crashed on my shoulders. The smell of fresh ink filled the air. A piece of parchment laid on top of the ledger, stamped with the Hyton seal.

A deal with the Duke of Lycaster, but for what?

My first step into the study creaked a floorboard and Father's head slowly rose.

I swallowed. "Father, I can help the family. I already have a plan to—"

"Never you mind about that." His glassy eyes fell to the shining blue wax of the Hyton seal. "Let the…men handle things."

I knitted my brows. "But I am the last Ravenwood and I can—"

"Go find your mother, Little Ember." He still refused to look at me. "She is out in the garden."

I bit my tongue. Fine. Father was the Baron of Ravenwood, a man of business. What would he know of the importance of marriage?

My footsteps were quieter as I walked through the manor to find my mother. She would be proud of me, at least. She had wanted me to charm Derrick and I did. I had eased his nerves, gained his confidence, and even stole a little of his affection.

I pictured our last night together—in the garden enjoying treats I had snuck from the kitchen. Starlight crested Derrick's cheeks as he laughed. His eyes were both as dark and as beautiful as the blue evening sky.

I traced the back of my hand with my thumb—where the memory of Derrick's kiss lingered like a promise—and the little spot of heat in my chest warmed.

I pushed on the door into the garden and caught a glimpse of Mother's dark hair through the shrubs. Pebbles crunched beneath my feet as I ran after her.

She turned as I caught up with her. With her toes in the dirt and her foraging basket tucked in the crook of her elbow, she was only my mother and not the Baroness of Ravenwood. She had abandoned the beautiful mask she had worn with Duke Hyton over the last fortnight and a hard look burned in her eyes.

I straightened my back. "I charmed him, just like you wanted."

She did not even smile. "Did you?"

What was wrong with her? Maybe she just needed to hear what I had done. "Derrick kissed my hand and said he was going to—"

"Lord Hyton," Mother said firmly. "You refer to him as Lord Hyton."

My voice hardened. "He asked me to call him by his given name."

Mother's mouth formed a fine line. A breeze rustled the leaves of the tall shrubs around us.

"You want control now that your brothers are gone, I understand," she said with a low voice, "but you cannot get your hopes up—"

"I am not getting my hopes up!" I snapped. "I know better than to do that after you told me that Erik and Endre would come back from the mountain—"

"Forget what I told you before." Mother's tone carried a cudgel of finality, but her eyes lacked any explanation. "Lord Hyton is not yours to choose. None of the men are, for any of us."

I gripped my skirt so tightly my fingernails nearly tore holes through the wool. "But you wanted me to look beautiful for him, and wear perfume, and smile—"

"And you had better do it." Mother tightened her dark green shawl around her shoulders. "Your survival hinges on his good favor. And his father's."

The warmth in my chest faded as the backs of my eyes stung.

How could I have executed every move perfectly and it was still not enough for her? How was it not enough to save me?

Mother turned toward the woods but kept her emerald eyes on me. "But good favor does not give you control. Keep your head down and your mouth shut."

She headed to the trees to stuff her basket full of mushrooms and I turned on my heel back into the garden. I shoved past the iron gate. Walls of green shrubs stretched into the sky around me.

I crashed to the ground and hid in the shade of a towering bush. Cold, grey numbness had trapped me for weeks, but now noise filled my head and my arms. My body was a needle, ready to poke and stab.

I would show them who was in control.

I slowly uncurled my tight fist on top of the garden path. I picked up a pebble and rolled it in my fingers, picturing that I was smashing that red spot of heat in my chest—that *weakness* Derrick had left within me. I dropped that pebble and picked up a larger one, mentally stacking it on top of the other.

Over and over I picked up pebbles and crushed the weakness. I was in control. My fate was *mine* to choose.

I threw the last pebble down with a crash, but the tension did not release. My breath escaped my nose in short puffs.

I hated the Hytons. I hated my parents. I hated my brothers for leaving me.

I hated the world that made me small.

Part One

Blood

and

Snow

Chapter One
Red

All I saw was red.

The frigid air stung my skin, but my blood blazed as I ran through the snow. My breath escaped my clenched teeth in short curls of mist. I gripped the Hyton dagger at my side as I chased my prey.

Daigen—the horned red monster of Nordingaard mountain.

He was supposed to make my fifteen-foot-tall husband the size of a normal man, but now, he was going to rescue Riyan from the Queen of the Giants. She had already taken my brothers from me, she was *not* going to take Riyan too.

Daigen sprinted farther ahead, his hooved legs moving faster through the snow than my short ones could carry me. His shock of white hair flowed out behind him as he disappeared behind a rock formation.

I turned as I followed him, finding a trail of hoofprints in the snow that led straight into the rocks with no way out.

I held my breath and listened for any movement. My golden blood bond twisted around my chest and cried out with every thump of my heart: *Save Riyan. Save Riyan. Save Riyan.*

I slowly stepped closer to the wall of rocks, scanning the grey and white formation for any trace of red. I reached past my blood bond and channeled the magic of the flaming white diamond in my heart.

Nothing responded. My magic was silent, but so were my footsteps.

I stalked closer as my grip on the dagger tightened. My eyes snapped to a boulder that moved up and down—it was breathing.

A smile crept up my lips. Daigen was a trickster, but turning invisible was not enough to evade me.

I reached into the depths of my throat to draw out my most commanding voice. "I caught you, beast. You have nowhere to hide."

Daigen's ugly red face appeared as his grey cloak of invisibility fanned away from him. He was even more terrifying up close. Shining black horns grew from his brow and curved toward his long hair. Thick, dark eyebrows framed his sharp golden eyes. His hands ended in claws instead of fingers.

Daigen's mouth contorted into a snarl. "You caught nothing, mortal. Do you really think a little dagger could subdue me?"

I twisted the dagger so it reflected moonlight in his eyes. "Do you really want to find out?"

His snarl turned into a smirk. "Mean little girls with flowers in their hair don't scare me."

I stopped myself from reaching up to the crown of blue flowers on my head—one of Riyan's last gifts to me. How dare that monster insult it?

The golden blood bond twisted in my chest. *Push harder. Save Riyan.*

I whirled the dagger to point at his throat. "The Queen of the Giants took my husband. You *will* help me get him back, or else."

Daigen crossed his arms. "No." A smile spread across his face. "What a silly little threat—you can't kill me. No one can."

I stepped closer until my dagger was inches from his crimson neck. "Then we will see if immortals can feel pain."

A flash of metal pulled my eyes away from his face—a curved knife was in his claws. The notches in the metal that formed faded runes must have been ancient, but the blade's edge was as sharp as a new day.

"You should never assume you're the only one with a knife," Daigen said. "How about this—let's drop our weapons at the same time and then we talk like civilized monsters."

Moonlit snowflakes fell around us. I channeled my magic, trying to force the red monster's blood to ignite like I had with a giant, but nothing responded.

Why was my magic failing? Was he just that much stronger than me?

Though questions made my heart race, my blood bond pumped courage through my veins.

I could not be afraid. I had to save Riyan.

Daigen shifted his weight. "I *promise* not to hurt you. On the count of three, we drop the blades. Ready?"

A curt nod was all I gave him.

He held the knife out to the side. "One."

I did the same. "Two."

Daigen smiled. "Three."

Just as Daigen dropped his knife, I plunged my dagger into his exposed side. The dagger tore his ragged wool tunic as I wedged the blade between his ribs.

His fangs gleamed in the moonlight as he hissed in pain. I yanked the dagger out with a grunt and his blood dripped off the blade like rubies.

"*Litlnadr!*" Daigen shouted as he clutched his wound.

No time to figure out what he had just said. I sprinted forward, ready to stab him into submission, when the icy air wrapped around my wrist and held me back.

My magic pushed against Daigen's enchantment but was too weak to throw him off.

Daigen's claws splayed out toward me and the air around my wrist trembled under the force of his enchantment. No more blood dripped from his shirt—his magic blood had already healed him.

His fangs gleamed as he smiled. "You really think I am going to help you if you keep stabbing me? You're not thinking this through, how unlike you."

My bond blazed golden fire in my chest. All I could think of was getting Riyan back, no matter the cost.

My furious breath puffed out in a swirl of mist as I tugged on Daigen's invisible hold. "I will not take 'no' for an answer. We are going to rescue Riyan, make him the size of a normal man, and then he and I will finally seal our damn blood bond!"

"Why should I care about you sealing that putrid blood bond?" He barely blinked as I struggled against his enchantment with all my might. "Who told you to seek out the scary red monster of the mountain?"

I pulled back, my feet dragging in the snow but my arm staying firmly in place. "Rosaline." I hissed. "She said—"

"Is that who Fraleigh's servant is these days?" He clicked his tongue. "How *naughty* of her to mention me. The Great Sorceress of Nordingaard doesn't want me anywhere near mortals."

I yanked my arm back so hard I might have dislocated it. "I do not care what Fraleigh wants!" Fraleigh had refused to help us. She could burn in the high halls of hell. "We are going to Ganora and—"

The snow suddenly swallowed my feet. I only had enough time to look down before it shoved me backward.

The back of my head hit the cold powder and I opened my eyes to the waning moon against the dark sky.

Daigen's voice cut over the wind. "So demanding and yet you don't even know what you truly want." His hooves crunched in the snow. "You don't even know who you are asking, either."

The snow pushed me back up to my feet. The frigid air wrapped around my neck, holding me in place while the snow gripped my ankles.

He canted his head. "I could suffocate you right now and you're not even trying to get out of it." His thick brows knitted. "What if I tried to turn you into a white bear to match your House emblem, Baron Serafina Bloodstone? Would you try to run then?"

I clenched my teeth as my blood turned dark, like Daigen had invaded my body and snuffed out the light. The golden blood bond pushed back, screaming through my muscles to fight the darkness.

Save Riyan. Save Riyan.

"Still no sense of self-preservation. How disappointing." Daigen smirked. "Fine, you want my help…but what would you give me in exchange for my services?"

The gilded flare of the bond pushed my answer out of my strained throat. "Anything!"

His enchantment forced my arms against my sides and I dropped the dagger into the snow.

"What a predictable answer," Daigen said cooly. "Anything? Would you tear down Hyton Palace brick by brick?"

The Hytons were monsters. "Yes."

Daigen's eyes flicked down to my skirt. "What about those two golden House pins? Would you give me control of the North?"

What good was ruling the North without Riyan to rule it with? "Yes."

Daigen shook his head. "That doesn't sound right, not after everything I have heard about you."

I struggled against his hold. "What do you mean? Take the damn House pins and take me to Riyan!"

He slowly circled me. "The Serafina I heard of would have never let go of that power. She would have lied and squirmed until she could shelter in the cozy embrace of the Hyton bulls."

The wind screamed through the craggy rocks and Daigen smiled. "I have my price."

My chest rose and fell with my strained breath. "Name it."

Suddenly the wind went still and Daigen's eyes gleamed. "Your blood bond."

His magic released me and I gasped. My feet staggered in the snow, but my hands flew to the center of my chest.

"Didn't expect that?" Daigen lowered his hand. "I bet you've experienced a lot of things you didn't expect over the past eight days. Sudden attraction to a stranger. Erasure of reasonable fear. An unexplained desire to touch."

Daigen's lies could not fool me. I had not known Riyan for long, but he was so handsome, of course I was attracted to him. I was afraid at first because he was nine feet tall, but I overcame that because I—

"Do you really love him?" Daigen's wicked smile did not falter. "Or is Fraleigh's enchantment doing exactly what it was supposed to do—push you to feel *everything* you needed to consummate the union?"

I refused to believe him, but how did he know what I was thinking? I had heard Fraleigh's voice in my mind before, but that would mean…

"Get out of my head!" I shouted.

"You let me in."

His golden eyes flicked up and I followed them. An invisible rope that I sensed through my magic sprung out from between my eyes and connected me to Daigen. His eyes glittered like he had discovered treasure.

I swatted at that rope, but my hand just passed through the falling snowflakes.

Daigen clicked his tongue. "Can't break the connection, not when the little Serafina in your head still wants help. Wants the truth. Wants—"

"Enough!" I just wanted his aid, not to be flayed open and *seen*.

He raised an eyebrow. "So you accept?"

My marriage enchantment was the most precious possession I had. Not only was it the only barrier keeping me from being the property of the Hytons under Lycaster law, it was the tie that bound my heart to Riyan's.

Because of my blood bond, I could feel again. I could cry again. I could *breathe* again.

And Daigen wanted to take it away?

I kneaded my crimson wool cape, smelling the lingering scent of nectar and wheat and the memory of Riyan's warmth filled my chest. Even as I savored Riyan's smell, Daigen's words took root in the back of my mind.

No, I could not even consider his accusation. I loved Riyan. Fraleigh's marriage enchantment had nothing to do with it. I loved his dimpled smile, and his twilight eyes, and his voice…

The memory of his voice, both rich and smooth as satin, filled my mind. *"Anything you want, you can have it! Just let Serafina go!"*

I let go of my cape and let out a pensive breath. Riyan had not questioned the price of my freedom with the Queen of the Giants. How could I question the price of his?

Whatever Daigen had planned to do with my blood bond…Riyan's freedom was worth it.

My shoulders sagged but I raised my chin, looking Daigen in the eyes. My voice was sharp as my blade that lay in the snow. "Take it."

Daigen let out a breath and dropped his hands. "What a good, sacrificial heart." He raised his claws again. "Brace yourself."

I raised my chest and closed my eyes. Hopefully Riyan would not feel any pain on his side of the bond.

"Open your mouth," he ordered.

Slowly, I parted my lips. A claw colder than the icy wind shoved past my tongue and down my throat.

My hands flew to my neck. I held my trembling throat as the claw gripped that golden rope around my heart.

The claw pulled.

Dark ice burned my insides and I screamed. Just when I thought the pain could not be worse, the claw pulled again.

Tears wet the corners of my eyes. Golden light sapped from my toes, my fingers, my legs, then my arms. It pooled in my chest, winding tighter and tighter like a spool of thread.

"Let go!" Daigen shouted. "You have to let go of the bond!"

Deep within the diamond in my heart, a tiny red spot glowed. I followed that small heat and my chest opened like an uncurled fist.

A gasp reverberated through my whole body. The claw dragged the ribbon of golden light away from my heart and out of my throat. My jaw opened so wide I thought it would unhinge.

The lingering golden fire from the bond warmed my tongue before it dissipated off my lips.

I took in a ragged breath and my knees gave out as I folded forward.

Cold snow bit my palms as I panted, but little air filled my lungs. I pressed my hand against the hollow chasm in my chest, checking to ensure he had not carved out my heart.

Hooves crunched the snow beside me. "How does it feel to no longer be married?"

I pushed onto my knees and glared at him. I reached into the bleakness, looking for an insult to lob at him, but where I should have found a passionate anger, I felt nothing.

My face fell. I pressed my hand against my chest again, feeling against my sternum like I was rifling through an empty wardrobe. I searched for sadness, hope, pity, fear, longing…anything I had felt with Riyan before, but instead I felt nothing.

I felt *nothing*.

No, I loved him, I…thought I loved him.

My stomach dropped like I was falling backward. Nothing existed within me. Riyan was truly gone.

He was *gone*.

A crinkling sensation slithered across my brow and I slowly lifted the crown of flowers off my head. The twisted vines of blue flowers had withered and died, the now brown petals crumbling off the crown like ash.

"Why?" I pulled my eyes from the ruined gift to Daigen's ugly face. "Why did you want my blood bond? Why would you take him away from me again?"

Daigen lowered onto his haunches and rested his forearms on his knees. "Did I really take him away when you never chose him? He was forced on you."

Tepid tears lined my eyes. "Riyan never forced—"

"*Fraleigh* forced it," he said with disgust. "Her marriage enchantment has been corrupted for centuries, yet thousands of people are still bound under duress."

Why would a monster on the mountain care about the noble marriage enchantment? Was he just a rival to Fraleigh's magic?

The dead vines crinkled as I gripped them. "Do you really hate Fraleigh so much that you want to take her gifts away?"

Daigen's eyes gleamed as the wind pushed his white hair around his horns. "Fraleigh was the start of your problem. Don't you think the Queen of the Giants is deeply unsettled that her only sister is enslaved?"

That could not be right. Fraleigh, known to all as *her majesty*, could not be a…a slave.

And the Ganora was her sister?

Impossible, all of it. The Queen of the Giants did not have a sister. The Great Sorceress who dripped with jewels and lived in a palace of gold was no slave.

"But…Fraleigh is all-powerful?" I asked.

"All-powerful does not mean all-wise," Daigen answered with a scowl. "She made a bad deal with the Hytons centuries ago and ended up permanently in their service. Ganora has been taking it out on the Dukedom ever since."

What kind of a deal would a sorceress have made? I could not shake the memory of that piece of parchment with the Hyton seal on Father's desk seven years ago.

A bad deal with the Hytons.

Daigen's voice softened. "You made your payment, now you get my help." He held out his hand. "Ganora took something from you, the Hytons took something from me. If you just trust me, we will both get what we want by the time the moon is full."

My eyes traced the faint white scar in the center of Daigen's palm. The mark was nearly identical to the blood bond scar on my left hand, but it was…purer, like it was formed with a different kind of magic.

I had completely surrendered to my own blood bond and let it ground me in a new, warmer reality. I thought my love for Riyan had changed me…but was it ever real?

Was *anything* between us ever real?

Within the dark chasm of my chest, the tiny white flame around my heart awoke. It flicked a small wisp of truth up my throat, dragging my shame with it. "How do I know if I ever loved him?"

He let out a gentle breath but did not lower his hand. "Love requires a choice. If you were ever meant to love him, you will without the bond. Trust me."

Never before would I have considered trusting the horned monster of the mountain, but what choice did I have? Before I had a blood bond full of love and light to guide me, but now I was directionless without the enchantment from an enslaved sorceress. Did Rosaline tell me to find Daigen because he knew the truth of the world?

Regardless of why I found him or what he wanted from me…at least he was real.

I *needed* something real.

I lowered the wreath of dead flowers into the snow and placed my left palm on top of his right, the scars from two different blood bonds meeting.

And I chose to trust him.

Chapter Two
Tears of Eternity

Daigen slowly helped me to my feet, even though my muscles shook and the cold wind blew around me.

He flicked his wrist and the snowflakes above my head melted away. "If you want to get your former husband back, *Litlnadr,* we have to get out of this cold first."

The hell did he just call me?

He took note of my quirked eyebrow. "Means 'little serpent' in Old Tongue."

Serpent? I could think of worse names for him. "The barbarian language?"

Daigen sneered. "Barbarian? If that is what you call those who were here before the invaders from the south showed up, fine."

I wrinkled my nose. Alastar the Conqueror had founded the Dukedom of Lycaster more than four-hundred and fifty years ago, that would make Daigen…

"Yes, I am quite old," he said.

I jerked my hand out of his. "I told you to get out of my head."

He crossed his arms and smirked. "I didn't need magic for that one. Part of the fun of being ancient is that I know what most people are going to say before they even open their mouths. Humans are much more predictable than you want to think."

I scoffed and knelt in the snow to retrieve the Hyton dagger. The frost creeping across the bronze bull's-head hilt bit my palm as I picked it up.

"You're a sorceress who wields a power stronger than steel or silver," Daigen said, "and yet you still reach for that ugly thing."

I glared at Daigen as I rose. Derrick had given me the dagger supposedly as a symbol of his love and protection. I had strung him along a fabricated romance for seven years, but maybe I held some sentimental value for a weapon from a starry-eyed friend.

I tied the dagger to my belt of linen scraps. Friend. Derrick was not my husband like I had planned nor my lover like I had wanted…he was just a friend.

Maybe even less than that since he was still a Hyton.

"Although," Daigen said with a fanged smile, "seems that you and I have a similar attachment to weapons."

With a flick of his crimson claws, his curved blade appeared in his hands. I turned my head to the spot where his blood still stained the snow. How had he retrieved his knife from all the way over there?

"*Se-ra!*"

I whipped my head around. I could barely make out the outline of two ravens against the night sky. The birds soared over the tall boulders and dove in the air toward me.

"*Se-ra! Se-ra!*" The birds croaked.

I huffed out a breath that swirled in the frigid air. Of course those ravens had to come back.

The last time the ravens showed up, poison like black fire had raged through my body. I had no idea how a bird could have poisoned me, but ravens were not a good omen. Even though they were my family's symbol, the rest of Lycaster saw them as bringers of Death and misfortune.

Daigen wrapped his claw around my left hand. "Not the opportune time for a reunion. Shall we take our leave?"

Before I could even nod in response, the air became heavy—no, the air was moving, like thousands of tiny beads trembled around us.

The ravens' great black wings flapped harder as they flew closer. "*Se-ra!*"

Suddenly, a memory of fragrant tea on a winter night entered my mind as the wind tickled my ears.

Before I could indulge in the memory, or even question where it had come from, the invisible beads in the air swirled around us. Sparkles of white and purple flashed in my vision.

I blinked and the swirling stopped. We were no longer near the tall rock formation, but instead at the glowing healing spring.

Daigen had transported us through the air.

He released my hand and walked toward the cerulean glow of the healing spring. "Feel any different?"

I held my cape closed. I hated that I knew exactly what he was asking. I was just at the healing spring with Riyan mere hours ago, but I felt like I was somewhere new.

Just like when I had poked my head into Erik's and Endre's empty bedrooms after they died, the surroundings might have been familiar, but the place was completely different.

The warmth and safety I had felt with Riyan in that spring was gone.

I bit down my sadness. If I had any hope of getting that warmth and safety back, I needed to focus. "So how the hell are Ganora and Fraleigh sisters—?"

Daigen grabbed my cheeks and silenced me. "First rule of our partnership—no direct questions. You have to gain knowledge at the right times."

He had just dropped world-shattering information into my lap and would not even give me the satisfaction of an explanation. Fraleigh had sold herself to the Hytons and Ganora was angry about it. How was I expected to trust him if those were the only clues he was going to give me?

Though the logical side of my mind screamed that I should not just quietly accept what Daigen told me, I had no other way to win Riyan's freedom. I was still unsure if I ever loved him, but he did not deserve whatever the Queen of the Giants wanted him for.

So I held my tongue and obeyed.

Satisfied with my silence, he released my face without so much as another word. He turned and walked to the healing spring, whistling a bouncing tune as his hooves clacked against the smooth rocks.

Although I wished I could have asked him why the hell he had started whistling, I recognized the melody—the song of the Man of the Mountain and how he lost his love. Despite the upbeat tune, the song was damn depressing.

"Stop that." I squeezed my arms—the request had come out much harsher than I had meant.

Daigen sat on the edge of the spring and dipped his furry legs into the steaming water. He did not need the spring to heal, but he looked ragged enough that a bath was a logical choice.

"So curious a moment ago," he said with a smirk, "yet you don't want to know the source of your magic?"

My hand pressed against the center of my chest. "I know where my magic comes from. The Man of the—"

"Wrong." Daigen splashed the water with his hoof. "He is the arbiter of magic and the judge of when and how we can alter reality, but he's not the source. She is."

The little white flame in the center of my chest sparked. She?

Daigen looked up, his golden eyes reflecting the cerulean glow of the spring. "The lost bride from the song. She was the first sorceress."

The *first* sorceress?

"Not much is known about her, sadly." Daigen rested on his elbows and looked up at the dancing bands of green light in the sky. "Over time, at least through the centuries I've been alive in, the legend has shifted to center around the poor man who lost his bride and how he grieves her."

I stepped closer to him, though my eyes traced the small stream that led into the mouth of the cave. "And the clever monster of the mountain *certainly* knows the real story…"

"The real story starts out the same as you know it." He shot me a smile. "Man falls in love with the sorceress who lives in his village. They run to the top of Nordingaard so they can bind together under an enchantment."

"Then she dies before they get there, I know."

"No," Daigen said. "*He* does."

That made no sense. The Man of the Mountain had taken me to the place West of the Moon and East of the Sun and held me in his arms.

"He was dead as could be, but the heartbroken sorceress dragged him to the top of the mountain anyway." Daigen's voice grew softer. "Used every scrap of her power to bind herself to him, hoping it would bring him back."

I flipped my left hand to reveal the faint pink scar across my palm. "She blood-bonded with him. Just like I did with Riyan, and like every noble man and woman in Lycaster has done for centuries."

He scoffed. "What she did was much bigger than Fraleigh's bond that lets you fuck whomever you want without consequences. The first sorceress's bond was so powerful that she summoned Death herself."

A chill ran through my arms and I closed my palm. "I suppose Death was not too happy to be summoned…"

Daigen's eyes met mine as he pushed himself deeper into the water. "Death is never happy, not really. She demands balance, as is the law of life and nature. The sorceress obliged Death's rules and made the first sacrifice…her life for his."

A bitterness coated my tongue. Riyan had done that for me.

I had felt a shift in the air and my magic had quieted when it happened. I could not fight against it. Riyan's agreement with Ganora to give his life for mine was seemingly unbreakable.

I walked around the healing spring and stood in the mouth of the cave. The trickling of the thin stream echoed around the rock as I took in the beauty of hundreds of Nordingaard crystals casting their cerulean glow in the cave's walls.

Just hours ago, I slept on top of Riyan's chest. He had guarded me for two days while my mind was with the Man of the Mountain. When I woke up, I felt so wonderful that I wanted to…

I bit my lip as heat flooded my cheeks. I could not believe I had tried to be *intimate* with him. Riyan was over fifteen feet tall, he would have hurt me, but that damn blood bond must have made me abandon my sense of self-preservation.

Daigen was right, Fraleigh's blood bond *had* manipulated me.

I moved my eyes to the spot where Riyan had pressed his arms into the cave floor rather than touch me. If the blood bond had pushed me toward him, what stopped him from responding the same way?

My mind pushed me to a memory of Riyan holding me in a shattered bed after our first attempt to be intimate had failed. He said his definition of love was putting someone else's life and happiness over one's own.

If the blood bond enchantment had pulsed pure desire through both of us but he never gave in, his legendary strength was not all that held him back…

"…he really loved me," I whispered.

"Of course he did, he got to *choose* you," Daigen said, his soft voice reverberating off the crystals around me. "That little bargain he just made with Ganora? A life for a life given in love—that is the most powerful magical bargain in existence. Nothing can stop it, not even Death."

I slammed my eyes shut to stop bitter tears from falling. Riyan had made an act of selflessness stronger than Death itself, and there I stood, hollow and confused.

Riyan had said I was his sun, but I was the coldest sun the world had ever seen.

"That is how our Man of the Mountain is still alive," Daigen said, "but do not think he was happy with that sacrifice. He escaped his fate to find his beloved dead next to him. He dug her a grave in the snow, just like the song…"

"*My tears did fall, my blood did flow…*" I mumbled flatly, keeping my eyes shut and my arms folded.

"…and I became Death's greatest foe," Daigen finished. "When the sorceress blood-bonded to him, she gave him all of her power. Every inch of him was filled with magic and he ascended the constraints of his own mortality."

Daigen let out a long breath. "He could have done anything with his new life and his nearly limitless power. He could have taken over kingdoms or be worshiped as a god, but instead…"

His claws splashed the spring. "He jumped into his beloved's grave and cried. And he never stopped."

I opened my eyes. The hundreds of crystals were now luminescent with a soft white light. I had never seen them do that before.

My eyes moved from crystal to crystal, trying to find the cause of their new glow, while Daigen's low voice filled the cave. "For more than a thousand years, he cried. He grieved his bride so passionately that the grave itself got deeper and deeper, until it became a place between worlds. The laws of our world could not reach him. Time. Morality. Everything but love and fear and truth."

The place West of the Moon and East of the Sun.

"But all graves have a bottom, don't they, *Litlnadr?*"

My eyes wandered up the tiny stream that bisected the cave. It, too, was glowing with the same soft light as the crystals. The stream thinned like a thread into the darkness of the cave until I could not tell if it ended or not.

If that stream fed into the healing spring, where had the magic of the healing spring come from?

If the Man of the Mountain was still at the top of Nordingaard, weeping for hundreds of years, and his body was filled with his sorceress's magic…

No. It could not be.

Even though I did not want to believe it, I knelt on the cave floor, my fingertips gently dipping into the cold, glowing water.

Little sparkles that I could not see pricked my skin. A melancholic essence traced my fingers in a languid dance, flowing with the gentle pull of the stream.

"Tears," I said in a breath. The magic of the spring was the Man of the Mountain's *tears.*

Daigen's smile brightened his voice. "The grave filled with millions of tears until it spilled over into this world. Bet you hated slurping on them during your marriage ritual! Disgusting, isn't it?"

My stomach turned, but eyes followed the flow of the tiny glowing stream until my feet caught up, leading me to the mouth of the cave. I leaned against the rough stone at the cave's opening as Daigen lounged in the spring, which was glowing a bright white.

Daigen swirled his claws in the water. "The tears of the mountain are complex. They are tangible bits of magic created from the most intense emotions a human can experience, but they're still water, so they act like water does. Flow into rivers, nourish plants, or even…"

He pointed into the mouth of the cave. "…crystallize into solid form."

I reached into my pocket and pulled out the gem Riyan had given me. It radiated warmth and soft white light in my hand. If the crystals were made of pure magic, then they must glow because magic is activated.

I certainly was not using my magic. Maybe Daigen was not merely taking a bath after all. "So, you are making the crystals glow."

A statement, not a question. His damn rule forced me to get creative.

Daigen canted his head. "I'm communicating with a friend. Many souls are trapped in the place West of the Moon and East of the Sun, and this spring is a direct channel to it. They get so lonely that sometimes I pop in for a visit, just like this. I might not be the best company, but being with me is better than swirling around in endless darkness."

I watched as the stream from the cave entered the pool of the healing spring. *That* was how the Man of the Mountain had taken my mind before. He reached out and dragged me all the way up to…

I swallowed. He took me to his grave.

Though…was it merely a grave, or was it also a perfect place to keep a prisoner?

I pocketed my still-glowing gem and dropped to my knees near the edge of the spring. I could not swim, so I certainly was not going to submerge myself like Daigen had, but if I just reached out—

"What are you doing?" Daigen asked with a smirk.

I dipped my hand into the warm water. "Trying to find Riyan. If he is trapped in the grave like others are, maybe I can reach him and figure out…"

The words failed on my lips as the magic swirled around my fingers. What would I figure out? Figure out where he was? Figure out how I really felt about him?

"Careful, you likely aren't powerful enough yet to find him," Daigen said as he leaned on the rocks. "Although something else could find you…"

I glared at him. "Watch me."

I called on the diamond in my heart and my white flame awoke. A slow heat that matched the hot spring filled my arms. I closed my eyes, focusing on the memory of the man with the golden hair and eyes like a twilight sky.

Even though my knees stayed firmly in the pebbles, my mind was being tugged down…or maybe up…but I was traveling.

Yes, it was working! My magic was working!

I kept focusing on that mental image of handsome Riyan. I pictured him sharing elskaberry jam with me in the field of red lilies and dancing with me under the moonlight.

Even though I still was not sure if anything we felt that day was even real.

The building heat in my body disappeared and a cold frost spread across the back of my mind. A wicked voice pricked my ears.

"*Looking for something, sorceress?*"

My breath froze in my lungs. The Queen of the Giants had found me.

"The bargain was sealed. His life is mine and he drifts in the place West of the Moon and East of the Sun. If you want him back, we must make an exchange…"

My free hand trembled as it wrapped around the pebbles below.

"*Unshackle my sister from the Hytons and he's yours. But if you don't do it by the next full moon, I will make my own blood bond and take full control over him…*"

My teeth chattered as the chill of each word bled through my body.

"*…and his spirit will remain in the place between worlds forever.*"

Chapter Three
Return of the Ravens

As soon as I thought I would suffocate on my own terror, Ganora released her hold on my mind.

I pulled my hand out of the water of the healing spring and crawled back on the smooth pebbles. My heart pounded as my eyes found Daigen's.

"G-Ganora, she—"

"This is what happens when you don't listen to me," Daigen said with a smirk as he rested in the spring.

I furrowed my brows and sat up. "She is going to blood bond with Riyan at the next full moon unless I unshackle Fraleigh."

Daigen ran his claws through his hair. "I told you Ganora cared about her sister…"

"Then tell me why!" The words seared my tongue. "Tell me why the Hytons enslaved her! Tell me how I can set her free! Tell me something, because if you will not let me ask—!"

Daigen quickly raised his claw and suddenly all the air from my throat disappeared. My hands scrambled to my neck as I tried to draw in air, but his brow stayed hard as he looked at me. "Your answers will come at the right time, be patient."

Why was he being vague when I had only three weeks to save Riyan from eternal enslavement? I shook my head and ran my fingertips along the ribbon of my choker as my lungs burned.

"Magic is not logic," he said firmly. "You *have* to just trust me."

He released his enchantment and I gasped. My palms spread across the pebbles as I coughed through the pain in my lungs.

All the questions I could not ask burned in my chest. Why did magic not make any logical sense? Why would Rosaline send me to Daigen as my answer to help Riyan? What had the Hytons taken from him that he would need my help to get?

"*Se-ra!*"

I looked up—the two black ravens beat their wings against the night sky, flying straight for us.

Daigen groaned. "Not this again!" He scooped up some glowing white water from the spring and dripped it against his forehead. The healing spring suddenly dulled into its normal cerulean luminescence. "I got the memory I want. Let's go."

He quickly leaped out of the spring and threw on his tunic and cloak as he shook his legs dry.

"*Se-ra! Se-ra!*" the ravens croaked.

I watched the birds as they flew closer. Why did they want to get to me so badly?

Daigen's hooves clacked against the rocks as he rounded the spring toward me. Steam curling off the surface of the hot spring warmed my face, and I swore I heard laughter as the steam kissed my ears.

Not just any laughter—the laughter of a boy on a summer afternoon.

I knitted my brows. I recognized that laugh…but it could only come from a memory…

Daigen's claws wrapped around my hand, but my eyes stayed on the ravens even as the magic in the air dragged against my skin.

In a flash of white light and a blink, a wall of icy rocks consumed my entire vision. Frigid wind blew past me and my hair whipped around my shoulders. I wobbled on the balls of my feet and I looked down.

Tree tops. I snapped my head up—we stood on a tiny ledge on the side of the mountain, only wide enough for my feet and not an inch more.

I gripped Daigen's hand and swallowed a gasp. He laughed.

"Not afraid of heights, are we?" He tugged me forward.

A goat bleated above us. Another answered from below, but I was too afraid to look at anything other than the back of Daigen's head as I tip-toed behind him.

Luckily, the perilous path was only a few steps long. With a click, Daigen pushed open a door and pulled me inside a small house.

Daigen flicked his wrist and a fire sparked to life in a small hearth. He locked the door and hung his cloak on a peg. Four other cloaks of dappled shades of grey, green, and brown hung near it.

How did he have *that* many cloaks of invisibility?

"I would love to learn how to become invisible," I said, careful to make my statement not sound too much like a question.

"I'm certain you can master the ability." Daigen looked over his shoulder and fanned out the grey and white cloak. "It's an ancient form of sorcery known as paint."

My fists gripped my wool cape and I shot him an icy glare.

He dropped the cloak and his smirk disappeared. "Can't even take a joke? You still have to learn how your power works, *Litlnadr.*"

"Just tell me—!"

Daigen held out his hand and silenced me. "Hand over that hunk of rock in your pocket and you'll know soon enough."

I held my cape tighter around me. My blood bond was gone and the flower crown Riyan had given me withered, why did he want my Nordingaard crystal too?

Daigen's brow hardened. "*Trust,* remember? I'm going to make it useful."

I let out a tense breath, but retrieved the rough crystal from my pocket. The crystal made a grating clink as Dagain's claws snapped around it.

He unsheathed his ancient blade from a scabbard at his hip. "Here, I'll hold your precious little trinket and you'll hold mine."

I tentatively held out my hand and he placed the worn leather hilt in my palm. I ran my fingertip down the ancient and tiny runes carved into the blade.

"*Reginbani*," Daigen said. The word sounded rough and ragged, must have been in Old Tongue. "That's its name."

Riyan had once told me men name their weapons to give them more power. I had no idea what *Reginbani* meant, but the weight of the name hung around the steel.

He turned on his hooves and slowly walked over to a small table that was littered with iron tools. He sat down and placed my crystal in a vise.

I tucked *Reginbani's* hilt into my palm and slowly walked toward the firelight to join him at the table.

He tapped the hammer to the chisel and a piece of the blue crystal chipped off.

I threw out my hand. "Stop! You will ruin it!"

My magic reached for him again, but nothing responded. A sneeze would have made stronger contact than whatever I had just done.

"Calm down." Daigen scoffed as he chipped another piece off. "These things aren't delicate like your sensibilities."

I sat on the stool opposite Daigen at the table. I focused on that little white fire around my heart that flickered slowly, like the single flame on a candle's wick.

What was the point of having the gift of sorcery if I could do nothing with it?

"Magic is based on your emotions, that is why you struggle with it," Daigen said as he calmly chiseled at the crystal. "When you want to change something—step through thin air, alter appearance, turn snow into flame—you have to *believe* in it. You have to want something so badly that you bend reality itself to satisfy that deep emotional need."

He gave the crystal a sharp tap. "For example, Fraleigh's damn blood bonds are supposed to be impossible to remove, but *I* have a deep emotional need to rid them from every mortal I come across…and here you sit, liberated from the corruption. You can thank me at any time."

When I last used my power, I allowed the pain of losing my brothers to warp my body until it did exactly what I wanted—destroy the giant that killed Endre.

Unlike then, my heartbeat now echoed in a hollow cavern. How was I ever supposed to use my magic if the grey numbness had taken over my body again?

"Thanks to your *liberation*," my voice broke and I swallowed, "I do not have a deep emotional need anymore."

I spoke but my words had no flavor. My voice had no melody. How could I know what I wanted if I did not even yearn for food, or sunlight, or…happiness?

Daigen sighed and put down his tools. "You are changing. Still very much mortal but…changing."

His hooves clicked as he rose from the table. He walked to a wooden shelf on the wall full of small glass vials. His claws clinked against the glass as he plucked a vial filled with white powder off the shelf.

"I used to be an alchemist's apprentice." He speared one of his claws into the cork and unstoppered the bottle. "I crafted remedies and illusions alike."

He poured a small pile of the powder into his left palm. His hand dipped slightly like he was carefully weighing the contents. "A couple of tricks here and there to amuse the simple-minded…"

He tossed the powder into the fire. The fire blazed blue. Hyton Blue.

I blinked. "The blue fire the Hytons use…was never Fraleigh's magic."

Daigen barked out a laugh. "No, though the Hytons do love to steal things. It was one of Alastar the Conqueror's favorite tricks of mine. His wretched son loved it too, among all the little feats and illusions I performed for decades."

His head slowly turned back to me, the blue fire casting a glow onto his white hair. "But the most important element of crafting illusions is not the materials I use, but *precision*."

He let the weight of his last word hang in the air amongst the crackling of the log in the fireplace. He leaned forward and splayed his claws on the table. "That is why I ask you to trust me. Everything I do is deliberate, *Litlnadr.*"

I quirked an eyebrow. "Everything *should* be deliberate."

Daigen let out a low laugh. "A little serpent with a mind like mine. Although we may think alike, our power manifests differently. I was formed in a time where I had to be discreet and unseen, so I developed an affinity for transformation."

He smiled, revealing his fangs. "I don't actually look like this."

I examined him from horn to hoof. "Then wear your real face. Surely you cannot be any uglier than this."

"This," he stomped his hoof for emphasis, "is a delightful curse from the Great Sorceress of Nordingaard. She wanted me so ugly, so fearsome, that no mortal would ever seek my help again."

So Fraleigh *did* have a rivalry with Daigen. Even while held captive by the Hytons, she must have somehow felt threatened by his power. "What a shame she forced you to look like this forever."

"I never said that." Daigen's smile grew bigger. "There is nothing more delicious than proving Fraleigh wrong, and since a certain little mortal sought my hideous face regardless of her curse, I finally have my opportunity to take the mask off…"

Daigen bowed his head slightly and his horns retracted. His hooves turned into feet and his claws became fingers. His red skin blanched into a pale white brushed with a lavender glow.

He opened his eyes—now violet instead of gold. His fangs had disappeared. Like Fraleigh, his features were too sharp to be considered beautiful, but he was no longer hideous.

A goat bleated outside. Dozens of hooves clattered on the rocks.

Daigen's violet eyes shifted to the small window. "I also have a talent for transforming others. Those enchantments tend to be more…permanent."

My stomach turned. "The goats are—"

"No, not them," Daigen said with a dismissive wave of his hand. "But others…I've hidden in the rocks around the mountain and turned men into mice. Girls into larks. Hell, I turned a couple of Bloodstone boys into white bears a few decades ago."

I folded my arms. "You robbed them of their lives!"

"It's better than being giant food! Though I will admit my insatiable need to help others is one of my worst vices." He sighed and sat down in front of his tools. "Anyone I turn into a goat runs away from me, those beasts outside just won't leave me alone. My father was a herder, guess it's just in my blood."

I rested my hand on my fist as I listened. I never needed to ask Daigen who he was, he was just…telling me. Despite his power, it was hard to be afraid of a cursed and bitter soul on the mountain who liked to help people.

Maybe he had a point about answers coming to me at the right time. Had he tried to tell me who he was before I saw his true face and his quaint home, I would have never believed him.

I had only known Daigen for a couple of hours yet I still *hated* when he was right.

A sharp tap rattled the window pane and the glass darkened. "*Se-ra!*"

The ravens had returned. How did they find us?

Daigen groaned and picked up his tools again. "Here we go. They're going to annoy us until they realize they can't break through glass."

I took in a breath—the smell of smoking herbs and charcoal dust hit my nose.

That smelled just like…it was impossible, but we were on Nordingaard, where the impossible had stared me in the face more than once.

My heartbeat quickened as I lifted myself from the table. "Just to make sure I understand you correctly—the Man of the Mountain's tears behave like water and live in the air around us."

Daigen lightly hammered his chisel against the crystal. "Yes."

A raven pecked its beak on the window pane and the wooden door rattled—the other raven must have joined in.

I took a step closer to the door. "You also took a memory from the healing spring. Since the magic comes from intense emotions…the tears can carry memories too."

Daigen blew the dust off the crystal and buffed it with his sleeve. "What a joy to hear that you're finally using your brain and figuring things out yourself. See what you can accomplish without asking endless questions like a snotty nursery child?"

I had picked up on the memories floating through the air with my magic, but why had the tears carried memories of my brothers any time the ravens were near? Were they just harbingers of my grief, haunting me with the fact that my brothers were dead?

Or what if…?

Sharp scratches echoed through the door. The hinges rattled again.

I could not pry my eyes off the door as the scratching got louder. "If you were on this mountain, then you must have been at the failed battle with the giants seven years ago."

"I was—wait, are they picking the lock?"

The door swung open and a raven screamed as it flew inside. It soared past me to attack Daigen.

Daigen cursed in Old Tongue and swatted at the raven, but it would not stop.

I snapped my head to the open door. The cold mountain air flooded in, carrying the scent of tea leaves with it.

Another raven, larger than the first, hung from the door handle. Its beak was clamped on the latch and a stick stuck out of the keyhole near its feet.

My breath caught in my throat and tears lined my eyes.

I knew him.

My throat shook and I could barely believe the name that left my tongue. "Erik?"

The larger raven flew toward me and landed at my feet. His glossy black eyes met mine and he said in almost a sigh, "*Se-ra.*"

Tears dripped down my lashes and my chest shook. I turned my head just as the smaller raven landed on the table next to me.

I fought back a sob as I said his name, "Endre?"

The smaller raven squawked and spread its wings as if it were about to give a hug.

Memories flooded the front of my mind. Muddy footprints in the foyer. Dozens of freckles on our cheeks after baking in the sun. Flying down a hill on our favorite sled.

My brothers were alive. They were *alive.*

But that meant…

I crunched my hands into fists and looked down, where Daigen was pulling himself up off the floor with bloody scratches marking his face.

He took them away from me.

My white flame ignited. Power surged through my arms like a river bursting through a dam. My empty chest turned into an oven, kindling my rage until it grew hotter and hotter.

And then one word screamed in my mind...

Burn.

Chapter Four
Heart's Desire

My chest flared with light and my hands lit up with heat. My eyes met Daigen's violet ones and all I wanted was to turn him into char.

Burn.

I released my magic with a scream. The surge of power I had sent toward Daigen bent back and flared through his house.

Fire crackled around me. Heat radiated through the air. My eyes stayed shut as my power thrummed through my body. Years of anger shredded my throat all at once and I could not hold it down.

"You turned my brothers into ravens!" I screamed. My temples ached. My muscles flared. "We thought they were dead! For *seven years,* we thought they were dead!"

I could not even sense Daigen through the blinding heat of my power. The bitter truth of my brothers' reappearance shoved itself to the front of my mind and the fire burned hotter.

The House of Ravenwood was destitute because its only heirs had died, so I had shouldered the impossible burden of the family's fate. I had schemed to become the Duchess of Lycaster, lied for years, and destroyed myself little by little to survive in the hell they left me in.

"*Se-ra! Se-ra!*" my brothers cried.

My heart raced. My breath escaped my clenched teeth in labored huffs. My body screamed with pain as the white flames raged through my arms, but I could not stop.

"*Litlnadr,*" Daigen's voice was infuriatingly calm over the roar of my flames, "keep going."

I hated him. *Hated* him.

I clenched my fists so tightly my fingernails cut my palms. Daigen needed to suffer. He needed to know *exactly* what he robbed from me.

I pushed the rest of the burning fury through my throat. "I refused to love *anyone* because they left me."

Suddenly whatever was fueling my fire had run out. The flames extinguished as my magic quieted. My knees buckled and I collapsed to the floor.

My eyes fluttered open. A smoking ring of char on the stone floor surrounded me. Daigen's wooden table had turned into a pile of ash. His iron tools were scattered through the remains and still glowing red. The Nordingaard crystal in the vise was a luminescent white.

The flutter of wings whispered near my ear. One of the ravens—one of my *brothers*—landed in front of my face. As soon as he started preening wisps of hair off my sticky cheeks, I knew it was Erik.

Daigen stood over me with the handle of a wooden pail in his hand. "Feeling drained after your little tantrum?" He shook the pail and water sloshed within. "Good thing you emotionally exhausted yourself, I was afraid I was going to have to give you a bath."

A loud squawk filled the air and the other raven—definitely Endre— flew toward Daigen with his talons out.

Daigen slammed the pail on the floor and shielded his face with his forearm. "I'm helping her, corpse reaver!"

I winced as Endre's talons sank into his skin, but Daigen did not even blink as he lowered his arm to bring Endre to eye level. "I am *helping.*"

Endre lowered his head and made a low sound like a growl. Erik croaked and Endre turned his head and croaked back.

Were they…talking to each other?

"I was going to let her find you, you didn't have to interrupt me!" Daigen said to Endre.

Endre hissed, but lowered his hackles and released his grip on Daigen's arm.

He fluttered to the floor and nuzzled his feathered head against my palm. I could not believe Endre was in front of me, *touching* me, and being playfully affectionate again.

I snapped my eyes up to Daigen. "Change them back!"

"Can't." Daigen moved his index finger over his sleeve—his wounds from Endre's talons had healed and he was stitching the torn wool back together with invisible magic. "It's easy to convince the magic to turn men into animals, since…well, most men *are* animals, but the other way around? I would have to know who they were as people to *make* them people again."

My heart fluttered. I knew who they were!

I placed my hand on Endre's smooth feathers and shut my eyes, focusing on the tiny bits of magic in his body that sparkled in my mind's eye.

Instead of letting rage fuel my power, I focused on memories of dark wavy hair and calloused hands. A dented dueling sword. Rude jokes our parents hated.

My whisper skated over my lips. "*Please.* Please come back."

The tips of my fingers tingled, but I opened my eyes and only found the shining black eyes of a bird staring back at me, not Endre's mossy green ones.

I huffed. Maybe Endre was just being stubborn. Typical.

I focused on Erik. I centered myself on the memories of his scolding voice as I snuck away from the manor past sunset, his charcoal sketches of the cat that lived in the kitchen, and him drawing my blankets over my shoulders on cold nights.

But my magic refused to cooperate.

I threw down my hands with a scream through my clenched teeth. "Nothing is happening!"

"Your flame is different from mine." Daigen lowered his arm with the perfectly-repaired sleeve. "You don't have the affinity for transformation, but you'll develop the skill eventually."

My heart sank as I looked from brother to brother. What did *eventually* mean? Would it be years before I heard their voices? Felt their arms around me? Laughed with them?

Tears lined my eyes as I drew my knees into my chest. It was like losing them all over again. Was love just something I could not have? Would it always loom just out of reach like an apple on a tall branch?

I looked up at Daigen, searching his violet eyes for an answer but finding none.

"I know you might hate me for it but…" Daigen sighed and his face softened. "What Ganora does to the people the giants carry through the pass…no one deserves it. At the first battle, I had nearly exhausted myself turning boy after boy into rabbits or what-have-you as soon as the fog from the pass hit their faces. But when I saw those Ravenwood green capes around their necks, it was very easy to convince the magic in their bodies that they would be better off as ravens than have their bones decorate Ganora's crown."

Endre dipped his head low and hissed.

Daigen pointed at Endre. "*You* had damn near crossed over when I saved you! Your inner self was *begging* for help. Death had almost taken you and you're still bitter—"

"Stop it!" My flame awoke again. I gritted my teeth and held onto the burn as my heart raced.

Then, like a cool breeze, a thought wisped to the front of my mind.

My brothers were *alive*. They might not be as I wanted them…but they were alive.

The small amount of energy that fueled my white flame sapped like I had sprung a leak at the base of my spine. A calm breath escaped my lips as I opened my eyes.

Daigen loosened the crystal from the vise in the pile of ash. The crystal had stopped glowing and had returned to its normal, deep blue hue.

The crystal disappeared into his palm and he lowered onto his haunches to look me in the face. "I heard your mind, *Litlnadr*—you've shut out your emotions for years. You're about to feel the harsh intensity of everything you've suppressed now that you're getting in tune with your magic. It's going to be uncomfortable, but you have to face it if you're going to get what you want."

I did not want to face anything. I just wanted…

I bit back a scream of frustration. I still did not know what I wanted other than to punch Daigen between the eyes.

Without my anger, my heart floated in a dark chasm. Directionless.

I looked up at Daigen as Erik and Endre rested at my knees. "I just want to know where to go from here."

Daigen pressed his finger in the center of my chest, right over the sparkling diamond the Man of the Mountain had placed in my heart. "Since your heart's desire guides your magic, I can't tell you what to do."

I wrinkled my nose. Heart's desire? That sounded like faerie story nonsense.

Daigen's violet eyes gleamed and he tapped the space between my eyebrows. "I can't lead your mind because your heart has to be in the right place. You have to *emotionally* arrive at the right conclusion every time. That's why I make you figure out the answers."

I clenched my teeth, holding back all the questions that spun in the back of my mind. How was I supposed to trust in a monster, believe in faerie story nonsense, and feel my emotions? How would any of that release Fraleigh from the Hytons? How would that free Riyan from Ganora's threat of oblivion?

What had happened to the careful woman who counted her breaths and waited until the perfect opportunity to strike? Each passing moment was unpredictable as lightning and Daigen was trying to drag me into a world where fickle emotion made the rules.

Daigen sighed and his face softened. "Trusting people has not been easy for you, I know. That's why I have something tangible for you to lean on."

My skin crawled. I hated how he could read me so well. I felt too *seen*.

My eyes flicked down to Daigen's hands as he pried a smooth onyx gem out of…my choker?

My hands flew to my neck and felt bare skin. How had he—?

He laughed. "I told you, I'm famous for my tricks."

With a quick shift of his hands, he deftly replaced the onyx stone with what had to be the Nordingaard crystal in his hand. He pulled the ribbon of the choker tight as he held it up.

My breath caught in my throat. What was once a rough stone was cut into a heart and secured in the center of the choker. The crystal threw firelight through its smooth facets, making spots of green and blue light dance around the room. Had I not known any different, I would have mistaken the collection of hardened magical tears for a normal, yet beautiful, gem.

"Told you I was going to make it useful." He slid his hands behind my hair and tied the choker so the crystal was flush against my neck. "Any time this crystal glows, you have found your heart's desire and are ready to bend reality to get it."

My fingers traced the smooth edge of the crystal. I looked down at Erik and Endre, who kept their black eyes on me.

I nearly looked away in shame. "I am so sorry. I am sorry I cannot—"

Endre hopped on top of my knee and butted his head against my chest. His wings fluttered as he looked up at me. "*Se-ra…love…you.*"

I sniffed and let a little smile bloom on my lips. Erik fluttered up to perch on my shoulder. He preened a few wisps of hair away from my temple. He was never one to dispense verbal affection, but he delivered the sentiment all the same.

I gently ran my fingertips down Erik's glossy back, then Endre's. Having some of them was better than none at all.

Daigen picked up his pail and walked to the fire in the hearth, which was losing its azure hue by the second. "If you have had enough of your little reunion, I have a reunion of my own that I need to get to."

Endre perched on my available shoulder as I slowly rose from the floor.

"I had no idea an immortal could be so impatient," I said.

Daigen tossed me a sly glance. "And I had no idea a sorceress could be so difficult."

He tipped the pail and doused the fire. I furrowed my brows.

Daigen glanced at my face and set the pail down with a clatter. "I already had to explain how water works, do I have to explain how heat works too?" He walked toward the pile of ash that was once his table. "Fire burns away all the moisture in the air around it, meaning there are too few tears around most flames for you to manipulate. Anything more than a candle is going to require normal mortal tools to snuff out."

How inconvenient.

He plucked *Reginbani* out of the pile of ash and slid it back into the scabbard at his hip. He pulled a pair of pants and a dusty pair of boots out of a cupboard and shoved them on.

Daigen finished the last knot on his boot and stood up. "Well, *Baron,* we'd best be leaving. There is a scared little girl at the fortress who just lost her parents and is needing some help."

My stomach dropped. Astrid. Nikkolas and Hilda Bloodstone had died more than three days ago. Poor Astrid was lost and confused on a normal day, how was she faring now that she was completely alone?

The bigger question, however, was why did Daigen want to go to her? Hilda had told me Daigen had cut Riyan free from his mother's womb, so he had appeared when Astrid was in peril at least once.

Did that mean she was in worse distress than I feared?

My hand slowly slid into the pocket of my skirt. I traced the threads of the three flowers embroidered into a scrap of linen, each one representing a promise I had made Riyan before he left.

Take care of Astrid. Take care of the North. Try to be happy.

I let out a breath. Even though I felt like I was failing Riyan with every passing minute, I could at least keep my promises.

I pulled out the golden Bloodstone pin bearing the snarling bear and pinned it next to the Ravenwood pin that held my cape closed. If we were going to the fortress, might as well announce loud and clear that I was the North's new Baron.

Daigen fastened a grey and green cloak around his shoulders. He held the door open for me as I stepped into the night.

Erik croaked in my left ear just as I was about to take my second step. I looked down and my heart leaped as my foot dangled in the air over the ledge.

I froze. Erik and Endre fluttered their wings against my hair as I almost took one step too many. The space outside the door could not have been more than six inches long—perfect for a sorcerer with hooves of a mountain goat, but not for a person! "The hell—?"

"Thought you were going to rely on me to get everywhere?" Daigen said. "This is another exercise in trust. *You* are going to trust in your magic to get back to the fortress and *I* am going to trust that you will not fall to your death."

Endre hissed and raised his hackles. I bit my tongue and was foolish enough to glance down. I could not even see how far up I was from the ground.

I turned around. Daigen leaned against the doorframe with his arms folded across his chest.

I could have punched him. "If I die, *you* will never get what you lost from the Hytons."

Daigen's smirk disappeared. His cheek twitched in his silence, as if he were carefully considering what he was going to say next.

Finally his eyes gleamed and he smiled. "I'm glad you finally figured out that I need you just as much as you need me, but the Man of the Mountain gave you the gift of sorcery for a reason. If you don't use your magic, you might as well sit next to Fraleigh at the feet of Duke Hyton's throne."

I huffed. "Duke Hyton cannot own me. I am a Baron!"

"Such silly mortals, inventing titles that mean nothing." Daigen straightened his spine. "Oh, you are a Baron? Allow me to cower in the presence of your golden pins! How is that going to stop the unyielding leader of the Hytons? Or his army?"

I furrowed my brows. "I have my own army! Bloodstone has dozens of soldiers—"

"And Duke Hyton has Fraleigh." Daigen's eyes turned deadly.

I swallowed. The Dukedom did not kneel to the Great Sorceress of Nordingaard out of mere respect. If the legends were true, Fraleigh could wipe out the Bloodstone army with just a sweep of her arm.

And if Fraleigh was truly that powerful, how could the Hytons have enslaved her in the first place? Nothing was adding up.

"You really think an army of mortals would make any difference when an army of giants couldn't?" Daigen said. "If you have any hope of freeing the prisoner in the golden palace, your magic has to get stronger than this."

I was starving for answers and Daigen was only feeding me crumbs. It went against every instinct I had, but if I were going to save Riyan, all I could do was follow each order blindly…

…even if it meant stepping off the edge of a cliff.

I let out a breath and tried to wake the white flame around my heart. I raised my hands and took a deep breath, trying not to shiver as I closed my eyes.

The tears sparkled like tiny beads in the air all around me. I could sense them even farther than my eyes could see. They were in the trees below the ledge. They frosted the rocks beneath my feet. I even sensed them inside the goats further up the craggy rocks.

Each tear vibrated softly. Waiting. Listening for my next command.

I closed my eyes and took in a breath, letting a few tears into my chest. Then I let them out slowly.

The crystal radiated warmth against my neck. The flame around my heart lit up with a calm, quiet energy.

Daigen's voice, smooth as ice over a pond, appeared behind me. "What do you want, *Litlnadr?*"

I took in a breath again, and I smelled the faint scent of Riyan that lingered on my cape. Nectar and wheat. Lilies and sunshine. Jam-filled buns and moonlit dancing. A comb through my hair. An arm to snuggle against. A broken bed and a mended heart.

Each memory was comforting, but tainted. How much of my memory was influenced by Fraleigh's enchantment and how much of it was real?

I let out a cool breath. "I want to know what was real."

Warmth pressed against my neck—my Nordingaard crystal was glowing. I had found my heart's desire.

Daigen's hand rested gently on my back. Wings ruffled against my hair on both sides.

"Then go to the fortress," he said.

I let out a breath and took a step off the ledge. Wind screamed around me and my eyes popped open.

My magic had failed. I was falling.

Chapter Five
Disgraced

Cold tears streamed from my eyes as I plummeted toward the trees. The ground grew closer and closer.

I was going to die.

Suddenly a hand snatched my cape and sparkling magic swallowed me. I gasped as my feet found purchase on grass and my head spun.

Daigen's horrible laugh cut through my ears.

I whipped around and my fists ached with how hard I clenched them. "You let me fall to my death!"

"No, I didn't." He folded his arms. "That was an exercise in trust, remember?"

My arms shook as I wiped away the frightened tears from my cheeks. "I was dead...I was falling..."

Daigen grabbed my chin and forced my eyes up to meet his. His touch was cold enough that I stopped shaking. "You'll step through the air when you want something bad enough that you'll split the fabric of the living world for it. Until then, you can trust that I will *never* let you fall."

He let go, but I kept my mouth closed as I tried to get my stomach to settle.

Morning mist crawled around my feet. I looked around and found tall square towers and a wall that stretched around us.

Daigen had dropped us in the center of the fortress courtyard. I looked up at the closed wooden doors at the top of the keep's steps as Erik and Endre settled on my shoulders. Endre hissed while Daigen snapped that he *technically* never put me in danger.

My heartbeat slowed as I forced myself to take measured breaths. If Daigen had sensed that Astrid needed help, I needed to be as calm as possible.

The golden Bloodstone and Ravenwood pins weighed on my sternum as my chest rose and fell. The North was mine. Magic was mine. But what did I have to show for it?

A toothless title and a worthless heart.

"By Ganora's mercy!"

"They appeared in mid-air, I saw it!"

"She's a–a-"

"Sorceress! Sorceress!"

Daigen's dark violet eyes swept across the courtyard. "I shouldn't keep poor Astrid waiting any longer." He shot me a wink. "Let's see if you can use your magic without burning anything down."

He stepped backward into the air and disappeared.

Endre lowered his head and extended his wing as I turned my head. Dozens of Bloodstone soldiers in their red uniforms ran toward me with swords drawn and arrows notched in their bowstrings.

My stomach dropped. So much for commanding my own army.

In sheer desperation, I held up my hands. The soldiers halted, some of them tripping backward over their own feet.

I might not know how to enchant them, but I could use their fear against them. "I-I am indeed a sorceress! And your new Baron! Do not come any closer!"

One of the soldiers gripped the hilt of his sword, but stayed still. "Oh yeah? Where's Riyan Bloodstone? Did you kill him and steal his pins?"

The company of soldiers rumbled with suspicion. Before I could protest, a voice I recognized piped up. "She couldn't have killed him, she's his wife!"

I turned toward the voice and a short soldier stepped forward. His face was much smoother than it had first seemed under torchlight, but he was the soldier who had played the flute as Riyan and I danced days ago.

A lankier soldier—the one who had played the lute—stepped beside the shorter. "But she brought omens of Death into the fortress!"

The soldiers murmured. Erik and Endre stilled on my shoulders.

The shorter soldier turned to the taller. "Then we let Captain Mydina handle it."

The rabble quieted. I swept my eyes over the soldiers and bit my tongue as my mind raced. Captain *Mydina?* How could the captain of the Bloodstone army be from the noble House of Mydina?

The shorter soldier jogged to me, but stilled as soon as he looked at Erik on my shoulder. His round eyes darted from Erik to Endre. "Uh, please come with me sorcer…uh, Baron."

He held out his arm but then quickly drew it back. He shifted on his feet and kept his eyes down. "B-Brandt Olson, at your service."

Maybe I did not need to frighten poor Brandt. I gave him a disarming smile as I followed him toward the keep. The eyes of every Bloodstone soldier drilled into my back the instant I ascended the first step.

Landing in the middle of the courtyard was a mistake I could not repeat. Any form of sorcery in Lycaster was a capital offense, though none of the soldiers would report me to the Hytons. The Bloodstone army merely existing was treason, a capital offense in of itself.

Still, I needed to tread carefully or else the superstitious soldiers might take an axe to my neck themselves.

Brandt tripped up a step and clumsily recovered. Easing his nerves might calm the rest of the army down too, so I put on a smile. "I remember you. Your flute-playing was wonderful."

A small smile flicked up his lips as he ascended the steps. "Well…I just followed Calder's lead—Calder Anson, I mean. We were bunkmates at the military academy. He was the one playing the lute and he has *much* better rhythm than I do."

I kept a polite expression and nodded. Anxiety made his mouth run like a river.

"And what about your captain?" I said as I reached the top step. "He could certainly play the violin well."

Brandt tugged on the iron handle of the heavy wooden door so we could slip through. "Oh, Captain is good at the violin. Best I've ever heard."

The violin was a logical choice for a noble son, but how did a noble son end up in the Bloodstone army? He should have graduated from Heaston Academy for Young Gentlemen unless he was kicked out and sent to the military academy.

The memory of Riyan's smooth voice entered my mind. *"Serafina, nice boys don't get sent to the military academy."*

If the captain was not a nice boy, maybe polite conversation was not the way to win him over.

Surviving after stepping off the edge of a cliff certainly made the idea of enchanting the mysterious noble son less frightening.

Brandt led me into the foyer and the warm smell of the keep entered my nose, reminding me of Hilda's loving embrace the first time I entered the fortress. I swallowed my sadness and grounded myself in my task. If I ensured Captain Mydina's loyalty, by whatever means, I was one step closer to freeing Hilda's grandson from the Queen of the Giants.

We entered the dining hall. A group of maids stood in front of the long dining table, the captain of the Bloodstone army facing them on the other side.

"I don't care what you do, just get her to calm down!" the captain huffed. "We just finished burying her parents and I am *not* digging another grave—"

Brandt cleared his throat. "Captain, we have an issue."

The line of maids parted as they turned toward us, revealing Captain Mydina's face. Before, I had been too distracted by the long scar that cut between his yellow eyes to figure out who he was, but I had finally put a face to the name I had suspected.

I had heard rumors about him—he was just a few years ahead of Erik in school when he had been thrown out of the House of Mydina and disinherited. What a *delightful* surprise to find him.

I could use his sordid past to my advantage.

My white flame flickered to life. Daigen had said to follow my heart's desire to get what I wanted, and my heart's desire was to keep my head.

Captain Mydina's eyes fell to the golden House pins on my chest, then they raised to Erik and Endre on my shoulders.

"Leave us," Captain Mydina clipped. "All of you."

The maids quickly shuffled away to the nearest staircase in the corner of the room, but Brandt lingered behind. "But Captain, she is a…a…"

"Sorceress," I finished with a cool voice and a smile. "And your new Baron. We have much to discuss."

Captain Mydina's eyes narrowed before they cut to Brandt. "Shut the gate. Make sure no one goes in or out until I get a handle on this."

Brandt saluted and left us alone in the dining hall.

My whisper skated over my lips as I turned my head slightly to Erik. "Remember him?"

A low croak of assent escaped Erik's throat. Captain Mydina spread his hands on top of the table and glared with suspicion at Erik.

"Can I trust him?" I whispered.

To my surprise, Erik gently preened a strand of hair in front of my ear.

I pressed my lips into a firm line. Erik likely meant "yes," but he was more rigid about morality than any man I had ever known. What did Erik sense in the captain that made him overlook his past?

Captain Mydina's gaze moved from Erik to Endre. "You must have caused quite a disturbance bringing *those* into my fortress."

My white flame flared around my heart. *His* fortress?

"My…companions from the mountain bring no harm." I took calm breaths so my indignation did not smolder into an inferno. "And did I hear you refer to this place as *your* fortress?"

The corner of Captain Mydina's mouth flicked up. "Nikkolas had me running most of the fortress's operations for him. He wanted someone to take charge in case his heir was…unable." He shrugged slightly. "And look where we are now."

The flame in my chest flared brighter. "Good thing someone has come to take charge. Riyan bestowed the power of the North to me, and you will do well to acquiesce to his wishes."

Captain Mydina chuckled. "You don't know the first thing about running a province, Serafina."

A smile crawled up my lips. "I know more than you think, *Evereon*."

Evereon Mydina's eyes widened and he held his breath. "How did you—?"

"Oh, you are quite infamous." I kept my voice low and calm as I moved around the long table toward him. "But I will admit, it took me a while to recognize you."

I let my fingertips trace the edge of the oak dining table as I rounded the far edge. "Coppery hair like your father's…" I flicked my eyes up to meet his gaze. "Yellow eyes and light brown complexion, just like your Sudrian-born mother, Baroness Mydina."

Evereon's throat bobbed as he swallowed. "Look, I don't know what you've heard, but—"

"I have heard many things, whispers mainly, all of them conflicting with one another." I rounded the second corner and stalked closer. "Your father kept most of the details quiet, but disinheriting a Baron's heir was quite a scandal."

I stopped in front of him, tilting my head up to look him in the eyes. To Evereon's credit, he did not cower.

"You can threaten me with whatever tricks you learned on the mountain," he said, "but I do not fear my past, I fear the future. What happened to him?"

I set my jaw. "You act quite concerned for someone who claimed this was his fortress. The disappearance of the last Bloodstone heir would be quite advantageous for you—a chance to have a Baronage again."

His face hardened. "I can't have a Baronage because I can't have heirs." His voice broke slightly, but his eyes stayed rigid. "I *can't*."

As soon as I felt the heat radiate against the front of my throat, my hand flew up to cover my Nordingaard crystal. I squeezed my fingers tightly to contain its light, even as warmth filled my palm.

At that same moment, a tiny pinhole of white light opened up between Evereon's eyes, right on top of the jagged white scar.

A moment later, I heard notes from a lone violin…but that was not possible. No one was playing music in the room. After a few more melancholy notes, I realized the music was in my mind, calling me closer to Evereon.

Power sparked in my fingertips. A few tears in the air sparkled and braided themselves into a rope that only I could see, connecting the white light on Evereon's forehead to my own.

Wait…it was not just white light…it was a door. A door into Evereon's mind.

Daigen had said that he had communicated with my inner self using a magical connection. Is that what I was doing?

As an answer, the violin music that only I could hear got louder and sadder. The music wrapped around my wrist and tugged me forward, like a child asking for help.

I swallowed and ignored the invisible magic pull. I had been so eager to use Evereon's past as leverage for my own security, but now I did not want to know. It felt…too deep and too sad.

I could scarcely handle my own emotions, I did not want to take on someone else's too.

My white flame retreated and the invisible magic connection weakened. Baron Mydina rejected his son because he could not have heirs, that I could accept. Evereon did not show any signs of disloyalty, so I would not need to enchant him after all.

I should have just trusted Erik's instinct.

Evereon's face stayed hard, unaware of the magical pull between us. "You and Riyan were the North's last hope, the last two people who could maintain our lineage and keep the Hytons from taking over. I need to know what you did to him on that mountain."

"I did nothing, I—" I swallowed and the numbness in my chest grew, suffocating my white flame. My magic hold over Evereon disintegrated. "The Queen of the Giants took him."

His eyebrows knitted and his nostrils flared. "What? What happened?"

My white flame awoke again, pushing my words out of my throat before I could stop myself. "He gave his life for mine."

Evereon's eyes were round as dinner plates. "He's dead?"

"No! No, he is still alive!"

He let out a relieved breath. "Still married, then? That at least gives us some stability—"

"No." My hand flew up over my throat. I did not mean to tell him my blood bond was gone. The answer just…came out on its own! How did that happen?

Evereon's face froze. "What do you mean, 'no?'"

Before I could try to come up with a lie, panicked footsteps echoed in the stairwell. I turned to see two white-faced maids running out of the stairwell and into the dining hall.

"Captain!" one of them panted, pointing backward toward the stairs. "A-a man is in Miss Bloodstone's room!"

"He's…he's purple!" cried the other.

Evereon wrapped his hand around the hilt of his sword as he marched toward the stairwell. He growled at the maids to get out of his way and then hauled himself up the steps.

I picked up my skirt and followed. I could not have him angering Daigen and getting turned into a goat or some other creature. Luckily, Evereon was slow enough that I could keep up.

Even though I was concerned about how the captain of the Bloodstone army would react when he found Daigen, a bigger question burned in my mind—why had I unwillingly given away harmful information? I had no control over my own tongue!

We reached the top of the steps and Evereon barrelled down the hallway toward Astrid's bedroom. He stopped at the door decorated with a rainbow of flowers with his brows knitted. I stopped in my tracks too.

What froze our feet was not a scream, nor the sound of a struggle, but a giggle, soft as butterfly wings.

She was not supposed to giggle, and yet…

With a croak of encouragement from Endre in my left ear, I pushed open the door to Astrid's room.

Hilda once said her daughter had lost her mind the day Riyan was born. Nikkolas had said she was broken and only knew five words, one of which being "monster."

But as I looked at Astrid Bloodstone, sitting in her wheeled chair in the center of her bedroom and tugging on Daigen's horns, the word "monster" was far from her lips.

Instead, her lips wore a smile.

Chapter Six
Shards of Memory

I never thought I would see Astrid Bloodstone smile. My heart swelled as I watched her play with Daigen in the middle of her bedroom.

Evereon did not feel the same.

He drew his sword. "Get away from her."

Daigen gently tugged himself out of Astrid's grip and glared at Evereon. "Oh, a lost little Mydina boy? Far away from the House of wolves, I see." He raised a hand. "Now would you be more or less ferocious as a wolf? Let's find out."

I stepped between Evereon and Daigen's potential enchantment. "Stop—"

Evereon stepped around me and kept his grip on his sword. "I will not let you terrorize Miss Bloodstone—"

Evereon pulled his sword only an inch out of its sheath before his wrist stilled. Before I could blink, Daigen used his invisible hold on Evereon's wrist to yank him forward. When Evereon's face was mere inches from his, Daigen opened his mouth and breathed out a dark frost. The moment the magical mist curled into Evereon's nose, his yellow eyes rolled back and he collapsed.

My breath caught in my throat as Evereon crashed to the floor. Astrid did not even blink.

Erik's and Endre's wings fluttered on either side of my head and made my heart jump. Erik perched on the top edge of a nearby wardrobe. Endre landed on Evereon's back and hissed up at Daigen.

"Calm down, wolf boy will wake up soon enough." Daigen's horns retreated back into his head. "I'm not a monster."

He looked down at unconscious Evereon and scoffed. "Terrorize Astrid, what a joke." He gently held Astrid's frail hand. "What did you say to me the first time we met?"

Astrid's grey eyes sparked like thunderclouds and a smile crawled up her face. "Eat shit."

Did…did I hear her correctly? Of the five words Astrid knew, I was fairly certain none of them were "eat shit."

I stepped closer and examined Astrid's flushed face. I looked up at Daigen and shot him another silent question.

Daigen kept hold of Astrid's hand. "I gave her a memory back—from my mind to hers. Along with the one I took from the healing spring." He gently stroked Astrid's temple with his knuckle. "She's got a few memories in there…bits and pieces that she's collected over the years visiting the spring."

My fingertips touched the cool surface of my crystal. If magic from the spring captured memories, that meant Astrid's mind had to be…

I caught my breath—her mind was in the place West of the Moon and East of the Sun. How had she gotten trapped there?

He lifted Astrid's hand toward me. "Care to take a look? I'm sure she'll let you in…she's horribly lonely."

I shot Daigen a look, but I understood. We did not come to the fortress because Astrid was distressed, we came because she had a memory I was supposed to see.

At least I was beginning to untangle Daigen's twisted logic.

Astrid's big eyes flicked up to me. She looked much older than thirty-nine but still seemed even younger than me.

She likely had no idea who I was, even though we had met before. I held out my hand. "Nice to see you again, Astrid."

Astrid let go of Daigen but did not reach for my hand. Instead, she reached for my crimson cape, gently feeling the wool between her fingertips. She closed her eyes and took a deep breath.

Did she even know that the scent that lingered on my cape was from her son?

"My name is Serafina," I said softly. "I married your son…once. I…I am trying to save him."

Astrid looked toward her bed, where portraits of childlike Riyan were nailed to the wall.

My eyes swept across the portraits of the yellow-haired child that Astrid had painted with her hands. She had screamed in terror when she last saw Riyan, but she would not have painted him as a child if she did not know him, at least a little.

She might even have known him better than I did. Maybe she would show me who he really was, at least a small clue, anything to give my heart some damn direction.

I held down a hopeful smile as my white flame awoke and my crystal warmed my throat. The light between Astrid's eyes that only I could see started shining and the magical tether between our minds materialized.

She released my cape and lifted her hand. Right before her fingertips touched my palm, a dozen butterfly wings fluttered in my mind.

Astrid let me in.

In a breath, I closed my eyes and the invisible butterfly wings led me into the darkness, submerging me like they pulled me underwater.

The feeling of water all around me made my heart jump. My eyes popped open to an endless black void. My arms and legs flailed, trying to swim through the water but failing.

A tiny light, like a broken shard of a stained glass window, twinkled in the darkness. Maybe I could use it to float on.

I frantically pulled myself toward it. The moment my fingertips touched the cool surface, my body tumbled through a fog.

The smell of fresh dew filled the air and morning mist crept through me. I did not have a body, which meant I was in a memory.

A quick survey of the surroundings placed me in the courtyard of Bloodstone Fortress. Servants in crimson livery milled about, but they looked like plain peasants, not trained soldiers.

Bloodstone did not have an army yet.

A girl that looked no older than sixteen swung a sword at a tree near the tall stone wall. Her golden braids danced along her back as she practiced her steady, yet fluid movements with her sword.

"Good morning, Miss Bloodstone," said a deep male voice.

Astrid startled and tripped over one of the tree's roots, landing on her backside hard.

"Fuck!" she cried.

Her eyes popped open and she clapped a hand over her mouth. Standing over her was a tall young man with white hair flowing down his back. His deep blue eyes were wide and unblinking.

"I mean…f-fortunate to see you this morning, Lord Hyton." Astrid pushed herself up onto her elbows. "I-I did not mean to startle, you are just so…large."

Her cheeks flushed red and she buried her face in her arms.

The young man did not chastise her for her impropriety, but instead he laughed. He laughed so loudly even the servants around the fortress stopped with their chores to listen.

Astrid's grey eyes peeked over her arms. A tiny smile raised her cheeks as the young man extended a hand to help her up.

The memory ended as if I had reached the end of a jagged cliff. I held out my hands and pushed, bringing myself up to the surface of the memory like I was floating on driftwood.

Although he was a teenager in the memory, there was no mistaking the white hair and Hyton Blue eyes. What was General Ragnar Hyton doing at Bloodstone Fortress all those years ago?

Mother had mentioned Ashmore students used to have summers at home just like the Heaston boys did, that was the only way Ragnar and Astrid could have met.

But why would a Hyton go to Bloodstone? Most of Lycaster avoided the Northern provinces.

I rested on my knees atop the glassy surface as I searched my own memories. Nikkolas and Hilda had brought up General Hyton's mother, Duchess Ilsa, over dinner on my first night in Bloodstone. Even mentioning the traitorous, murdering, alleged sorceress was illegal in Lycaster, but Nikkolas and Hilda talked about her as if she were an old friend.

And if Ilsa was a friend of the Baron and Baroness of Bloodstone, maybe her son had accompanied her on a visit to the fortress.

"I have what you seek, young thief."

I turned my head. That was Ganora's voice…but what was it doing in Astrid's mind?

Ganora's voice came from another floating shard of memory. The jagged glass glowed white with sparkles of rainbow light refracting off the edge. I stretched my fingertips toward the memory and used my magic to pull it closer.

The moment my fingertips touched the cold surface, I plunged into frigid air.

Snow was all around me. Astrid wielded her sword as four giants stomped toward her. The giants smashed their grey fists near her, sending snow flying high in the air. Astrid screamed and swung her blade.

Like the claps from a raging thunderstorm, the giants hit the ground again and again, but Astrid barely avoided them. She held a hand over her abdomen and rushed forward.

If I had a body, my heart would have ached the moment Astrid protected her belly. She was pregnant…and facing the giants alone.

She ran toward a large, swirling pit full of glowing water. Gold, violet, green, blue, and white light all sparkled in the depths and on the surface.

It was a giant well…no, not a well…the Man of the Mountain's grave, surrounded by frost-covered runes more than fifteen feet high.

Astrid panted as she raced toward the well. Tears and snot streamed down her ruddy face, but she kept her pace.

Then the giants went still. The temperature plummeted.

Astrid stopped mere feet from the edge of the well. Her watery eyes traveled up until she met the grey face of the Queen of the Giants. Ganora knelt by the edge of the well on the opposite side.

She raised her hands and invisible icy talons ripped Astrid's sword from her fist, then an empty water skein from her shoulders.

Astrid's eyes went wide the moment the skein disappeared into the snow. If the skein was empty, why did she panic?

Ganora's glowing eyes were hard. "I have what you seek, young thief." Ice laced her words. "Come take it."

Astrid's face hardened and then I understood. She was there to steal the Man of the Mountain's tears from his grave.

Astrid accepted Ganora's challenge and ran straight for the well.

She threw herself onto her hands and knees and desperately gulped down a mouthful of bitter tears. The moment she took a breath, her mind tumbled out of her body into the water.

The wisp of Astrid's mind swirled around the perimeter of the well and I swirled with her, taking in everything I could.

Ganora stalked toward Astrid's body and blew sparkling ice crystals into her nose and mouth. Astrid's belly began to grow.

Then everything went black—Astrid's mind plummeted into the depths of the place West of the Moon and East of the Sun.

I pushed myself out of the shard of memory. The weight of everything I had just witnessed sat in the center of my chest like a boulder.

Ganora had used the tears that Astrid had swallowed to enchant her baby. She made Riyan too large. It was *her* power in his veins that made him impossibly strong, lightning fast, and forced him to painfully grow every time he was afraid.

A screaming memory pulled itself toward me. Through the shining surface was a red face with black horns. I held my arms tightly over my stomach as I looked through the memory like a window, watching through Astrid's eyes.

Over the screaming, Daigen tried his best to soothe Astrid. "You'll be all right, I promise. Just trust me."

Daigen held up a gleaming *Reginbani.* The screaming got louder. I tightened my hold over my abdomen. Even though I was too afraid to touch the memory, I could *feel* the slice of the knife across my lower belly.

It was like being lit on fire.

The memory started to float away and the pain subsided. Right before the memory disappeared into the darkness, I spotted a giant, but underdeveloped baby in Daigen's claws.

Riyan.

My chest went tight. My limbs shook. It was too much.

Before I could escape, ribbons of voice surrounded me.

"How can I be with child, Ragnar? I am not married!"

"Do not worry, summer break is coming soon. As soon as Selection Night is over, I will sneak out of the palace and we will go up the mountain together. As long as we get those tears from the well, I can order Fraleigh to marry us."

A tiny fragment of memory floated by—Astrid hurriedly tying a crimson ribbon to a branch of a tree outside of Bloodstone Fortress. A leather skein was slung across her back and her sword was attached to her hip.

She was ascending the mountain—she needed the tears to marry Ragnar.

But why was she going alone?

Ragnar's voice whispered around me. *"I will come back for you, I promise."*

Astrid walked further through the woods outside the fortress and tied her second ribbon right above the mountain trail. The twin crimson signals clearly marked her path for someone to find, but Astrid looked over her shoulder and waited.

"I will come back for you, I promise."

Astrid's lip trembled, but she gripped the hilt of her sword and started her climb.

I slammed my eyes shut. I could not take it anymore. I had to get out.

"I promise."

I forced out a breath and let go of my magic. My white flame blinked out and I floated out of the tar pit of Astrid's mind.

I took in another breath and opened my eyes. My feet were on the floor. My hand was in Astrid's.

But my knees were weak…and I could not stand…

A hand with long fingers caught my back before I could fall backward.

"I thought you would have lasted longer than that," Daigen said as he set me down on a cushioned footstool. "You have the emotional capacity of a teacup if watching a few memories exhausted your power like this."

I glared at him, even though my vision was swimming. "Emotions made me weak, so I stopped having them."

Daigen scoffed. "You never stopped having them, you just suppressed them." He ran a hand through his white hair and sighed. "What did you see?"

My eyes found Astrid. "Ganora punished her…cursed her baby as punishment for stealing the tears."

"Good, you saw *that* memory." Daigen's heel clipped against the floor. "Now you know why your big boy was so big. Giants made from magic and mud were unstable. They could only travel a certain distance from the mountain before they crumbled. So, Ganora made a new giant out of flesh and bone."

I furrowed my brows. Suddenly Ganora's curse on an unborn baby seemed less like cruelty and more deliberate. Not only had Ganora made him big, but she also made him the strongest and fastest man alive. He was just like one of her giants, no, better.

Had she cursed Riyan hoping she could raise him to be her perfect weapon? Once Daigen had rescued Astrid from the well, did Ganora plan for Riyan to come back? Did she send her giants to destroy the North, hoping to lure him to her?

Was Ganora lying in wait all this time to take full control of Riyan and use him to free her sister?

Maybe the curse was never a punishment for Astrid, but for the Hytons. No better revenge against the royal House who made a "bad deal" with her sister than to turn one of their sons into a weapon against them.

I scrubbed my face with my hand. Just as I was thinking up a way to ask Daigen all my burning questions without actually *asking* him, the sight of Astrid's sparkling eyes stole my attention.

I turned my head to follow her eyes to the wall above me.

Of all the finger-painted portraits tacked onto the wall, the newest one was right above me. Astrid had painted it days ago—a man with blue eyes and long blonde hair.

Hilda had thought the man in the portrait was Riyan and so did I, but the hair was too long to be Riyan's…

It was Ragnar. Astrid had painted the father of her child the way she remembered him.

I swallowed and turned from the painting to look at Daigen. "He never came back."

Daigen laid his hand on Astrid's shoulder. "She doesn't know that. Her last memory of him is that promise."

The questions I wished I could ask hung in the air like a dense fog. Why had Ragnar never returned? Why had he been with Astrid in the first place?

The Hytons kept their vast number of secrets close enough to bury themselves in mystery. How could they be the most prominent family in the Dukedom and yet no one had figured out that their General had a secret son? Or that they held the Great Sorceress captive?

How could I force Duke Hyton to release Fraleigh if I did not even know what I was up against?

Evereon groaned as his body shifted on the floor, interrupting my thoughts.

Daigen looked down. "Oh look, the cranky puppy is awake."

Evereon's eyes were glazed as he pushed himself into a sitting position. I crossed the room to help him up. Endre soared past me, likely having the same idea.

Evereon's yellow eyes widened and he swatted at my brother. "Get away from me!"

Endre turned in the air and landed on a stool. He lowered his head and let out an indignant croak.

Evereon begrudgingly took my hand as I helped pull him onto his feet.

Daigen smirked at Evereon and gestured to Endre. "Is that how you treat a fellow Baron's son?"

Evereon's face blanched and his body went stiff. My mouth fell open. How could Daigen just—?

Daigen's violet eyes flicked over to me. "I took a secret from him, so I figured I'd give him one. It was only fair."

His hand dipped beneath his cloak and he retrieved a thick ivory envelope. My heart stopped as soon as I saw the bull stamped in the shining blue wax seal.

Daigen deftly flipped the letter over and turned his attention to Evereon. "Thought you could just hide this in your doublet and I wouldn't sense the stink of Hyton Palace on you?"

I did not even wait for Evereon to offer an explanation, my vision and mind focused only on my name on the front of the envelope. I knew that handwriting as intimately as if it had been marked onto my very skin— tall letters that crowded together, romantic curves and loops, and all inked into the parchment so strongly it might as well have been branded.

My heart raced and I suddenly could not breathe. Whatever was in that envelope came from Derrick.

Just like when he visited Ravenwood Manor seven years ago, the House of Hyton's only heir became the key to my cage of circumstance.

I only hoped he was the key to Fraleigh's cage too.

Chapter Seven
The Light

Rays of the setting sun weaved through the clouds. I rested on my forearms between two battlements on the southernmost tower of Bloodstone Fortress. Erik and Endre perched on the battlements on either side of me.

I had spent an hour convincing Evereon the lost Ravenwood sons were alive and not just some magical trick from the mountain. Afterward, we crashed on the chairs in Astrid's room, gently exchanging pieces of information and hoping to make sense of all that had happened over the past few days. He told me Nikkolas and Hilda had been laid to rest by their sons. I told him the truth of Riyan's parentage.

I had hoped that somewhere in our conversation I would find a clue as to how I would get Fraleigh away from the Hytons, but the day had almost ended without a conclusion. Daigen was right, what good was the Bloodstone army when the Hytons had Fraleigh at their disposal? What benefit was my magic if I could not use it when I needed to and barely withstood it when I did?

I had more power than I ever could have dreamed of and yet I was still stuck. The next full moon was creeping closer by the minute and I had no time to waste.

Derrick's letter crinkled in my hand. I unfolded the parchment, hoping to find something I had missed.

Serafina,

I worry every day that you are safe. I beg you, do not attempt to be intimate with Sir Bloodstone. I would not be able to go on if you left this earth and left me behind to grieve you for eternity.

Enclosed is an invitation to the Darkest Night ball, held every year on the new moon after Selection Night. Please attend, if only so I can know you are alive and unharmed.

I love you.

Eternally Yours,
Annalisa Thornebow

Derrick was no longer signing his secret letters as "Midnight." He had escalated from sneaking lines in his twin sister's letters to completely pretending to be her. To his credit, no one at Bloodstone Fortress was familiar with Annalisa's perfect penmanship to know the thin script did not come from her hands.

I sighed. Derrick was once my only salvation. I used to comb his letters and find clues of his feelings, his dreams, and his fears. I took his vulnerabilities and used them to make him fall more in love with me. *That* was my sense of direction over the past seven years. If he loved me, I had the crown.

But now that I was back in the grey, directionless void, what did his letters hold? A desperate plea to not seal my blood bond and an invitation to a stupid ball!

Hinges creaked behind me and the trapdoor into the keep slammed closed. Heavy footsteps grew closer, but I did not turn.

The spiky smell of burning herbs hit my nose. Evereon held a tiny rolled-up parchment that was smoldering on one end. He put the roll up to his lips and inhaled deeply, then he breathed out a puff of smoke. "A hell of a day."

I hummed in assent and eyed the parchment. "Endre used to use those too, for when his breath was short and his chest hurt."

Endre croaked and fluttered his wings.

Evereon let out a low chuckle as smoke curled around his face. "This is for a different kind of chest pain. Want some? Of all the ways people in Lycaster try to dull their pain, this is one of the least dangerous."

I tried not to breathe in the repulsive smell and shook my head. Thin wisps of smoke curled around Evereon's face as my eyes ran along the diagonal line of his scar. The scar stretched from forehead to jaw and cut perfectly between his eyes.

The corner of his mouth flicked up. "It's from the military academy."

I dropped my gaze to my folded arms as my cheeks heated. I should not have been staring. "I heard stories of General Hyton's methods at the academy. I…never thought he could be so cruel."

"General Hyton didn't slice me up," he said with a wan smile. "Riyan did."

I looked back up and the sight of his scar made my stomach turn. With how deep the cut must have been, I could not convince myself it was an accident.

Evereon shook his head slightly, but his soft smile stayed on. "General Hyton wanted the two noble sons to spar and Riyan would always do anything to impress him. *Anything.* Makes me wonder how much worse he would have been had he known the General was his father."

That did not sound like the man I had married. Riyan had a notorious reputation as "the Beast." He had killed twelve giants, two of them before my very eyes, but I had never thought him capable of carving open a man's face.

He had only ever shown me kindness…but that was with the blood bond. If the magic of the blood bond had bent my own hardened personality, how much had it altered his?

I bit my tongue as my blood ran cold. "Did…you know anything else about him?"

"Not really." Evereon leaned against the battlement. "He was an angry child when I was at the academy. Then he was smitten with you when he came back to the fortress. Not much more to him than that."

A tense breath hissed out of my nose. Another dead end.

My eyes fell to the soldiers patrolling the wall. Evereon had convinced the army I was a benevolent sorceress and loyal to the North, but a few still had their reservations.

"Did Nikkolas ever tell you what the army was for?" I asked.

He took a deep breath. "I was one of the first soldiers hired on. We were all fresh out of the military academy, so we thought the House of Bloodstone just wanted some men with weapons training to defend against the giants. Nikkolas made me captain after a few months once he realized I was one of the few soldiers who could read."

A moment of uneasy silence fell over us as Evereon looked over the wall. "I was too old to be considered a Bloodstone son, so I didn't even go up the mountain when all those boys went to fight the giants seven years ago. None of the soldiers did."

My stomach twisted. I could not imagine how my brothers must have felt hearing Evereon's confession. They had led thousands of Northern sons up the mountain, seen the horrors of slain boys just as Riyan had, spent seven years as *ravens*…and there was a whole army sitting around nearby?

What was the point of an army if not to fight the giants?

Evereon took a long drag from his parchment. "Then I noticed giants never came around the fortress. We spent most of our time stockpiling weapons and food. We were just…preparing."

I slid my hand into my pocket and pulled out the golden House of Ravenwood and House of Bloodstone pins. I stared at the snarling bear and cautious raven on the pins as I recalled the last conversation I had with Nikkolas Bloodstone.

He had stressed that I had to consummate my marriage with Riyan because the Hytons would take control of the North if Bloodstone had no heirs.

His gravelly voice wove through my mind. *"They cannot have access to our magic—not after what happened to Ilsa Ravenwood. The Hytons are monsters."*

I ran my thumb over the wing of the raven pin. "He was preparing for the Hytons to take the North."

Evereon nodded and glanced at my letter. "I grabbed that as soon as it arrived at the gate so I could check it for a threat. I wondered if Duke Hyton was going to make a move after merging Bloodstone and Ravenwood."

It always came back to the Hytons. Every conversation, memory, or threat all led to the royal House of Hyton and their desperate need for control—control of the provinces, of Fraleigh, and of how everyone perceived their legacy.

Even if it meant letting the sword fall on one of their own…

All at once, every directionless thread in my mind wove itself together. My white flame awoke and danced circles around my heart.

The Hytons were stubborn, unyielding, and had triumphed over every challenge in history. With the Great Sorceress of Nordingaard in their arsenal, they were seemingly untouchable.

In truth, a single person had cracked their foundation so deeply that they had to cover up her existence. Made her name illegal. Erased her from history. Crafted lies about her. If the Hyton legacy was a grand tapestry, all I would have to do is pull a single thread for it all to unravel.

The Hytons had cast out the memory of Duchess Ilsa for a reason, I just had to find out what that reason was.

I pulled out the invitation for the Darkest Night ball. The calligraphy was perfect, detailing a lavish masked ball to take place during the new moon—only seven days away.

Derrick had just handed me the key to the palace…but who would look after the North in my stead?

Exhilaration spoiled into worry in an instant, but I swallowed my feelings and kept calm. I weighed the two pins in my right hand before I held them out to Evereon.

He leaned away slightly from the pins. "You know I can't—"

"I promised Riyan I would take care of the North." I put on a small smile and pushed the pins closer to Evereon. "Someone needs to run the fortress while I am gone."

His brows furrowed. "And where are you going?"

"The ball, it would be quite rude to ignore the invitation." I cleared my throat as the backs of my eyes burned. "Besides, the longer the Hytons believe Nikkolas and Hilda are still alive, the longer the army can merely…prepare."

Evereon swallowed. He stared at the pins as if they were coiled serpents, ready to strike.

"Just until the next full moon, at most," I reassured.

He let out a long breath. Slowly, he gathered the pins in his hands, accepting full control of the Northern provinces. "I…I heard too many stories of what goes on in that palace. Even my father didn't like it." His eyes flicked up to my face. "I'll keep up communication with you, just to make sure you don't get…lost.

He gave me a tight-lipped smile and turned away, the House pins clinking as he shoved them in his pocket.

I gently stroked Erik's back with my fingertip. Endre hopped down from his perch and nudged Erik out of the way with a croak. He greedily nuzzled my palm with his feathered head.

I could not hold back my smile, even though despair seeped through my chest. "I cannot bring you with me. Walking into Hyton as a sorceress is dangerous enough. Having ravens at my side would instantly raise suspicions."

The trapdoor creaked open and Daigen appeared. "Talking to birdies is a great way to get yourself killed."

I rolled my eyes as he joined me to look over the courtyard. The wind ruffled his hair around his shoulders and he gave me a pointed look.

Sure would be nice if I could ask for his advice, but I would just have to see if I came to the right conclusion on my own.

I swallowed. "I am returning to Hyton at first light tomorrow."

He folded his arms and raised an eyebrow. "Now why would anyone want to go to that clifftop cesspit voluntarily?"

"I need to uncover the truth of Duchess Ilsa." I straightened my spine. "She was no sorceress. I may not know exactly where the truth may lead, but it has to be enough to damn Duke Hyton if he spent all these years hiding his own mother."

Erik let out a concerned croak. Endre let out an exuberant one. Daigen's smile grew and my body thrummed with energy—I was going in the right direction.

I glanced down at the soldiers patrolling the fortress walls. "If Duke Hyton gave Nikkolas enough money to raise his own army so long as he stayed quiet about Riyan's parentage, he might offer me something even better once I find the truth."

Daigen leaned on the side of the battlement and lifted an eyebrow. "The sorceress is going to the Duke for Fraleigh's freedom? Of course you would immediately resort to extortion, *Litlnadr*."

"Then you suggest what I should do."

"You know I can't."

I turned away and stared south, where red sunlight clashed with the dark blue sky. Damn the nonsensical magical rules! Although, could I really expect magic based on the tears of an ancient man to be straightforward?

My eyes fell to the crumbled remnants of the wall where Riyan had fallen through it days ago—where the curse in his blood had forced him to grow fifteen feet tall and he accidentally killed his grandparents.

Magic was not logic and it was not always good. Riyan certainly had never understood it, in fact, he seemed like he hated it.

All the more reason to figure out what exactly Fraleigh's damn blood bond had done to us.

I turned back to Daigen. "Fine, then I have to go to Hyton because I need to find my heart's desire. I *need* to control my magic."

His violet eyes flicked down to the letter in my hand. "And you're so sure your heart's desire is there?"

I frowned. "You said love requires a choice, and I cannot choose Riyan until I know who he is." A dark pit grew in my chest, marking the absence of the warmth I had shared with him. "The person who knows him better than anyone else alive is in Hyton Palace—his father."

Daigen hummed. "A logical conclusion."

"And once I learn more about him…" I swallowed, gathering my strength to face the dreaded unknown. "I will know if my heart ever desired him at all."

My palms started to sweat, but I grounded my feet on the bricks below. Daigen smirked, weighing me with his gaze as the evening breeze traced my ears.

For the first time, I did not even care if he was rifling through my head again. I just needed to know I had gotten something right.

"Ilsa is the right place to start," he said softly. "The truth shall always set you free."

I smiled, but Daigen held up a finger to stop my excitement. "But before you embark on your righteous quest to the den of vices, I have one more thing I need to tell you about your magic."

He stepped closer and poked me in the center of my chest. "Remember when I said you are changing? The Man of the Mountain's gift flows through your blood, connecting you with him even though he resides in the place West of the Moon and East of the Sun. He not only sees all the truth of the world, he demands it."

A flare of my white flame singed the base of my throat as my stomach knotted. I did not like where he was going…

"*Litlnadr,*" Daigen said with mock concern and a smile, "you can't lie."

Daigen withdrew his hand and my heart skipped a beat. When the Man of the Mountain told me my silver tongue would no longer do me any good, I thought he just meant in front of him. Lying was the language of survival in Hyton! How could I navigate the palace as an illegal sorceress, wielding an illegal crystal, and trying to uncover the truth of an illegal woman without the ability to lie?

A dozen solutions flashed through my mind in an instant…but each one ended with an axe through my neck.

I held my breath and counted my heartbeats, trying to calm down. Riyan would have known what to say. He would have wrapped his massive hand around my back and made a light quip to make me smile. Or combed my hair and sang a ridiculous song. Or shoved a delightful treat in my face.

Darkness has always surrounded me, but he was my one light. He was my moon, waxing and waning with his moods, but always there.

Though that was with the blood bond. Now…now I had no light, but the light I had was not even real!

When Riyan had left me, I had tried so hard to tell him that I loved him, even though I had enchanted myself into silence to keep myself safe from the giants. Though my throat was frozen, my mind screamed "I love you too."

But was my tongue silent because of my enchantment, or because I could not speak a lie?

I threw my hand in my pocket instead of crying out in frustration. My fire cooled as I pulled out the tiny scrap of linen from my pocket and traced each flower.

I grounded myself in each tiny bump of the threads, reminding myself of the promises I had made to Riyan before he disappeared.

Take charge of the Northern provinces.

Evereon had control. The North was secure.

Take care of Astrid.

Daigen had put a smile on Astrid's face and kept her calm.

Try to be happy.

The fog of numbness crept around my ribs. Even if it was just an enchantment, I missed that golden light Riyan and I had shared. I missed feeling happy. I missed that part of myself I thought I had found before the magic of the blood bond made me doubt everything.

The scrap of linen fell back into my pocket. I closed my eyes and let the gentle wind dance around my cheeks.

Snow fell in my memory. I was fifteen again, staring out the window on a January afternoon. I sat in a stiff armchair hugging my knees, watching thin snowflakes drift to the earth like ashes.

I had stared out that window for two hours, accepting that I would never be truly happy again.

I took in a breath and my white flame danced. My blood warmed, melting away the memory. Soft words floated to the front of my mind:

Untouched by the endless winter,
I am warm even now.

Winter would no longer dig its icy claws in my chest. The Queen of the Giants would *never* take anything from me again. Regardless of how I truly felt about him, Riyan deserved his life back.

So I had to be brave, just like he once told me I was.

I opened my eyes and the sun had disappeared, leaving behind only the cool twilight and a few flickering stars.

Three stars twinkled brightly in the sky. My eyes traced them as I marked each one with a new promise.

I would find out who Riyan truly was. I would free Fraleigh. I would…

The flaming diamond in my heart sparkled as I traced the Nordingaard crystal over my throat.

I would still try to be happy.

Part Two

Mirrors and Masks

Chapter Eight
Faerie Wine

My heart raced the moment we crossed the bridge into Hyton and I ran my thumb over the facets of my Nordingaard crystal to ease my worry. Daigen had wanted me to keep the crystal on my skin as much as possible while I was still new to my magic, but I could not risk being seen with it.

Any evidence that I was a sorceress would lead to an immediate death sentence.

I untied the ribbon of the choker and slid the crystal deep into my trunk that sat on the opposite carriage bench.

"Only a little while longer before we reach the palace, Madame Bloodstone!" Brandt called.

Paranoid Evereon had insisted someone accompany me to the palace and Brandt volunteered. Although judging from how he spilled his life's story multiple times to the poor coachman over the hours-long journey, he was more nervous about the plan than I was.

The carriage rattled as the dirt path of the country turned into the cobblestones of the city. I pulled out Derrick's letter from my trunk and ran my eyes over the parchment until I stopped just above the signature.

"Eternally yours."

My heartbeat slowed down. Even though I was mere minutes away from committing several crimes, I had one lifeline.

The heir to the House of Hyton still loved me.

The carriage stopped. I quickly folded up the letter and placed it in my trunk. Starlight filled the carriage as the door swung open and Brandt smiled as he offered his hand to help me out.

He and the coachman wore plain peasant garb so no one suspected either of them of being part of an illicit army, but I wore a deep crimson dress, proudly bearing the color of the House of Bloodstone. I had altered the dress during the journey so that the hem skated just above my feet, perfect for a night of dancing.

If I could even make it that far into the palace without being apprehended.

Brandt kept a gentle hold on my hand as he escorted me to the palace steps.

I looked up at his boyish face. "Will you be joining me inside?"

He shook his head. "Someone like me doesn't belong in there. I'll meet up with a few of my old mates from the military academy, but I'll be checking in on you."

I smiled. "Because Captain Mydina will ream your ass otherwise?"

"No," he replied with a smile of his own, "because you are the North's last hope."

His words weighed on my heart as he released my hand. The doors swung open and candlelight flowed out into the evening. His eyes flicked toward the doors. "I would wish you luck, but you don't need it—I've seen how well you can dance."

I turned from Brandt and chewed on my tongue as I stared at the open palace doors. Duke Hyton was inside…but so were the answers that would lead to Riyan's freedom.

I could not waste a second more. I picked up my skirt with shaking hands and ascended the first step.

The sounds of cackling laughter and swirling music drew me in, making each step feel lighter and lighter. Fragrant perfume tickled my nose. I could nearly taste the sweet wine on the cold edge of a silver goblet.

The promise of the dazzling spectacle within was almost intoxicating.

My slippers met the marble floor of the foyer. The palace doors closed behind me, sealing me inside.

My heart beat faster as I stepped through the foyer and into the halls. I passed a large tapestry of Fraleigh wielding her green and golden flames as the soldiers of the Sudrian empire begged on their knees for mercy.

Fraleigh had defeated the largest army in the continent yet was still trapped with the Hytons. The famous battle happened centuries ago, but it still made no sense.

The din of chatter and revelry grew louder and louder. A few nobles lingered in the hall outside the doors to the palace ballroom. Their eyes snagged on my crimson dress before they turned to their companions. Their lip paint crinkled and their teeth gleamed as whispers filled the air.

"The half giant did not eat her after all!"

"Do you think she consummated her marriage?"

"Of course not! She is still walking!"

I swallowed the bitter words that my white flame tried to push out my throat. Two servants in Hyton Blue livery each opened a door with a gloved hand and welcomed me inside the ballroom.

A lively violin tune bounced off the marble columns around the room. Starlight streamed in through the tall windows. The candles in the iron chandeliers were ablaze beneath the mural of prancing bulls on the domed ceiling. A rainbow of House colors swirled on the black and white tiles of the dance floor.

My stomach turned when I spotted Duke Hyton. He was sitting on his throne with a golden goblet in his hand.

I tore my eyes away from him and scanned the crowd for any sign of the tall man with hair like snow under the midday sun—General Hyton.

He was the only person in the Dukedom with knowledge of his mother and his son. He was not too keen with me the last time we spoke, but maybe I could find a way to loosen his tongue. If General Hyton gave me the right information, I could escape Hyton long before the moon fattened in the sky.

No sign of the General, but a smile flicked up my lips as I watched the dancing feet and flaring skirts in the center of the ballroom. It was a cadleigh dance. We had practiced them in school, but I had never seen a real one before.

So many colors. So many smiles.

"Sera!"

Sharp hands grabbed mine and I looked up. Annalisa.

"You came back!" she squealed. She wore a white dress draped with a Thornebow grey overskirt and had pulled her blonde curls into a knot on the back of her head.

I flicked my eyes to the dancing men and women. "Surprised to see you are not in the middle of it all."

She shrugged. "I was actually sneaking out when I saw you."

Annalisa sneaking out of a party? That did not sound like her at all. "Really?"

"Nothing is lonelier than a room full of people." She flashed a smile and tugged on my hands, pulling me deeper into the ballroom.

My stomach twisted. I was there to find the General, *not* dance in front of everyone!

"Would you young ladies like some refreshment?"

We turned our heads. A balding man held two tiny glass cups in his fingers. I took a quick note of his yellow cape and the golden pin of a deer that held it closed—Baron Amberfield.

Annalisa accepted a cup and peered at the clear liquid that filled the glass. "What is it, Uncle Thorin?"

"Faerie wine, perfect for you fawns just starting out." Baron Amberfield gave me a wink. "Gentle stuff, just do not overdo it."

I took the tiny glass and held back a recoil. Faerie wine did not *smell* gentle.

Baron Amberfield laughed. "Do not taste it! Just swallow."

I glanced at Annalisa. She gave the drink a considering look before she knocked back the glass and gulped it down.

I looked at my own glass. The firelight refracted off the cut glass edges and made the clear drink glimmer. I had no time to waste, but if I refused a drink from a Baron, I could look suspicious.

With a flick of my wrist, I dumped the prickling cold liquid down my throat. I forced myself to swallow and discarded the glass.

Annalisa laughed and grabbed my hands. "Come on! We have to dance!"

Before I could protest, Annalisa pulled me to the dance floor. She deposited me on one side before rushing to the other. A man and a woman grabbed my hands and I looked down, trying to remember the steps to the dance. Just as I got the rhythm, a man thrust me across the black and white tile as people threaded themselves from one side to the other like laces on a bodice.

Little glasses of faerie wine appeared in my hand any time it was free. I tossed glances over to Annalisa on the other side of the line, only downing a drink each time she did.

Had to make sure I did not "overdo it," whatever that meant.

I spun around with a beautiful woman wearing a purple dress and let myself smile. I had no idea my first night in the palace would be so fun!

A man yanked me into another group before he was supposed to and I accidentally stepped on his toes.

"Just relax, Madame Bloodstone!" said my partner.

Another man took my hand and spun me around. "I can help her relax."

Suddenly a pair of lips mashed against mine.

My heart stopped. The man pulled away and I blinked as I recognized him. Gerond Pebblebrooke, Camille's husband. He just…kissed me?

He released my hand to another man in the group, but I deserved an explanation. "The hell—?"

I caught a flash of red hair in the side of my vision before another kiss crashed against my lips. I yanked my hands out of his hold and pushed against his chest.

It was Myles Amberfield, Dinah's husband.

He laughed. "Calm down, you act like I bit you!"

Those two married my classmates and thought they could just kiss me?

Just as I was about to slap Myles, Gerond grabbed my wrists and forced me to keep dancing. "Do you not know? You kiss all the brides in your Selection class for good luck!"

Myles took my hands and spun me. "Just to make sure you have no hard feelings."

"Because we did not marry you," Gerond added.

I furrowed my brows. If anyone had hard feelings, it was *them* for not getting to choose a bride first.

"We had to land one on you while the half giant was gone," Myles said as he danced. "We just have Lady Hyton left."

Gerond shoved me across the dance floor to the other side of the line. A woman caught me and weaved me into her group, but my head spun.

Gerond and Myles kissed me. Lady Hyton was next. Lady Hyton was…

Brietta.

I caught a glimpse of auburn hair on the other side of the ballroom. Brietta wore a golden diadem and Hyton Blue fabric that cascaded from her shoulders. She walked behind the line of dancers, her head higher than anyone else's in the crowd. Her brown eyes met mine right before someone threw me into another spin.

My throat went dry. I had not expected to see her so soon after entering the palace. I did not even reply to her last letter because I was so angry with her for consummating her marriage with Derrick when we had agreed to annulments.

Though after the Man of the Mountain had shown me what had really happened…the magical pull of the blood bond must have overtaken Brietta and Derrick. They did not have a choice.

But I could not take back what I had screamed at her when I was blinded by rage. Our friendship was over, I just had to manage the situation the best I could.

During the carriage ride, I rehearsed the inevitable meeting with my former best friend. I would keep it cordial, letting Brietta think I was no threat and hopefully she would stay out of my way.

I moved further and further down the lines of people as I danced. The violin music grew louder. Brietta followed me, her brown eyes never moving away from me.

Pale yellow curls and a large golden crown appeared at Brietta's side before I spun again.

What was Duchess Hyton doing talking to Brietta?

The ballroom swirled around me as my feet found purchase on one of the white tiles. My hands were free. My legs were still. I had finished the dance!

I could have run to the beginning of the line to begin again like I was supposed to, but the notes of the violin traced my ears and held me still. I turned toward the music and found the man playing the lively tune.

Tall. A golden coronet atop his dark curls. A Hyton Blue cape down his back.

Derrick.

His eyes were closed as he played. I stepped closer and my chest warmed. Maybe the faerie wine was hitting me.

Derrick took in a breath and his dark lashes fluttered open. He caught sight of the hem of my crimson dress and his beautiful blue eyes snapped up to my face.

He lowered his violin as his smile slowly grew. "Finally, a wish that came true."

His hand cupped my face, his thumb brushing against my jaw. Heat flooded my cheeks and I could not breathe. A tiny speck of warmth in my heart blinked to life.

Oh, the wine really *was* hitting me.

Before I could take a breath, someone crashed into me and I fell to the floor. Warm liquid ran down the front of my chest and soaked my belly. I pressed my hand against the wet spot and withdrew it—my palm was stained red.

I froze. Had someone stabbed me? Did I reveal myself as a sorceress? Was I about to be dragged away in chains?

"My, how clumsy of me!" said a familiar voice.

I tore my eyes away from my red palm and looked up. Duchess Hyton stood above me with an upturned golden goblet in her hand. A drop of deep red wine dripped from the goblet's rim onto my skirt.

I let out a small sigh of relief. Just wine. Just an accident. No one had discovered my secret.

Derrick knelt to help me up, but Duchess Hyton grabbed me by the elbow and hauled me to my feet.

Her blue eyes raked over my dress. "Oh dear, what a mess. We need to get you cleaned up right away."

"Mama—" Derrick protested, but Duchess Hyton waved him off.

"Hush." She started to pull me away and looked over her shoulder. "Keep playing, lest your damn father think I caused a scene."

Before I could help it, I flicked my eyes up to the dais. Duke Hyton was looking right at us and rising from his throne.

Shit, *no!* I needed to look innocent, needed to hide, needed…

I turned back to Derrick, silently begging him to keep his father away.

Derrick looked from his mother to me. "But—"

"*Perform,*" Duchess Hyton hissed across her teeth. "You know your role."

A few voices rang out, demanding that the music return. Derrick swallowed his words as his mother dragged me off the dance floor. His eyes did not leave me as he lifted his violin to his shoulder again. Derrick grew smaller and smaller until he had completely disappeared in the crowd.

As soon as my eyes left Derrick's, my stomach knotted. Duchess Hyton pulled on my arm with more insistence than just someone wanting to clean a dress. Her feet hit the tile too strongly for her to be pulling some drunken antic.

Duchess Hyton was not escorting me, she was *taking* me.

Chapter Nine
Bristles and Bathwater

Duchess Hyton kept a strong grip on my arm as she tugged me through the palace halls. I tried to explain that a maid could escort me to appropriate quarters, but she had none of it.

"We have a room ready for you," Duchess Hyton said as she kept her eyes forward. "Now that the whole palace knows Sir Bloodstone is not joining us, I can finally burn that disgusting giant mattress my husband had put together."

I hoped the "room" the Duchess mentioned was not a dungeon, but I forced myself to keep calm. I came to the palace with an invitation, I had not performed any sorcery, and I at least appeared completely innocent. So long as I kept my mouth shut, I should be fine.

After climbing three flights of stairs, Duchess Hyton walked me down a hall with blue carpeted runners that I recognized as the royal family quarters. A couple of maids opened a pair of doors and soon I was in a small room with a porcelain tub in the center.

At least Duchess Hyton had taken me to a bathing chamber instead of a cell in the Western tower. The room was papered with a pattern of blue birds soaring through pink damask. Fresh white and lavender blooms puffed out of vases like clouds.

Although appearances could be deceiving.

Duchess Hyton slumped onto a cushioned stool near the tub. Her voice was dry as parchment. "She had an accident. Clean her up."

I pursed my lips. I did not expect company while I bathed, but apparently privacy was a luxury only the poor could afford.

One maid unlaced my dress while two others filled the tub with steaming water from a kettle.

I dared to look at Duchess Hyton again. She took long sips from her golden goblet while peering over the rim at me.

I threw my gaze down to the pink patterned rug. Hopefully the Duchess was just thrusting me into an odd post-Selection Night ritual like Gerond and Myles had done with their kisses.

The maid freed me of my dress and undergarments. I crossed my arms over my breasts and kept my eyes down as I stepped into the tub. The warm water on my skin felt like paradise.

The door clicked open and Brietta walked in. I gritted my teeth and tightened my folded arms. Who else was going to watch me bathe?

Brietta's hands were tightly clasped in front of her belly as she kept her eyes on Duchess Hyton. "We collected her clothes."

Two maids appeared behind Brietta and placed my trunk on the floor.

I gripped the edge of the tub but kept my face still. My Nordingaard crystal was in that trunk.

My heart thudded. I thought I would have had some time to properly hide my trinket before confronting any of the Hytons.

Tingles of magic in the bathwater danced around my legs and belly as my white flame flickered around my heart. I tightened my grip on the edge of the tub and bit my tongue.

I did not want to use sorcery in front of the Hytons! Why the fuck was my magic activating?

Duchess Hyton waved a hand at the maids. "You girls are dismissed. Let Madame Bloodstone have some privacy."

The maids bowed their heads and left us. I cut a glance to Duchess Hyton, who did not move from her stool.

Privacy, my ass.

Duchess Hyton's blue eyes flicked down to the bathwater. "What joyous news, another one of my kittens does not have an heir on the way."

Kittens? I followed her eyes to the trail of crimson swirling up from my hips in the water.

Shit! My cycle had started. I should have been keeping track!

I looked away and the magic in the water quieted.

Duchess Hyton scoffed. "Oh, do not be embarrassed. The longer you can go without getting pregnant, the easier your life will be—right Brie?"

Brie? When did Duchess Hyton start calling Brietta by her shortened name?

Brietta's voice was stiffer than I had ever heard it. "Right, Freya."

Freya turned back to me. "Not that you had to worry about that—you still have that virginal look in your eyes."

The flames inside me burned hotter and a scowl broke through my stoic mask. I was not completely untouched, but a couple of Riyan's fingers coaxing an orgasm out of me was apparently not enough to satisfy the terms of Fraleigh's blood bond.

Even though it had felt…very good.

The memory of Riyan's massive hands gently parting my thighs invaded my mind. He had tugged on my hair while his other hand explored me, my mouth grazing his as I gasped, my fingernails piercing his arms as I…

Then I remembered where I was and my cheeks burned. Freya took one look at my face and cackled in effervescent glee. What a ridiculous old drunk.

"Well," she slurred, "looks like you two are still synced up from Ashmore."

I held down a smile. Despite Brietta and Derrick sealing their blood bond, Brietta was not with child.

"The monthly curse is a blessing now." Freya sat on the edge of the tub. "Just as I was telling Brie, these men will keep you happy because you are the *only* person in the world that can give them what they need—an heir."

She gestured to Brietta with her goblet. "Thanks to that damn blood bond, the heir to Lycaster *has* to come from her. Keep holding out and even the strongest man in the House of Hyton will bend over backward to get you anything you want. But the instant you push out that male heir… all your power is gone."

Freya tipped back her goblet and her voice echoed in the metal. "Gone, gone, gone…it is all gone."

A tiny bell tinkled and Freya removed her goblet from her lips. "Ah, His Excellency came to join us."

I covered my chest and crumpled into the bathwater. The Duke was in the bathing chamber too?

Freya barked out a laugh. Brietta glanced down and said, "She means the cat."

Brietta bent over and lifted a large mound of brown fluff with green eyes and white paws into her lap. The gigantic cat nudged Brietta's palm as she stroked its ruff and ears. "Magnus the Bed Warmer, or Magnus for short."

"I call him 'His Excellency,'" Freya said, "because it pisses my husband off."

The door creaked open again. My stomach tensed until I realized it was only Merri, Freya's personal maid. She held a ceramic cup and saucer in her hands and glanced at Freya expectantly.

Freya nodded toward me. "Give it to her. She must be starving after that long journey from Bloodstone."

Merri politely dipped her head and walked over to the tub. I obligingly lifted my wet hands out of the water and placed them both around the warm cup. Inside was what looked like cream with flecks of brown dust on top.

Soft steam tickled the bottom of my nose. The promised taste was tantalizing, but I was not foolish enough to drink it—not with both Freya and Brietta watching me like a pair of eagles.

Freya scoffed. "You will knock back faerie wine but worry about this?"

She snatched the cup out of my hands and took a drink. She handed the cup back to me while pointedly licking the cream off her top lip.

She might have been a drunk lunatic, but the Duchess of Lycaster would not willingly poison herself. I lifted the cup to my lips and swallowed.

Every part of my body from my lips to my chest was suddenly warm—like I was getting a hug from my mother. I savored every moment of it until I was sucking the dregs from the edge of the cup.

"What a good girl," Duchess Hyton said with a smile as I lowered the cup. "Good to see someone else enjoys my little invention."

I licked my lips, searching for any remaining drop of cream or tingle of spice. "Invention?"

"The heaviest of cream," she replied wistfully. "A Meadowshyre spice blend. And the secret—hunter's root. Ground so finely that you cannot taste it, but enough of the hearty root to fill you up."

I smiled. Hunter's root was all over the forests in Ravenwood. Our cook who was fond of spirits after dinner once revealed that my mother had ordered her to mix hunter's root in my porridge every morning because she was concerned with how scrawny and small I was.

Too bad the damn root never made me grow taller than five feet.

The delicious drink turned in my stomach. I had greedily slurped down their offerings and yet I was there to extort the Duke.

Although the Duchess would likely not be too upset if I threatened her husband with anything, especially the truth of what had happened with his mother.

Regardless, I had a contingency plan should the House of Hyton come crumbling down. I would take the innocents and run to Bloodstone Fortress. Maybe my magic would be under control by then…hopefully.

Hopefully I would not leave the Dukedom in chaos, either.

I gritted my teeth and set my empty cup on a nearby table. The fate of Lycaster was not my problem. The star that guided me through the hazy night was the thought of getting Riyan back from the Queen of the Giants.

If Riyan gave everything for me, I had no problem *taking* everything for him.

It was…the right thing to do. It was a repayment for his sacrifice, justice, or even merely giving him the second chance at life he deserved.

No matter how much I tried to honey my reasoning, my motives were still cold.

I let out a frustrated breath and looked over at Brietta. Magnus had somehow left her lap without me noticing. She straightened her spine and glanced over at the Duchess. "I can take things from here, Freya."

Freya let out a sloppy yawn. "I am certain you can. I need to acquaint my face with my pillow anyway."

She left her stool and slunk into the darkened doorway of what I could only assume was her bedchamber. Magnus's bell tinkled as he dutifully followed her, his fluffy tail dragging behind him.

That was…odd, but so was every encounter with Duchess Freya Hyton.

Out of the corner of my eye, I caught Brietta extending her hand. I hesitated for a moment before I took it and she helped me out of the tub.

This was not the cordial reunion I had planned for.

She wordlessly handed me a towel and I patted myself dry. I put on undergarments and menstrual wrappings as the wordless tension grew heavier.

Silence was my symphony, but it was a foreign tongue from Brietta's mouth. The longer she went without talking, the more suspicious I became.

Just as I was about to start a polite conversation about palace life, Brietta handed me a folded nightgown. The hem tumbled to the floor as I held it and my heart stopped.

It was not just any nightgown, it was *my* nightgown.

"Took it from your trunk while you were eating," Brietta said.

I swallowed and slipped the nightgown on. Maybe she had not rifled through my trunk to find the damning evidence of my treasonous actions. She knew me for too long to suspect anything. All I had to do was act normal and I could slip past her.

"We were friends for six years, Sera," Brietta said. "We have a lot to talk about…"

She pulled her hand out of the pocket and my stomach dropped. She held up my choker, the illegal crystal catching the candlelight.

"…and you had better not lie to me this time."

Chapter Ten
Lies of Men

Of all the ways I had prepared to be confronted with my sorcery, standing in my nightgown fresh out of a bath was not one of them.

I stared at my Nordingaard crystal in Brietta's hand and kept my face schooled. Brietta had always kept my secrets in the pocket I had sewn in her heart, but that was when I was her friend and not a threat to her new House.

Just the crystal was enough evidence that I was using sorcery. If she turned on her heels and took it to Duke Hyton, my head could be on the chopping block by sunrise.

The magic in the bathtub glimmered in my mind's eye. Maybe I could enchant her to forget it, but the crystal would glow if I used my magic. Then I would truly damn myself.

Brietta's eyes were hard. "I was raised in the House of Elvar. I know every gemstone that is mined in the Dukedom or traded across our waters. *This* is not any of them. This is—"

I held up my hands. "Brietta, I—"

"You know everything is different now." Her lip quivered for only a moment. "It's *Lady Hyton*."

My shoulders curved forward. Brietta had always towered over me, but I had never felt smaller until that moment.

I *hated* how she made me feel small.

"I watched you drink *five* glasses of faerie wine," she said. The ribbon of the choker rippled as Brietta's hand trembled. "I have carried stacks of books that weigh more than you—that fourth drink should have knocked you on your ass by now! What happened to you?"

My white flame burned the bottom of my throat, trying to push out an answer I did not have. The magic in my blood must have made me more resistant to spirits. Daigen should have fucking explained how my body had changed!

She took a step forward. "What happened to your husband? We all know he is not here."

The answer flew out of my mouth. "The Queen of the Giants took Riyan."

I clamped my teeth down. Fuck! Why had my body forced the answer out?

White fire swirled around my chest, growing bigger and bigger. I had to keep still. I had to hold firm. I could not lose control in front of the future Duchess.

"*The Queen of the Giants* took your husband?" Brietta's lip curled. "Why are you still lying to me?"

My white flame exploded.

"It is not a lie!" My blood was alight, the flames from my magic burning the walls of my chest. "I cannot...I cannot lie anymore!"

White light flared from the crystal. Brietta yelped and dropped the necklace onto the rug.

Brietta stepped away, her eyes not leaving the crystal on the floor. "Sera, what are you—"

"A-and he is not my husband anymore!" I could not stop. *Could not* stop. "My blood bond is gone! It is fucking gone!"

The water in the bathtub was suddenly ablaze. My breath quickened. I shut my eyes and tried to focus, but words flew out of my mouth like arrows. "Nikkolas and Hilda Bloodstone are dead! The North is going to collapse if I do not get Riyan back!"

Why was I spiraling out of control? What did my heart want so badly that it was forcing my body to combust?

Suddenly I heard whispered poems against my ear. Then shared laughter in the lecture hall. My fists loosened, and I felt a dinner roll that I had passed beneath the dining table in my hand. I felt hands braiding my hair. Wet tears on my shoulder. A warm hug against my cheek.

I just wanted to unload the burden of the past few days. I wanted help from someone who once knew me.

I wanted Brietta. I…wanted to be her friend again.

The inferno within cooled to a warm glow. The fire in the bathtub snuffed out. My limbs were weak as I opened my eyes. Brietta's back was to the wall, her palms flat against the pink paper.

"You…" she stammered, "are you some kind of—?"

"Sorceress." The damning admission left my lips. Fatigue weighed me down, but I shifted onto the balls of my feet, as if ready to run from an executioner the moment I said the word.

I had just put my entire life—and Riyan's—on the line. Before, I would have slithered my way out with a string of lies, but the flame inside me was too bright for the darkness of my deceit.

I *had* to trust Brietta with my secret.

Her lip quivered. Her eyes darted from my face to the crystal and back. "Sera, you cannot—"

"And unless you want me dead, you cannot tell."

The silence that followed nearly strangled me. After a couple of thudding heartbeats, Brietta tilted her chin up.

"Fine, sorceress." The imperious gild to her voice suited her, although it sounded strange coming from her lips. "I will keep your secrets if you can keep mine. Freya and I did not just bring you here for a bath."

I let out a shaking breath. I was safe. She would not turn me in. I was fine. Just fine.

Brietta turned around, placed her hand against a green bird on the wallpaper, and pushed.

With a heavy clink and a soft sigh, a panel opened up in the wall to her left.

I had slipped into a secret passageway in the palace before with Mother, but this opening had more sophisticated mechanics than a small door hidden behind a tapestry.

Brietta took a candlestick off a nearby table and stepped into the dark stone hallway behind the pink wallpaper.

The flicker of the candlelight in the dark made her round face look almost dangerous. "Lycaster is nothing like we thought. Follow me."

I picked up my choker off the floor. The moment the crystal met my palm, I let out a slow breath. My knees were still weak, but I was somehow calmer.

Slowly, I entered the shadows with Brietta. She pulled a rusted lever and the bathing chamber wall moved back in place with a groan.

I followed Brietta through the hallway that was so narrow, I was surprised her shoulders did not scrape the stone walls. Her fingers traced the wall until they disappeared into what looked like nothingness. She turned sharply and suddenly she descended.

I followed the light of her candlestick down a tight spiraling staircase.

"Do you remember learning about 'Alastar the Good' in school?" Brietta said as her feet softly tapped on the stone stairs.

"The second Duke of Lycaster?" I ran my hand along the soft stone to keep balance. "The Baron council named him 'The Good' after his death because he freed all the barbarians his father had enslaved, right?"

"That is what our matrons taught us, anyway."

"I suppose you also learned that our matrons lied?"

We spiraled another full turn before she responded. "Talking with Freya has been…enlightening."

Just as I was getting dizzy, Brietta stopped. We entered another dark hallway and she marched forward. Her circle of candlelight was our only bubble of safety against the unknown.

"Alastar the Good abolished one form of enslavement, sure." Brietta groped along the wall until she found an iron handle of a door. "But he wrote into law another one, a sneakier one, one that we still use today."

Did she know about Fraleigh's captivity? Maybe I should not tell her everything I knew just yet. "What slaves are in Lycaster?"

Brietta ducked under the doorway. The candlelight lit up her brown eyes like amber gems. "You think you would know—considering you are one."

My hand floated up to my neck, stroking the bare skin there. What was she talking about?

"Every noble girl is shipped off to Ashmore Academy the year we turn fifteen," Brietta said. "No one has a choice—that is the law. They keep us in that prison, stuff us full of lies, and as soon as we are ripe, they auction us off to men to do whatever they please for the rest of our lives."

Brietta turned and I followed. We walked through the much wider hallway that was lit with gently burning sconces. Polished wood trim and marble floors lined the halls.

A low, slow buzz filled the air.

"Then what is our fate?" Brietta gestured to her left. "This."

The buzz came from a snoring man who rested on a small bench in the hallway and was using a woman's rear end as his pillow. The woman's hair was tousled, her lip paint was smeared, and her bosom was half-exposed over her tight bodice.

Was she even breathing?

"Constant parties until the next full moon," Brietta grumbled as she started down the hallway again. "Where the men trade wives like they are just another bottle of wine to pass around."

I slowed my pace, eyeing a sleeping woman on the floor who was smashed between two unconscious men. "Surely Derrick has not—"

Brietta snorted. "No. He makes his obligatory appearance at every party and then retreats to the North tower."

I let out a relieved breath. Of course Derrick would never treat Brietta with such disrespect. He only loved me, but he was still not that cruel.

Brietta stopped at a large tapestry of hunters with spears surrounding a doe. "But if you think Derrick is a beacon of decency in this depraved morass…" She pulled back the tapestry, revealing another door. "…you are wrong."

She pushed the door open. Brietta's candle lit up a small room with a row of four plush leather chairs. All four chairs faced a series of windows that led into…

I held in a gasp. It was a window into the dressing room that we prepared in before the Presentation.

Riyan had confessed that he had seen me before the Presentation through magic mirrors, but were they really magic? My Nordingaard crystal warmed in my fist and I threw out a quick sweep of my power over the glass.

Nothing responded.

I walked over and touched the glass. It felt completely ordinary. How was it possible to be a window on one side and a mirror on the other?

"They pile all the suitors in here and tell them these are magic mirrors that will show them our true selves." Disgust dripped off Brietta's voice as she stepped into the room. "All bullshit, Freya told me everything. The mirrors are not magic—it is just some trick with metal. Duke Hyton just tells them the mirrors are cursed so that the suitors' cocks will fall off if they ever tell a woman about them."

I tapped the glass with my fingernail, trying to figure out the trick.

I used to be an alchemist's apprentice. Master of illusions.

Daigen. He had said he performed services for the former Dukes of Lycaster—the mirrors had to be one of his illusions.

Brietta kept her distance from the mirrors. "All the suitors have watched every bride at her most vulnerable for hundreds of years. While we sweat about the biggest moment of our lives, they leer at us and they *laugh at us.*"

I stared at the exact spot where I had dressed mere days ago and a shiver crawled up the back of my neck.

Her voice broke. "I always knew we were property. Being slaves to our husbands made sense when Freya explained it…but I never realized how powerless we were until I saw this room. They will not even let us have privacy. We solely exist for their use, for their entertainment, and for their consumption until we finally give up and die."

I ran my thumb over the ridges of my crystal as I looked at the worn vanity tables and stools. Riyan had watched me. He had…participated in all this.

He was too large to fit into any of the chairs, so he must have just sat on the floor behind them, watching the entire spectacle like it was cheap theatre.

He had watched me backhand Annalisa and order Camille and Dinah to help me fix Brietta's dress. He had told me I impressed him, that I was so commanding and strong that he had to marry me.

What had Riyan thought while Brietta cried because Ilsa's dress did not fit her? He was supposed to choose her, but did watching her tears make him select me as his bride instead?

No, Riyan had said he wanted me from the moment he saw me through the mirrors. I looked through the window at the row of white doors in the dressing room. My eyes locked on the door that I had stepped through not even two weeks ago.

There. That was when he first saw me. He had known *of* me, the younger sister of Erik and Endre Ravenwood, but he did not know me. He could have never known me or seen me had it not been for the centuries-old trick of glass and metal.

Such a strange duality. The opportunity to spy on the brides so the suitors could see "our true selves" was infuriating and unjust…but had Riyan really seen my true self through those mirrors? Was I truly commanding and strong?

Riyan certainly thought so, anyway.

I folded my arms and hissed out a breath. The mirrors were a reflection on one side and a window on the other—how fitting. Riyan got to see all of me, but I still did not know who he truly was…other than that he was a leering bastard like the rest of the men.

As much as I hated to admit it, Daigen was beginning to make sense. Riyan loved me because he got to choose me. He got to look through the glass, reject Brietta, and pick me to marry. He got to see me at my most vulnerable and decided that *I* was right for *him*.

But I never got the same choice…and of course the creator of the mirror illusion knew that.

I wanted to punch those damn mirrors until they shattered into a thousand pieces.

Brietta gently stepped across the room until she stood at my side. "The humiliation and pain after Annalisa's ball was horrible but…" Her knuckles turned white as she gripped her candlestick. "They *all* saw me in here."

Her voice was tempered, but her chest rose and fell faster.

"There is nothing Annalisa, Dinah, or Camille ever did that made me feel as low as knowing all those men watched me break down from the shadows like I was just…meat."

Brietta let out a breath. "I will *never* feel that low again, and neither will anyone else. What Freya and I are planning…it will change the fabric of the Dukedom forever."

I dragged my eyes up to hers—they glistened with rage and a glimmer of determination. If her anger matched mine, maybe I could trust her with not only my secrets, but Fraleigh's as well.

She took a long breath like she was about to jump into the ocean. "Full citizenship for every woman in Lycaster—not just the nobility. Women will own property, inherit titles, and Selection Night will be nothing more than an embarrassing chapter in the history books."

My eyes widened. Maybe I did not have to sneak around Hyton Palace to uncover Ilsa's secrets after all. The women of the House of Hyton were already working on plans for liberation that perfectly aligned with mine.

I lifted my chin slightly and matched her measured tone. "Would those plans of citizenship include the Great Sorceress of Nordingaard?"

Shock flashed across her face. "No, Fraleigh…"

"Made a bad deal with the Hytons long ago and ended up in the same place as us," I finished. "*That* is why Ganora took Riyan, she wants to use him as a weapon to finally free her sister."

Her mouth fell open slightly as the machinations of her mind processed the impossible. After a moment, Brietta looked away from me. "The situation may have just become more dire, but I am glad you are here. You played a crucial role in our plans…"

I furrowed my brows. "What did you have planned for me?"

She swallowed. "I cannot get pregnant. You heard Freya, the only scrap of power I have right now is an empty womb. My cycle ends soon and…I want you to keep Derrick as far away from me as possible."

I scanned her face, looking for a clue for what she meant, but for once I could not read her. "Exactly *how* do you want me to keep him away from you?"

Her eyes stayed on the rug. "He is still obsessed with you. He has barely looked at me since the…incident." Her hold on her arms tightened. "I want to keep it that way."

Now it was my turn to stare at the swirling filigrees on the rug. Derrick certainly had not put his feelings for me aside when he had married Brietta. We had kissed, my hands had wandered along his chest, and I had wanted to go further, but we never did.

Did Derrick still want me like he had before? Everyone believed I was still married to Riyan, but that did not matter. Despite what we were taught in Ashmore, fidelity was not a pillar of any Lycaster marriage.

But Brietta never specified how she wanted me to distract Derrick. He was still…just my friend, after all.

I finally pulled my gaze away from the rug and looked up at Brietta. "We cannot take long. The Queen of the Giants gave me until the next full moon to free Fraleigh."

Brietta hissed out a breath. "That is in less than three weeks…no time at all."

I shook my head and suppressed a smile. Brietta could act tough, but she still had no idea how to manipulate people. "If you want the Duke to give you what you want, you have to threaten him with a larger cudgel than an empty womb."

Brietta arched an auburn brow and I let my smile finally break through.

"You threaten him with the truth of what *really* happened with his mother," I said.

She gave me a sly smile and extended her hand. "Allies?"

Allies. Not friends.

I bit back my disappointment and took her hand. "Allies."

She squeezed my hand. "I will schedule a tea with Freya. We can see how much she is willing to say about Ilsa."

I smirked. "Better fill her teacup with wine."

She sighed. "Whatever it takes." She turned to look through the window again, peering into the darkened dressing room with carpets stained with stale tears. "I am through with the lies of men."

Chapter Eleven
Under the Rainbow

The Duke of Lycaster was still a threat even in his sleep.

As Brietta and I walked through Hyton family quarters, my eyes stayed glued on the rearing bulls carved into the twin doors at the end of the hallway. Duke Hyton was behind those doors, I was sure of it.

I fought the shiver that skittered up my spine, but not because the Duke was mere paces away. A sickening feeling that I could not name pulled at my chest and I could not tear my eyes off those carved doors.

Maybe that sickness was because my mother was likely there too. My stomach turned and I fought the urge to gag.

"Are you sure you are all right after that faerie wine?" Brietta said stiffly. "Five glasses is more than most can handle."

I nodded, though my heart ached at the absence of the usual warmth in Brietta's voice. "I just followed what Annalisa was—"

"Brie!"

Brietta and I both turned to the thick-tongued shout. Annalisa finished dragging herself up the stairs. Her curls slipped out of her knot as she stumbled toward us.

"Brie—Brietta!" Annalisa's eyes were glassy and drooping, but her voice was sharp with urgency. "I am sorry. I am sorry I used to act like such a cu—"

Annalisa gagged and bent at the waist, heaving the contents of her stomach onto the floor.

My hand flew to my face, but the smell of the faerie wine already stung my nose. Annalisa dropped to her hands and knees and retched again.

Brietta wrinkled her nose, but her brow softened. "Oh, Anna—"

"Lady Hyton," a man whispered behind us. "It is past curfew."

We both turned. A palace guard slowly approached us, his eyes on Brietta. I tightened my grip on my Nordingaard crystal, completely hiding it from the guard.

Brietta's brow hardened again and she gestured to poor Annalisa. "Can you not see that the heir's twin sister is in distress?"

The guard caught up to Brietta. "You know His Excellency's orders—"

He gripped her elbow but Brietta yanked her arm away. "Do not touch me!"

Her voice echoed around the hallway and the guard's eyes went wide. He looked over his shoulder at the door with the carved bulls.

The last thing we needed was for Duke Hyton to appear. I quickly knelt beside Annalisa. "I-I have her, Lady Hyton."

Brietta gave me a stiff-lipped, yet approving look before whipping her head forward and lifting her chin. She walked further down the hall, the guard only two paces behind her.

She slammed Derrick's bedroom door shut as I helped Annalisa onto her feet. The guard reached for his belt and the jingle of keys echoed in the hallway. A lock clicked.

Annalisa started crying, but I rubbed her back and kept my head down. "Where is your bedroom?"

"T-to the left." She hiccupped. "Three doors down."

I wrapped my hand around the handle of what Annalisa said was her bedroom door and pushed. The door opened without so much as a creak.

Strips of moonlight peeked through curtains. A stiff-backed couch and a low table sat near the left wall. On the far right was a large wooden bed.

Annalisa gagged again and I rushed her inside. I grabbed a pot from the floor and held it under her face just in time.

Her knees buckled and she crashed to the floor. I quickly set the crystal on her vanity so I could catch her.

I wrapped my arm around her shaking back and held her hair up. She spat in the pot and sobbed. "That damn wine…made me feel…I want it to stop. I want it to stop!"

Annalisa had gotten sick from the wine from the Ashmore kitchens before, but never so bad that she cried. Maybe I could distract her.

I looked over at the bed and what I had mistaken for a canopy was actually a large tree painted on the wall—but it was not a normal tree. Streaks of red and pink formed the bark. The leaves were blue, violet, and orange. Doves with periwinkle feathers perched on the branches. Two lilac chipmunks poked their heads out of a hole in the trunk. Green fawns with white-dappled backs nibbled on orange grass near the baseboard.

I spied a golden vixen that peeked out near the bottom of the bedpost. "Why are none of the animals their normal color?"

Annalisa sniffed. "Why should it be? The ugliness of the real world does not belong in my bedroom."

With Annalisa's poetic babble, it was a wonder that she and Brietta were ever enemies in school.

My eyes wandered up the painted tree where the leaves morphed into flying birds on the ceiling. I found two ravens flying over the bed, their black feathers highlighted with green and their beaks a shining gold. Ravens painted in green and gold? How very…Ravenwood.

Maybe it was a sneaky tribute to her grandmother, Ilsa Ravenwood.

I could not help myself. I had to know. "Look at those ravens, they are lovely—"

"No!" Annalisa shrieked. She skittered away from her bed until her back slammed into a chair. Tears crept down her cheeks.

I dropped to my knees in front of her. "Anna? What is wrong?"

Her lip trembled as her eyes stayed bolted forward. "The wine made me forget…but it all came back. It all came back again!"

Her breathing quickened and I grabbed her hands. "What came back? Anna, tell me!"

Annalisa slammed her eyes shut and cried. The patter of raindrops echoed in my ears. I glanced out the window—it was a clear and cloudless night.

Though if Evereon let me into his mind with the song of a sad violin and Astrid did the same with the flutter of butterfly wings…

I looked back. The light between Annalisa's eyes that only I could see shone like a tiny beacon.

She was calling for me…

My Nordingaard crystal started glowing on the vanity and my heart leaped into my throat. I had to break the magical connection. What if Annalisa saw the crystal's light?

I pulled my hands away and my white flame quieted. Annalisa quickly grabbed her knees and pulled them tightly into her chest.

"*Raindrop, Raindrop, make the rain go away,*" she sang into her knees. "*Your rainbow will come some other day.*"

I let out a silent sigh and gently guided Annalisa to bed. She protested when I eased her onto her back, so I rolled her onto her side in case she got sick again.

I crossed the room to the vanity and snatched up the crystal like it would run away. My trunk was nowhere in sight. I had a room prepared somewhere, but I could not just go around opening doors around the palace looking for it.

Looks like I had to stay with Annalisa.

I silently climbed into bed. I stuffed the crystal beneath my pillow and settled in next to her.

I was no stranger to sleeping beside Annalisa since we used to be dormitory mates. On her sixteenth birthday, she had cried into her pillow for so long that I even let her sleep in my bed.

I had just wanted her to finally be quiet, and hopefully write to her twin that I had been kind so I could curry some favor, but a shared bed became part of her birthday ritual every year.

She just hated being alone, though she would never admit it.

Her twenty-second birthday was in two days, might as well start the tradition early.

I rolled over and faced Annalisa's back. "Just like Ashmore, huh?"

Annalisa was still sniffling softly. Maybe I could change the subject to something more pleasant. "What were you singing earlier?"

She rolled over and faced me. Her eyes were glistening. "Mama calls me Raindrop…because I used to cry a lot."

I gave her a smile. Annalisa had cried more in the past two weeks than in all the seven years I had known her. Selection Night was rougher than any of us had expected, and everything that happened after…

Well, I understood. Deep within the bleak coldness of my chest, I understood.

A thin smile pulled at Annalisa's lips. "Mama used to sing '*Raindrop, Raindrop, make the rain go away*' to help me calm down. Then my sisters started singing it to…do the opposite."

Her six older sisters all shared names with gemstones, but they sparkled like sewage. Ashmore had collectively sighed with relief every time one of them graduated.

I eyed a peacock with sunset-colored feathers in the tree above us. "Your sisters are horrible."

"No, they were right. Hytons cannot cry." She sighed. "*Your rainbow will come another day.* Too bad my rainbow never came."

My white flame pulsed with a gentle heat around my heart. Maybe just like with Brietta earlier, finding my heart's desire was not just about finding Riyan.

I could not risk more people knowing about my sorcery…but my friend needed me and I wanted to help.

I kept my eyes on the ravens and thought of my brothers. "Maybe your rainbow is coming."

She snorted. "Not in Lycaster. The storm never ends."

Chapter Twelve
Traitor's Bane

Isolation. Darkness.

But then there was music.

I could not place the tune, but I danced alone in the dark. I slowly moved my limbs to the sweeping notes and gentle melody.

And then a voice made my feet freeze.

"Keep that crystal on your skin, *Litlnadr*. And tell the truth as it benefits you."

I opened my eyes. I was in Annalisa's bedroom and my fist was wrapped around my Nordingaard crystal.

Daigen had somehow invaded my dream and talked to me. Annoying, but about damn time he gave me some advice.

I pushed myself up from the mattress to see Annalisa at her easel. I was not eager to wear the illegal Nordingaard crystal around the palace, but Daigen was deliberate—what little information he gave me was important.

Trusting an old sorcerer from the mountain was testing every ounce of sense that I had.

I slipped the crystal under the blankets. Daigen had only said to keep the crystal on my skin, he never specified where.

As I watched Annalisa to make sure her eyes did not leave her canvas, I pulled up the hem of my nightgown and tied the choker just above my right knee. Unless someone committed the unspeakable offense of lifting my skirt, the crystal would go undetected.

Annalisa's eyebrows raised at the sound of me shifting on the mattress and she peered over the canvas to look at me. "How are those giants supposed to look?"

I stretched like I had just woken up. "Grey. Fifteen feet tall. Lumpy." I shot her an incredulous look. "Why are you painting giants? I thought you said the ugliness of the real world does not belong in your bedroom."

Her face disappeared behind the canvas. "This is a portrait of Grigory's victory on the mountain, a present for when he returns from his secret assignment."

Grigory's victory? *Riyan* had slayed all the giants.

Annalisa's brush flicked across the canvas. "He assured me in his most recent letter that he should be back for me soon." She sighed. "He misses me so much."

Despite the Hyton and Thornebow rivalry, Annalisa and Grigory seemed to have fallen for each other. Their marriage was already consummated, so I could not blame her feelings on Fraleigh's enchantment.

Maybe the affection her and Grigory shared was actually real.

Annalisa peered around her canvas again. "Get over here. I need you to pose for me."

I rolled my eyes and climbed out of bed. Annalisa pulled me in front of her easel and positioned my arms to look like I was holding an invisible bow and drawing back an arrow.

I felt ridiculous. "Grigory is going to come out looking rather small."

Annalisa scowled. "You know I always use more than one reference."

I looked down at the table next to her. Beside her collection of paints was a faerie book, open to an illustration of the heroic Prince Haldar. The book was an older version than the one I grew up with, so instead of his signature dark curls, Prince Haldar had hair down his back with braids framing his face like an ancient warrior.

I smiled. Riyan had said Prince Haldar was his favorite faerie story growing up. He definitely emulated Prince Haldar's gallant qualities.

Yes, that was something I remembered liking about him. I looked back down at the illustration—the handsome Prince Haldar stood in a field of flowers as he journeyed to slay the giant.

Handsome. Heroic. Gallant. *That* is what I remembered about Riyan.

My chest started to feel warm for the first time in days. My eyes traced the red flowers on the illustration in the faerie book and suddenly a song filled my head.

"Just as blossoms bloom and whither…" I sang.

Annalisa stopped painting. "What are you doing?"

Great question. It was the same tune as the song in my dream, so maybe I had invented it. "Oh, appreciating Prince Haldar."

She scoffed. "Really? Everyone knows *The Snow Princess of the North* has the superior protagonist—you cannot beat talking to animals and coming back from the dead!"

My womb cramped like a fist wrapped around it and I lowered my arms. Annalisa probably had a vial of motherwort nearby, her cycle always started a couple of days before mine.

"Hurting, huh?" Annalisa said as her brush stippled on the canvas. "I will have a maid bring up a cup of tea to help."

A cup? Just one?

I pressed my hand against my lower belly to help with the pain. "What about you?"

Annalisa did not look up from the grey and white splotches in front of her. "Mine has not come yet."

A loud knock rapped on the door. That did not sound like a maid.

"The General summons Madame Bloodstone."

My heart stopped. The General had been so insistent that I go to Bloodstone Fortress and stay with Riyan, it was no surprise that he would want to inquire about me returning alone.

"Uncle Ragnar can wait until we have breakfast," Annalisa replied. She swirled her paintbrush in a small jar of oil with an annoyed *clink.*

"He requests her immediately."

"I request that you *go away* immediately."

It was a rude hour to call upon a lady, but I needed to speak to the General anyway. I could not fault him for promptly giving me an opportunity to find out more about Riyan.

I quickly put on a pair of Annalisa's slippers and grabbed a dark blue robe hanging on the side of a massive oak wardrobe. Hopefully Annalisa would not mind me borrowing her clothes.

I slung the robe across my shoulders and pulled the satin belt tight. "Anna, quit making a fuss. I am sure your uncle just wants to ask me about Sir Bloodstone's whereabouts."

Tell the truth as it benefits you.

I could not lie and I had no idea if my magic would even work on the General, but I had one weapon in my arsenal if all else failed—I knew Riyan was his son.

A stone-faced guard stood on the other side of the door. I pulled the edge of the robe tighter across my chest and followed the guard down the hallway. The snores of the other Hyton daughters filtered under their doors as we passed.

The guard stopped at a seemingly random spot in the middle of two doors. He pulled the metal bracket of a sconce and a thin panel opened up the wall. He slipped into the secret passage as I made a quick note of its location—across the hall and four doors down from Annalisa's room.

The guard sealed the panel shut behind us and we were within the walls again.

All the smoldering sconces on the walls were identical and the roughly hewn bricks in the passages were a monotonous grey. How did anyone find their way?

I kept pace with the guard as I nibbled on the skin around my thumbnail. The moment the coppery tang of blood hit my tongue, I swiped my thumb on the stone.

The slight twinkle of magic in my blood sang out to me as I left it on the wall. The small tear in my skin healed almost instantly because of my magic, so I bit my thumb again.

I repeated the bite, bleed, and smear over and over as we traveled through the narrow halls and down a set of spiraling stairs. As soon as the guard opened up a door and the smell of crisp morning dew filled my nose, I placed my hands demurely in front of me.

My crystal warmed against my thigh and I threw a quick sweep of magic behind me. The trail of blood on the stone glimmered like moonlit pebbles in my mind.

A smile flicked up my lips. I had a path out of the palace.

The guard wordlessly led me to a small castle built into the wall surrounding the palace—the guard house.

Horses whinnied in the stables as we approached the guardhouse door. The guard reached for the door handle when a shadow washed over us.

"Not the front door, Jonson. This is no place for a lady."

The guard whipped around. General Hyton stood behind us, his towering height blocking the rising sun. The sun's rays gave the General's white hair a golden glow, making him look nearly identical to his son.

If Riyan were not fifteen feet tall, anyway.

General Hyton quickly unpinned his cape from his shoulders. "And I told you to wait until the lady was properly dressed." He wrapped the cape around me, shrouding everything below my neck in Hyton Blue. "No one should see the wife of the future Baron of Bloodstone in her nightclothes. What were you thinking?"

The guard swallowed. "You said—"

General Hyton's eyes flashed a deadly look. The guard mumbled his apologies and then disappeared.

The General turned to me and warmth filled his voice. "My deepest apologies, Madame Bloodstone. Please, join me."

I placed my fingers in the General's waiting palm. Even though the top of my head did not even reach his shoulder, he was careful to keep pace with me as he led me around the guard house to a more secluded door.

The door led to a staircase lined with Hyton Blue banners bearing the House emblem—the rearing bull. We passed so many bulls as we ascended the steps I felt like I was in the middle of a stampede. At the top of the steps was a single door which the General unlocked with a small iron key.

The room on the other side of the door looked more fit for a prince than the General of the Lycaster army. A four-poster bed sat on a raised platform. The blue and white striped Lycaster flag hung above a crackling fireplace. A tapestry bearing Alastar the Conqueror with his signature spear and shield stood guard over the room.

General Hyton led me to a small table where I sat in a chair carved with snowflakes and flying birds. No desk—he did not conduct official business in the room. Regardless of whatever General Hyton had in mind, he intended to make the meeting look like a friendly visit.

As if to illustrate my point, he crossed over to the fireplace and removed an iron kettle from the fire. He poured the tea into two waiting cups that sat on a nearby cupboard.

While his back was turned, my eyes darted around the room—taking in as much information as possible. A map labeled "Nordingaard" was nailed to the wall next to the Alastar the Conqueror tapestry. A lock of red hair laid on the edge of the night table. Below it, the tail of a crimson ribbon peeked out from the top drawer.

The floorboard creaked. My eyes snapped forward and my gaze fell on his perfectly-made bed.

General Hyton set the glazed teacup in front of me. I kept my hands folded politely in my lap, even as the rising steam tantalized my nose.

He moved around the table to sit across from me, setting down his teacup with a tiny clink.

He rested his forearms on the table. "Imagine my surprise to hear you came back so soon, even after my warning about the…delicate situation the House of Hyton is in."

General Hyton had told me to go to Bloodstone and leave the Hytons behind, but it was not for my safety. They were just concerned that I would keep Derrick from consummating his marriage to Brietta. Since the future Duke and Duchess of Lycaster were irrevocably bound, my presence was no longer a threat. Why was he so concerned?

"We have not had a war with another country in centuries." General Hyton raised an eyebrow slightly. "What, then, do you think my job is as the General of the Lycaster army?"

I took in a breath, smelling the fragrant tea. "Well, I know you run the military academy and I assume you oversee the palace guard." I dipped my head slightly to look up at him through my eyelashes. "But a man of your caliber is capable of so much more."

He gave me a small smile. "So young and yet so clever."

Nothing like a dash of flattery to disarm a General.

He rose from the table and slowly stepped toward me. "I am the head of the Dukedom's law enforcement."

I held my breath as he got closer.

"Sure, every province handles their own petty crimes, but the serious affairs all come to me."

Like sorcery.

He softly ran his fingers along the edge of the table. "A nice young lady like you could not imagine how many criminals there are—or should I say *were*—in the Dukedom."

He passed me and stopped at the wall. I let out a breath as my eyes followed him.

A massive sword hung on the wall beside General Hyton and his deep blue eyes did not leave the blade. "When my father died, I devoted my life to protecting my family. I never graduated from Heaston and never had my own Selection Night—all to keep the House of Hyton secure."

I kept my mental calculations hidden behind a polite mask. If my arithmetic was correct, Riyan was born mere days before Baron Thornebow murdered Alastar the Wise. Did the General even know about his son then?

He turned from the sword and his eyes met mine. "On the morning of my brother's coronation, *I* executed Baron Thornebow."

I did not have to feign the shock in my voice. "But you would have only been twenty!"

"And because I was young, I was messy." His eyes were hard, but his mouth flicked up in a disarming smirk. "Three swings of the axe before his head came off."

He ran his knuckle along the flat edge of the sword's blade. "I do not like messy things, so I had this smithed—Traitor's Bane."

Another weapon with a name. Unlike Daigen's knife, at least the General's meaning for the sword was clear. My stomach twisted into a knot.

The General turned from the sword to me. "Those charged with high crimes face numerous forms of execution…but for the last twenty-two years, every single traitor to the crown has died by this sword."

There was the threat.

I shifted my knees and grounded myself in the weight of the crystal against my leg. He had just served up a death threat like breakfast and I was somehow still calm.

Maybe the crystal did more than just tell me when my magic was ready.

Regardless, the General knew nothing. Brietta would not sell me out without ruining her own plans. No one else was around to hear my confession of sorcery in the bathing chamber, either.

Well, if he wanted to threaten me with no evidence, I could show him how to issue a threat with some teeth.

I smiled. "You are the perfect executioner, just like your son."

General Hyton remained firm. I mirrored him, even though the air around us suddenly snapped tight.

The fact that he had not taken the sword off the wall and hacked off my head proved that the General needed me. I had information he wanted and I could not talk if I were dead.

I held my breath as the General took a step forward. "When Nikkolas told you…" Another step. "Did he realize the cost of what he had done? Does he realize the danger he put you in?"

My throat was warm with my white flames. "Nikkolas is dead."

I quickly closed my mouth, but it was too late. How had I just let that secret out? This was not like when I was hiccupping my feelings to my oldest friend. The *last* thing I wanted to do was inform the Hytons that the North was in chaos and was vulnerable to invasion.

I bit my tongue as my mind spun. Maybe Daigen's rule against asking him questions held more meaning. If the Man of the Mountain's magic would not let us lie with our tongues, we could not lie with our silence either.

I *could not* refuse direct questions.

General Hyton's jaw ticked and he quietly crossed to his end of the table. He grabbed the back of his chair with one hand and his teacup with the other. My heart slowly pounded yet I was frozen in place as he dragged his chair over to rest *right* beside me.

He gently placed his teacup on the table and sat down. Even his seated figure was imposing, but the somber look in his eyes softened him. "Riyan had another one of his accidents, didn't he? That is why you are here."

I kept my lips closed as the white fire scorched my tongue, compelling me to answer. I could answer the General's question in the affirmative, telling the truth as it benefitted me…or I could go even further.

If General Hyton wanted to merely scare me into giving him information, he would not have brought me to his quarters and served tea. He wanted to know what had happened to his son in the North? We could make an exchange.

I forced my heated breath to cool with my measured words. "I will tell you…in due time."

His brows knitted. "You dare refuse your Gen—?"

"You ask so many questions of me, yet my own questions go unanswered." The flames spun within me. "And I am *tired* of not having answers. If you want another answer from me, you have to give me one."

His Hyton Blue eyes examined me slowly, agonizingly slowly. I felt like I was going to vomit molten lead with every second I withheld the truth.

Finally, he conceded with a smile. "An answer for an answer. Ask your first question."

The fire within me cooled, as if the magic in my own body agreed to our deal. "What was Riyan like at the military academy?"

The General shifted his shoulders and looked down at his folded hands for a few moments before answering. "He was…obstinate. A young man of his size with the strength of ten men needed a firm hand."

From what Riyan had told me, "a firm hand" was a light way of putting it. He had made his own son hold up the bridge into Bloodstone on his back.

He took a sip from his cup. "Just when I thought I had him under control, he defied my order to marry Brietta Elvar." He glanced at me.

"Not that I have any objections to you, Serafina. Only when Riyan has no control…he is dangerous."

I picked wool fibers off the cape as I remembered the axes thrown in anger, the barrels of wine he drank one right after the other, the shattered bed, the bend of my ribs when he did not realize he was crushing me…

I swallowed. "Riyan grew again and…fell. That is what killed Nikkolas and Hilda."

The General's cheek pitted like he bit it. "Where is he?"

I let my eyes wander to the map of Nordingaard on the wall. "Ganora took him…he gave his life for mine."

His eyes widened only slightly. Riyan had once told me the General had sent soldiers up the mountain for years, gathering information about the giants and their queen. I carefully studied his stoic mask for any clue that he understood the sacrifice Riyan made and what it meant, but if he knew, he did not show it.

Though beneath his hardened surface, his eyes gleamed and his breath was still. He had his next question ready and he was desperate to ask.

I took advantage of the General's desperation and risked my most inflammatory question. I tried not to think of the scar that split Evereon's face in two as I asked, "How many people has Riyan hurt?"

A muscle in the General's face feathered. "More men than I can count, but that was by their own choice."

I did not like that answer. "What do you mean?"

"That is two questions, Serafina."

"Then I owe you another answer." I pulled the cape tighter around me. "What do you mean it was the men's own choice?"

The General let out a long breath. "Like I said, I oversee the executions of the Dukedom. For the worst crimes, I gave prisoners a choice: the gallows or five minutes in a room with 'the Beast' and a chance to survive. No weapons, just man-to-man physical combat. Many prisoners…chose to die the hard way."

The floor fell beneath my feet. I thought Riyan was a perfect executioner of *giants*…not men!

He killed someone, *many* someones…in less than five minutes each.

Suddenly he was nothing like the gallant Prince Haldar at all.

The General's eyes softened. "They were the worst criminals, Serafina. They deserved everything Riyan did."

My skin crawled, imagining the same hands that combed my hair and gently stroked my skin beating the life out of another person.

Even those memories were tainted. Stained with blood.

General Hyton leaned on his forearms. "Did you consummate your marriage?"

A horrible shiver crawled down my spine and I squeezed my knees together. The hand that had been *inside me* had ended countless lives.

My throat trembled as I finally gave the General his answer. "No. He was fifteen feet tall and we could not…"

He scowled and hissed out a tense breath. "I have until the full moon, then." His eyes focused again. "Many do not understand the magic of Nordingaard. Depending on what he felt for you, he may have invoked something more powerful than even he is."

My brows knitted. He knew the rules of magic? The power of the bargain of a life made in love?

Maybe his admission was a clue. Ilsa might not have been a sorceress, but she was from the North. She knew the old lore, and she must have passed it down to at least one son.

I wanted to press for more information, but I could not trust the General just yet. He might have been Riyan's father, but he was still a Hyton—wielder of Traitor's Bane and loyal to his House. A few morsels of honesty between us was not enough for me to let my guard down.

General Hyton gestured to the tea in front of me. "Drink it before it gets cold—it's motherwort."

Motherwort? My fingertips shook as I placed them around the cup. He drank from the same kettle so I was certain the tea was not poisoned, but…

"You knew I was—?"

"I know everything that goes on within those palace walls."

Shit. I wasted a question and owed him an answer, but at least I knew *just* how closely he was watching me.

The General leaned on his forearms again, looking me directly in the eyes. "I need you well for when I finally bring Riyan back. Your marriage *cannot* annul."

I placed my lips on the edge of the teacup with painted larkspur. The bitter sting of the motherwort coated my tongue, but it was perfectly brewed.

Nothing the General just said was a direct question, so I was safe in letting him assume that I was still married.

"Just stay out of trouble and let me take care of finding him," he ordered.

The last thing I planned to do was stay out of trouble, but if all my scheming led to the safe return of his son, the General might just forgive me for upturning the House of Hyton.

I just had to stay on his good side.

My stomach was still in knots as I took another drink. It might have been foolish to ask another question and owe the General *two* answers… but I had to know.

Before I left the privacy of the General's quarters, I needed something of Riyan that was…good. Untainted by magic or death.

"General…" I instantly hated how vulnerable my voice sounded. "I know this sounds absurd, but…was he ever gentle?"

General Hyton was silent for longer than I wanted, but then his eyes found mine and he smiled softly. "He sang at night, like the lone wolf howls at the moon. Low and soft, just to fill the silence."

My mouthful of tea felt warmer as I remembered Riyan's voice. He had hummed into my hair as he stroked my back. He came up with silly songs out of nowhere. He sang to me while I slept for two days, calling out to me as the Man of the Mountain held me in the place West of the Moon and East of the Sun.

Riyan was a murderer. He had killed more men than the General of the Lycaster army could even count. He was…gruesome.

Gruesome. Barbaric. Merciless.

And though all that was true, no sound in the world was warmer than his voice.

I stared into my empty teacup as I swallowed. My heart sank and my Nordingaard crystal cooled against my skin.

Even a voice as warm as his was still not enough to make me love him.

Chapter Thirteen
The Trials

 As soon as the palace guard opened the wall into the Hyton family quarters, Brietta passed in front of us.

She wore puffed sleeves and skirts that flowed like seawater—dressed too splendidly to be pacing in the hallway alone.

Her brown eyes went wide and she unclasped her hands. "Ah, Serafina! I have been looking everywhere for you. We are late for tea with Her Excellency!"

She was never a good liar. She had obviously been wringing her hands with worry ever since the General demanded my audience.

Brietta might have looked the part of the future Duchess, but she still needed me to give her radical ambition some fangs. She might want to disguise the interrogation as a midday tea, but I had no time to waste on pleasantries.

If the loose lips of a drunk woman were my best lead, I would get Freya to talk our way to freedom.

The guard gave Brietta a dutiful bow before leaving us alone. Brietta reached for my hand but drew back.

My heart sank a little at the reminder that nothing was the same between us.

She refused to look at me, but quickly moved further down the hallway. I followed. Brietta stayed quiet and stopped at a door near the end of the hall. She opened it to reveal a dark bedroom and quickly beckoned me inside.

She shut the door with both palms and clicked the lock. "What happened?"

"He questioned my arrival and I told him the truth." I looked up at her. "You may have noticed my new…form does not allow me to refuse direct questions."

Her face paled, but I stopped her before she could spiral. "He asked nothing about you."

She sighed with relief and I turned to see where she had taken me. Unlike Annalisa's bedroom that was a rainbow of pastel shades, the room had dark wood furniture, a lush green bedspread, and a curved white chair with a matching footstool that sat by the sunny window.

Simple and comfortable—a sharp contrast from everything else in Hyton Palace.

I eyed a small tapestry decorated with maidens and raven feathers on the wall. "Whose bedroom is this?"

Brietta crossed over to a polished wardrobe, not meeting my eye. "It was supposed to be yours."

She flicked the latch and opened the doors. Dresses in shades of Hyton Blue filled the wardrobe, but glimpses of earthy green and creamy ivory peeked out in between. I walked over and touched a green sleeve—the fabric was so soft, I immediately wanted it on my arms.

I bit my tongue. Only Derrick knew how much I loved gentle green colors. The chair at the window was perfect for hours of comfortable embroidery. The room was far enough away from the stairs that noise would not have invaded my peace.

Derrick gave me the perfect refuge and it all went to waste. I was never going to be his Duchess.

Brietta stepped away from the wardrobe and folded her arms. "Look presentable. We have to go into town after tea, then we have dinner with the entire House of Hyton afterward."

I pursed my lips and rifled through the wardrobe. "I did not realize you would organize a full schedule for me."

She bristled. "*You* were the one who said we did not have much time. Besides, the dinner was all Derrick's idea. He wanted to celebrate your…safe arrival."

Meaning he was elated that I had come back to the palace without Riyan.

I selected a deep purple skirt and bodice that was embroidered with creeping ivy. Brietta kept her arms folded and stared at the willow leaf pattern on the wallpaper as I dressed. Every garment fit perfectly, even the slippers.

I had just finished tying back my hair with an ivory ribbon when Brietta spoke up. "Freya has already had a bottle of wine. She is ready to talk."

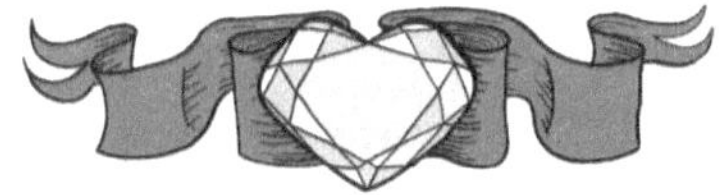

The teacup's glaze glistened in the sunlight from the tall windows. Eiders cooed outside as they glided over the waters of the Western Sea. Magnus the Bedwarmer softly purred in Freya's lap.

Freya slurped down the rest of her wine and set the empty bottle on the table with a sigh. "You will have to pour your own tea, kittens, I banished the servants. Cannot risk any hungry ears around."

Brietta and I glanced at each other from across the small round table. Both of us had our hands clasped firmly in our laps as we silently choked on the risk Freya was about to take.

Freya looked from Brietta to me and sighed. "Fine, I will say it." She took a breath. "Ilsa! Ilsa! Ilsa!"

Brietta and I recoiled as her words echoed around the small sunroom. Freya nonchalantly reached for the steaming teapot in the center of the table.

"See?" She poured herself a cup of fragrant tea. "No one is running in with an axe. Unclench, will you?"

Brietta and I still held our breaths. Freya scoffed and grabbed Brietta's teacup. She produced a small vial from between her breasts and poured a few drops into the cup. "Here—a little gift from the faeries. Mix it with the tea."

Brietta's saucer rattled as Freya clumsily set the cup down. She snatched my cup and gave me a helping of whatever was in her vial.

Freya shoved the cup back in my hands and gave me a wink. "Made by the Viper, the best potion maker in Lycaster."

Nothing made by someone named "the Viper" seemed trustworthy, but Freya still upended the rest of the vial into her own cup. "All right, ask. Which one of you is braver?"

Brietta cut me a fearful glance. I supposed the brave one was me.

My hands trembled slightly as I poured my tea. "Did…the former Duchess really murder Alastar the Wise?"

"Might have." Freya took a loud slurp from her teacup. "She only loved her Little Diamond."

Little Diamond? "Did she have some jewelry that she was fond of?"

Freya snorted. "Yes, but that is not what I am referring to. The entire Dukedom called Ragnar the 'Little Diamond' because he was so damn pretty."

I bit my tongue to keep from smiling. General Hyton was handsome, sure, but I could not imagine anyone considering him pretty…or little.

Freya rested her cheek on her fist. "Ilsa had iced Derrick out from the beginning. I cannot imagine why."

I furrowed my brows just as Brietta piped up, "Derrick?"

"Alastar Derrick Pervale Hyton, yes," Freya slurred, emphasizing every part of the name. "I named my Midnight after the best damn Duke that Lycaster ever had."

Midnight? She used *my* Derrick's secret name too?

Freya hiccupped and smacked her fist on the table. "And yes, I do include the Conqueror in that statement!"

No one ever dared to say Alastar the Conqueror was anything less than wondrous. He founded the Dukedom, reigned for sixty-five years, and became a legend. All of his mighty accomplishments flooded to the front of my mind as if I were about to write yet another exam at Ashmore.

Freya lazily stirred her tea. "When everyone else saw me as just the vessel of a potential heir, Derrick saw a brilliant mind. We read together. Played table top games. Discussed new ideas. I was the daughter he never got to have."

She sniffed and raised her spoon, watching intently as droplets of tea dripped back into the cup. "But even I can admit he had a monster in him, all the Dukes do. 'Spirit of the Conqueror,' and all that."

Alastar was not a true name but a title, traditionally earned in a series of trials to determine who would be the next Duke of Lycaster. Whoever won had the "spirit of the Conqueror" and would become the Alastar.

The spirit of the Conqueror was merely an idea that defined what it meant to be an "Alastar," but Freya described it as if it were a living, breathing thing.

Drunk old fool.

I took a sip of the foul tea out of politeness, though I wished Freya would steer the conversation back to Ilsa. How was learning about a dead Duke going to help us?

Brietta huffed out a breath. "I never understood the 'spirit of the Conqueror' idea. Why should our next ruler be determined by who could perform the best feats of strength in an arena? Alastar the Steadfast was right to end them."

The Alastar trials might have ended, but the Hyton peasants still craved entertainment. Heaston filled in the gap, creating a Spring Exhibition where the noble boys would show off their dueling skills. I only remembered the history because Endre had talked about the Spring Exhibition all the time—he was certain he would duel circles around the entire school once he was old enough to compete.

I had no idea Brietta had paid so much attention in history lessons. Maybe she really was scribbling notes instead of lines of poems.

Freya snorted so loud Magnus hopped off her lap. "Feats of strength in the Alastar trials? Oh, I forgot that is what those biddies at school teach you."

I put down my teacup. What else could the trials have been other than feats of strength? Although…our lessons never mentioned the Hyton sons who had lost the trials. Maybe they traveled to different kingdoms or became adventurers? Or maybe…

"They all died." My stomach was hollow as I said it. I looked up at Freya. "The Dukes of Lycaster were not merely declared winners…they were just the last brother standing."

Brietta's mouth fell open.

Freya's eyes gleamed. "There is only one bull in a herd."

I gripped my hands as I imagined Derrick and Riyan facing off against each other in an arena…

Derrick would not have stood a chance.

Freya took another sip of her tea. "Derrick…er, Alastar the Wise, was the first Duke of Lycaster to not have to fight in those bloody trials, but his six older brothers killed each other anyway—like they still had to prove themselves strong enough to rule."

Freya scratched Magnus's ruff and smiled. "The irony—all those centuries of fratricide and the crown ended up with the quiet brother who hid amongst the books." Her smile fell. "But even he could not hide from the cold hands of murder."

I seized the opportunity. "But how could Ilsa have murdered—"

"But the trials returned!" She took another slug from her teacup. We were losing her. "Sure, Anders did not have to murder anyone in an arena, but he became a performer on a stage with no end—constantly having to prove himself worthy of the crown. And when men of Lycaster cannot have blood, they crave sex instead."

I squeezed my knees together as I tried to think of how to steer the conversation back to Ilsa.

Brietta's lip curled and she avoided Freya's eyes. "They lock us up in Ashmore for seven years to keep our chastity intact yet *immediately* expect us to be receptive to—"

Freya's booming laugh startled Brietta so much that she jumped. "Oh, am I the first to tell you the chastity requirement is all a lie?"

Brietta's face hardened and my stomach dropped.

It…it was a lie?

"What?" Brietta cried. "But they would not let us see or talk to any men because our chastity was necessary—"

"Necessary to not get pregnant," Freya replied with a dry laugh. "Do you think the Heaston boys were kept on a chain? They get to play around just like all boys do while *you* get to spend your early fertile years in a cage."

Brietta's eyebrows creased and she let out a low breath.

Of all the lies the Ashmore matrons told us, the chastity requirement hurt the worst. They held us prisoner, suppressed all of our…urges, and told us all of it was necessary to have any place in society.

Worst of all, they had lined us up in front of Fraleigh and forced us to endure her "chastity examination" so we were allowed to get married.

"That is disgusting," Brietta hissed. "The boys got to have as many lovers as they wanted?"

Freya licked her teaspoon and tossed Brietta a look. "Do not tell me you are ignorant of the oldest laws of men. Sex has always been power to them. The more they have—or *say* they have—the more powerful other men believe they are."

I stirred my tea just to distract myself from the fire that raged beneath my ribs. I wanted to sprint back to Ashmore and kiss a guard just because I *could.*

"But Derrick never had to play that game—he owned the Diamond of the North," Freya said. "She was the most beautiful and valuable woman anyone could possess, so men respected him for that alone."

Back to Ilsa. I opened my mouth for another question, but Freya barked out a laugh. "But Anders? I am no diamond. Constantly being pregnant gave Anders some credibility as far as his virility was concerned…but then I only made daughters. He had to seek out…other venues for validation."

Her blue eyes slid over to me and my stomach turned over. "Of all the things I will never forgive my husband for, buying your Mother is at the top of the list."

That could not be true. Freya was just drunk and rambling. Mother was…intimately involved with the Duke, sure, but she was married to my father. Duke Hyton could not just buy her!

A feline smile grew on Freya's face. "Oh, you think I am lying, little kitten? Are you ready to hear the truth of just how replaceable we all are?"

As much as I did not want to believe Freya, I thought back to the shining blue wax of the Hyton seal on top of Father's desk seven years ago.

A bad deal with the Hytons.

No. Father had always kissed Mother's cheeks and told her she was the honey in his tea. He bought her new and foreign seeds for her herb garden. He never even so much as raised his voice to her.

I shook my head. "He loves her, he—"

Freya threw her head back and cackled. "Loves her? Do you think that would stop a Duke from getting what he wanted?"

I looked over at the once romantic Brietta as warmth drained from my face. Her eyes were wide and she covered her gaping mouth with her hand.

Freya slowly shook her head like she was swimming through a cloud. "It was my fault. After Derrick died, I…lost myself. I could not leave my room. Could not face the public. Could not do…anything."

Her hands curled into fists. "But your father was the one who fucked up. He pleaded that Anders take care of the giants at a meeting of the Baron council. He embarrassed Anders, making him look like he did not have complete control of the Dukedom…idiot! Frederick had always wanted to swoop in and play the hero, but what did that get him? He lost everything…and so did she."

Before I could change the subject back to Ilsa, Freya suddenly rose from the table. She grabbed both my wrists and leaned down.

Her eyes watered as her wine-stained breath skated across my face. "You listen to me—men are always the most dangerous when they think they do not have control. It all goes back to control—always! The monster consumed my husband, all it wants is control!"

My eyes darted across Freya's face. I did not know what to say, or even what to think. Was the faerie potion warping her mind like it had with Annalisa? What was the monster she was talking about?

Freya gripped my wrists harder. "Anders is a catapult—he will do as much damage as possible with one move. He does not care about consequences. He has no limits. He is going to eat my baby too!"

I had no other choice but to follow her logic. "Who is going to eat your—?"

"Stay away from the monster!" she cried. "Run! Run!"

Her hands started to shake and I caught a glimpse of Brietta behind the Duchess. She put a hand on her shoulder. "Freya, please—"

Freya released me and turned to Brietta, gripping her arms just below her shoulders. Her eyes were wide with urgency. "You have to do it, Brie. You have to run! You have to keep the dream alive!"

Brietta's lip trembled as she tried to hold Freya upright. "Yes, we are trying. We are trying—"

Freya broke into sobs and collapsed to the floor. The faerie potion had finally overtaken her.

I knelt beside Brietta as she rubbed Freya's back.

"Freya, get up, please," she begged. "We still have more to learn."

I lowered my head as I tried to meet her eyes. "Your Excellency, what more do you know about Ilsa—?"

Freya's head snapped up and her eyes locked on my face. "Adalia, I am sorry!"

She thought I was my mother. Was she going mad, or was the faerie potion that strong? "Your Excellency, I am not—"

"Save him, and then do what you have to do," Freya sobbed. "End it, once and for all. Let the kittens run. I should have been stronger for you. I am sorry. Sorry! Sorry!"

She fell into a delirious babble. Magnus pawed at Freya, nuzzling into her side as his fluffy tail swished across the floor. Brietta and I tried to calm her, but her cries got louder until a group of maids burst into the room to collect her.

Freya shook as the maids helped her out of the room. Brietta and I exchanged weary, defeated looks. Our tea had turned cold, and all we had to show for it was the tears of the Duchess.

We had to find another door to the truth, but if Freya was too far gone and the General was too close to his brother, where else could we even look?

Chapter Fourteen
Hers to Mold

Brietta and I stared out opposite windows in the Hyton carriage as we rode to the dressmaker's shop in the center of town. She had only given me a brief explanation that we needed to get our costumes for the Darkest Night ball, but otherwise kept silent.

Neither of us wanted to say much about our disastrous tea with Freya. Not only did we have nothing new about Duchess Ilsa, but also we both nursed the wounds of another lie.

Our chastity requirement was all bullshit.

The gems on Brietta's rings flashed in the sunlight as she turned to me. "What would you have done differently at Ashmore had you known?"

A spot of warmth glowed in my heart as it compelled me to answer the question. I thought of Derrick's lips on mine when he snuck me away after the Suitors' Ball. And his hands around my waist. And his teeth on my neck.

He had not just wanted me as a future wife, but wanted me in the way a starving man seeks a meal. Despite how intense he was, it felt…*good* to be wanted.

I stared at the passing stone buildings through the window as my cheeks heated. As much as I wanted to modestly deny it, my magic would not let me swallow the truth. "I would have found a way to be with Derrick, at least once."

A mixture of sensuous memories and the fantasies I had weaved through the years flashed through my mind. I shifted on the velvet cushion as pressure grew in my hips. I could not be feeling like *this*, I had answers to find. I could not just retreat to my dormitory for fifteen minutes and hope no one came in like I used to.

I bit my tongue as my mind wandered from dark curls and gorgeous eyes to golden tresses and massive biceps. I thought those inconvenient… *feelings* would go away after the marriage enchantment, but maybe even Fraleigh's magic had not been powerful enough to temper the frustrated knot within me.

The blood bond might have not exactly *forced* me to want Riyan's body, after all. Maybe having a red-hot desire was just part of me.

Desire—that was what I must have felt for Riyan. Love had nothing to do with it. After all, Father loved Mother with all his heart…and he still sold her to the Duke.

Love was a lie in Hyton. How the hell did I ever think I would have it for myself?

Brietta's soft voice pulled me out of my thoughts. "I would have been with any man, so long as it was my choice. Just…anything different than what my first time really was."

The memory that the Man of the Mountain had shown me through her eyes flashed through my mind—waking up confused on a couch with white-faced Derrick on top of her.

The air tightened around us, but I gathered the courage to pull my eyes over to Brietta. Her arms were folded across her chest and she stared down at her feet.

I could almost see piles of stones on the carriage floor as we silently built our walls. I had done this before—stacked the stones and shut out love. I once thought the fortress around my heart kept me safe, but the world had still caved in anyway.

Shutting out the warmth of what love might have been was not going to help me this time, either.

I let out a breath and imagined that wall crumbling at my feet. I could not just retreat, I had made a promise.

Try to be happy.

If I could not reconcile my ideas of love with my feelings of desire, I could at least try to find small bites of happiness. I was going shopping with my fr…the future Duchess. We could have fun again.

My eyes flicked over to Brietta. Maybe I could even see her smile again.

The carriage came to a stop. Brietta sat up and gracefully stepped onto the street and I followed.

We entered a dressmaker's shop in one of the more posh parts of the city. The dressmaker was an older man in spectacles, wearing a berry-colored doublet and shoes with shining buckles.

The dressmaker's eyes gleamed as he bowed with a flourish. "Lady Hyton, we've been expecting you. Your costume for the Darkest Night is nearly as splendid as you are!"

Brietta kept her shoulders back and her lip stiff. "That is all well, bring out Madame Bloodstone's costume first."

My costume was already made?

"Ah, yes, the Midnight Dream!" the dressmaker said with glee.

He turned and pushed past a glimmering curtain that led to the back of the shop. Two bleak-eyed women emerged from behind the curtain and led us to a private area. They helped me onto a round pedestal while Brietta sat on a luxurious couch behind me.

I glanced at my reflection in the large mirror in front of me and my heart leaped into my throat. I had not expected them to undress me!

As soon as the women left, I yanked up the hem of my skirt and quickly pulled the ribbon of my choker. The Nordingaard crystal slid into my waiting palm as I turned toward Brietta.

Her eyes met mine and I tossed her the crystal. She flinched as if I had thrown a spider at her, but caught the crystal and shoved it behind her back.

Without the crystal on my skin, my heart started to pound.

Footsteps echoed into the room and a flash of silver caught my eye. Four young women entered with black—no, dark blue—fabric in their hands that had glitters of silver sewn in. All the women had lines around their eyes, but somehow seemed to be close to our age.

Two of the women took off my bodice and skirts while the others held the fabric that looked like the folded night sky. I flinched as a hand touched the sleeve of my chemise.

"These too, Madame," the woman said softly.

I grabbed my arms. "What do you mean? I have to have my undergarments."

The woman dropped her eyes. "Dresses for the Darkest Night are different."

I looked over my shoulder at Brietta and raised my eyebrow.

She looked down and cleared her throat. "The Darkest Night is not a normal ball. You get married on the full moon, but on the *new* moon, you find the person you want to *be* with…at least for the night."

I blinked in disbelief. Surely she was not suggesting…

Shame pricked my cheeks and I dropped my voice to a whisper. "Are you telling me this ball is just a giant orgy?"

Brietta nodded. "The entire House of Hyton has to attend."

I scoffed and crossed my arms. "I am not going."

Her eyes snapped up to meet mine. "You came to Hyton Palace accepting the invitation. You would *greatly offend* His Excellency if you did not attend."

And by "greatly offend," Brietta really meant that I would tip him off that something was amiss.

Maybe I could work my way around it. "But it is a *masked* ball. His Excellency will not know if I am there or not."

Brietta's eyes went dark. "He will know. Do not test him."

A chill ran down my arms. She was right, I still needed to stay inconspicuous if we were going to gather information.

"Freya said the ball is for us newlyweds, anyway—designed as an incentive to hurry up and seal our blood bonds." Her voice turned bitter. "Now we get to celebrate the joys of consequence-free sex with everyone else. Supposedly, the masks help the new blood feel less insecure."

But I had no blood bond, and despite the tight knot sitting in the center of my hips, I certainly did not want to have sex with anyone there!

Brietta must have read the fear in my eyes. She dipped her chin and said, "Though if one is feeling…*bashful,* no one is required to participate in anything. Just provide good company, that is all you need to do."

I released the breath I had held in. Brietta's message was clear—if we all had to attend the Duke's orgy, I needed to keep Derrick the hell away from her.

Derrick would not *want* to be with Brietta that way…but that had not mattered before.

I turned back to the large mirror on the wall, silently hoping it was not another window in disguise as my hands slowly rose to my shoulders.

I closed my eyes and removed everything but the wrappings around my hips. My eyes stayed shut as I stood on that pedestal with my arms folded over my bare breasts.

The women tied layers of organza skirts around my waist. Delicate slippers slid onto my feet. My arms slid through puffed sleeves and a bodice encircled my ribs. The inside of the bodice was whisper-soft against my bare skin.

Only when the maid had finished lacing the bodice in the front did I open my eyes.

I held in a gasp. I looked like a dream.

The dark organza was a gorgeous contrast against my pale skin. The bodice squeezed my bust to make it look fuller. Best of all, the overskirt was embroidered with hundreds of silver stars.

I held my breath as I moved my hips. The stars shimmered in the afternoon light that streamed in through the gossamer-trimmed windows.

I swallowed—no one but Derrick could have commissioned the dress.

I waved the overskirt in a beam of sunlight, making the stars twinkle. "What did Derrick even intend for my costume to be?"

Brietta scoffed. "You really do not remember?"

I knitted my brows at Brietta's reflection. "I never claimed to have a sterling memory."

She tightened her grip on her arms. "'*A thousand wishes will never change what was written in the stars.*' He wrote that for your birthday last year."

Poetic nonsense. No wonder I left that for Brietta to handle.

She narrowed her eyes. "We responded, '*And so we shall shine forever.*' Might want to remember that while you are…with him."

I suppressed an eye-roll. I could not wait to shout lines of poetry at Derrick and hope the sounds of the orgy would not drown me out.

Brietta glanced at the women who quietly stood against the wall. "Thank you, please allow us to inspect the dress in private."

The four women demurely bowed and left, closing the door behind them with a soft click.

Brietta waited until their footsteps disappeared before she pulled the Nordingaard crystal out from behind her back. "What does this even do?"

I turned to face her. "Radiates warmth and light when I use my magic. Captures memories." My heart pounded. "Somehow keeps me calm."

I yearned for that crystal to be on my skin again.

I turned back to face the mirror and caught a flash of skin through the edges of my bodice. I took a closer look. Despite being snug against my ribs, the bodice did not close completely in the front. Beneath the criss-crossing midnight blue ribbon was a sliver of my skin and the slight swells of my breasts.

Is *that* why I was not supposed to wear my chemise?

My cheeks heated. I gripped my skirts, only to find that they weren't complete. With a little tug, the layers of organza parted on each side, revealing slits in the fabric that ran all the way up both of my legs.

Surely Derrick would not have requested such an indecent design.

I turned to Brietta so I would not have to look at my nearly-naked form in the mirror. "Do you think I could alter the dress to look less…scandalous?"

She let out a mirthless laugh. "That dress is closer to our Ashmore uniforms than the normal Darkest Night costume. Derrick wanted you covered up!"

The heat in my cheeks spread to my ears. "Then what is *your* costume?"

"A peacock." She uncrossed her legs and gestured across her bust. "Shimmering gold fabric will drape across my body and dozens of imported peacock feathers will cover whatever skin is left bare."

I folded my arms. "And do you plan on participating in the Darkest Night?"

She did not even blink. "Maybe. The Darkest Night is one of those rare times we can make a choice, or many choices, depending on one's mood."

The romantic Brietta I once knew really was dead. "So you intend on gobbling up your choices like a feast?"

Brietta spread her hands out on the couch cushions. "So long as I hold the fork and knife instead of being the roasted boar on the table. It might be a tiny taste of freedom, but I want to gulp it all down until I can refill the chalice myself."

I looked down. How could she want to go to the Darkest Night, scarcely dressed, after…everything that had happened? "But I still do not understand your costume. All the men will see you—"

"I want them to see me." She stood up from the couch. "All of me, on my terms. Mine. I will banish the image of the girl crying bitter tears into Ilsa's Presentation dress from their minds forever. I cannot control these men, but I will control how they see me."

She took a few powerful steps until she stood beside the raised pedestal. We looked at our reflections, my eyes the same level as hers for once.

Brietta eyed my dress, opened her full lips, and recited:

"A dress of white turns into shackles of gold,
She is his to have, but he is hers to mold."

My eyes slid from Brietta to my reflection. We were to be dazzling illusions of complacency, obeying commands yet playing by our own rules.

Maybe I could follow Brietta's example and find power within the manipulation.

I took a deep breath, watching the small mounds of my breasts swell against the tight bodice. Instead of the midnight satin of the costume, I imagined Riyan's hands encircling my waist like he had before.

My cheeks reddened. The organza in my hands crinkled as I slowly lifted my skirt, widening the slits on either side. The silver-beaded toe of my slipper peeked out and the dark organza parted as I revealed my foot, then my ankle, then my bare calf from the split in the night sky.

Gooseflesh bloomed across my skin as I reveled in the memory of Riyan on his knees, kissing the insides of my legs as his hands traveled higher…

I dropped my skirt and swallowed the lump in my throat as the knot within my hips tightened. At least I was confident that the desire I had felt for Riyan was *very* real.

I chewed on my tongue as I tried to calm my racing heartbeat. Brietta was right, though the event itself was disconcerting, our costumes for the Darkest Night were certainly better than a tear-soaked Presentation dress.

My heart stopped for a moment. Tears. Ilsa's Presentation dress.

Tears.

I turned to Brietta. "Do you still have your Presentation dress?"

She raised an eyebrow. "I shoved it into the back of Derrick's wardrobe after…after it was removed. Why?"

The words flew out of my mouth as my thoughts raced. "What if you were not the first person to cry in that dress?"

Her brows furrowed and her voice dropped. "Does this have something to do with sor—"

"Magic holds memories." My heart raced as my white flame danced. "And magic is everywhere water is—in our bodies, in our tears. If I can just touch the dress, maybe I can find—"

"No time tonight." She glanced at the closed door before turning back to me. "We have to go straight to dinner with the House of Hyton and then Derrick and I get locked in his room for another night. But tomorrow…"

Then a smile finally broke through Brietta's lips. I smiled back, my chest alight with righteous white fire.

Tomorrow, we would get acquainted with Duchess Ilsa.

Chapter Fifteen
Little Rabbit

By the time Brietta and I had arrived back at the palace, the Hyton daughters were already entering the dining room. Each of the beautiful, blue-eyed women were dressed in dark fabrics with fine embroidery, wearing tiaras studded with gemstones corresponding with their names.

I quickly counted the women. Amethyst, Emeralda, Garnet, Sapphira, Rubia, and Pearl were all there. No Annalisa.

Derrick was chatting with Amethyst when his eyes met mine. He left his sister and quickly stepped over to us. Before he even had a chance to say anything to Brietta, she turned and entered the dining room without so much as a blink.

Derrick ignored the rebuff and smiled at me. "You look splendid."

My cheeks heated and I ran my hands down the front of my bodice. "You mean underdressed?"

"Nonsense—this is just a normal dinner." He took my hand in his. "I have to enter with my father, but find me after. We have much to discuss."

He gave the back of my hand a soft kiss and left.

A normal dinner. As long as I leaned into my years of etiquette training from Ashmore, no one would suspect that a sorceress was at their table.

I clasped my hands, my thumb tracing the warmth that lingered on the back of my hand, and entered the dining room.

The dining room was silent as all the women stood behind their chairs. Apparently, I was to sit at Freya's left and Brietta would sit at her right.

I quietly took my place.

Rubia and Sapphira glared across the table at the empty spot between Pearl and I—Annalisa was nowhere to be seen.

Freya entered the dining room dripping in regal splendor. She glided across the room with flawless poise to her place at the end of the table. Her eyes were cold and clear, as if her breakdown at tea had never happened.

She smiled. "What a delight to have all my kittens in one place." Her eyes flicked to the empty chair. "Well, almost all of you."

I tightened my hold on my hands. I was not a kitten, I was a serpent in the herd of Hyton bulls.

The door to the dining room opened again and Derrick entered. He gave me a quick glance and a warm smile before taking his seat at what would be the Duke's right-hand.

General Hyton entered the room, the candlelight skating across his white hair as he stood at the spot across from Derrick.

A gleam of gold caught the corner of my eye and my back stiffened—the Duke had arrived wearing the golden crown of Lycaster atop his greying hair and gold chains studded with gems across his chest. I turned to face Alastar Anders Hyton as he entered the dining room but then my stomach dropped. He was not alone.

Next to the Duke was my mother, wearing a simple Hyton Blue dress with her dark hair swept up on top of her head. Duke Hyton's hand was on her back as he led her to the table. Her dark, heavy lashes veiled her eyes.

My chest caved in like I had been punched. Since Duke Hyton had stripped Father of the Baronage of Ravenwood as punishment for high treason, Mother was no longer Baroness Ravenwood.

Even though she had been bought and sold, she did not even have the dignity of a title. Nothing separated her from a common whore.

My *mother* was just a Hyton whore.

Mother silently took her place between General Hyton and Garnet. Duke Hyton sat and the rest of us followed, the carved chairs groaning as we all took our seats.

Servants went around the table and filled our goblets with wine, but no one else dared to move as Freya stared knives across the table at her husband.

I glanced past my mother to look at General Hyton and I could still see bits of Riyan in his face. My mind crafted an image of Riyan as the size of a normal man replacing his father at the end of the table. His long honey-colored hair was neatly combed and a Hyton Blue cape draped across his back.

The imaginary Riyan tugged on the too-tight collar of his doublet and gave me a wink, silently beckoning me to abandon the dinner and meet him in a dark hallway.

My thumb stroked the back of my hand as I bit my tongue.

The dining room door creaked open and then slammed shut, banishing my fantasy. Footsteps pattered across the floor before Annalisa plopped in the chair next to me. Her hair was still piled on top of her head and her hands were speckled with paint.

Rubia took one glance at Annalisa's dusty blue dress and wrinkled her nose.

Sapphira scoffed. "Cannot even show up on time."

"Or dress properly," Pearl added with a sneer.

Annalisa leaned back in her chair and folded her arms, countering Sapphira with a frosty glare.

Duke Hyton stood up and held out his golden goblet. "A toast!"

I wrapped my hand around my cup and lifted it. Duke Hyton's horrifying blue eyes found me amongst the forest of raised goblets.

"To the newest member of the House of Hyton." His eyes swept to my mother's, who returned with a tight painted smile. "And to dear Serafina's safe return."

Bile rose in my throat, but I forced it back down. Duke Hyton brought his cup to his lips and the rest of us followed, some mumbling "to Adalia," and "to Serafina."

Just as the edge of my goblet touched my lip, Duchess Hyton gave Brietta a pointed glance. They both pantomimed swallowing a mouthful before setting their goblets down.

I did the same.

Plates clinked as the servants brought out the first course—some sort of stew. My eyes swept across the table as Derrick's sisters dug into their bowls. I gently stirred my spoon as I watched the others take mouthful after mouthful. Even Brietta and Freya slowly picked at their stew, so it must have been safe to eat.

The thick gravy was warm on my tongue as I swallowed a spoonful.

Mother accidentally took a drink from General Hyton's goblet and laughed it off, replacing his wine with hers before getting back to her own stew. The General gave her a small half-smile.

I had seen Mother and the General speak before, but something about that small exchange seemed…friendly. I did not think either of them was capable of being friendly.

Duke Hyton folded his hands. "Are my precious gemstones enjoying the stew?"

"Yes, Father!" Pearl beamed.

"Absolutely wonderful," Rubia added with a bat of her eyelashes.

Emeralda tipped her goblet back but gurgled in assent.

Duke Hyton smiled. "Can any of you guess what the meat is?"

The spoon became cold in my hand. I did not like this dinner game.

"I know it is not beef," Amethyst said as she patted her pregnant belly. "My Tadpole would force back up if it were."

"Is it venison?" Rubia asked.

"Duck?" chimed in Sapphira.

Garnet remained pointedly silent.

A sly smile crept up Duke Hyton's lips. "No."

My stomach turned. Were we eating rats? Bear cubs?

Duke Hyton glanced in Derrick's direction. "It is rabbit."

Oh, rabbit was not bad.

Derrick leaned back against his chair and let out a tense breath. General Hyton snickered.

Freya put her spoon down with a clatter. "Really, Anders?"

Emeralda leaned forward with sleepy eyes. "What? Am I missing something?"

"Oh, so you have not heard that my heir earned a new name at court?" Duke Hyton shot Derrick a pointed look paired with a wicked smile.

Derrick's cheeks reddened and he stared down at the table like he wanted to disappear beneath it.

Freya's hands balled into fists. "Anders, do not—"

"Since Derrick made such a spectacle of himself at the ball last week with his *fast performance,*" Duke Hyton boomed, "everyone started calling him Little Rabbit Hyton!"

My hand clapped over my mouth. Derrick and Brietta had left Annalisa's ball and reappeared in what seemed like a blink, but was it really that fast to notice?

General Hyton burst out laughing. Mother's chest rose with tense breaths as she stared at her stew. Annalisa cursed under her breath. Brietta's cheeks flamed and she shrunk down. Derrick's older sisters squealed in disgust except for Garnet, who had her nose stuck in a book.

"Stop it, Father!" Derrick hissed. "You are embarrassing Brietta! And Serafina should not hear—"

"She should be embarrassed!" Duke Hyton shouted as he gestured to Brietta. "The whole damn Dukedom knows her husband can only last *one minute!*"

Brietta covered her scarlet face with her hands. She had not remembered anything that happened between her and Derrick that night, and for the Duke to bring it up in front of everyone…

My hand left my lips and curled into a fist under the table.

Freya put her hand on Brietta's shoulder and spat venom. "Of all the disgusting stunts you have pulled over the years—!"

Duke Hyton slammed his fist on the table. Everyone other than the General flinched. "Damn it, Freya! We are in a family crisis and I will address it as such! All the Barons now believe the sole heir to the House of

Hyton is an impotent little pup! You know what that means for the rest of us!"

Pearl slammed her hands over her ears the moment her father said "impotent," Garnet slipped another book from underneath the table and passed it to Emeralda, and Rubia and Sapphira shrieked in disgust.

"Father!" Rubia cried. "Stop talking about our baby brother like that!"

"I am going to throw up," Annalisa growled.

I could practically feel Derrick's burning embarrassment from the other end of the table. Duke Hyton reached for Derrick and made fast, stabbing motions like he was poking him in the chest.

"You. Are. The. Heir. Damn it!" he shouted. "If the Barons are not convinced that you are a virile bull, they will think you are weak—they will think *all of us* are weak!"

It was exactly as Freya had told us—the Alastar trials never ended. Just as the Duke had to constantly prove himself worthy, so did his entire line.

But Duke Hyton's entire line was *just* Derrick.

Sapphira pushed up from the table and bared her teeth. "Stop it, Father!"

Duke Hyton ignored his daughter. "Until you start producing some heirs, you will continue to be a pathetic joke!"

I forced myself to look at Derrick. His eyes were down, even as his father held him by the collar. His chest rose and fell, but he stayed firm.

My white flame surged in my chest. Derrick was *not* pathetic.

My hands curled into tight fists beneath the table as the magic awoke in my veins. I should have grabbed my crystal from Brietta before we got back to the palace. I could not lose control of my power in front of the entire House of Hyton!

Duke Hyton leaned in close to his son and a growl shredded his throat. "Hate me all you want, boy, but this is only the beginning of the torture you face."

Amethyst threw her arms around Derrick's shoulders. "Enough, Father! Leave Der-bear alone!"

Der-bear? My white flame quieted from the secondhand embarrassment plunging through my chest.

"Let go, Amie," Derrick grumbled through his teeth.

Amethyst planted a big kiss on his cheek that he tried to resist. "We love you and think you are perfect!"

Rubia, Pearl, and Sapphira agreed, adding sweet words and "Derbears." Emeralda sloshed wine out of her goblet and started slurring praises. Even Mother shot him a pitiful glance and a smile.

Annalisa twisted the tines of her fork on her plate, making skin-crawling squeaks. "Derrick, Derrick, Derrick," she mocked. "Everything always has to be about *Derrick.*"

Sapphira snapped her head toward her youngest sister. "What was that, Anna?"

Shit. I had endured enough Ashmore dinners to know what was about to happen.

Before I could stop her, Annalisa threw down her fork. "You have your own sons you could fawn over, you know. That is, if you ever stepped away from the gambling halls, *Empress Sapphira.*"

Sapphira slammed her palms on the table so hard her cutlery rattled. A brown curl popped free from the tight braid around her head. Annalisa did not even flinch.

"Little Annalisa, always acting out for attention." Her blue eyes shot over in my direction. "Did you ever wonder why she is the only one of us without a gemstone name? From the moment she was born, even our mother knew she was just a worthless little crybaby!"

Annalisa's chair flew out behind her and she was on her feet. Metal flashed in the corner of my eye and I turned—Annalisa held out her knife.

"I could do all those rebels in your crumbling empire a big favor right now and end you," she growled. "Call me worthless *one more time.*"

I placed my hand on her forearm. I could not risk trying magic, but I had to intervene. "Anna, calm down."

Rubia gasped as Sapphira picked up her own knife. Her chest heaved as her mouth twisted in a predatory snarl.

"Worthless. Little. Anna." She leaned on the table, the knife gleaming under the candlelight. "Last-selected. Married to a nobody. You are not even a Hyton any longer, you Thornebow rat. Enjoy the rest of your life with those traitorous, useless, Thorn—"

Annalisa lunged onto the table with a scream. Sapphira followed. Goblets flew out and bowls toppled over as they collided on the table.

Freya cried at them to stop. Sapphira snarled and held her knife in the air just before Rubia grabbed her wrist and knocked the knife away. Pearl grabbed the hem of Annalisa's skirt and I grabbed her ankle as she thrashed with her knife.

Emeralda threw her book at Annalisa and missed. I tugged Annalisa's leg and she slid back on the table before Sapphira could punch her in the head.

I heaved her back one more time before an arm wrapped around my waist and forced me to let go of Annalisa.

With a quick spin, the arm released me and my palms found the papered wall before my face did. I whipped my head around just as Derrick grabbed Annalisa by the laces of her dress and yanked her off the table. He threw her into the wall so hard that it shook.

I gasped and stepped away. Annalisa's skirt flew up as she kicked him, but Derrick held her in place with his forearm against her chest. He forced the knife out of Annalisa's hand and it clattered on the floor.

"The hell is wrong with you?" he shouted.

Brietta's hands found my shoulders and she led me out of the dining room. I glanced back to see Rubia, Emeralda, Pearl, and Freya holding nearly-feral Sapphira against the opposite wall. Duke Hyton disappeared through another door with his arm around my mother's back.

My chest heaved as rabbit stew ran down the front of my bodice. Amethyst rushed past us, crying that the fighting was not good for her growing baby.

Just a normal dinner, Derrick had said.

I did not want to think about how true that statement still was.

I rested on my back on Annalisa's bed as I mentally traced the veins on each colorful leaf she had painted on her tree. Brietta had given my Nordingaard crystal back and it rested securely against my leg.

After that horrible dinner, it was nice to feel calm again.

I smoothed my nightgown over my belly. I had already…*taken care of* those aching feelings that had plagued me all day. I could have just stayed in my own bedroom, but I did not want to leave volatile Annalisa alone after her whole family went into a frenzy at dinner. She might even light the palace on fire if someone were not there to talk her down.

The door unlatched and I sat up. Annalisa trudged in, her curls a mess and her blue dress smeared with dark splotches of rabbit stew. A few red scratches marred her face, but I found no evidence that she had received a kiss from the empress's blade.

Instead of greeting me with an insult or complaint like I expected, she yanked her unfinished painting off the easel and ran to her window. Before I could stop her, she threw the window open and hurled her canvas into the night with a scream.

"Anna! Why would you—?"

"It was awful!" She whipped around, tears streaking down her cheeks. "Horrible! Grigory deserves better—"

A hard knock echoed on the door. Annalisa stomped over to answer before I could take a single step.

She yanked the handle but only left a crack in the door. "What?"

"Is Serafina there? She was not in her bedroom."

I furrowed my brows. The voice belonged to Derrick but it did not sound like him.

"Everyone has had enough of you for one day," Annalisa snapped.

"I need her."

Something about his clipped words sent a shiver down my spine.

"Go away, Derrick!" Annalisa shouted, slamming the door in his face and locking it.

Her whole body clenched and she screamed behind her teeth. She stormed over to her window and gripped the windowsill. Her curls danced in the gentle night breeze.

I quietly joined her and gently pulled on the loose laces of her dress. Camille and Dinah usually fawned over Annalisa after a spat with one of her sisters when we were in school, but now I was all she had.

Annalisa complied as I slid off her bodice and then untied her skirt, but she just stared into the night as the waves crashed against the cliffs below.

She seemed so…hollow. I had to fix it.

I placed my hand on her shoulder. My crystal radiated a gentle warmth against my leg as my magic activated—maybe she would let me in. "You are not worthless, Anna."

She let out a shaking breath, but did not respond.

I kept my hand on her shoulder and joined her at her side, letting the soft sea air kiss my cheeks. "You are the most talented artist I know. You are brave and honest, even when no one wants to hear it."

I was only honest because magic forced me to be.

I leaned my head further out the window so I could look into her eyes. "*Never* underestimate the freedom honesty gives you."

Annalisa's lip trembled. "'Der' was my name for him. 'Lis' was his name for me. We had our own made-up language."

She choked on her words as her eyes brimmed with tears. I stroked my thumb on her shoulder and rain fell in my mind again.

She let me in.

"He is my twin, the other half of my soul…but now he hates me too."

The rain fell harder and my vision swam. I closed my eyes and over the sound of the rainfall I heard two small children giggling and stomping in puddles.

"*Race you to the bull statue, Lis!*" A small boy called over the rain.

Annalisa turned and I let go of her shoulder. I opened my eyes as the magical connection between the two of us broke. Annalisa had just sent me a memory, but she did not seem to realize she had done anything.

She crossed the room where a thin castle tower painted on the wall stood guard near her dressing table. A long vine of rainbow flowers curled up the tower.

Annalisa traced a blue flower on the vine with her finger. "Emperor Orlon is twenty-five years older than Sapphira. He bought her when we were still in school."

Her finger dropped to a crimson flower. "Two princes had a bidding war over Rubia when she was a child."

She turned her attention to a bright green flower.

"Emeralda gets passed around the nobility of her kingdom. She drinks to forget about it."

A purple flower.

"Amethyst is thirty years old and she has been pregnant eight times. All of the pregnancies have failed."

A white flower.

"Pearl's kingdom drained their treasury to buy her, but she has not given her prince an heir yet. The king beats her with a rod when her cycle starts."

Finally, a deep wine-colored flower.

"Garnet has not spoken a single word since she was sent away."

My heart ached. I never knew what happened to the Hyton daughters once they graduated from Ashmore…but I never could have imagined such horror.

Even with all I knew about them, not a single one of them deserved it.

A gentler hand knocked on the door and I answered. Merri was on the other side, a silver tray holding two cups of spiced cream in her hands. Annalisa hiccuped as Merri gave her head a pat and her cheek a kiss.

I filled my belly in silence as I reflected on the memory Annalisa had sent me. In her worst moments, was Derrick what she thought about? Was he truly the other half of her soul?

The bigger question was why was my magic only responding to the sadness of those around me? Divining the secrets of Ilsa and braiding that knowledge into a scourge would be much more useful.

Why was my heart's desire to be sympathetic instead of productive?

I swallowed my frustration with the last of the warm drink. As much as I hated to surrender to fickle emotion, I had to follow my magic's direction to win Riyan's freedom.

Annalisa put out the candles and we slipped into bed. As I rested on my side, looking at the mural of the tree behind us, I counted two of every animal Annalisa had painted. Two ravens, two foxes, two fawns…

…every animal had a twin.

Annalisa pulled the blankets tighter around her, her arms and knees tucked in close to her chest. She had been mean in school, but had she only reached for knives so she would not constantly reach for what she was missing?

Maybe I could help her find what she needed to be complete again.

My white flame slowly danced around my heart and my crystal warmed against my leg. I had ended the day no closer to freeing Fraleigh than when I had arrived at the palace, but maybe the path to liberation did not begin with the destruction of the House of Hyton.

The Hytons were doing a fine job of destroying themselves without me, anyway.

My eyes rested at the bottom of the mural, my eyelashes fluttering closed at the image of two little rabbits.

Chapter Sixteen
Two Stars

Treason could wait until after breakfast.

If Brietta was going to take her time clearing Derrick out of their bedroom so we could look for memories within Ilsa's Presentation dress, I might as well eat.

Annalisa sat beside me on her couch and picked at the tray of iced buns on the low table in front of us. As soon as I lifted a warm bun to my lips, the memory of Riyan's voice traced the back of my mind. *"Take a bite, you'll love it!"*

I sighed and put the bun back down on the painted plate. As good as the bun looked, it was not filled with delicious elskaberry jam. I was not in the middle of the Bloodstone lily field enjoying them from a wicker basket, either.

I was still in Hyton Palace, wondering if each meal could be my last.

Brietta entered Annalisa's bedroom without so much as a knock. "Come, Sera, we must go to tea."

Annalisa shifted on her couch and gestured to the breakfast tray. "But we have tea right here."

Brietta did not look at either of us. The belt of her robe was tightly cinched around her waist, but her auburn braid was mussed.

I did not have to make a magical connection to know something was wrong.

"This is a different tea," Brietta said. She turned on her heel and left the room, forcefully shutting the door.

Annalisa shot me a quizzical look, but I rose from the couch and followed Brietta. I hated leaving Annalisa, but I could not risk her asking a question that I could not ignore.

Brietta marched across the hallway so quickly I had to pick up the hem of my robe and run just to keep up with her. She flung her bedroom door open and I followed her inside.

The blankets on the elaborately-carved bed were still tousled from a night's sleep. The couch at the foot of the bed where Brietta had said Derrick slept looked undisturbed. The room seemed sparse, like some furniture was missing.

Brietta slammed the door shut and wedged the back of a nearby armchair beneath the handle. She waved her hand over her shoulder. "The wardrobe is over there."

She was not acting like herself, but maybe she was just nervous because I was about to perform sorcery in front of her.

I opened the carved wardrobe and the soft scents of oak and vanilla filled my nose. I gently thumbed through the Hyton Blue brocades when my hand found a black linen sleeve. He had worn that shirt during the Presentation—I must have been close to where they had stashed Ilsa's dress.

My fingers dropped to the cuff of the sleeve and I froze when a threaded pattern traced my fingertips. I lifted the sleeve—two embroidered black stars rested on the inside of the right wrist.

When we were in our fourth year of school, Derrick caught troll pox. The whole Dukedom was in a panic. Annalisa was inconsolable.

Once his letters became less frequent, I knew his illness was serious. Feeling helpless, I had quickly stitched two stars on a small rectangle of linen and sent them to him along with his letter.

I had forgotten I had done it—hell, I was not even sure *why* I had done it. Did the two stars symbolize him and I? Or him and Annalisa? Was it supposed to just be a wish of good health?

Regardless of why, Derrick had kept the little gift for years. Even though the stars were lopsided and sloppily done, he had them sewn on his wedding clothes.

I held my breath as my thumb traced the stars once, then I pushed past the shirt.

A glimmer of silvery blue peeked out between more black clothes and my heart jumped.

Found her.

I gently reached into the back of the wardrobe and pulled out the heap of fabric. The dark green ribbons that I had torn from my own Presentation dress were still attached to the sleeves, but the makeshift laces were gone. I laid the dress out on the floor and sat beside it.

Brietta stood over the dress with her arms tightly folded. "What are you supposed to do?"

I lifted the hem of my nightgown and loosened the ribbon from around my leg. "Not entirely sure, but I think this will help."

I tied the choker around my neck so the crystal was flush with my throat. Calmness washed over me and I closed my eyes. I was powerful. I was in control.

The crystal warmed against my skin and magic tingled my fingertips as I reached over the dress. Each of the Man of the Mountain's tiny tears awoke in the fabric, sparkling in my mind's eye like a river on a sunny day.

But I was not just looking for the Man of the Mountain's tears, I was looking for Ilsa's.

I kneaded the dress, searching for young Ilsa—that future Duchess who had no clue what her life would become.

The sound of flipping pages entered my mind and I followed the trail my magic was leading me down. I did not find tears, but instead cold sweat.

Good enough.

I smiled and leaned into the memory's pull.

"*Let me get you out of this. I will not touch you, I promise.*"

I recognized that voice…

Male hands untied dark green laces on the back of the dress. "*No matter what happens, I will bring honor to your name, Brietta. I swear it.*"

It was Derrick's voice—*my* Derrick. I had not found Duchess Ilsa's memory, I found Brietta's!

I bit my tongue and released my hold on the magic.

"*You are the most noble friend, the best—*"

I pulled out of the memory and looked around, reorienting myself in Derrick and Brietta's bedroom.

"Well?" Brietta asked stiffly.

I look back down at the dress. "Wrong person's memory."

"What did you see?"

My lip trembled as I gave the answer I could not refuse. "Promises made but not kept."

Her eyes widened slightly and her grip on her arms tightened. "Try again. Make sure the memory is hers this time."

I closed my eyes and my magic swept through the dress again. Ilsa, Ilsa, Ilsa—what did I know about Ilsa? Mother of Anders and Ragnar. Wife to Alastar the Wise. Icy beauty.

She had iced Derrick out from the beginning.

Maybe Freya had given us a clue after all. My hands traveled up to the square neck of the bodice.

The light beating of feathery wings traced my mind—my magic had found tears.

"*I cannot do this!*" cried a young woman's voice.

I soared into Ilsa's memory on the back of white raven's wings. The wings disappeared in a flash of light and I took in my surroundings— plush pink and blue furniture, girls in their undergarments milling about, and a wall full of tall mirrors.

I was in the moments before the Presentation.

A tall woman with long white hair sat sullenly at a dressing table—Ilsa Ravenwood.

The shimmering dress fit snugly around her curved frame. A beautiful blue diamond pendant sat on the dressing table behind Ilsa. Even though the room was abuzz with other women lacing up their dresses and trying not to cry their makeup off, Ilsa's violet eyes did not move once.

A woman with light brown hair walked over to Ilsa, her petal pink dress swishing around her ankles. Her lips parted as she admired the necklace. "Oh, Ilsa, is this what your father bought you for the Presentation? It is beautiful."

Ilsa shrugged. "That is nice, I suppose. Not that I can appreciate it for myself."

The woman in pink frowned. She picked up the pendant and held it in front of Ilsa's face. She angled the blue gemstone so it caught the sunlight from the windows and scattered sparkles across Ilsa's violet eyes.

The woman in pink gave Ilsa a warm smile as she moved the gem back and forth. "How about now?"

The fractals danced across Ilsa's unmoving eyes and she smiled. "Thank you, Hilda."

Hilda! I should have recognized her smile. If I had a body in the memory, I would have wrapped my arms around the young Hilda Bloodstone.

Hilda gently placed the crystal around Ilsa's neck so it rested on her heart. "Who do you think is going to pick you?" She bounced with delight. "Richard Thornebow was absolutely enamored with you at the Suitors' Ball yesterday!"

"He was quite nice," Ilsa said fondly. Her face fell. "But with my fame, we all know who will actually choose me."

Ilsa's voice broke and then tears streamed down her cheeks. She wrapped her hands around her stomach and leaned forward as she sobbed.

"I cannot do this!" Ilsa cried. "He cannot force me to marry him!"

The other women shot green glares as she cried. I might have even glared at her too had I been there. All I had ever wanted was to be Duchess of Lycaster, and she was sobbing at the opportunity?

Hilda swiped the tears from Ilsa's cheeks and took her hands. She guided the incredibly tall Ilsa from her chair and led her to the wall of mirrors.

Alastar the Wise was sitting right behind those mirrors, hearing everything. Hell, Nikkolas Bloodstone was there too.

And so was the doomed future Baron Thornebow.

Hilda gently straightened Ilsa so she stood squarely in front of the mirrors. She wrapped her hands around Ilsa's arms and smiled at their reflections.

"I am not sure how much you can see right now," Hilda said with a smile, "but you are radiant."

Could Ilsa…not see?

"Today might be hard but—" Hilda's smile grew bigger. "—you can still love him. It will just take time."

Ilsa's countenance hardened and I swore the temperature in the room dropped. Her cold gaze set on her reflection, unknowingly facing the man who would become Alastar the Wise.

"He can force me to marry him, but I will *never* love him."

Ilsa's words put a stamp of finality on the memory, so I released my magic.

My mind returned to an ice-cold body. I fought back a chill as I tried to comprehend everything I saw.

"It was the Presentation." My heart raced as I panted. Searching through the memory took more energy than I expected. "She did not want to marry Alastar the Wise and refused to love him."

Brietta gave me a considering look. "Why? She had to have a reason."

"She…just did not want to be forced."

Brietta hissed out a breath and looked down at the dress. "A feeling I share."

"She was right at the mirrors when she said it—and Alastar the Wise still picked her?"

"The future Duke just needed a valuable diamond, not a happy one."

Diamond. "She had a diamond too—a large blue one."

Her eyes widened. "What? A diamond that size and color would be worth thousands, no, hundreds of thousands of marks. If something like that is in her vault—"

"Do you know where the vault is?"

She tightened her hold on her arms. "No. And no one will tell us unless they want to lose their heads. But if the Hytons had sold a jewel like that, my family would have known about it. It has to be in the palace."

And if the Hytons were willing to hide away a diamond worth a small fortune, what else were they hiding in that vault?

I pushed up from the floor with a huff. Finding the vault would be the next move. We still had no definite answers, but we at least had a lead.

"Anything else?" Brietta asked.

"She was blind, at least I am fairly certain she was."

Brietta wrung her hands together and paced across the room. I suddenly noticed the knuckles on her right hand were red and swollen.

Had she hurt herself? I followed behind her as she paced, but she stopped in her tracks.

"She did not kill him," she said.

I crossed my arms. "Are you really saying it is impossible for a blind person to kill her husband?"

"No, what I am saying is that I *understand* her." Brietta looked over her shoulder at me. "She might have been forced into the marriage. She might not love him, but…no matter what he did, even if it was horrible… she would not find it in herself to kill him. Even if she had found a way around the blood bond."

She suddenly turned away. I stepped around a couch to try to look her in the face when something caught my eye.

A pile of broken wood was shoved into the corner of the room— shattered pieces of a chair. One of the legs was splintered, the end stained with dark red spots.

Blood.

My mouth fell open. "What happened?"

"Nothing!" She turned on her heel and headed for the door. "If you cannot get anything more from that damn dress, you can leave."

I ran my eyes up and down Brietta's body—no injuries other than her knuckles. Was she hiding anything under her robe?

Or…was *Derrick* the one who was injured?

She opened the door, but I did not move.

"No, tell me!" I said. "You really think I believe—"

"I do not care what you believe!" She gripped her arms, her swollen knuckles turning white. "Get out. Give me some time to fucking think so I can fix this damn Dukedom!"

My heart sank. She did not sound like the Brietta I knew. She sounded like…

…me. She sounded exactly like me.

I looked at Brietta and did not see my friend, but a fortress.

She had completely shut me out, just like I had done to the rest of the world for years.

Nothing I did not deserve.

I had turned my back on her when she was vulnerable on that velvet couch. I chose to make her my villain instead of reaching out with the same helping hand she had given me for years.

But if Brietta was suddenly like me, I was too late to say sorry.

Slowly, I stepped out of the room. Though my feet obeyed the future Duchess's order, my white flame swirled around my heart, beckoning me to speak.

I could still try to find my friend again.

As soon as my feet found the blue carpet in the hallway, I turned to the still open door. "Brie?"

Brietta's hand froze on the door handle.

I swallowed and the Nordingaard crystal radiated a gentle warmth against my throat. "I see you, Brie. I see those walls you have stacked up."

Her brown eyes flared. No one liked to be seen, but she had to hear it.

"I had a wall just like it, for years," I said. "It's lonely, but you think you are safer in there." I shook my head. "You are not safer. Or stronger. Just colder."

The gleam returned to Brietta's eyes and I recognized her again. "How…poetic."

"I learned from the best." I gave her a soft smile. "You were there for me when I was behind a wall and…even though I know I am part of the reason you have that wall…I will be here if you want to come out."

Her lip trembled, her eyes growing glassier by the second. "Thank you, Sera."

She slowly closed the door and clicked the lock shut.

My smile stayed on as I remembered my last promise to Riyan—*try to be happy.*

Though my insides were still bleak, reaching out a hand to Brietta was at least a start.

I looked down the long hallway as the crystal stayed warm on my neck. For the first time, my magic felt stable. I could not waste the opportunity—I had to chase this little spark of happiness to whatever end.

Logically, I should have started looking for Ilsa's vault, but magic was not logic. As the crystal pulsed warmth against my skin, my heart's desire was pulling me on a different path. I wanted to help Brietta, and Annalisa, and…

I let out a shaking sigh. Just as I had once hastily sewed two stars into linen, I needed to make sure Derrick was all right.

If I could even find him.

Chapter Seventeen

Healer

I never thought the heir to Lycaster would be so hard to find.

None of the Hytons had seen him. He was not holed away in his music room or his bedroom. He had not gone for a ride on his horse.

He was just…gone.

After hours of searching, I crashed into a chair in yet another small room in the maze of the palace. I slumped over, my belly full from a quick dinner, and tried to think.

Bloody pieces of a shattered armchair were stacked in the corner of Derrick and Brietta's room. The blood bond meant Derrick could not be dead, but he was hurt.

I *needed* to find him.

"I thought you were taught to have better posture than that."

I whipped my head toward the noise. Standing between two suits of ancient armor was a floating white head—a phantom.

No, it was not a phantom, it was…

"…Daigen?"

He had followed me to the palace?

He stepped away from the wall, his cloak that perfectly matched the blue damask wallpaper fluttering around him. "Much calmer of a response than normal. Looks like you heeded my advice about keeping that crystal on you."

I was not about to admit he was right. "Is invading my dreams not good enough? You have to harass me in the halls too?"

He kept his arms folded as he stepped over. "Watching you wander around the palace like a lost sheep was too painful to bear any longer. I could not wait for you to pass out."

I hissed out a breath. "You could actually teach me how to get inside dreams instead of sneaking around, you know."

"It's easy." Daigen mussed the hair at the crown of my head before I could flinch away. "You just stand over someone while they are sleeping…" He tapped me between the eyes. "…and go right through that open door. You drool a little, you know."

He had watched me sleep? "You are vile."

"I am *effective*." He hooked his ankle around the leg of a chair and dragged it across the floor beside me. He sat down with a flourish, resting his feet on top of a low table. "People are much more vulnerable when sleeping."

I wrinkled my nose at his boots on the furniture. "Noted."

He folded his arms behind his head. "How is following your heart's desire going?"

I held back a scowl. "Leading me in unproductive directions. All I know is that Riyan is a murderer and Ilsa might not be."

Daigen slid his feet off the table and rested his elbows on his knees. "We know anger fuels your power, but when do you connect with your magic the most?"

Evereon had let me in when he was talking about how he was kicked out of Heaston. Astrid had let me in to see memories of Ragnar. Annalisa's raindrops poured on me any time she mentioned her siblings.

"When someone is sad," I said. "Usually they send me memories— things that should be happy, but an underlying bitterness sours it."

Daigen gave me a soft smile. "Seems like we know what your affinity is."

"Sure would be nice if you gave me a clue."

"My magic speaks to me when I need to change." Little horns poked through his temples to prove his point. "Your magic speaks to you when others need to change. My affinity is transformation, yours is *healing.*"

I scrunched my nose. I was never clever with medicine nor did I know how to wrap a sprain or make a compress. I excelled in our childcare classes at Ashmore, but I was never drawn to making sick people well again.

"Healing makes no sense," I said. "I rarely cared about anyone other than myself."

I clamped down my teeth and shut my eyes. I did not mean for that bit of ugly truth to come out, but I could not help it.

Daigen laughed. "Still having trouble with the compulsive truth?"

I shot him a glare. "You never said this would be a problem. I am going to lose my head if I keep hiccupping up damning truths!"

"Just accept your truth so the magic does not force you to! For example…" His skin began to flare red. "You will never see me wear someone else's face. The magic only reflects what I truly believe I am."

I crossed my arms. "A monster."

His violet eyes were still. "A son of a goat herder who cannot hide no matter how hard he tries."

I bit my tongue…what did *I* truly believe I was?

Was I a bride? A daughter? Friend? Liar? Magic danced within my veins, making me a sorceress…but did my gift from an immortal man really answer my question?

No matter how much I achieved or reflected on my inner turmoil, I still did not know myself…or Riyan, for that matter.

Would he have even believed that I was a healer?

Daigen's voice suddenly pulled me out of my thoughts. "By the way, the young Alastar is prowling within the walls, just like I was."

I suppressed a groan—as if I could find Derrick in an even darker maze.

Daigen rose from the chair and flipped his cloak to reveal a grey side. He wrapped the darker fabric over his shoulders. "His behavior is *very* predictable—he generally is in the same place every night."

I hissed out a breath. Not very helpful.

He stepped toward the fireless hearth. "Think of this as another trust exercise. Just as you float on your back in the middle of the lake, I am the gentle tide that pushes you in the direction of your heart's desire."

I folded my arms. "I cannot float! Or swim."

He rolled his eyes. "The art of a good metaphor is lost on you."

"Just tell me!"

"Just *feel* something!" The air tensed, as if Daigen had suddenly taken command of all the magic in the room. "Stop demanding answers and find them. Your emotions *will* put you on the right path."

Daigen stepped into the ashy hearth and turned to face me, his back against the bricks in the fireplace. "I have too much at stake for you to go the wrong direction. Just trust me."

He leaned against the bricks and they instantly swallowed him. I had no idea how he had done it.

He was the master of illusions and a complete pain in the ass.

My head fell into my hands. If merely looking for Derrick had not worked, I had no other option but to heed Daigen's advice.

My white flame snaked around a little spot of warmth within my heart. Derrick was hurt. I wanted to heal him, if I could. He was predictable, but where would he run off to night after night where no one could find him?

Then the realization hit me like a jolt of lightning. I knew where he was…or at least where he would be.

I stood on the balcony of the North tower as the stars twinkled above me. I kept darting my eyes between the door and the pile of pillows and blankets in the corner of the balcony.

Brietta had said Derrick was able to escape to the North tower, but maybe a guard had grabbed him and locked in his bedroom for another night.

The thin crescent moon loomed above me. Time was running out.

I propped my arms on the balcony railing and gazed at the faint peak of Nordingaard in the distance.

How was Riyan faring in the place West of the Moon and East of the Sun? Was his spirit merely swirling around in endless darkness like the other lost souls?

I sighed and looked down at my hands. Trusting Daigen was difficult, but if he said following my emotions was the way to Riyan, I had no other choice.

Wings flapped next to me like a whisper. I turned—a raven had perched on the balcony.

I looked over my shoulder to make sure no one was around before I asked, "Erik?"

The raven raised its hackles and flapped its wings. Wrong—it was definitely Endre.

Endre raised one of his talons, showing off a tiny-rolled up piece of parchment attached to his leg. I untied the parchment and a sliver of charcoal fell into my hand.

Was Evereon contacting me already? I unrolled the parchment.

Yoo gud?

I wrinkled my nose. Evereon had said he was one of the few soldiers who could read and the writing was too sloppy for me to believe it had come from the hands of a noble son, even one who had not finished school.

I turned to Endre. "Did Brandt send this?"

Endre bobbed his head and I smiled. "Where was he?"

"*Guard-house,*" Endre croaked.

Brandt must have been staying with former cadets from the military academy. He was taking a huge risk to send messages by raven, especially a talking one.

All to make sure I was all right. How sweet of him!

I flipped over the parchment and wrote a simple "Good" along with a small heart, in case he could not read.

I secured the parchment around Endre's leg. "Give him a little kiss for me when you see him."

It was supposed to be a joke, but my voice came out hollow. Could I still talk to Endre like I had before?

I pulled the twine into a tight knot. "Was it a tough flight from the fortress?"

Endre shook his head and the ruff around his neck fluffed up. His wavy hair used to always be so messy, no comb could fully tame it.

Slowly, I reached over and stroked his neck and tried to smooth the ruff. "I just found out that all you Heaston boys got to play around while the Ashmore girls were locked up. How many lovers did *you* have?"

Endre looked over his shoulder and narrowed his eyes. I swore he was smiling.

"*A-lot,*" he croaked.

I scoffed and flicked him on the back of the head. "You men are absolute boars."

Endre opened his beak and spread his wings, as if to say, "Not me! I am a raven."

Hinges creaked behind me and Endre took to the skies. Derrick stood in the doorway, gripping the handle of the tower door. He had a red and purple ring under his left eye.

My heart ached. What had happened to him?

He dropped his gaze. "I did not know you would be here, I—"

He caught his words and stopped. He shifted back into the tower, but I reached out my hand.

"Derrick, what did Brietta do?" I asked.

He froze in place and swallowed. "Nothing I did not deserve."

Did they have an argument? Had he somehow discovered our plans? Did he know I was a sorceress?

My palm pressed against my heart and I took a step closer. "What do you mean?"

His eyes stayed low. "I cannot remember."

I knitted my brows. He said he could not remember consummating his marriage with Brietta either, but how could he be black and blue and not remember what had happened?

Derrick's throat trembled and he hissed out a breath. "Look, it is late, you should go to bed."

No, I was not going to let him shut me out too. "You were looking for me last night—you said you needed me and here I am."

He looked up at me and raised an eyebrow. "I…I did?"

The ache beneath my ribs deepend. How much could he not remember?

He turned his shoulders toward me, keeping his fingers hooked on the door handle. "I suppose I wanted to make sure you were all right." A ghost of a smile flicked up his lips. "You certainly are doing better than I am."

Being direct was not going to help, maybe I needed to change the subject and then he would open up.

I glanced at the pile of pillows and blankets. "Do you sleep out here often?"

His Hyton Blue eyes finally met mine. "Every night since you left."

He had told me his eyes would stay north until I came back to the palace. I thought he was just being poetic.

"Seems foolish, I know," he said, "sleeping outside like a dog and watching over the mountain…but I just could not stop worrying."

He walked toward the balcony's edge. He slumped down onto the railing, his eyes on the dim outline of Nordingaard. "When the moon was full, I could almost see that damned fortress with you locked inside. Then the moon thinned night after night, so I stopped trying to see. I just listened—listened for a scream."

I joined him at the balcony railing. His eyes were bolted north as if he were tracing Nordingaard's peak into his memory. "I knew you had my dagger with you. I knew you were smart enough to escape him and strong enough to fight back if he…"

He swallowed. "I just waited for a reason to go out there and save you, my father's laws be damned." His hand found mine, holding me so tightly my hand folded in on itself. "Everyone knew what was going to happen to you if he tried to seal that blood bond. All those bastards at court treated it like a joke, but it destroyed me every time I was reminded that monster had you."

My stomach felt hollow. I had carefully penned every letter to make Derrick need me so he would choose me. I had never considered what would happen to Derrick if he *could not* choose me.

"You were *mine,* damn it." His voice broke. "They all knew I loved you, that I had waited for you for seven years. There was *only* you."

He had the freedom to do as he pleased throughout our time at school. He could have had another lover in town, or been with any woman eager to please the heir to Lycaster…

…but he chose to wait for me.

Derrick's throat trembled. "I grew up believing love was the greatest power in the world, but when I watched you ride away in the black Bloodstone carriage like you were going to your own funeral, I realized that was all a lie. I was the Duke's heir, but losing you made me feel as powerless as a….as a…"

His voice dropped. "…as a little rabbit."

I pried my hand out of his grip and placed both hands over his pounding heart. I had to make this better. I had to help. "You did not lose me. I am right here."

Derrick finally looked down. Slow, careful notes of a harp echoed in my mind. The pinhole of light slowly opened up between his eyes, but the horrible bruise on his eye captured all my attention.

"I hate that you are going to look like this for your birthday tomorrow," I said.

He sighed. "Father is throwing another ball to celebrate, he is going to be furious when he sees me."

The hell he would. I might not be able to mend the wounds in his heart, but I could at least try to mend his face.

I could not bear to see his horrible father call Derrick weak again.

He gave me a little smile and pulled out a small round tin from his pocket. "Thanks to the Viper, this is helping, at least. I use it for all my… cuts and scrapes."

He handed me the tin. I opened the lid and the fragrance of the balm inside hit me like a fist. Smelled just like home. I swiped my thumb in the creamy balm. "Close your eyes."

Derrick obeyed and I raised up on my toes. My hand rested against his cheek and he exhaled.

I spread a little balm underneath his eye. "Why did your mother call you Midnight?"

His smile was soft. "I used to have a lot of nightmares when I was little, mostly of a horned monster. Midnight is usually when I would wake up from them."

The door into his mind opened more under my touch. Every bit of magic inside of Derrick sparkled, lighting each of his blood vessels up like a roadmap. His entire body thrummed with magic, waiting for my orders.

I paused for only a moment to appreciate it—the heir to Lycaster was under my command.

The crystal warmed my leg. Even though the image of Duke Hyton's tight fist around Derrick burned in the back of my mind, what made my white flame dance was not anger. I was not even sure what emotion I was channeling, but I did not care.

Derrick lit up even more. "But really, I think Mama just wanted something else to call me. Anything but Alastar. Anything but Derrick."

The music in my mind got louder, like we were in the middle of our own dance floor that my magic had created. I closed my eyes. Power pulsed in my fingertips and Derrick's blood grew warm beneath his skin as I touched his wound.

"You have many names, Midnight," I whispered.

"I am whoever I have to be."

I pictured his handsome, unmarked face when I saw him for the first time at the Suitors' Ball. My heart had stopped, my stomach fluttered, and I had wanted nothing more than to be with him. I took that memory and sent it through my heartbeat, pulsing through my blood to my fingertips.

White light glowed behind my eyes. The magic was listening, and so I commanded:

"*Change him. Fix him. Heal him.*"

After a heartbeat, everything went still. I moved my hand from his cheek to his shoulder and opened my eyes.

I smiled—the bruise was gone.

Derrick opened his eyes. He had no idea what had just happened, but he smiled back. He leaned down and kissed me on the forehead. His warm lips on my skin sent a symphony through my mind, the notes lifted and peaceful.

My heart pounded with triumph. My magic was building. My muscles felt stronger. Somehow, I even felt a little taller. I was not just a sorceress, I was a *healer.*

Whoever the Viper was could take credit for healing the bruise. I was just happy that…well, I was finally a little happier.

Daigen was right, following my heart's desire would lead me down the right path, even if it seemingly made no sense.

My eyes found the crescent moon that was slowly disappearing amongst the stars. I only hoped my heart's desire would give me the right answers soon.

Chapter Eighteen

Commander

My feet were light as I danced on the waves.

The low song of the sirens vibrated under the seawater, but I was not afraid. Light from the full moon crested on each rolling wave.

"One of these days, I will teach you how to swim. You just have to wake up."

Even though the voice from the sea felt as delicious as a satin ribbon against my ears, I stopped dancing. Why would I need to wake up?

My eyes felt like they were weighed down with boulders. I slowly rolled my head, feeling the pillow beneath me.

I was in bed, not in the sea.

I slowly opened my eyes and oriented myself in the pastel shades of Annalisa's bedroom.

My heart skipped a beat as I recalled my dream. I had heard Riyan's voice. For the first time since he left, I heard his voice.

But how? Daigen was in the room when he had invaded my dream. If Riyan was in the place West of the Moon and East of the Sun, how had he connected with me at all?

I slid my hand under the blanket toward my leg. Maybe the Nordingaard crystal had something to do with…

Wait…where was the crystal?

My hand touched the bare skin of my leg and my heart stopped. I lifted my pillow. The crystal was nowhere in sight.

"Looking for this?"

I slowly looked over my shoulder to see Annalisa standing next to the bed and dangling my choker in front of her.

I just needed to tell the truth in a way that benefitted me. "It was a gift from the North. It reminded me of home and it is very precious to me—"

"Do not lie!" Annalisa snapped. "You think I do not know exactly what this is? You were kicking around in the middle of the night and *this* was glowing on your leg!"

My heart raced. Annalisa could be cruel, but she would not turn me in to her father. Not after everything we had been through.

Her deadly eyes glistened. "You will end up like *her.*"

She was too afraid to say the name, but I knew she meant her grandmother.

Even though her brows were furrowed like twin arrows, Annalisa was not angry with me. She was scared for me.

My hands rested over my heart. "I know." The truth of everything bounced around in my chest, waiting to find its way to my lips.

And I let it out. Not because I was not strong enough to keep it down, but because my friend deserved to know everything.

Most of all, I *wanted* her to know everything.

Annalisa sat on the bed and listened while the rosy dawn turned into bright golden rays. Her brows furrowed in confusion when I told her my blood bond was gone. She smiled when she heard about my adventure to the Bloodstone lilies. Her hand found mine when I told her of our journey up Nordingaard mountain.

"Grigory told me all about Nordingaard—such a strange and frightening place," Annalisa said. "I wish he were here. He would know how to make Ganora pay for taking Riyan."

Though the crystal was back on my thigh, my stomach clenched. Had her bond affected her too? "How did you fall in love with Grigory if you were only together for two days?"

She looked down at the floor and smiled. "After the…*you know what* happened, he stayed up all night and talked to me. He listened to me. He…he thought I was important and worthy." She hugged her middle and her cheeks pinked. "If that is not love, I do not want anything else."

A gentle knock echoed through the room before the door swung open. Merri entered carrying a small box with a bright pink bow on top.

The corners of Merri's eyes crinkled with her warm smile. "Happy birthday, Madame Thornebow."

In Annalisa's mind, her birthday was not until the evening. Every year, just before a quarter past five, Annalisa would whisper "Happy birthday, Derrick" and wait exactly twenty minutes before it was *her* birthday. As soon as she reached that magical time, she would tear open whatever gift Derrick had sent to the school.

I had to witness the odd ritual for years, but Annalisa apparently was fine with breaking tradition for Merri. She ran to Merri and crushed her to her chest before taking the box in her hands.

Annalisa's eyes sparkled. "A pink ribbon? It's from the finest jeweler in Hyton square!" She pulled the pink ribbon from the top of the box when another, younger maid walked into the room carrying a large tray filled with breakfast delights.

The maid's chestnut hair was neatly coiled into braids on the back of her head, but I did not miss the crystal blue in her downcast eyes—Rosaline.

What was Fraleigh's servant doing in the palace disguised as a maid?

Rosaline set the tray on the table in front of Annalisa's couch. Merri gestured to the tray as Annalisa tore through the box. "I brought all your favorites."

I left the bed and crossed to the couch as Rosaline met my eye, raising a single finger to her lips.

If Rosaline had told me about Daigen in the first place, maybe she was part of his "gentle hand of guidance."

Annalisa's squeal tore my eyes away from Rosaline. She held up a golden pendant of the House of Thornebow emblem—a fox in an oval frame.

"Look, Sera!" She held the pendant flat on her palm and thrust it under my nose. 'Annalisa Thornebow' was engraved at the bottom of the oval. She dropped the pendant into my hand. "And he sent me a letter with it!"

She held up the fine parchment and proudly read: "Happy twenty-second birthday, precious. I wish I could be there with you, but wear our crest over your heart and know that you have my heart no matter where I am. F.W.A.B.Y.B.T.M."

I furrowed my brows. "F.W.A…what? What nonsense is that?"

Annalisa rolled her eyes, but her smile stayed on. "An acronym for Grigory's special phrase for us—'fate will always bring you back to me.'"

She pressed the parchment against her heart and squealed. She lovingly placed the note on the table and spun around, holding her curls on top of her head to expose her neck. "Put it on me! Put it on me!"

The pendant was surprisingly heavy, but I wrapped the chain around her neck and opened the clasp. I glanced back to the couch, but Merri and Rosaline had silently left the room.

As soon as my fingers left the back of her neck, Annalisa ran toward her dressing table and sat in front of the mirror to admire her new gift.

I smiled. Riyan had told me Grigory used to be a heel with women, but as the new Madame Thornebow looked at her reflection with stars in her eyes, I was sure he had changed his ways.

A flash of black flew in the open window. Annalisa screamed and whipped around.

A raven with another roll of parchment on its leg stood on the windowsill.

Shit, I had forgotten to explain the ravens to Annalisa.

I ran up to the raven. "What are you doing here?"

Annalisa got up from her dressing table chair. "Are you talking to that thing?"

It was all too much to explain. I had never mentioned my brothers around Annalisa, or even told her their names. "Yes. I…I grew up with a love of ravens."

Not a lie.

I turned to the raven and dropped my voice to a whisper. "You could have come when I was alone, Endre!"

The bird growled. Wrong—I was definitely speaking to Erik.

"Do not get that tone with me," I whispered. "I cannot tell you two apart!"

Annalisa stood next to me, looking between Erik and I. "This is by far the strangest thing you have ever done, Sera. The bird has a name?"

I sighed and gestured to my brother. "This is Erik. I know another raven named Endre and even though they look identical, they get testy when you mix them up."

Annalisa scoffed and looked down at Erik. "I understand, I have a twin brother."

She walked over to her easel in the corner, which she never tidied. She picked up a brush out of her jar of dirty oil and a small pot of pink paint. She quickly dried the brush on the side of her nightgown and dipped it into the paint.

She walked over to Erik. "Mama did this to me when I was a baby. Derrick and I looked indistinguishable as bald little infants when we had gowns on, so she put a drop of paint on my head."

Erik hopped away from the incoming brush.

"Hold still!" Annalisa commanded. "If you cooperate, I will share my breakfast."

Erik stood still as Annalisa painted the top of his beak pink. I could not believe my eyes, but seven years of being an animal must have made him never refuse the opportunity for food.

Annalisa returned her paint supplies to her art corner and then sat down on her couch in front of the breakfast tray. She patted the armrest to her left and Erik flapped over and perched on it.

Annalisa held a grape between her fingers and extended her arm toward Erik. He snatched the grape with his beak and Annalisa flinched. "You greedy thing!"

I smiled, picturing tall and stoic Erik in human form taking a grape out of Annalisa's hand. I walked over to Erik as he ate and untied the parchment from his leg while Annalisa poured herself a cup of tea.

Once the parchment was safely in my hand, I leaned down and whispered, "Behave, today is her birthday."

"Ugh!" Annalisa scowled, pulling her lips from the edge of the teacup. "That new maid has no clue how to make tea. This is way too bitter!"

Erik flapped his wings and flew out of the window. Few things were more offensive to Erik than bad tea.

"Hm, he must not have been that hungry," Annalisa said before popping a grape in her mouth.

I stepped over to Annalisa's dressing table and unrolled the parchment. I ran my eyes over the inked scrawl that had to be Evereon's.

Still have two feet on the ground? Soldiers getting restless.
We need you back.

I rolled my eyes. Freeing Fraleigh was taking longer than I had thought, but his impatient ass could wait.

Unlike Brandt, Evereon had not included charcoal for me to respond. I set the parchment on Annalisa's writing desk and dipped a quill into the inkwell.

I flipped the parchment over and scribbled my reply.

Making progress. Be patient.

I rolled the parchment back into my hand when the whisper of wings entered the room.

Erik landed on the table with a small vine of yellow cone-shaped flowers in his beak and hopped over to Annalisa's teacup. He ran his beak down the length of the yellow petals, squeezing drops of nectar into the tea.

After repeating himself with a second flower, he tapped on the edge of the cup with his beak. Annalisa warily picked up her cup and drank. She raised her eyebrows and hummed in delight.

She smiled and stroked his back with her fingertips. "What a clever bird you are!"

I held the parchment in my hand as I sat next to Annalisa on the couch. I could not help but smile as I poured myself a cup and watched Erik drip nectar in my tea. I took a sip and savored the light sweetness that balanced out the burned leaves.

Tears lined my eyes as I drank, and not from the steam of the warm tea. I had never liked tea after Erik left. I only ever drank it out of politeness or forced it down when I needed medicine.

Tea was finally sweet again.

I wiped a tear away with the inside of my wrist as Annalisa continued petting Erik, completely ignorant to who he was and what he meant to me.

"You are such a pretty bird," Annalisa said with a gentle smile. "I always liked ravens, even though the rest of Lycaster hates them. I never saw them as bad omens because…well, because my grandmother was from Ravenwood."

Erik cocked his head, like he was actually listening.

I leaned my cheek on my fist. I had not seen Annalisa that serene… ever. Maybe she just needed a pet.

"I am named after her, at least my middle name." Her voice went from an airy calm to pensive. "I have gone through life with a part of myself that I was supposed to be ashamed of…even if none of it was my fault."

The door clicked open and Brietta walked in, her Hyton Blue robe around her nightgown and her hair still in a braid. She closed the door behind her and locked it with a sigh. "Finally escaped that damn room. We have a big party planned for tonight and we need to strategize."

Annalisa scowled. "*We?* What is this 'we' shit?"

Brietta folded her arms and sat in the chair across from us. "All the nobility will be there and now that we know about Derrick's new name—"

Her brown eyes widened when she found Erik. She looked over at me, silently demanding an explanation.

The white flame spun beneath my ribs. I could not slither my way out of that commanding stare.

I swallowed and gestured to the raven on the table. "This is Erik." The white flame pulsed hotter. "My…my brother. He never died, he was transformed into a bird."

Brietta's mouth fell open. "What?"

"He is a man? Ew!" Annalisa swung her arm and smacked Erik in the chest, sending him flying backward through the room. He crashed into the wall with a pained squawk.

Annalisa turned to me. "Why did you not tell me he was your brother before I *fed* him?"

I gestured to Erik as he rolled over onto his feet. "You would have thought I was raving mad!"

"What is he even doing here?" Brietta asked.

I answered by unfolding my hand and showing her the roll of parchment. "Communication with the House of Bloodstone, since…" The flame burned my insides again. Fuck, I had to tell her. "…since I became the Baron."

Annalisa scoffed. "Great, another secret."

Brietta blinked and then she smiled. "You are the Baron? Not Baroness?"

"Essentially." I folded my arms across my chest. "Do not sound so happy that Nikkolas and Hilda are dead. They were wonderful."

Brietta held up her hands. "I am certain they were but…" Her smile only got bigger. "You are the leader of the Northern provinces! You are *exactly* what Freya and I are trying to achieve."

Annalisa sprang up from the couch. "What are you talking about? What are you plotting behind my back?"

Brietta stood, rising to her towering height. "No one is going behind your back when *you* never leave your room."

"No, Grigory was right!" Annalisa stamped her foot. "You two are not really my friends! Not when you keep secrets like this!"

Erik flew to the table and stood between the teacups, shooting me a judgmental look. I wanted to kick him back across the room.

Brietta looked at me expectantly. Since when was I supposed to be a diplomat?

"We have not been fair to you, Anna." I reached out to touch her arm. "We are just scared."

Annalisa backed away from me with a scowl.

Brietta chimed in. "Your mother warned me that changing the laws to make the women of Lycaster true citizens was dangerous and we did not want you getting hurt."

Ice clung to Annalisa's voice. "You already hurt me by lying to me. And by ignoring me. And not inviting me to tea."

Brietta and I exchanged looks. For once, Brietta was brave enough to speak first. "Fine. The three of us tell each other the whole truth from now on."

Annalisa refused to meet my eye, but I offered the first bit of truth. "Both of you already know I am a sorceress."

"And I…" Brietta squared her shoulders and took in a deep breath. She closed her eyes. "I…I gave Derrick a black eye."

"What?" Annalisa roared.

I threw out my arm to stop her from giving Brietta a black eye of her own. I turned to Brietta, keeping my voice soft despite holding Annalisa back. "Tell us what happened."

Brietta bit her lip and nodded. "The night after the family dinner, he was acting very strange."

"My brother is strange, what else is new?" Annalisa spat.

"He…" Brietta's voice trailed off, like she struggled to find her voice. "It was like he was someone else. He only wanted one thing, and he was not taking 'no' for an answer, and I was trapped in that room…"

Brietta wrung her hands. "After I defended myself, he got sick—like he was purging all the evil from his body."

I thought back to the memory the Man of the Mountain showed me of Derrick right after he had consummated his marriage with Brietta. He was violently sick and shaking.

I had first thought he was sick because he had drank too much, but maybe it was not how much he drank but *what* he drank. Brietta also had some special wine from Duke Hyton's private stores right before the ball.

What if it was not the magic of the blood bond that had forced them to be intimate with one another? What if it was…

"Poison." I looked up at Brietta. "Did Duke Hyton poison you on the night of—?"

Brietta nodded, tears shining in her eyes that looked only at the floor. "That is why neither of us can remember what happened. I have never drank anything Anders offered me since, but at the dinner…Derrick did."

A chill ran down my body. Derrick did not sound like himself that night when he came to Annalisa's room. His voice was strained with a ravenous edge and the only thing that would satisfy him was…

Me. In his lust-poisoned state, he first wanted *me*.

If Annalisa had not slammed the door in his face that night… No, I did not even want to *imagine* what the man who was not my Derrick would have done.

My throat trembled. "Derrick would never—"

"I know," Brietta said, hard and fast. "And I will not let him apologize each time he tries. We drank the same poison. If he admits fault, then so must I. And I *refuse* to believe—"

Brietta sucked up her tears and threw her shoulders back. "That is why we need to strategize. If Anders is turning his son into a monster because he is desperate for an heir, we have to get him under control."

A thought pulled on the back of my mind, where Freya had said a monster consumed her husband…

"Under control?" Annalisa snapped. "Are you going to put my twin brother on a chain?"

Brietta tightened her hold on her arms. "What do you suggest, then?"

Annalisa laughed—not what I expected. "You two want to play the games of the House of Hyton? You need someone who was raised as a Hyton."

She crossed to her dressing table, dipped her fingers into her water bowl, and started smoothing her curls into perfect ringlets. "First of all, everything in our family starts and ends with my father. If you can manipulate my father, you have control of the House of Hyton."

She was only confirming what I already knew. I just needed more information on his mother to back him into a corner and force him to release Fraleigh from whatever deal that held her in captivity.

Brietta loosened her grip. "So we need to get into your father's head? Maybe with Sera's magic—"

"Wrong." Annalisa twirled a strand of hair around her finger. "My father lets no one in, but he has shown his hand for once. The only thing he cares about right now is Derrick and how the nobility perceives him."

Brietta and I glanced at each other. Everything she stated was obvious, how did it help us?

Annalisa took note of our silence and scoffed. "Make Derrick look good. If Derrick looks good, my father is complacent. If he is complacent, he is not making moves against anyone. If he is not making moves, *we* can make moves against *him*."

Annalisa was never a strategist nor was she a planner. She had always struck first and asked questions later—sinking her teeth into the jugular with no cares in the world other than herself.

Erik perched on the edge of the dressing table. Even though Annalisa was the one preening herself like a bird, I could not find the school bully I grew up with. Instead, I saw a commander giving orders to her soldiers.

Annalisa rested her hands on the dressing table and looked down at Erik. "I have spent twenty-two years dealing with my father's bullshit. I am tired of trying to win his affection, now I want to earn his hatred."

She looked over her shoulder at us. "If you want any hope for the control you seek, Derrick had better have the best damn birthday of his life tonight."

Chapter Nineteen
Gilded

Were beads distracting?

I stood in front of my wardrobe and ran my hands over the periwinkle beads sewn onto my bodice. The white lace over my forearms contrasted nicely with the billowing dark blue sleeves and skirt. The dress was not exactly Hyton Blue, thank goodness, but had enough of Derrick's favorite colors to catch his eye.

From what I had heard, the ball was not going to be a large affair. Everyone was too excited for the Darkest Night in three days to bother with the heir's birthday.

Still, my job was to capture as much of Derrick's attention as possible to keep him away from Brietta. I needed to be more…extravagant than anyone else.

I adjusted my breasts so they formed little mounds on top of the bodice. Yes, extravagant. That was the word I would use.

The door to my bedroom clicked open and Brietta poked her head in. She was in her usual uniform of Hyton Blue and as much gold that she could fit on her body. The gems on her tiara sparkled as she gave my outfit a once-over and an approving nod.

I kept up with her confident stride as we walked to the ballroom, but my hands picked at the beads at the bottom of my bodice.

I had decided to leave my Nordingaard crystal in my room—I could not risk wearing it in front of all the Lycaster nobility. What if it fell onto the dance floor? What if it glowed and people could spy it underneath my skirt? What if someone already suspected I was a sorceress and the crystal was just the damning proof they needed?

Though it was necessary, I had needles beneath my skin the moment I removed the crystal from my leg. My mind was spinning so much, I had sent Erik to check up on Brandt at the guard house to make sure he was all right.

Might have been risky to send another raven to the guard house, but I would have done *anything* to quell the unease. I needed the confirmation that Brandt was merely visiting with his old bunkmates from the military academy and no one suspected him of being part of a treasonous army.

Treason. I might have been dressed in shades of blue, but I was still committing treason. Just like Brandt. Just like Evereon.

And then we would all die and Riyan would be stuck in the place West of the Moon and East of the Sun forever.

Fuck, I needed to forget the word "treason" before I vomited on the staircase.

We had just made it down the steps when Annalisa's irate voice echoed through the hall. "No, I will not take it off!"

Brietta and I turned our heads. Annalisa glared up at Derrick with her arms folded and her Thornebow crest gleaming over her bosom. Derrick's golden coronet gleamed in the fading sunlight from the nearby windows. His back was facing us, but I could still see a white box with a pink ribbon in his hand.

"All I am saying is you might like this more." Derrick held out the box. "Come on, it is five o' clock. Just take it—"

Annalisa stepped back and her glare sharpened. "What? You think you can just replace him by throwing your money around?"

Brietta and I shared a quick glance.

"That is not what I—"

"I am a *Thornebow*—you will never change that." She lowered her voice. "And if you cannot accept my new blood, if you cannot accept *me* after all these years, then do not bother speaking to me again."

Derrick hissed out a breath and turned on his heel. "Fine."

He stormed past us without so much as a glance in our direction and flung Annalisa's gift out of an open window.

My eyes followed him down the hall. Damn it, Annalisa! Whatever happened to making tonight the best birthday of Derrick's life?

My white flame twisted around my heart—I had to fix it.

Brietta's lips parted to speak, but I cut her off. "I will take care of this."

I picked up my skirts and ran to catch up with Derrick. I could cajole Annalisa into apologizing and calm Derrick down. Maybe a servant could go fetch the box before half-past five. We had too much at risk to not have the evening go smoothly.

"Derrick!" I panted as I caught up to him. "She is just fond of the Thornebow pendant because she misses Grigory. I am sure she—"

He whipped around. "It looks like a fucking brand!"

My heart stopped. He looked so...unlike him with his brow hard and his eyes harsh.

He cleared his throat and his face softened. "I am so sorry, Serafina. Forgive me, I just—"

"Lord Hyton," a servant said as he meekly peeked around the ballroom door. "Beg your pardon, but it is time for your entrance with Lady Hyton."

Derrick let out a measured, but still frustrated breath as he adjusted the golden rose pin on his black doublet. "I will see you inside."

I could not let him go that easily. I had to be alluring, damn it!

I put on a smile and forced my clenched fists to release my skirt. "Would it be too bold to ask for a dance later?"

He smiled back, returning to the Derrick I knew. "Of course not."

He kissed my hair and then his soft whisper skated across my forehead. "Every second you are here mends my heart a little more. Thank you."

My heartbeat slowed down even as he pulled away. "Happy birthday, Derrick."

He gave me one last smile before following the servant.

Just like I had planned, even with Annalisa's hiccup. All I needed to do for the rest of the night was hang on Derrick's arm, bat my eyelashes, and make him look good enough to ease Duke Hyton's nerves about his heir's image.

Freya's explanation of my body as currency was spine-chilling, but Brietta and I needed to temporarily play by the rules if we were going to break them.

I just needed to get Annalisa in the game again.

Brietta had already moved to the ballroom to make her grand entrance, so I followed the echoes of sobbing to find Annalisa curled up against the wall with her head on top of her knees.

I swallowed most of my frustration and put my hand on her back. "Come on, Anna. We have to go in. Remember what we—"

She snapped her head up. "I know, damn it! We have to gild Derrick's laurels even more."

She shoved herself off the floor and wiped away her tears with the back of her hand. I ran behind her as she marched to the ballroom. My stomach flipped—was Annalisa about to break something? Was she going to cause a scene in the ballroom?

Wide-eyed servants quickly opened the ballroom doors as Annalisa barrelled for them. I caught up to her just in time to grab her hand.

"Just stay next to me," I panted. "At least until Derrick makes his entrance—"

"I know." Her chest rose and fell with her furious breath. "I *always* know he comes first."

We moved through the edge of the crowd as Derrick and Brietta slowly danced together, keeping each other at arm's length.

My heart sank a little as I watched them. Their tight smiles and refusal to meet each other's eyes was a far cry from the way they laughed and twirled at the Suitors' Ball.

"Happy birthday, Derrick," Annalisa whispered to herself.

I looked around—not a single clock in sight, but somehow Annalisa still knew the time. Even though her full lips were pursed in disdain, her eyes that matched her twin's were glassy as she watched him dance.

I had once missed my brothers so deeply that hating them was easier than grieving. Maybe Annalisa was grieving a brother that was still living.

My chest warmed with white light. I was a healer—I could help.

The hands of a clock somewhere in the palace were inching ever closer to Annalisa's birthday. I did not have a box with a pink ribbon to give her, but I had something more valuable.

Maybe Annalisa would not feel so ashamed of her grandmother if she finally knew something about her.

I raised on my toes to get closer to her ear, keeping my words soft as feathers so they were only for her. "Your grandmother had hair white as snow cascading down her back."

Her brows softened, even as Duke Hyton entered the dance floor.

He flashed a smile to the crowd. "Could he get any more stiff? Let us get him some better company!" He yanked Derrick away from Brietta and threw him into a chair that had been pushed onto the dance floor.

Laughter cracked around the ballroom. Derrick looked up at his father with wide eyes, but Duke Hyton turned to the crowd with his arms out like the beginning of a show. "How about we celebrate the heir turning twenty-two years the Hyton way?"

The Hyton way? My heart raced, but I kept focus on Annalisa. "She also had lavender eyes."

Annalisa's lip trembled, but she stared at the dance floor.

Someone whistled over the din of the crowd. A few men howled. Sharp footsteps tapped against the dance floor.

I turned to see what the commotion was about and my heart stopped—it was Mother.

Mother stalked onto the dance floor with a tiny fluted glass between her fingers. She was not dressed in a fine gown or simple jewelry like she had as the Baroness of Ravenwood, but instead wore a black dress that was barely more than undergarments. The scant fabric of the dress was thin and clung to every part of her body, revealing…*everything*.

My hand flew to my mouth. What was she doing?

Mother's sultry lips were blood red and her eyes were rimmed with black. She lifted her skirt, completely exposing her right leg, and straddled Derrick's lap.

The crowd hollered. I could not see his face, but Derrick's hands gripped the bottom of his chair so hard that his knuckles turned white. Mother swirled her head around, her dark hair streaked with silver feathering out behind her. She arched her back and grabbed his chin with her free hand.

I gasped, frozen in place as my mother kissed Derrick on the lips.

My knees went weak and I fought to keep myself upright. Annalisa clutched my hand so hard her fingernails dug into my skin.

Mother slowly pulled away, her lip paint smeared and her eyes half-lidded. "Happy birthday, Lord Hyton."

Whistles cut through the air like whips as Mother thrust Derrick's head back and tipped her little glass of faerie wine down his throat.

I pried my eyes from my mother to look anywhere else and found Freya. She sat on her throne and glared daggers at Duke Hyton, clutching her golden goblet like she was about to crush it. Derrick's six older sisters stood around the dais, their faces frozen in shock and disgust.

Duke Hyton paid them no attention as his voice boomed over the raucous crowd. "My son got the first potion, but now everyone can join in for Ravenwood *Rota!*"

What the hell was Ravenwood *Rota?* I did not even care, I wanted to leave.

A servant wheeled out a cart topped with a circular tray that held dozens more tiny fluted glasses in a circle around the outer rim. Each glass held either faerie wine or dark purple liquid.

Duke Hyton wrapped his arm around Mother's waist and lifted her off his son's lap. "The Viper whipped up some special treats for tonight! Let us make some magic happen!"

Mother kept her smile painted on, but her eyes were glassy.

A crowd of men rushed for the tray and I lost sight of Mother and the Duke. Derrick pushed his way out of the crowd, his face colorless except for the red paint smeared across his lips.

His eyes found mine for a brief moment before they snapped up to Annalisa. Her hand was like granite around mine, but even from the edge of the ballroom I saw Derrick's shoulders start to shake.

I had to get him out.

Before I could even take a step toward him, General Hyton clapped a hand on Derrick's shoulder and led him away.

Even though my limbs were frozen, my chest was raging with white fire. Duke Hyton was a monster. I wanted to roast him alive. I wanted to…

No. I had to stay in control.

I yanked my hand out of Annalisa's and gripped my skirt. I closed my eyes and counted my pounding heartbeats, forcing myself to calm down.

My usual tricks were not working. I was about to combust. I was mere seconds away from igniting every glass of faerie wine and dooming myself.

Then I looked deep within, focusing on the fractals of the diamond in my heart. Annalisa needed a friend just like I did. Making her happy could calm me down.

The crowd had rushed for the dance floor. The din of laughter and clinking glass would drown me out.

"Anna, your grandmother…" I opened my eyes and looked up at her. "She was strong. She was stubborn. And…she did not need to see herself to know she was beautiful.

The fire within me calmed and my limbs started to weaken. My heart's desire had led me down the right path again.

Annalisa swallowed, considering. She eyed a nearby servant holding a silver tray. "You know what I really want for my birthday?"

She grabbed the poor servant's arm and dragged him next to us. The gleaming silver tray held at least a dozen tiny glasses of faerie wine.

My eyes danced across the shimmering cut glass. "Anna, but remember last time—"

Annalisa picked up two glasses. "I want to forget everything we just saw. Everything that we feel."

She handed me a glass and I bit my tongue. Drinking the faerie wine was risky. I could spill secrets. I could get sick like Annalisa had.

But the last time I had faerie wine…I was happy. For the first time since my blood bond had been removed, I had finally felt warm.

My heart ached as I stared at the glass, yearning to feel warm again.

My upbringing had been a lie. My mother was a whore. Derrick was heartbroken. Brietta was no longer my friend. Ilsa was still a mystery. Riyan was still little more than an executioner.

And I was still *so* unhappy. And exhausted. And frustrated.

Once, I had scorned Riyan for drowning his woes at the bottom of a bottle, but I finally understood him. It was foolish and dangerous...but I just wanted to forget it all, at least for one damn night.

I took the tiny glass from Annalisa. We locked eyes before we poured the faerie wine down our throats. Then we took another. Then another. I grabbed two glasses and downed them. I could not stop. I took more and more.

Stars tickled my belly. Sunlight filled my veins.

And I was finally warm again.

Chapter Twenty
Dusted

Bodies and hands moved all around me like I was treading through
the sea.

Cackling laughter bubbled through the air around the ballroom. My
feet twisted in a dazed tangle across the dance floor.

I ran my fingertips along my lace sleeves. My whole body shivered—
the texture was *delightful.*

More and more people tipped the tiny glasses to their lips. Some
started tearing at each other's clothes. Others mashed up against the wall
in an amorous tangle, not caring that everyone was around.

What a decadent romp it all was. I tilted my head up, spinning so the
prancing bulls on the ceiling danced with me.

Strong hands gripped my shoulders and placed me squarely in front of
a silver tray full of tiny glasses.

"Spin, girl!" a man commanded.

I stretched out my fingertips…only they did not feel like mine. I
touched the edge of the tray and it was cooler than I thought it would be,
deliciously cold. Suddenly the tray was spinning, sending the little glasses
of the purple and clear drinks spiraling like a dazzling night sky.

My vision blurred, but then focused on the little cup of the sparkling clear liquid in front of me.

"Faerie princess it is!" the man hooted. More laughter sparked around me. They sounded like a flock of birds.

I picked up the tiny glass and a sharper hand gripped my shoulder. "Seraaa! There you are!"

Annalisa. Her glittering cheeks were ablaze.

"Dinah is telling everyone she is pregnant!" she slurred. "The Amberfields are celebrating their new heir!"

"What?" I hiccupped. "She is pregnant? Good for her…"

Annalisa's eyes went as wide as ponds. "She would have only barely missed her cycle! If she is pregnant, then that means that I—"

Too much talking. I hopped up on my toes and poured the tiny glass into her furious mouth. "No more angry. It is your birthday!"

Suddenly, Annalisa and I were in the middle of the dance floor, moving our bodies to the sensuous music in all the ways we were never allowed to. Cheers spiraled around us. I picked up my skirt and twirled. The lace on the hem of my stockings fluttered. My garter ribbons caressed my calves.

I caught a flash of red hair in my vision. Brietta's head was higher than any of the dozen men around her as she danced. Myles's yellow cape flashed like a daffodil as he spun with her, only for Gerond's sky blue cape to overtake him as he shoved him out of the way.

Brietta dipped her head to kiss Gerond. Then Myles.

Eat them alive, Brietta.

"She is sure having a good time!" cried a familiar voice.

I turned around to a wall of black and gold.

"Derrick!" I wrapped my arms around him.

He hugged me back, crushing me against him so hard my cheek mashed against the golden filigrees on his doublet.

"I looked everywhere for you, darling!" he cried.

I pushed off him, picking up my skirt in both of my fists. "Watch me spin!"

Candlelight swirled around me, but my ankles failed and I toppled to the left.

Derrick caught me and I looked up at him. The black pits in the center of his eyes had swallowed up everything but a thin ring of blue.

His delicious scent of oak and vanilla drew me in. My hands found his chest, his heart pounding like a drum against my palm. His lips were so close to mine.

I wanted him. For *so* long, I had wanted him…

But then the memory of what my mother had done tore through my mind.

I spread my hands against his chest. "I hate your father! He made my mother kiss you!"

Derrick's smile did not falter. "What?" Then he blinked and shook his head. "Right! This helps me forget!"

He held out a thin silver canister that looked like a tiny flute. I picked it up—it was colder than an icicle against my fingertips. "What is it?"

His smile stayed on but his breathing was shallow. "Uncle Ragnar said it makes the pain go away."

My thumb flipped open the lid. What a clever contraption! The metallic tang of silver hit my nose, but was it all silver? Something was underneath it…something stronger.

I took a deep sniff and breathed in a cloud of dust.

Fluffy pink clouds floated around us. Winged babies sang. Derrick and I swirled together, dancing in a dream. Every fiber of my body was awake and asleep at the same time.

"Derrick." Even my sigh was a song. "Derrick, is this the first time we have danced?"

"Yes, my darling." His voice wrapped around my waist and pulled me in closer. "A thousand wishes will never change what was written in the stars."

"And I will shine forever," I answered. "Because I am the sun."

Someone had likened me to the sun once…too bad I could not remember who.

Derrick's watery eyes made me gasp. "Derrick! You cannot be sad on your birthday!"

His lip trembled. "A thousand wishes. I should have made a thousand and one more. Then maybe it could have been us."

"No, Derrick!" My hands searched his doublet until I found the pocket with the tiny cold flute. "Make the sad go away! Make it all go away!"

His hands found my jaw and lifted my face. I raised onto the tips of my toes as his lips found mine.

He tasted like an endless dream.

Derrick kissed my jaw, then my cheek. I was limp in his arms as his lips traced my cheekbone to the shell of my ear. He nipped my earlobe and I choked on a gasp. Every hair on my arms stood on end as he whispered, "*Mine.*"

The flying babies sang higher as he dipped me backward. Magical little dust sprinkled on the column of my throat. Derrick's tongue followed the dust in a line, tasting me all the way up to the underside of my jaw before his mouth found mine again.

His tongue traced the dust against mine until stars exploded behind my eyes.

My breasts pressed against my bodice. Hands explored the laces on my back. Lips and teeth caressed my neck as my chin tipped up toward the night.

This was our dream, sweet and pink and beautiful. No one else was amongst the clouds but me and Derrick, my Midnight.

His breath caressed the shell of my ear. "I love you, Serafina. Do not seal your blood bond. *Please.*"

Blood bond? Oh, silly Derrick! "I do not have a blood bond anymore."

Derrick jerked back and grabbed my jaw. His eyes were new moons as he examined me. "Is he dead? Did the plan lwork?"

Was *who* dead? "No. The blood bond is gone. Magic of the mountain." I raised my hands, pushing away the pink cloud that was floating between us. "Poof!"

"Poof." Derrick blinked. "Are…are you sure?"

A smile stretched across my face. "I cannot lie, Midnight."

He laughed, bright and exuberant, and suddenly I was in the air. His hands were around my waist. We were spinning.

Suddenly, my right shoulder and arm ached. My breath was gone. Somehow, I was on the floor.

Derrick was on the floor too, but he was still laughing. He got up and straddled me, bracketing his arms around my face. How did I get on my back?

Sweat glistened on his brow. "Why is it so hot? I am burning up!"

I tugged at his Hyton Blue cape. "Then take your clothes off, silly!"

Then he kissed me, gentle as a whisper. I closed my eyes and savored the feel of his cape brushing against my lace sleeves, his silken curls against my fingers, my stockings across his belt as my legs hooked around his hips…

I wanted him. I had *always* wanted him.

"Lord Hyton?"

Candlelight and shrieking laughter broke through the pink clouds. I gripped his doublet and shut my eyes. My dream was collapsing.

"Lord Hyton, I am sorry to interrupt, but—"

A growl rumbled through Derrick's chest. "What?"

"Um…your performance, my Lord." The voice was small—must have been a mouse.

Derrick groaned. He slowly pushed up and helped me onto my feet. He lifted his coronet from his head and placed it on mine. The warmth of the gold surrounded me like a halo.

Derrick winked. "Hold onto this for me, darling."

He slowly walked through the crowd toward the other musicians as his Hyton Blue cape slipped off his shoulders.

No, I could not let him leave me. Derrick was the beginning and the end. I was his dream. He was my star.

It was always supposed to be us, damn it!

The air dragged against my face like honey as I pushed through the crowd, following the gold on Derrick's clothes.

Gold. Gold. Gold.

I found gold. A man wore a crown of gold around his silver hair. His goblet was gold. His eyes were the deep blue of the sea.

I gripped his sleeve. "It was supposed to be us."

The man furrowed his brows. "Serafina, what the hell are you doing?"

My lashes were wet. "He was supposed to be my forever. He waited for me…he waited for me."

The man gripped my face so hard my teeth scraped my cheeks. He leaned closer, his eyes searching mine for an answer I did not know the question to.

He bared his teeth like a lion. "Who dusted you?" He turned his head. "Someone get Adalia!"

"Attention, people of Lycaster!" Derrick shouted.

The man turned his head again and his eyes became big as saucers. Derrick stood in the center of the dance floor, his violin in his hands and his shirt missing.

"Oh, *fuck*." The man tore away from me. My hands stayed flexed, open where his puffed sleeve had just been. My eyes followed the man wearing deep blue as he dragged Derrick off the dance floor, then my feet followed him.

I needed Derrick. I was going to be the next Duchess of Lycaster. That horrible man could not take him away from me!

He pulled Derrick behind a stone column, but I was not too far behind.

"The hell are you doing?" The scary man hissed. "Where are your clothes? Why are you letting other men get fistfuls of your wife?"

"Leave me the hell alone for once!" Derrick yanked away from the man. His face glistened like he just rose from the lake. "Do I not get one night—?"

"No! Baron Amberfield's *grandson* just announced that he has an heir on the way and here you are with that stupid violin and no shirt! The damn Amberfields look stronger than us tonight!"

I pressed my fingertips against the cool stone. Maybe I could push the column over and knock the scary man on the head. I would save Derrick from the monster.

The monster would *not* eat my Midnight!

"It took *you* nine years to make an heir!" Derrick argued.

"And I almost lost the throne over it! I do not want to use Adalia like that again, so please fuck Serafina all you want. Just remember you *cannot* look like you love that girl in front of the Barons. You *cannot* show that weakness—"

"I do love her!" Derrick shifted, but I could not see what he was doing. "And I know something you do not know..."

"Boy, put those back on—!"

"Attention, everyone!" Derrick stepped around the column, gesturing with his violin bow.

The crowd gasped, but too many people blocked my view for me to know why. I pushed my way between two men and then I saw it.

Impressive.

I pointed at Derrick, naked as the day he was born. "That is no little rabbit!"

Everyone laughed for some reason, but Derrick smiled and spread his arms wide—proud as he should be.

The scary man appeared behind him and smiled tightly. "Behold, the...virility of the House of Hyton!"

I clapped. Only a few people clapped with me.

Derrick's teeth gleamed as he smiled. "I dedicate this song to the newest member of the House of Hyton!"

I gasped. Who could that be?

"The Beast is defeated! Her blood bond is gone!" He raised his violin to his shoulder. "My darling Serafina is a HYTON!"

Gasps and cheers echoed around me. My fingertips flew up to the coronet on my head, savoring the warmth of the gold.

I was a Hyton—I won.

Derrick's bow flew across the violin strings. The music lifted my feet and I bounced with each quick note. I spun around and around, twirling my skirt in the way I knew he loved.

The words of the nobles danced around me though their bodies kept still.

"How is it possible? Was it the magic of the North?"

"Does it matter? Bloodstone will have no heirs!"

"The North has fallen!"

I stopped mid-turn when my eyes found General Hyton's. He stared at me, unblinking.

He probably hated me. Oh, well. Back to dancing.

Derrick sawed away at his violin, the sinews in his forearms flexing as he played faster and faster. His hair was damp with sweat. He flashed me a triumphant smile but did not stop playing.

He would never stop. We would never stop. He was my forever.

But why was I still so empty?

My brows creased and the emptiness turned into darkness that spread through my chest, then up to my eyes.

Before I could scream for help, the darkness swallowed me again.

Chapter Twenty One
Notes of Blue

The night was still. Water gently lapped against my ears, carrying a gentle voice with it.

"*You should be all better now. The poison is gone.*"

My head swam, but my eyes slowly peeled open. Dark green tones filled my blurry vision. A soft pillow was beneath my head. A warm quilt covered my shoulders.

I must have been in my bedroom.

I blinked and found Annalisa asleep in my ivory armchair. Her curls were a blonde bramble. She wore nothing but her undergarments and her golden Thornebow pendant that gleamed in the hazy afternoon sun.

Slowly, my eyelids grew heavier and heavier until they closed.

"*Are you dreaming, Sera? Are you dreaming of the life you could have had without me?*"

The voice disappeared as water dripped across my eyelids. I slowly opened them to a dark room.

Someone tenderly dabbed a damp rag over my forehead. The smell of warm herbs hit my nose. A gentle hand rubbed medicine on my chest.

"Mother?" I murmured.

Then I tumbled into the blackness again.

"You should have killed me. Then you never would have ended up here."

I chased the voice, but awoke to another golden afternoon. Freya's drunken warbles echoed through my door as she sang:

"The sand is running down, but we dance all through the nights,

For the lioness loves the viper, even though she bites."

She retreated to her room and left me in peace to fall back asleep.

"Wake up, please! It's been two days! Wake up!"

Riyan. The voice was Riyan. How was he reaching out to me again? Why did he sound so desperate? Why did I need to wake up?

I pushed against the dark veil over my mind. Riyan was speaking to me for a reason. I needed to wake up.

"Wake up, Serafina!"

My eyes popped open.

Two days. I had consumed so much at the party, my body took two days to recover.

"No one is sure how you are still alive," Brietta said.

She sat in my armchair with her hands folded in her lap. A cup of spiced cream warmed my hands as I sat in bed. I took small sips to calm my hunger pangs as she explained what had happened at the ball.

My cheeks burned with embarrassment and I gripped my cup so tightly I thought the ceramic might crack. I thought letting go would have made me feel more at peace, but all I had done was make my situation harder by sniffing that damn dust.

Brietta told me faerie dust was a notorious substance at the Duke's parties. It was a fine white powder that caused hallucinations and memory loss along with heart-racing euphoria. Faerie wine came from mixing a small amount of the dust with clear maiden wine from Pebblebrooke. The wine was mostly harmless, the dust however…

"Derrick should have never gotten his hands on it," Brietta said bitterly. "He collapsed right after you did. Luckily your mother had an antidote on hand to keep his heart from bursting. Everyone is trying to guess how you are half his size and survived after getting dusted, especially now the whole Dukedom knows you had no blood bond to protect you."

I hissed out a breath. I was so fucking stupid. Faerie dust or no, how could I have spilled that secret in front of everyone? Hopefully the gossips could invent a better explanation for my iron constitution than magic in my blood.

Worst of all, everyone knew the North was vulnerable.

I was stupid, stupid, *stupid!*

I shifted my legs under the blankets, my Nordingaard crystal catching the linens. Annalisa had tied the crystal onto my leg after the palace guards carried me into bed—she had wanted me to feel better, apparently. Maybe I would not have acted so foolishly at the ball if I had the crystal to keep me calm and in control.

"Do you think we still succeeded?" I asked. I needed some good news, if only to feel some sort of ease in my soul. Hopefully the party was so good that Duke Hyton would lower his hackles.

"*We* did just fine." Brietta scoffed. "Derrick was the one who embarrassed himself again. Anders is worse than ever, trying to fix it all."

Well, fuck.

She rose, saying she needed to confer with Freya again. She reached the door before she put her hand on the frame and looked over her shoulder. "He calls for you in his sleep, by the way." She looked down. "You are playing your role well."

The door clicked shut. I stared at the willow leaves on the wallpaper, letting my mind spin until the afternoon faded into darkness and starlight crested the bedposts.

At least my cycle had finally ended, but the new moon was nigh and I was no closer to getting Fraleigh out of her enslavement.

Maybe I was wrong about Ilsa being the answer. I was a powerful sorceress, what if I just lit Duke Hyton on fire until he released Fraleigh? Or used magical bonds on his wrists like Daigen had used on me? Maybe I would even get angry enough to turn him into a toad.

But my magic was barely strong enough to ignite a bathtub without me collapsing. If I tried and failed, I would kiss the chopping block before the sun rose.

My magic could not answer any of the questions around Riyan, either. Was I really hearing him in my sleep, or was I just dreaming of his voice?

I wanted to pull my quilt over my head and hide, but I had wasted enough time in bed. I needed an answer, any answer.

"Now would be a good time for a gentle hand of guidance, old man," I said into the air.

Nothing responded. Maybe Daigen was lurking in the walls somewhere else.

I chewed on my tongue. Daigen seemed just as desperate for me to arrive at the right conclusion as I was. If I were not close, he would not have let me languish in bed for two days without at least invading my dreams.

Maybe I already had direction.

With nothing else to rely on, I closed my eyes and channeled my magic. My crystal warmed against my leg.

My mind and my heart spoke to the magic within my body, searching for what I might have missed. I asked for direction, for an answer, for *anything*.

And then I heard music.

The music was soft and low, like it was far away. The melody tugged on my heart and before I knew it, I had shoved off my quilt.

The music in my mind pulled me into the hallway. The blue damask wallpaper surrounded me like a dark forest as I crept along the hallways with only the dim light of the sparse sconces lighting my way. The flame in my heart pushed me forward, though I did not know where I was going.

But the music in my mind was getting louder.

Silent as a phantom, my feet slowly dragged across the soft carpet runners until they pressed against cool marble.

I blinked and looked around. Somehow, I made it into the ballroom. I dragged my eyes to the dance floor in the center of the room, immediately finding the crack like a bolt of lightning amongst the black and white tile.

My knees kissed the cold tile and my fingers traced the break in the ceramic where Riyan's head had hit the tile when we fell while dancing.

I had not noticed the crack when the room was full of people, but how could I have forgotten it? I had been so angry with Riyan for dropping me because he had gotten too drunk to hold me.

I had screamed at him in the garden over a simple accident just for me to make a worse intoxicated mistake a week later.

I wished I could speak to him. I would apologize for being so hateful before and…for continuing to fuck up even more now.

Then the music started again. The thinnest sliver of the crescent moon cast its soft glow over the tiles of the dance floor. The faint blue luminescence looked so magical, so inviting…

So I danced.

I moved my feet in time to the song in my mind as my heart warmed. My arms swept through the air as I weaved around an invisible partner. No one was around to grab me, or critique my steps, or force a drink into my hand. The lovely song filled me from head to toe, and I was safe.

My breath was calm, a smile lifted my cheeks…

Then the faint notes left my mind and traced my ears. They were slow and soft, like feathers in the air. I looked around—no one else was in the ballroom.

I was not even sure if I was hearing the same song that was in my mind, but my feet dragged across the tile as I followed the music. I slipped past the ballroom doors and the music got louder.

A gentle run of notes up the scale sent a pleasant shiver down my arms—it was a harp.

I traveled down the hall, following the notes to a door that was left ajar. I wrapped my fingers around the door and slipped into the small room behind it.

The drapes were pulled over the windows. The modest furnishings and decor were visible only from the light of a single candle in the far corner of the room. In the glow of the candlelight was Derrick, strumming a large ebony harp.

I let out a relieved breath. His face was sallow and his cheeks too sharp, but at least he was all right after collapsing.

Derrick's eyes were half-lidded as he played. Blue starlight danced along the strings and crested his features. He moved with the harp in time with his breaths and with the slow, sweeping song.

I quietly stepped closer. His hands moved up the strings, the notes getting higher and sweeter, and then a floorboard creaked under my foot.

Derrick's hands stopped and he looked up with wide eyes. My heart missed a beat as we looked at each other. I had no shoes and wore only a nightgown, I must have looked ridiculous.

"Serafina, what are you…?" he asked breathlessly. He looked to the floor. "I did not think anyone would…"

"I liked it." My cheeks warmed and I stroked the tail of my braid. "I heard it outside and…"

I let myself trail off. What was I doing? Why had my magic not led me to Ilsa's vault? Or maybe evidence that Riyan had been more than a mere executioner?

Why did my heart's desire push me to *Derrick?*

He rested his hand on the black wooden frame. "Did you just wake up too?"

I gave him a tight lipped smile and nodded.

He looked down and started strumming again. "Your mother assured me that you were healing fine, but I was still worried. I thought the music would help ease my mind."

He plucked a few strings. I fidgeted with my braid as he played, but my white flame stirred, urging me to keep talking. "I was always so impressed that you could play the harp. I never could. My arms are too short and my hands too small to reach all the strings."

His hands fell from the harp and he shot me a disbelieving look. He silently beckoned me and I tentatively stepped over.

Derrick gently wrapped his arm around my waist, guiding me to sit on his left leg. "Never say you cannot do something, Serafina."

My cheeks blazed, but I heard Brietta in my head saying, "*Play your role.*"

Was this what my magic was trying to tell me? Was I only supposed to keep Derrick occupied so Brietta could uncover the truth of Ilsa and win our liberation? Would the General eventually open up about Riyan if I acted like a good, complacent Hyton?

Was I really *that* useless as a sorceress and a healer?

Derrick placed his left hand on top of mine and then lifted it to the taut harp strings. "All right, you are going to be my left hand."

I swallowed at the feel of the strings beneath my fingertips. The memories of the other girls mocking me for being too small to reach rang in my ears.

His lips grazed my temple. "When I play this…," His right hand played a short, high-pitched melody. "…pluck these to complete the phrase."

He directed me to hook three strings using my fingers and my thumb. He placed his left hand around my arm, trusting me with my part in the song.

Derrick played the short melody and then I tentatively strummed the final three notes.

He let out a short laugh. "You can do better than that. Listen to how the music is feeling and try to match it."

I tried not to roll my eyes. His nonsense sounded similar to Brietta's. I could not match a feeling using my *hands*.

He played again. The melody was a sweet and hopeful tune, but not exactly triumphant. Like the first star of the evening, a tiny red ember in my heart glowed. I channeled the warmth from the ember into my fingertips and strummed the last three notes to match.

The final note vibrated in my ears and the warmth from the ember intensified.

Derrick smiled against my skin. "Just like magic. I knew you could do it."

My hand dropped into my lap. A small flicker of triumph made my own smile appear again.

He wrapped his arm around me and started playing, surrounding me with a slow, lovely tune. "The poems in your letters inspired me to play, you know."

The poems Brietta wrote. I swallowed all the lies I could never tell again. "How?"

He was quiet for a moment, letting the music fill every empty space in the room.

"When I was younger, words would often fail me." The melody dipped lower. "Music was the only way I could be heard, so my hands would say what my mouth could not. And when you sent me the most beautiful lines in your letters…I loved them so much that I wanted to hear them for myself. Even though we were separated for seven years, I heard your voice reciting those lines in my music."

I bit my tongue. He had imagined my voice speaking Brietta's words.

The music picked up tempo. "I used to be so terrified of even opening my mouth. But then I started practicing your lines in the mirror."

His breath warmed my neck as he recited:

"For you I hope for, for you I yearn,
If I do not have you, the whole world will burn."

I held my breath. Damn, Brietta.

He laughed. "I recited that one over and over until I no longer tripped over the words. Even Father was pleased that I started speaking better. Your words were my salvation."

I was a damn snake.

I shifted in his lap. The truth that I had not actually written the poems bubbled up in my throat, ready to spill.

"But I fell in love with you long before the poems."

He *what?*

I tried to make the question sound easy, like banter between old lovers, but it came out shaky. "When did you fall in love with me?"

His hands slowed and the notes were long and spaced out. "Ravenwood Manor."

My plan for seven years had been to trap him into falling in love with me so he would choose me as his future Duchess. If he had been in love with me that whole time, all that plotting had been for nothing.

My hands began to tremble, but Derrick's melody became long and light, like a dewy meadow in the early morning haze.

"It was my last night there," he said. I was in the garden and you came around the iron gate with a sack full of treats that you stole from the kitchen. You had this determined glint in your eyes and a wicked little smile. And just like that, my heart was yours."

I still could not breathe. My mouth went dry as I whispered, "You love me because I am wicked?"

"No, I love you because you are powerful." He kissed my cheek. "Your disregard for someone else's rules proved you could hold your own as the Duchess."

He plucked a low note that reverberated in my chest. "Besides the practical aspect…every time I remembered that sly little smirk of yours, my heart fluttered. Thinking of another boy holding your hand made me feel sick. I dreamed of you nearly every night."

I slammed my eyes shut to stop the incoming tears as the claws of guilt shredded me from the inside. I had lied to Derrick for *nothing*.

"I only learned romantic lines to match yours," Derrick said with a hollow mirth. "I just wanted to impress you. Sure, the Selection Night choice was mine, but I wanted something no Duke of Lycaster had for generations…"

A tear rolled onto my lashes as the music swelled.

"…I wanted a wife who was in love with me."

The sob that rattled out of me was a sour note in Derrick's melody.

He set the harp down and placed his hand on my cheek. He wiped my tear away with his thumb. "I know. None of this is fair."

I shook my head. Nothing was fair because the world was cruel and so was I.

He had no idea how much I had used him.

Derrick gave me another sorrowful smile as he wiped away another tear. "Midnight just wanted to be with Birdie."

Midnight and Birdie—our code names in our letters. We had both played roles, sending romantic fluff back and forth. Though underneath the syrupy prose and coy banter of Midnight and Birdie, there was still Derrick and Serafina.

And Derrick loved Serafina—sneaky, wicked, and powerful as she was.

The white flame seeped through my chest, forcing up every ounce of my shame, my sorrow, and my guilt until I could not hold back.

Is *this* what my magic was compelling me to do? Purge my guilt?

"I hate this," I sobbed, wiping away a tear with the back of my hand. "I hate what I have done."

Derrick's eyes glistened. "Do not be ashamed of what happened at the ball. I…I know what it is like to wake up confused and sick, but none of it was your fault."

Even after all my manipulation, he was still only concerned for me. I was worse than a snake.

"I embarrassed myself," he said, "and my father will see to it that I mend my reputation in front of the Barons." Revulsion dripped off his words. "I would rather cut off my own hand than go to the Darkest Night tomorrow. I do not know if he will sneak more Cupid's Blood into my drink and let that monster loose on the crowd or if he will force me to fuck your mother while everyone watches."

My stomach turned. "Cupid's Blood?"

Derrick swallowed and looked away. "The potion that forces you to forget everything you are and fixate on only one thing. I have retched it up enough times to be very familiar with it."

He leaned away from me, his eyes still downcast. "Ever since…what almost happened to Brietta the other night, I am too scared to even eat or drink anything."

I turned toward him as much as I could with how close we already were. "Derrick…you have not eaten in four days?"

He shook his head, but still refused to look at me. "I cannot do it. Even still, Father could still trap me and force something down my throat like he did on my birthday. I can do *nothing* about it."

The fear and anger that cut through his voice made my skin crawl.

"I will go with you," I blurted out. "I will go to the Darkest Night with you."

Derrick had said my letters had made him brave. If I could just give Derrick that small bit of security back, a small amount of his power back…maybe I could start to heal the wounds guilt left within me.

The white light brightened in my chest and I followed its energy.

"It might be a masked ball, but you will find me," I said as the fire swelled within my soul. "Look for the Midnight Dream dress."

Derrick lifted his eyes and a small smile flicked up his cheek. "I would know you even in a mask, Serafina."

His hands found the harp strings again and he started strumming a slow and sweeping tune.

I shook my head. "How many songs do you have memorized? I do not know what this one is called."

"You have no way of knowing," he replied as the melody picked up. "No one has ever heard it before. I wrote it just for you."

The ache in my soul deepend. "You did?"

His right hand plucked the higher stings near his face while his left hand crawled along the lower strings. "I call it *Musica Trans Sepulcrum Amatores.*"

He must have noticed the lift of my eyebrow. "I named it from the language of my ancestors," he explained. "The translation into Lycastrian is not exact, but it means 'Music will carry my love beyond the grave.'"

Then Derrick played his heart for me, his eyes closed, fully leaning into the music as he embraced both the song and my body.

That little ember flickered in my chest, flaring four times.

If my affinity was healing, maybe healing all the wounds on Derrick's heart would finally make me happy, truly happy.

I just had to get him through the Darkest Night.

Chapter Twenty Two
The Darkest Night

The moon had vanished, yet none of the stars across the night sky were as luminous as the stars on my dress.

I stood in the center of Annalisa's bedroom, adjusting my breasts in the bodice of the Midnight Dream. My stomach turned over at the thought of all the nobility seeing that much of me, even though I had my crystal on my leg to keep me calm.

I parted the slit over my right leg and tightened the satin ribbon so the Nordingaard crystal was flush with the back of my thigh. I had paced around Annalisa's room a dozen times to ensure any onlookers would only see a peek of the satin ribbon if the slit parted, but I was still worried.

After I had lost control at the last ball, I could not risk leaving the crystal behind. I had to stay completely grounded so I could keep Derrick safe from anyone sneaking him potions.

Brietta would be safe from Derrick, Derrick would be safe from his father, and everyone would be happy…at least for one night.

Once the Darkest Night was over, we would try to look for Ilsa's vault at least.

Annalisa opened the box my costume had arrived in to fetch my gloves. She had her curls pinned on top of her head and her arms and dress were covered in paint.

She had her brush dipped in paint pots all day, finalizing touches on her sisters' masks and brushing swirling designs on their skin.

Since Annalisa was no longer a Hyton, she did not have to attend the Darkest Night. Still, I hoped she would at least stay with me for a little while so I did not have to navigate the debauchery with Derrick alone.

"You sure you do not want to go?" I said to Annalisa as she slipped the first long, dark blue glove onto my arm. "A night of costumes and bad behavior seems perfect for you."

She let out a snorting laugh. She adjusted the top of the glove on my arm and a thunderclap roared through my mind the instant her skin touched mine. The door between her eyes suddenly widened. My crystal glowed on the back of my leg.

Annalisa removed her hand and gave me a wry smile. "I will not go without Grigory."

I furrowed my brows. "The whole point of the ball is to *not* be with the person you married."

Annalisa reached for the other glove. "I am not a person who hides behind a mask."

She slid the glove onto my other arm and the sound of rain crashing into a windowpane rang in my mind.

Over the rainfall, a voice hissed, *"Don't even think about going to that damn ball while I'm gone."*

The voice was too rough to sound like Grigory, but I did not know who else it could have been. Annalisa looked up at me and I glanced away. Her door was still wide open, but what she had unknowingly sent me felt too intimate, like I had walked in on someone naked.

Something two people should never directly address.

Annalisa turned to grab my silvery mask, commissioned to have glittering stars around the eyes. She placed the mask on my face and I caught my reflection in her dressing table mirror. Annalisa had painted my lips a berry shade and smudged my eyes in black so they looked heavy. My eyes might have been covered, but the rest of me was so…exposed.

But if Brietta had said my costume was modest, I hated to imagine what everyone else would wear.

Brietta and I entered the Darkest Night at the same time. Music with a low, pulsing beat echoed around us. Women who wore nothing but ribbons danced in the air using swaths of silk that hung from the ceiling. Masks of dogs, horses, and birds peeked out amongst the flashes of scant fabric.

Refreshment tables lined the edges of the room, holding silver platters that spilled over with clusters of Pebblebrooke's finest grapes and small stacks of cheeses from Amberfield. Not a couch or a bed in sight—the partygoers would have to rut like animals somewhere more private.

Brietta was a glorious vision in her shimmering gold dress and peacock feathers, showing off most of her breasts and nearly her entire left leg. Her mask was blue and had a delicate golden beak over her small nose.

We both held glass goblets of maiden wine. If anyone slipped a potion in our cups when we were not looking, the crystal clear wine would reveal the trick before we took an unknowing sip.

Her lips that gleamed with a purple stain turned up into a smile. "Ready to make some choices?"

"You know exactly why I am here." I folded my arm across my chest, covering up as much of myself as possible.

As careful as I was to stay inconspicuous, Brietta strutted about the room, beaming as everyone's eyes roamed over her gilded bosom. She was the feature of the party, I was just the virginal guardian at her side.

But where was Derrick?

My eyes wandered from Brietta to the crowd, watching the throngs of people mix with one another. No one was doing anything normal society would consider dancing—just a fluid motion of limbs and hips in time with the heavy beat.

In the center of the crowd, a lithe girl in green was being doted on by nearby eyes and hands. She had leaves painted on her limbs and pink petals over her breasts, her golden waves shining as she danced…oh, it was *Camille.*

My classmate who had turned red as amaranth after mere mention of physical intimacy wore *nothing* but a sheer pink skirt over her hips.

I tore my eyes away as my cheeks grew hot beneath my mask. A sealed blood bond had burned all her shyness away, apparently.

"Of the many peacocks I have seen, this one is the most splendid. Would you agree, Myles?"

Brietta and I turned around to find two men—one wore a fishnet over his chest and hips and the other had fluffed up his red hair to resemble a lion's mane.

"I would agree, Gerond," said the lion, who was clearly Myles. "Especially paired with the lovely night sky." His eyes slid over to me. "What are we even supposed to call you now that your marriage suddenly dissolved? Miss Hyton?"

I took a step back. "Must you defeat the point of the masks?"

Gerond rolled his eyes behind his fish scale mask. "Must you be an obvious virgin?"

I was about to call him an asshole when Brietta let out a velvety laugh. "Are you just frustrated because your little wife is getting more attention than you are?"

Gerond smirked. "Camille can have her fun. My concern is my quarrel with Myles."

Myles tossed Gerond a sly look. "We were arguing over who would approach you first, Lady Hyton. We figured whoever you did not choose would get a foray with stardust over there, but she is clearly in a poor mood."

My cheeks went hot. "As if I would *ever* consider—"

"Why should I choose?" Brietta asked wryly. "Should the future Duchess not get everything she desires?"

I could not believe what I was hearing, but then I looked up at Brietta. Her shoulders were back, her head was higher than the men's, and her wry smile was genuine. I had seen her enrapture a lecture hall full of girls with her poetry before, and this was no different.

I looked over at Gerond and Myles, whose eyes stayed locked on her as if her curvaceous body draped in gold was poetry of its own allure.

Brietta was letting them see her exactly as she wanted to be seen. For once, she had control.

She just needed some encouragement to finally *take it.*

I smiled. "I think that is a splendid idea, Brietta."

Myles pounced on the opportunity. "A few benches in the garden are unoccupied."

Gerond stepped in front of Myles. "Better hurry, a prime spot is sure to get taken soon."

Brietta's peacock mask hid her expression, but concern still lined her voice as she turned to me. "But Derrick is still not here. I cannot leave you—"

"The refreshment table is calling to me. I will be fine." My smile grew as I looked past her mask into her brown eyes. "Get drunk off that freedom, Brie."

Brietta smiled back. She downed the rest of her maiden wine in one gulp and handed me her empty glass.

I watched as she weaved her way through the dancing crowd, Myles on one side and Gerond on the other.

Brietta might have been dressed as a bird, but no cage could contain her.

I sipped my maiden wine as my eyes swept the crowd. Even though I caught more flashes of skin than I would expect in public, embarrassment did not sting my cheeks. Maybe seeing Riyan walking around nude in the wilderness had desensitized me to human anatomy.

With his distaste for clothing, Riyan would have fit right in at the Darkest Night.

"*Nice dress, sweetheart,*" imaginary Riyan whispered into my ear. "*Looks good enough to tear off.*"

Heat spread across my cheeks and I tipped back the rest of my wine.

Despite the ballroom being packed, I had not seen Derrick anywhere. I looked down at the empty goblets in my hands. If Derrick found me at one of the refreshment tables, maybe I could persuade him to eat.

I pushed my way across the ballroom, trying to maneuver through the throngs of the masked crowd. I caught myself before I nearly ran into a man with a mask that covered his entire face.

I gasped as he grabbed my arm. "Get out of here, *Litlnadr.*"

Suddenly, a laughing woman crashed into me, knocking me to the floor. I lost one of the goblets and it shattered on the tile. I pushed myself up and suddenly I was lost in the crowd. I swiveled my head, trying to find my bearings amongst the smeared paint and torn clothes.

A meaty hand grabbed my wrist. Another grabbed my skirt.

I blindly pulled away from the hands. "Stop!"

A shrieking laugh tore through the air. A low cackle followed. More and more people joined in, dressed as birds and beasts and monsters. They tugged me by the arms through the menagerie of sickening smiles.

"Look at her sparkle!"

"Is this your first time?"

"We can show her how to play!"

My heart raced. I planted my feet and pulled myself out of the greedy hands. "Leave me alone!"

"There you are."

A large palm gripped my ass and I froze.

My captor spun me around to face him. An older man with a mask like a blackened sky with numbers painted amongst the stars towered over me. Behind the mask was a pair of unmistakable blue eyes.

Duke Hyton.

"Oh, it is just little Serafina!" Duke Hyton chuckled. "My goodness, you look exactly like your mother."

I kept still, hoping he would leave and look for my mother, but, to my horror, he did not move. Instead, he flashed me a crooked smile. "Can you guess what my costume is?"

I timidly shook my head.

He held out his arms, showing more numbers painted on the skyscape of his dark robes. "I am time. I may not wear stars as brilliantly as you, but I did make a good attempt."

I tried to steel my voice and give a charming smile. "Y-You did, Your Excellency." I swallowed. "If I may ask, where is Derrick?"

His eyes gleamed. "He should be along…eventually."

My breath stayed frozen in my throat. What had he done with Derrick?

"You know, I have not officially welcomed you into the House of Hyton." Duke Hyton pulled a flask out of the pocket of his robes. "Let us make a toast."

He unstoppered the flask. With a smooth flick of his wrist, he poured a thick, dark purple liquid into my empty goblet.

Cupid's Blood—it had to be.

My heart raced as I looked at the goblet. If I acted girlishly timid, maybe he would feel too guilty to make me drink it. "Thank you, Your Excellency, but I was not going to partake tonight."

His smile turned wolfish. "Oh, do not worry. My special drink takes the edge off the nerves. We want you to have fun, after all."

My eyes darted around the edges of my mask. The crowd was tightening around us. Even if I could be fast enough, there was nowhere to run. Daigen could not pull me out and take me away, either.

"Yes, Serafina, they are all looking at you," Duke Hyton said. "In fact, I see five young men just waiting for you to take that first sip."

At once, it all clicked into place. This was not mere cruelty. Duke Hyton's plan was not to poison Derrick, he wanted it to be *me* who lost control in the middle of the Darkest Night. The Barons would all see me. I would no longer be the holder of the heir's heart and a threat to his control, but just a silly girl for everyone to play with.

Even though the Duke himself stared me down, I dared to channel my magic. My white flame blazed. The Nordingaard crystal warmed my thigh. A few tears in the air and even within my goblet activated.

I gently reached for the Duke's mind, but no door opened between those Hyton Blue eyes. I could not silently get into his head. I could not light him on fire with all those eyes on me. What was the point of having sorcery if I kept getting backed into a damn corner?

I might have worn the cosmos on my hips, but I was no more than a rabbit in a snare.

No, I would never admit defeat. I had another way out.

The magic in my blood made me more immune to poison. I had survived faerie dust, I was a damn sorceress, and I was going to stay in control.

Duke Hyton chuckled at my hesitation. "What an anxious little lamb you are." He flashed a sweet smile. "We will take a drink at the same time. On the count of three?"

I gripped my goblet. I was powerful. I was not going to lose myself in a lustful frenzy.

Even still, I looked for someone to save me.

"To your first time, even though my poor son will miss it." He raised his flask. "One…"

I looked for Derrick.

"Two…"

I looked for Daigen.

"Three."

And before the goblet touched my lips, I nearly cried out for Riyan.

The Cupid's Blood was sweet on the tip of my tongue. It was so delicious that I could not help myself—I poured the entire contents down my throat and the sweetness coated my tongue.

Duke Hyton pulled his flask from lips and smiled. "Good girl. Now take your pick from all those handsome young men."

The trail of sweetness down my throat suddenly turned bitter. I coughed as the aftertaste burned my tongue. I hunched forward, ready to throw up.

"Careful!" Duke Hyton rubbed my back as I coughed. "This is strong stuff, but a big girl like you can handle it."

A low but strong voice rumbled through the air. "Leave her alone."

I looked up and saw a tall man with light hair, a square jaw, and a red cape.

At first I thought Riyan had somehow returned…but the eyes beneath the bronze mask were too blue to be Riyan's

General Hyton stood next to me dressed as an ancient war god, wearing a breastplate of bronze that was fitted perfectly to the contours of his muscles and a red tunic around his hips.

A single heartbeat passed before I realized the armor was not armor at all…it was bronze paint.

My mouth suddenly watered and I looked away. How was he that muscular?

"Did you forget your shirt, Ragnar?" Duke Hyton sneered.

"Did you forget your age, Anders?" General Hyton shot back with a crooked smile—Riyan's smile. "You are old enough to be the girl's father."

Duke Hyton gave his brother a sly grin. "Like you would know anything about being a real father. Now back off, the *young* men had already formed a line for the girl."

Out of the corner of my eye, a woman in a viper mask broke through the crowd and appeared at the Duke's side.

Duke Hyton glared at his brother for a moment more, but the woman tugged him by the arm and he retreated through the crowd.

General Hyton grabbed me by the forearm and dragged me away from the men who shouted their protests.

My feet struggled to keep up with his pace. "Why are you pulling me around?"

"No one here gets to lay a hand on you." His shoulder bumped into the back of a delirious man's head, making him fall over. "I need to get you out of here."

My heart raced even faster than my footsteps as General Hyton yanked me to the closed ballroom doors. He jerked on the handle, but the door was locked.

"Damn you, Anders!" General Hyton hissed. He looked around the ballroom. "Where are my guards?"

I pulled my glove out of his grip. Bronze paint stained the dark fabric. "I will be fine." I had to be. I *had* to be. "Why would it matter anyway?"

His brows knitted and the corner of his mouth flicked up. "You have no idea how many people are eager to bed a Hyton. The noble men will harm nothing but your pride, but a few of these opportunistic servants could take advantage of your newly available womb now that you have no blood bond. Just stay with me and—"

Ragnar's words melted before they reached my ears as I focused on his full lips.

A low burn bloomed beneath my stomach. The burn spread through my limbs like lavender honey. The hair on my arms stood on end.

How had I never noticed how handsome he was?

My lips were flush and heavy. "You look just like him. How has no one ever guessed your big secret?"

Ragnar's eyes widened. "Serafina, keep your voice down."

The command made my knees weak. The small growl in his words sent a shiver down my spine. "But Riy—"

He clamped his hand over my mouth and my heart leaped. Suddenly my back was against the wall. A tower of bronze was all I could see. The metallic tang of the paint on his skin filled my nose.

"I have not forgotten that you owe me." His heartbeat pulsed in his palm as he lowered his eyes.

My breasts pushed against my bodice as my chest heaved. I was ready to tell him to take whatever he wanted when his warm breath caressed my forehead. "An answer for an answer, remember? You owe me two."

I nodded as he removed his hand from my flushed lips. My heart was pounding. My bodice was too tight.

Candlelight glinted in his eyes. "You survived the deadly faerie dust and your blood bond has disappeared with no logical explanation."

My thighs shifted together, the insides were slick and I *needed* friction between them.

"If I asked you a direct question, you could not refuse me, right?"

My vision was blurring, but I answered, "Yes."

Anything to please him. Anything to get him to touch me.

His hand parted the slit in my skirt. The instant his fingertips caressed my skin, I threw my head back and gasped. Pleasure hit me like lightning, sending heat straight to my core. His strong hand massaged my thigh as white light flared behind my eyes.

But it was not enough. I needed more.

Ragnar withdrew his hand and it was like someone dunked my head under water. My eyes popped open and I found his handsome face smiling at me.

"So tell me, Serafina…" He held up a black satin ribbon with a blue crystal in the shape of a heart that threw fractals of firelight. "…are you a sorceress?"

A ball of pure warmth pushed up my throat. "Yes."

"Get off of her."

The wall of bronze moved and the sensuous smell of oak and vanilla filled my nose. Derrick stood behind his uncle, dressed in black, and his eyes were on fire behind his dark mask.

General Hyton glared at Derrick and took a breath like he was going to say something.

"What are you doing, Ragnar?"

Even though my insides were practically molten, I looked up. A tall, red-haired man folded his arms and glared at General Hyton beneath his golden mask.

General Hyton's chiseled face smoothed and he put on a smile. "Merely playing nursemaid, Tyreon." He tossed Derrick a look and smirked. "But now that the children found each other, we should get some refreshment."

The red-haired man's mouth softened and he turned, his purple robes swishing around him. The General followed closely behind.

The burning sensation spread throughout my body, pooling with white-hot intensity in my hips. My skin shivered as Derrick rested his hands on my jaw and lowered his face near mine.

Fury burned in his eyes as they flicked down to the spots of bronze on my glove. "Did he hurt you?"

I savored his breath warming my cheeks as I answered, "No."

"Did he give you anything to drink?"

"No, Derrick." His name tasted *so good* in my mouth.

"Good, I have not had anything to drink either." He let out a relieved breath. "Father told me what was happening and let me into the ballroom."

His shirt was open at the collar, revealing a hint of dark hair on his chest.

"I am so sorry," he said. "I should have been here sooner."

My fingers twitched, aching to touch him as my eyes roamed his chest. An embroidered silver star rested on each side of his collar.

Two stars. All black ensemble. His costume was suddenly obvious.

A smile pulled at my flushed lips. "But you are here now, Midnight."

He smiled. "Midnight was always there for you. I did not want tonight to be any different."

My mouth watered. I could not take it anymore, I needed to touch him.

I traced one of his stars with my finger. His throat bobbed as I drew a line from his neck to his chest. Heat pulsed between my legs. "Derrick, I want you."

His chest rose and fell faster. He looked down at me and swallowed. "Serafina, I know what tonight is supposed to be and…I have *always* wanted you, but are you—?"

I raised on my toes and my lips crashed against his as a desperate whimper escaped my throat. Now. I needed him now.

He pulled away and his breath skated against my swollen lips. "Are you sure?"

"Yes." I wrapped my arms around his neck and pulled him into another kiss. He bit my lip and I nearly collapsed. My heart drummed faster and faster.

"Right here," I breathed between kisses. I wanted him to take me on the floor. Tear off my skirt. Give me everything.

He picked me up in his arms. His body became the entire world. Dark silken curls tickled my cheek. A strong hand caressed my right breast. An aching heart beat against my own.

"Patience, darling," he whispered onto my lips. He pulled out a brass key and held it up. "Your first time will not be in front of a crowd."

Chapter Twenty Three
Kneel

Derrick's quick footsteps echoed through the palace halls. His heartbeat pulsed under my lips as I kissed his throat. My hips wriggled against his chest as he held me.

I needed him *now.*

"Derrick," I whimpered against his skin. My body burned with so much desire it hurt.

He shoved his shoulder into a door and the latch clicked open. He set me down on the closest table. My heart pounded against my ribs. My inner thighs were slick.

But I was still *burning.*

He tore his mask off, then his gloves. I let out a little gasp as he grabbed my jaw and forced me to look up at him.

"Take that damn mask off." His lips were stained scarlet from my smeared lip paint. "I want to see *all* of you."

My hands flew to the ribbon on the back of my head, but they were too heavy to untie the mask.

"Damn it!" I cried. "I cannot get it—!"

He deftly untied my mask with his free hand and threw it across the room.

With a smirk, he grabbed my right wrist. He bit the fabric on the tip of my middle finger and slowly pulled the glove off with his teeth. I closed my eyes as the fabric slid off my arm, then my hand—the sensation was overwhelming.

He kissed me gently on the inside of my wrist. My arm trembled as he placed kisses all the way up my arm before biting me on the inside of my bicep. Stamps from his red-stained lips lined my arm like tiny rose petals.

Every kiss was like another shock straight to my hips. I was going to tear my skin off if I did not get some satisfaction soon.

"Derrick," I panted. "I need—"

He grabbed the back of my neck and brought my lips to his, kissing me like he shared my fire.

"So impatient," he scolded, his breath hot against my lips. "I waited for this for *seven years,* but I can wait a little longer so I can play with you. Would you like that?"

"Yes." My heartbeat pulsed between my legs. "But—"

He kissed me again and silenced me. He pulled away and left me gasping.

"I want to take my time, darling." He wrapped his hand around my left wrist. "Little Rabbit dies *tonight.*"

I squirmed as he worked the glove off my left arm. I bit my tongue and whimpered as his hot breath made the skin on the inside of my arm tingle.

He released the glove from his teeth and his hungry eyes flicked down to my bodice that strained under my heaving breaths.

He eyed the thin laces criss-crossing on the front of the bodice and leaned down. His teeth scraped the skin in the center of my chest as he bit down on the laces, loosening them as he slowly pulled away.

Cool air kissed my breasts as the bodice fell away from my sticky skin. His lips found mine, his tongue gently sweeping into my mouth as his hands massaged my breasts. I arched my back and raised my chest. The organza of my skirts crinkled as I locked my legs around his hips, feeling his hard bulge press against my pulsing center.

Fuck, I was going to die if I did not get him inside me.

"I cannot take it!" I pushed my hips against his. "I need you now!"

Derrick slid his hands under my thighs and picked me up. "As you wish."

He turned me around and walked a few steps, his hands gripping my ass for leverage. I caught the sight of his harp in the corner of the room as he gently laid me on a chaise.

He kissed me, his chest pressing into mine. My hands gripped his silken curls and explored his back as his hand ran up my leg. His fingertips stroked me between my legs as he gently discovered what the most intimate part of my body felt like.

Not enough. I moved my hips in time with his hand, bucking up against his belly and the hard bulge below it. The small friction was the only relief, like tiny gasps of air.

Oh, it felt so damn good. I pulled away from his lips, tipping my head back against the cushion, and let out a soft cry.

"Shh, Serafina," Derrick whispered. "You need to be quiet so no one can find us."

His fingers slowed down. Pain replaced the soft satisfaction from his touch, filling up my chest like I was drowning.

Derrick leaned in, his lips tracing my cheekbone. "Do you want me to make you come?"

"Yes," I said through my heavy breath.

He gave me a quick, ravenous kiss and then moved down to my neck, then between my breasts, then my belly.

Derrick pushed himself up from the couch, standing over me for a couple of pounding heartbeats.

My vision blurred, the candlelight getting darker as my heart thudded. I was dying. I could not get satisfaction. I was going to drown on my desire.

Satisfaction or death. Satisfaction or death.

"The heir to Lycaster bows to no one." Derrick dropped to his knees at the edge of the couch. "But I will kneel for *you,* Serafina Helia."

He hooked his arms around my legs and jerked me toward him.

I yelped as I slid on the chaise, but I quickly covered my mouth. Derrick looked at me with a crooked smile and raised eyebrow.

"Good girl." He parted the draping fabric of my starry skirt. "Now try to stay quiet for me."

His head dipped between my legs and he kissed me there just like he had kissed my lips.

A wave of satisfaction rolled over my whole body and I gasped.

I closed my eyes and moaned into my palm, containing my screams of delight to the inside of my throat. One of Derrick's fingers joined his mouth and tongue, gently exploring inside of me. I wiggled my hips with the rolling pleasure, but Derrick's other arm held me down so I could not squirm away from him.

He bit the inside of my thigh and shot me a look before he put his mouth on me again. The pressure built inside me, about to reach its peak. Passion raged through my whole body, pushing me closer and closer to that sweet release I needed.

Satisfaction or death.

I tipped my head back on the chaise, my entire upper body arching up as Derrick feasted on me.

"Derrick!" Stars flared behind my eyes. My legs trembled. I had to have him. I had to finish. "*Derrick!*"

With a flick of his tongue, he sent me over the edge, crashing into release like a wave against a mighty cliffside. My legs shook in his grip and I gritted my teeth, biting back my screams.

Then everything went still.

I blinked and the filigreed medallion on the ceiling came into focus. My entire body shook, no, *shivered,* like I had just walked inside after a torrential downpour.

Why was I so cold?

My stomach turned and my throat constricted. I clamped my teeth down as I held sickness back.

Derrick panted against my thigh and then he rose to his feet. He looked down on me hungrily, a satisfied smile across his devious lips.

What was he doing? Why was I on my back?

I glanced down and my eyes widened. My breasts were bare and my nipples were peaked. All I wore was my starry skirt.

Oh no…the Cupid's Blood. *The Cupid's Blood.*

I watched in horror as Derrick unlaced his shirt.

"I will go slow," he said. "I will be very gentle."

Tears pricked the backs of my eyes. I was not ready, I did not want to, but I had still *been* with him.

Suddenly noise erupted outside. People were running.

"Lord Hyton!" a voice shouted.

Derrick turned toward the door with a raised eyebrow. "What the hell—?"

The door crashed open and a group of palace guards rushed in.

"Get out!" Derrick yelled as he shielded as much of my body as he could.

I sat up on the couch, covering my breasts with my arms.

One of the guards stepped forward. His face was white and his eyes were wide. "My Lord, you have to come with us."

"The hell I am!"

"My Lord…Y-Your Excellency," the guard stammered. "Your father was killed."

Part Three

Spear

and

Shield

Chapter Twenty Four
Roar of the Lioness

In the moments when my heart should have been beating, I could only focus on three thoughts.

My breasts were bare. I had been poisoned with Cupid's Blood. Anders Hyton was dead.

I sat on the couch with my arms over my naked chest. I was too stunned to move, even as the palace guards approached Derrick.

Derrick…the new Duke of Lycaster.

The guards placed their hands on Derrick's arms but he jerked away. "What are you doing? Get off me!"

"Orders from the General," one of the guards replied. "We have to keep you safe while we investigate Alastar XI's death."

The color drained from his face as he put everything together. His shock made him compliant and the guards wrapped their arms around his back.

I should have said something, *anything*, but my body was still frozen.

Derrick's throat trembled as he swallowed. "At least let me say goodbye to my mother." The guards forced him out the door. "Let me see my mother before it is too late!"

The guards ignored his desperate plea and suddenly my fire awoke in my chest.

I had to get him to Freya before her blood bond sent her into Death's arms.

I swung my legs off the chaise and tried to get up, but my legs refused to move. The room spun and my stomach churned. I gripped the edge of the couch and slammed my eyes shut as I forced myself not to vomit.

"Lis!" Derrick shouted down the hall. "*Lis!* Find Mama!"

I shoved myself off the chaise. I stumbled, but picked up my starry skirt and ran out of the room.

No time to put the rest of my clothes back on.

I gripped the doorframe as I tried to find my balance again. A narrow passage had opened at the end of the hallway. Derrick's face peeked over the blue uniform of the guard's shoulder as his eyes found mine.

"Serafina, find my mother!" His voice cracked and his eyes glistened. "Tell her I love her. Please!"

The guard sealed the passage shut, the brocade wallpaper masking any seams in the wall.

Though I had no idea where the guards were taking Derrick, there was no point chasing them through the maze in the walls when Freya had *minutes* left.

My bare feet pounded on the tile in the hallway as half dressed monsters in paper and lace masks ran screaming past me. I shoved my way through the oak doors and raced across the empty ballroom.

"Freya!" I cried, scanning the ballroom that was littered with glass bottles and discarded masks.

Maybe she was in the garden. I pushed on the glass doors leading to the garden and ran out into the summer air.

"Frey—!"

My lips froze in a silent scream. Anders Hyton was skewered on the right golden horn of the rearing bull statue—impaled through the stomach like he had fallen out of the sky. His unmasked face was frozen in eternal surprise as he faced the moonless night.

I trembled as my eyes followed the trails of blood that ran down the stone bull.

My stomach twisted and my throat burned. I bent over on the stone steps and retched. My sickness was purple and slimy as it rolled down the steps toward the gored Anders Hyton.

My throat burned as if I had vomited molten iron. Tears ran down my face as I released the Cupid's Blood from my body.

It tasted worse than anything I had ever experienced. The poison coated my tongue with the bitter sting of shame.

Derrick's mouth had been on me…and *in* me. How could I have let it happen?

I heaved and shook as the last of the Cupid's Blood left my body. Standing on shaky limbs yet seconds away from breathing fire, I slowly raised my eyes at the corpse of Anders Hyton. I spat out the last remnant of the poison from my mouth.

Good fucking riddance.

I wiped my mouth on the back of my hand and ran back into the ballroom. I ran up the stairs toward the Duchess's dressing room when a shrieking roar echoed through the hall.

I shoved open the dressing room door and immediately found Freya sitting on a couch. Her curls trembled around a radiant golden crown. Her pink robes were soaked with crimson at her belly and blood pooled at the hem around her ankles. Amethyst and Sapphira were holding her hands. Emeralda, Pearl, and Rubia—unmasked but still in their gauzy costumes from the ball—knelt beside her and gripped her robes as they wept their final goodbyes.

"Bri-etta?" Freya choked, her eyes still squeezed shut. Black streaks ran down her cheeks as her makeup mixed with her tears. Blood dripped from her mouth.

"No, Mama," Amethyst said in a breath.

I ran forward, stopping before I stepped in the growing puddle of blood. "Derrick loves you, Freya. Your Midnight wanted me to tell you he loves you."

The door flew open and Annalisa ran in, pulling an unmasked Brietta by the arm. "Mama! I got her!"

"Freya!" Brietta shrieked. She knelt beside Freya and blood stained her knees. "How can I—what can I—?"

Freya peeled open her eyes and her whole body shook. Blood stained her teeth. "My desk. Find the letter. You know where."

Brietta nodded as tears rolled down her cheeks.

I waited for Annalisa to join us as we helped Freya into the next life, but instead she quietly crossed the room. Garnet, the only person other than Annalisa not dressed in a costume for the ball, silently wept in the far corner. Annalisa gently took her older sister by the hands and led her over to us. "Come on, Gar. We need you too."

Annalisa and Garnet stood behind their formidable mother as she rattled with her final breaths. Annalisa had one arm around Garnet and then she threw the other around Sapphira's shoulders. The rival sisters' foreheads touched as they leaned into each other.

"You can rest Freya," Brietta whispered as she blinked out tears. "We will take it from here."

The door flew open again and a group of palace guards rushed in.

"Duchess! Come with us," one of the guards ordered.

My heart jumped as the guards wrapped their hands around Brietta's forearms.

"Let her go!" Freya roared, shaking as she forced herself onto her feet. "I still breathe, damn you!"

Brietta's brown eyes went wide as the guards led her out of the room. She did not even bother fighting them off.

I had never seen Brietta look more afraid.

My head whipped around as Freya crashed into the pool of her blood. Seven pairs of arms surrounded her failing body—embracing her with the love of seven hearts.

My white flame ignited. Power surged through my veins.

"I got her," I said as my final promise to Freya Hyton.

Suddenly the magic in my body trembled as a wash of cold passed through me. The ragged breaths that skittered across the pool of blood stopped.

Death had come…and had taken Freya.

I forced back tears and ran into the hallway, focusing on the two young guards on either side of Brietta's arms. As soon as her frightened eyes met mine, my white flame twisted and bent, morphing into something bigger and stronger.

No matter how hard I clung to it, manipulated my way to get it, or craved it until my heart ached, I kept losing my control. I lost control with the Cupid's Blood and the faerie dust. I lost control when Ganora took Riyan. I lost control when Nordingaard stole my brothers.

And I was tired of losing control. If I could not hold onto it, I would just *take it*.

My chest was ablaze with righteous fury. Power sparked in my fingertips. The tears in the air vibrated as I reached out my arm. "Let her go!"

The guards turned their heads. "Orders from the Gen—"

Each guard stopped, their mouths falling open and their eyes dropping to my breasts. The tiny pinholes of light shone between their eyes as their mental doors opened, beckoning me in.

I took advantage of their ogling eyes and twisted my hand, the tears in the air braiding into an invisible rope between their minds and my mouth. This was not a connection of empathy, it was one of pure control.

Their minds were mine. *Mine.*

My throat quivered as if my words were quiet thunder. "I am the Duchess's greatest friend. I will keep her safe for the General."

The invisible tether vibrated as it sent the message to the guards' inner selves. Each blinked, one after the other, as if they accepted the enchantment.

"*The Duchess is safe*," echoed sleepily in their minds.

A satisfied smile raised my cheeks. "You did your job well. Now report to the General."

The guards gently released Brietta. They shuffled along the carpet like their feet were as heavy as boulders. They passed me, slowly blinking with soft smiles on their faces.

My vision blurred as I held the tether over their minds. My heart pumped that white-hot power through my veins, but my muscles ached from the intensity.

As soon as they turned the corner, I released my magic with a soft gasp. Brietta ran over and grabbed me before I collapsed. She heaved me up and ushered me into the Duchess's bedroom.

The door slammed shut and the lock clicked. I dropped onto the plush cushions of a couch as pain screamed through my muscles.

I peeled open my eyes and caught my reflection in a gilded mirror across the room. The weight of the shame crashed onto my shoulders as my eyes flitted from my smudged black makeup to each mark Derrick had left on my arms and chest.

That was the powerful sorceress—nothing more than the new Hyton whore.

Tears lined my eyes. My chest rattled with a sob. How could I have let it happen? I had more power than most women, most *people,* in the world and I still fell. I still succumbed to the poison.

A fist wrapped around my chest. I suddenly could not breathe.

If Riyan knew…if he only knew how weak I really was. He never would have given his life for mine.

I could leave, no, I *should* leave. Brandt could come from the guard house and take me away from this wretched palace for good. I could disappear and no one would have to bear witness to my shame. My guilt. My failure.

Warm water caressed my arms as Brietta wiped off the scarlet stains with a rag. Her own lip paint was smeared, but her mouth was shut tight as she cleaned me.

Tears rolled down my cheeks as my chest shook. "C-Cupid's Blood," I sobbed, giving Brietta a sorry explanation for my emotional state. "Anders…he…"

"I should have stayed with you," she whispered. She moved the rag to the other arm, but did not look me in the eye. "This is my fault."

"No," I hiccupped. It was my fault. *My* fault. "I had too much faith in myself. I should have resisted more."

Brietta moved the rag up to my neck. "Fighting would have done nothing. Cupid's Blood is just…very strong."

And *I* was supposed to be stronger.

A bead of water trickled between my breasts and magic twinkled against my skin. What was the point of magic if it failed me when I needed it the most? What was the point of having power if someone could just take it away?

Brietta offered me the damp rag and her eyes flicked down to my hips. "Are you hurting?"

"No," I sobbed. "He was…good to me. We did not even do…*everything*."

Her auburn brows knitted. "You remember?"

I nodded. My magic held onto the memory of every ounce of shameless pleasure I had drenched myself in.

"I…I wanted it," I said. "I had *always* wanted it…but not like that. Not when Anders forced…"

Brietta put the rag in a nearby porcelain bowl. "Derrick has no idea, does he?"

I shook my head. Derrick never saw me drink the poison, and from his view, what was there to suspect? I had spent seven years showing him I was in love with him. I kissed him at his birthday party. I sat in his lap while he played the harp.

Giving in to desire was expected because *I* had made him expect it.

My throat was sore from sickness and shame. "I made him want me. This is my fault."

"Serafina, no!" Brietta's shining eyes finally met mine. "Do not say this is your fault!"

"I am supposed to be saving Riyan, repaying him for what he gave me," I cried. "But *every day,* I fail. I am not a powerful sorceress, or a Baron, I am just another stupid whore!"

Her arms wrapped around my shoulders and her auburn waves brushed against my sticky cheeks.

"*Never* call yourself that," she commanded. "You did nothing wrong."

But her voice broke. The magical tears sparkled in the water on my chest as Brietta's skin brushed against mine. Her bosom heaved and suddenly I heard parchment flipping in my mind.

The door to Brietta's inner self slowly creaked open.

The flipping parchment got louder. Brietta may have always been an open book, but she had glued some of her pages together, hiding her own shame.

A swirl of magic pulled me toward Brietta's open door. I closed my eyes and eased into the memory written in those glued pages.

Yellow wallpaper formed the cage of the memory. Brietta heaved into a bowl, getting the last of the Cupid's Blood out of her stomach. The purple sludge in the bowl blurred as tears filled her eyes.

Freya rubbed her back. "You did nothing wrong, Brietta."

"I betrayed my friend," she cried. "I do not remember, but I…I hurt her."

Brietta rubbed away her tears and Freya's face came into focus. Freya's glacial blue eyes shone like glass.

No, not glass…a mirror.

Freya's voice was gentle as wool but sharp as a blade. "I will stop this. *We* will stop this. Never again."

Brietta's lips trembled as she repeated, "Never again."

I left the memory like an exhale, closing the book on that chapter. I returned to my body and pressed my cheek into Brietta's skin.

"You did nothing wrong, Brietta," I whispered. "You never did."

Brietta's arms trembled. A tear hit my shoulder. Then another.

Her mask of quiet confidence finally came off as soon as the first muffled scream tore from her throat. She cried into my hair and I cried into hers, unleashing the roars of two wounded beasts held on chains.

We apologized to each other over and over, understanding each other in a way we never wanted to.

A door clicked open and Brietta and I looked up. Annalisa had walked in from the dressing room. Her face was white and her dress was stained red.

She looked at us like she was looking through us. "They took Mama. The funeral is at sunrise."

Her hands flew to her face and she sobbed.

Before I could get up to comfort her, a bell tinkled in the air. Magnus rubbed against Annalisa's legs and let out a soft meow.

Annalisa pulled her hands from her tear-stained cheeks. "Go away, Magnus!"

Magnus prowled over to the dressing room door. He meowed and scratched at the door, swishing his fluffy tail.

"She is gone, damn it!" Annalisa cried. "Mama is gone!"

I got up from the couch and held her as she sobbed. She did not even care that I was half-naked, she clung to me like I was driftwood in the open sea.

I looked past Annalisa's curls to find Brietta at Freya's desk, reading a piece of parchment. Brietta's eyebrows knitted and she placed her hand over her mouth.

She softly walked over and handed me the letter. I rubbed Annalisa's back as I examined it. The letter was addressed "To the new Duchess of Lycaster" and was sealed not with the seal of the House of Hyton, but with a beautiful fuschia wax with a lioness emblem.

"Freya's personal seal," Brietta softly explained.

I gently unfolded the letter and read:

Brietta,

Anders was never going to sign a reformation. My Midnight
always held our liberation. Do NOT give him an heir until
he releases all women of Lycaster from bondage—that is
your only power over him.
Yes, I knew I would never see my own freedom, but
my dream was dead until I met you. You will be
Lycaster's salvation.
You are no longer kittens. You are lionesses.
Stay strong.

The parchment crinkled in my hand as I read the lines over again. That was not a letter Freya had in her desk just in case of her demise. She wrote that letter knowing her time was coming, and soon.

But *how* soon?

Annalisa's sobs calmed as I handed the letter back.

Brietta's once sorrowful eyes gleamed with determination. "Derrick is going to change the laws. The Baron council may resist, but the Duke has the ultimate say."

"Ultimate say?" Annalisa yelled. She pushed away from me and faced Brietta. "Do you two have any idea how much pressure he is up against now? The Barons will not just let him—!"

"I do not care what the Barons say." I rose to my feet as my fire raged beneath my ribs. "Derrick *will* sign a reformation and he *will* free Fraleigh."

Annalisa's lip curled into a sneer. "And how do you know—?"

"I *make* him want it." I splayed my fingers and all the magic in the air awoke at my command. "Brietta keeps her womb empty and I whisper into his mind until he gives us everything we want."

Annalisa's brows knitted and her lip trembled, but she bent down to pick up Magnus. She nuzzled into his thick fur and choked on her last sob.

We changed out of our costumes, throwing the blood stained fabric in a pile on the floor—hopefully to be burned. We slipped on Freya's nightgowns and fell into the Duchess's large bed.

The three of us clung together in the center of the mattress with me in the middle. I shifted my head on the soft down pillow and stared at the canopy as my friends slept.

The soft scent of powder and lavender perfume clung around the collar of the nightgown. Freya had just laid in that bed not even a full day ago, and we were what was left in her place.

A new Duchess, a heartbroken daughter, and a…

I let out a breath and closed my eyes. I tried to push it away, but the word echoed in my mind like a scream:

Whore.

I opened my eyes again, staring at the dark canopy above me. Freya did not want Brietta to feel this way. Brietta did not want me to feel this way.

And I never wanted anyone else to feel this way ever again.

I could no longer just run around the palace chasing Ilsa's ghost or Riyan's memories. The game had started all over again. This time, I was not going to manipulate Derrick into giving me the Duchess's crown, I was going to get him to change the world for me.

Derrick wanted me, he desired me, and he would kneel only for me. I had his heart, I just needed his head.

Being Derrick's friend was not enough. If I were to get close enough to bend his will, I needed to become his mistress.

Just like my mother.

I let out a breath. No, not like my mother. I was finally in control.

I was no whore—I was a fucking lioness.

Chapter Twenty Five
The Bold

The sky was still dark when glassy-eyed Merri entered the Duchess's bedroom and roused the three of us. Brietta solemnly unraveled from our tangle of limbs, rising from the bed as the new Duchess of Lycaster. Magnus nuzzled Annalisa's arms as she awoke into a nightmare where her mother was dead.

Merri said the maids had selected modest dresses to wear underneath our black shawls of mourning. I spoke up, specifically requesting one of my Hyton Blue dresses for the funeral.

I did not want the Dukedom to think I merely belonged to the new head of the House of Hyton, I wanted to be seen as a Hyton.

Even though my plan was to become his mistress, Derrick did not have me, *I* had *him.* His heart was mine and his head would soon be mine too. I just had to get access to him again.

Merri directed the two maids in the group to fetch our dresses. When they returned, Rosaline was with them.

I kept my lips pursed as Rosaline dressed me. If she was supposed to be part of Daigen's "gentle hand of guidance," she was doing a shit job. Hell, Daigen was at the Darkest Night and he could not even save me from…

I let out a silent sigh as Rosaline slipped my bodice on. It did not matter. I could not change it. All I could do was get Fraleigh out of captivity. As long as Derrick played into my hand like he should, it would be easy.

Then I would bring Riyan back from the mountain and hopefully forget any of this ever happened…if he would even want to look at me once he found out.

Rosaline tied my laces at the back of my dress. She leaned in close and whispered so quietly no one else could have heard, "Fraleigh wants to see you."

I held my breath. Even though my main task was to free Fraleigh from the Hytons, I did not think I would speak to her again.

What could I even say?

Rosaline disappeared back into the fold of maids as I wrapped the knitted mourning shawl over my shoulders. Whatever Fraleigh could say to me, I just hoped it was enough to free us all.

Merri stood on a footstool as she worked the comb of a sheer black veil into Brietta's hair.

"You will walk with His Excellency behind Duchess Freya's coffin," she said. "No one is to see your face until the coronation."

Brietta rolled her eyes before the veil fluttered over her face.

Once Annalisa had found an embroidered handkerchief to carry, the three of us walked hand-in-hand out of the Duchess's bedroom. The other Hyton sisters slowly joined us in the hall of the family quarters. Each sister was shrouded in black and completely silent.

Despite footsteps running through the halls like rain, the palace was still somber and grey. All nine of us huddled at the bottom of the foyer steps, waiting to face the Dukedom.

Stiff-backed soldiers marched through the foyer at the direction of General Hyton, who was dressed in his military uniform. He did not have so much as a scrap of bronze paint left on his skin from the night before, but his body shone with all the brass regalia he could fit on his chest and shoulders. The only part of him that did not shine was the black scarf tied around his right arm and the lavender rings beneath his eyes.

"I bet a hundred marks Derrick does not have to cover his face," Brietta grumbled beneath her veil.

Annalisa wrung the handkerchief in her hands. "Where *is* Derrick?"

General Hyton crossed over to us. I quickly glanced away as my cheeks warmed.

It was almost *him.* After I drank the Cupid's Blood, I had thrown myself at Riyan's *father.*

I had to stop myself from retching as General Hyton bowed to Brietta. "Come with me, Duchess. We must begin the procession."

Brietta's eyebrows knitted beneath her veil—she was the only woman tall enough to look General Hyton in the eye. "Derrick is supposed to be here."

General Hyton's voice softened. "He is safe. We found that Alastar XI's death was an accident, but His Excellency is in a secret location because he could still be in danger."

Accident or not, Anders's gored corpse flashed through my mind. Only the snap of Annalisa's teeth pulled me out of the horrifying image.

"*Bullshit,*" she said. "How convenient that the man next in line for the crown is keeping the new Duke locked away? Quit acting like you—"

"Do you want to walk behind his coffin next?" General Hyton's eyes turned deadly. He dipped his chin and faced his youngest niece. "While you are painting your silly pictures and dancing at the fourth ball of the week, the rest of the world is in chaos. The Sudrian empire is crumbling."

Sapphira spat a curse in High Sudrian that I could not translate. Rubia grabbed her arm to keep her from charging at the General.

General Hyton paid no attention to the scorned empress and kept his eyes on Annalisa. "Your brother is the last of his line. You never know what an ambitious few would do to the last Hyton heir, especially when he is in such a fragile state."

I gripped my skirt. Fragile?

General Hyton looked up to address the rest of the family. "The House of Hyton is in a precarious situation." He shot me a quick, pointed glance. "If you want to make it out alive, you will listen to me."

I swallowed and shut my eyes, but his footsteps drew nearer. General Hyton bent at the waist until his face hovered near my left ear.

"We will talk later," he forced something hard into my hand, "*sorceress*."

My hand instinctively wrapped around my Nordingaard crystal, but every other part of my body froze. In the bloody frenzy of the Darkest Night, I had forgotten that I had even worn the crystal.

General Hyton walked away as if nothing was amiss and offered Brietta his arm. Brietta quirked her chin up and walked beside him, but Annalisa shot me a worried glance.

My heart thudded, but the familiar crystal on my skin sent a gentle whisper of serenity through my body.

General Hyton held the Duke himself somewhere unknown and gave the Duchess orders. He commanded all the palace guards and the entire army.

No wonder he had never made any moves for the crown. He was already the most powerful man in the Dukedom.

If he wanted the sorceress dead, I would not be standing in the foyer with an illegal crystal in my hand. I had to be useful to him…somehow.

With a wave of his hand, General Hyton signaled for us to join them outside. I quickly stashed the crystal inside my bodice and held Annalisa's hand as we walked into the cold dawn. The rest of the Hyton sisters paired up, gripping each other's arms as we all joined the funeral procession.

Six soldiers each carried two oak coffins and stood in a line in front of the palace gates. The coffin at the front of the procession had the Lycaster flag draped over it and the Duke's crown on top. The second coffin had a modest wreath of fuschia flowers laid upon the wooden surface.

Brietta stood right behind the second coffin. She took a breath, straightened her spine, and sent her shoulders back.

She stood alone, but she could not be weak.

A line of the six Barons wearing their colorful House capes stood behind us. Baron Tyreon Elvar wore rich purple and chains of diamonds. His eyes swept from General Hyton to Brietta—the richest man in the Dukedom now had the Duchess for a niece.

General Hyton whistled and my head whipped forward. Legions of soldiers snapped into attention at once. I quickly scanned the soldiers for

Brandt's round face. The entire Lycaster guard seemed to be present—had Brandt thrown on a uniform to stand with them? Or was he sitting in an empty guard house?

I needed to check in on him as soon as I could. I had not heard from him, or Erik for that matter, for too long.

After ensuring his soldiers were properly positioned, the General walked to the front of his brother's coffin—he would lead the entire cavalcade.

As if waiting for General Hyton's signal, the Great Sorceress of Nordingaard appeared beside us as she walked to the front of the procession. The Hyton sisters all held their breaths as she passed and so did I, but for a different reason.

Before, Fraleigh had been a walking legend, a pillar of ancient power, and the greatest ally the House of Hyton could ever have. Now, even though the cerulean luminescence of her skin was the only color in the bleak morning, I could not pry my eyes away from the golden collar around her neck that I had never seen her without.

I tried to swallow but my mouth was too dry. The evidence of her servitude had been right in front of our faces, and yet none of us had ever noticed.

But why would we? Even as she walked to stand behind the Duke's coffin with her golden eyes bolted forward, she still carried an air of omnipotence. The soldiers bearing Anders's coffin even stiffened as she approached.

Though I knew the truth, the question pulled at the back of my mind—how was a sorceress as powerful as Fraleigh still in servitude? Why could she not fight back?

Trumpets and pipes blared, so my mind went quiet. The iron palace gates creaked open and the procession began.

So we took the first step into a new world where Derrick reigned.

Annalisa gripped my hand as we passed through the palace gates and walked the long path to Hyton city square. The citizens of Lycaster lined the streets of Hyton in somber reverence as their fallen Duke and Duchess passed them one final time.

We slowly marched through the square as the pipes sang. Cobblestones turned to grass as we arrived at the cliffside overlooking the Western Sea. Annalisa shook with silent sobs as we stepped into the royal cemetery.

Stone markers of every Duke and Duchess of Lycaster stretched to the sky, standing tall as giants. Each marker was in pairs except one—"the Wise" stood alone.

Ilsa was not even allowed to rest as a Duchess. From what I had heard, her corpse was burned like a peasant—no trace left behind.

We passed "the Wise" to two freshly-dug graves. A whole team of diggers must have worked all night to have them ready.

General Hyton ordered us to stand next to Freya's grave. Brietta took a step to go first, but then Annalisa tugged me along to walk past her. Brietta stood to the side, allowing Annalisa to stand closest to her mother's final resting place.

Annalisa stared at the hole in the ground as Brietta joined me at my left side. I took Brietta's hand in mine, finally ending her tragic solitude.

The eyes of the growing crowd turned to me and I wanted to hide, but I had to be a pillar for the friends who clung to my hands. Out of the three of us, I never thought *they* would rely on *me* for strength.

The burden of being their support in front of all those eyes was sudden and heavy. Was that how Riyan felt as the Hero of Lycaster?

I had once thought his stony countenance before a crowd made him heartless, but that was likely just his way of staying strong for the people. He was steel when I needed him to be, and he had not faltered once.

I never gave him enough credit for the pressure he had faced.

The other Hyton daughters filed in behind us as the six Barons appeared, standing in a line by Anders's grave. All of them had their eyes on the veiled Duchess.

I glanced out into the crowd of noble mourners and saw my mother, standing near Anders's grave and clutching a small bouquet of fuchsia flowers. Her eyes sparkled with tears. Even though Anders was dead, she still had to play the part of the dutiful mistress.

General Hyton stood in the space between the two graves and his voice rang through the stale morning air. "We gather to say a final farewell to

Alastar XI—a brother, father, and friend—who reigned over Lycaster for twenty-two years."

"All hail the Duke," the line of Barons chanted.

General Hyton's eyes swept over the crowd. "Before we begin, it is only right that all of Lycaster knows what became of our ruler. After a lengthy investigation last night, we found that Alastar XI fell from the balcony in his chambers. He was trying to get a better look at some…*activity* in the garden and lost his balance."

Brietta gasped and gripped my hand. Even the black veil could not hide her scarlet cheeks.

The Barons exchanged glances, some hiding their amusement better than others. Whatever Brietta had done with Myles and Gerond at the ball was apparently anything but private.

General Hyton cleared his throat, silencing the snickering Barons. "We also say our final goodbye to the bearer of the Lycaster heir—beautiful, faithful and dutiful."

On cue, the soldiers approached the grave with Freya's coffin.

"Hail the Duchess," the Barons muttered.

I bit my tongue. They would not even say Freya's name.

Two of the soldiers around Freya's coffin stepped back as the other four lowered Freya into the ground.

The notes of Annalisa's song with her mother skated quietly over her lips as she stepped toward the grave. "*Raindrop, raindrop…*"

She gave her handkerchief a kiss before releasing it on top of the grave. "*My rainbow will come some other day.*"

I watched the handkerchief fall and whispered, "Goodbye, Freya."

Brietta sniffed. "Goodbye, Freya."

Annalisa stepped back to us and I grabbed her trembling hand.

The crowd parted for Fraleigh as she glided across the grass behind Anders's coffin. Fraleigh took her place at the end of the grave with her eyes forward and her hands clasped in front of her.

Six soldiers held the coffin above the grave. The Duke's golden crown gleamed in the rays of the morning sun.

General Hyton turned to the line of Barons. "What say you, Barons of Lycaster?"

Baron Elvar stepped toward the coffin. "The Barons of Lycaster wish a triumph over Death to Alastar the Bold."

"Hail Alastar the Bold," the other Barons chanted.

The Bold—that was the best they could come up with? I had a list of names that would have been more fitting for that conniving worm.

But none of the pageantry had to be honest, it was all just ritual. No one could really triumph over Death, anyway.

Well, none but a select few.

Fraleigh kept her eyes on the grave as Baron Elvar took the crown of Lycaster off the coffin. The rest of the Barons chanted "the Bold" over and over.

The rest of the mourners joined in, their voices rising like an incoming storm over the sea.

"The Bold!"

"The Bold!"

"The Bold!"

As they chanted louder and louder, Fraleigh stepped forward to the edge of the grave. The sleeves of her robes billowed out as she waved her arms and the crowd instantly silenced.

She held her hands in the air and closed her eyes before placing her palms on the wood of the coffin. She bent at the waist and gave the flat surface of the coffin a kiss.

My stomach turned, but the General stole my attention with his booming voice. "With the blessing of her majesty, the Great Sorceress of Nordingaard, we return Alastar the Bold to the earth—to be part of Lycaster forever."

Blessing? What blessing? I did not feel any vibrations of the tears in the air or even the barest sparkle of magic.

I stared at Fraleigh, her face the picture of composure. Like the chastity examinations, her blessing was just another lie.

I could have even conjured up something wondrous to impress the crowd if I tried. Maybe nothing more than a little flame, but at least something people could see. Something to sell the lie.

Did that mean…Fraleigh had even less power than I did?

Fraleigh took a step back from the grave and dropped to her knees as the soldiers lowered Anders in his grave. The lower the coffin went, so did Fraleigh. She pressed her palms into the earth and lowered herself in a bow so deep her forehead was in the grass.

I felt like I was looking through the altered mirrors again, but instead of seeing a dressing room, I was watching a slave in the dirt while everyone else saw the Great Sorceress performing a grand ritual.

My skin crawled. How had I never seen it? How had *none* of Lycaster seen it?

The legend who had scorched armies on a battlefield was long gone, all that knelt in the grass was a mere husk, like her flame had…suffocated.

My own flame danced around my heart. Maybe no one realized Fraleigh had no power because none of them knew what powerful sorcery looked like, or felt like, or how it singed the air and made it tremble.

The only magic Lycaster ever knew was the magic of a Hyton lie.

"Today, the sun will set on Alastar the Bold," General Hyton said. "But tomorrow, the sun will rise on our new ruler—the young, new Duke of Lycaster!"

"Hail Alastar XII!" the Barons shouted.

Alastar XII—not Derrick, not Midnight, not Der. Another Alastar.

And we did not even know where he was.

General Hyton ended the funeral by plunging an iron sword into the earth at the head of the grave—a weapon to fight Death. The mourners trickled out of the cemetery. Baron Elvar carried the crown of Lycaster away, ready for the coronation at the next sunrise.

Even as all the Barons and the Hyton daughters left, Fraleigh stayed on the ground in reverence to the fallen Duke.

Only my mother crossing the cemetery could tear my eyes away from the Great Sorceress in full submission to her last owner. Mother laid the bouquet of flowers at the head of Freya's grave and I swore I heard an apology escape her lips.

She tugged her black shawl closed and followed the line of mourners back to the city.

I stroked Annalisa and Brietta's hands with my thumbs. "I have to stay behind and speak with Fraleigh."

Brietta let go of my hand and held it out to Annalisa. "Come on, Anna. I do not want to walk by myself again."

Annalisa sniffed and took Brietta's hand as they walked past the tall graves.

As soon as they left, Fraleigh and I were alone. For a few heartbeats, I just stood above her and listened to the waves of the Western Sea crash into the Hyton cliffsides. Mist crawled around the gravestones. Sea birds cawed over us. Clouds moved peacefully overhead in the grey sky.

Fraleigh pressed up from the ground, but refused to look at me. "I hear you came to save me."

I gripped my hands. "I…I am. Your sister said she would release Riyan if I—"

"Don't."

I furrowed my brows as the sea crashed against the cliffs in the distance. Fraleigh's eyes stayed north as I struggled to find words to say. Why would she not want me to free her?

"I am…restricted on what I can say," Fraleigh finally said. "Everything must happen at the right time, and in the right way…but you still get a choice. Remember that you get a choice."

I dared step closer. "What choice?"

Fraleigh paused, carefully selecting her next words. "Carrying the Man of the Mountain's gift is a heavier burden than most people at the edge of a wishing well could ever imagine. What seems like a key is actually a lock."

Did she think I was as weak as she was?

I straightened my spine. "My life has been nothing but a series of locks, one right after the other. Iron locks. Doors slammed on my nose. Bricks of stone that crash in front of me. I still find a key every time."

Fraleigh finally turned, her golden eyes gleaming as much as the collar around her neck. "I believed that once too."

She let out a breath and extended her left hand to me, where a faint scar crossed her palm. The white light twinkled between Fraleigh's eyes.

The Great Sorceress had let me in.

My stomach turned at what I was about to see, but I stepped forward. My left hand met hers, my fresh scar brushing up against her centuries-old one. The moment our skin touched, the shrieking of the winter wind filled my ears.

I closed my eyes and let the scream of wind push me down the tether into Fraleigh's mind.

Then I opened my eyes and saw snow.

Chapter Twenty Six
Gift of Sorrow

Wind. Ice. Panic.

I floated beside Fraleigh in her memory as she ran through the snowy peak of Nordingaard mountain. She looked about seventeen and her skin was pale instead of luminescent.

How strange to see her so…young.

Fraleigh's amber eyes flitted amongst the rocks, looking for perfect handholds in the slope. She took a leap and began to climb. Her dark hair whipped behind her as the wind nearly pushed her down, but she kept going.

"Fraleigh, slow down!" another girl cried.

A younger girl—maybe fourteen years old—followed behind. She puffed out a frosty breath through her round cheeks as she struggled up the rocks. Her blonde hair loosened from their braids as she struggled to catch up.

No…that could not be…

"Hurry, Ganora!" Fraleigh cried.

All at once, I floated next to the two girls in an open snowy plain. An opening in the rocks loomed ahead with a dense fog rolling out between them. Fraleigh sprinted toward the passage without a moment of hesitation.

Ganora huffed as she ran behind. "How do you know he will help?"

"Trust me!" Fraleigh's voice echoed through the fog.

The fog opened up to a large well in the snow, swirling with glowing water. Tall runes circled the well, bearing carved images of suffering, lost love, and even Death.

The grave of the Man of the Mountain, the same place from Astrid's memory.

Fraleigh stood at the edge of the well and looked into the water. "The bad men killed Papa. They killed him so we could get away. I…I know what that means."

Who was she talking to?

The water glowed so brightly Fraleigh had to shield her eyes. The air around us suddenly turned heavy.

She took a small knife out of a scabbard attached to her belt. "I was scared before, but I'm ready. It's the only way to stop the bad men from killing us all."

She winced and dragged the blade across her left palm. Tears blossomed in the corners of her eyes. "My tears fall, my blood flows…"

"Fraleigh!" Ganora cried behind her.

Fraleigh closed her eyes. "…now we become Death's greatest foes."

She stepped into the well and sank beneath the surface.

Ganora ran to the edge of the well as soon as Fraleigh's dark hair disappeared into the swirling water.

"No, Fraleigh!" Cold tears ran down her shaking cheeks. "I can't lose you too!"

I could not believe the helpless girl in the memory was the future Queen of the Giants. How had she become the legendary monster the North feared?

The water glowed a blinding white and Ganora scrambled away from the edge. Ancient wails of a grieving man spiraled around the runes. Ganora clapped her hands over her ears and screamed.

Every bit of air was filled with a voice that was impossible to block—a voice sharp as ice and gentle as a low flame.

A voice I knew all too well.

"*Through love, I defeated Death,*" the Man of the Mountain whispered, "*through your passionate love, you hold my gift of sorrow on your lips. Walk the earth as my heart, destroy all that would hurt your beloved, and live through eternity as I wished my bride could have.*"

Fraleigh rose from the water like she floated out of it and took a strong step into the snow. She looked unharmed, but…sharper. Stronger. Angrier.

She ran toward cowering Ganora and placed her hands on her shoulders. "I'm all right. I'm going to protect the village."

"What?" Ganora cried. She grabbed Fraleigh's wrists. "They'll kill you!"

Fraleigh's face hardened. "No, they won't. I cannot die."

Ganora tightened her grip. "They can do worse. I won't let you go."

With a pained grunt, Fraleigh shoved her sister into the snow and raised her hands.

"Stay here," she said, her voice heavy. "Stay here until it's safe."

The snow brightened and formed warm green and gold ribbons that wrapped around Ganora's wrists.

The ribbons shortly disappeared, but Ganora grabbed her left wrist with wide eyes. "What did you do?"

Fraleigh's lip trembled, but then she straightened her back. "I did this for you."

Ganora opened her mouth to protest, but Fraleigh ran for the passage. My consciousness followed Fraleigh, but I caught a glimpse of Ganora desperately chasing her older sister through the passage.

But Fraleigh ran faster. Four seconds passed before Ganora's scream shredded the frigid air.

The future Queen of the Giants had reached the end of her enchanted tether.

A flash of white engulfed my vision and then the memory warped.

Snow turned into flame.

Huts made from pinewood and animal hides were ablaze. Each snowflake fell to the earth bathed in golden fire. Children cried. Women screamed.

But Fraleigh stood in the snow, her eyes lit up with righteous fury as her magic wrapped around the neck of an invading soldier. Fraleigh closed her fist and the soldier fell in breathless death, his blue plumed helmet clattering against the ground..

Three more soldiers ran after her with their swords drawn, but with a wave of her arm, Fraleigh bathed them in a tower of flame. They died screaming as their steel chainmail cooked them.

A young but tall man barrelled through the lines of men in the village. His dark curls peeked out from beneath his helmet as his blazing blue eyes looked around.

I could not believe it, it was Alastar the Conqueror himself!

Fraleigh's memory was his conquest of Nordingaard, his final battle before he claimed Lycaster as his. I had to memorize every recorded detail of the battle in school, but I was watching the real history play out.

Alastar raced forward and yanked his father's shield off a nearby wall where it had been displayed as a trophy—the famous Taurus shield.

His father, Cassius, was a Latiman general who fell at the first siege of Nordingaard. His partner and fellow general, Marcus Janus, had sent Cassius on a doomed mission up the mountain so he could rule the soon-to-be conquered Lycaster by himself.

Alastar the Conqueror's taking of the mountain was not just the final push to form the Dukedom, it was his vengeance for the betrayal of his father.

Alastar let out a scream of triumph as he fastened the shield bearing three rearing bulls to his arm and held his spear aloft.

The soldiers of Alastar's army flooded into the village faster and fiercer.

Even though I knew they were going to win, I still choked on terror as I watched the snow turn scarlet.

Volleys of arrows soared through the air, piercing Fraleigh's skin one by one. She yanked an arrow out of her chest, but there were too many for her magic to stop.

She tried to run, but an arrow pinned her to the wooden wall of a house behind her. Then another. Then another.

She was trapped—pinned to the wall like a butterfly. Sparkling blood poured out of each wound as Fraleigh panted with her eyes closed. Her wounds tried to heal themselves around the arrows, but she could not free herself.

My consciousness stayed beside Fraleigh as her head lolled down. She must have exhausted her power.

The victorious Latiman soldiers rounded up the village elders and threw them to their knees before Alastar the Conqueror. Some of them had missing eyes or their lips were stained red with blood.

Alastar barked at the cowering men, but they could not understand him. I had to study the Latiman language in school, but I had never heard it spoken in conversation. It sounded much less formal and more…harsh.

The men before him babbled in panic, but Alastar was growing visibly frustrated with their barbarian tongue. Alastar pointed at Fraleigh. The man in the center of the line spoke up.

"The mountain!" He pointed toward the mountain pass. "She gets her power from the mountain! Go up the mountain!"

Alastar's blue eyes gleamed with understanding. He helped the man onto his feet, who looked relieved.

Then Alastar drove his spear into the man's chest. The man crumpled to the ground as blood pooled into the snow.

Death did not faze Alastar. He walked over to Fraleigh and gently plucked the arrows out of her tired body. On the final arrow, Fraleigh folded forward into Alastar's arms. Alastar picked her up and her half-lidded eyes met his.

Alastar sneered and his eyes cut to the bleeding body in the snow. "*Proditor.*"

Even without the context, I knew what that word meant.

Traitor.

A flurry of snow blanketed my vision and soon Fraleigh and I stood at Nordingaard's peak again. Alastar held her in front of the swirling well. Even if she had any energy to run, his grip on her arms was too tight for her to escape.

Alastar barked at his soldiers and pointed at the well. Half a dozen ran to the edge with leather skeins, gathering up as many tears as they could.

Ganora appeared from behind a rune with Fraleigh's discarded knife in her hand. Her eyes were lined with tears and ablaze with rage.

"Free my sister," Ganora commanded.

"*Lamia?*" Alastar said with a wicked smile.

I remembered that word—sorceress.

He motioned for his soldiers to seize Ganora.

"Ganora! No!" Fraleigh cried as she struggled against Alastar's iron hold.

Ganora's eyes found Fraleigh's and the weight of the air crashed around us. "And this is for you."

She sliced her left palm and ran into the well. She fell through the surface of the water without even a splash.

Ancient screams of anguish swirled around the frightened soldiers.

"*Through the fear of lost love, I hold the magic of Nordingaard,*" the Man of the mountain said. "*Through your fear, you hold its power. Turn your fear into rage, live eternally as the magic always will, and destroy all who try to corrupt my gifts.*"

The ground shook as Ganora emerged from the well. Her hair had bleached into a scream of white, her eyes were icy and bright, and her skin had become as grey and unfeeling as stone. She was no longer a teenage girl, but a huge, snarling monster.

Ganora's fear had turned her into a giant.

The soldiers all loosed arrows, but they merely bounced off Ganora's skin. Ganora swiped through the air, her magic freezing the blood of the soldiers and snapping their necks in a blink. Their bodies crumbled to the snow as Ganora's eyes turned to Alastar.

My consciousness snapped backward as Alastar threw Fraleigh over his shoulder and ran back through the pass.

Ganora's pained screams echoed through the fog. "Fraleigh! *Fraleigh!*"

Fraleigh's eyes watered as the realization that she had trapped her baby sister spread across her face.

Even though I was merely witnessing her memory, I could still feel heartbreak hardening within Fraleigh's bones like permafrost.

The Great Sorceress's sacrifice was all in vain.

And so the Queen of the Giants began her reign.

A flash of white whisked me away into a new memory. Iron bars spread across my vision as I floated beside Fraleigh within her small cage.

Her manacles rattled as she trembled. Soldiers in blue marched around her, laughing and slurping down skeins of mead as they enjoyed the spoils of their conquest.

Waves crashed against the cliffs to the west. The sea of tents turned into stone buildings further inland with banners of blue hanging from the rooftops. Chains of the barbarian slaves dragged across the grass of the Hyton camp. All the people Fraleigh once knew as neighbors kept their eyes down as Alastar the Conqueror spoke with an old man with a long white beard. Fraleigh might not have understood his words, but she still recoiled when Alastar pointed at her.

The old man responded in Latiman, tripping over his consonants and mixing up words. After his tongue failed him, the old man pulled a boy forward, one with white hair and deep eyes. The older man gestured to the boy and I could make out the words "good" and "mind."

The boy spoke up, speaking in near-perfect Latiman that even brought a smile to Alastar's face. Alastar gestured to Fraleigh and the boy cautiously walked over.

The boy stopped when he was three feet in front of Fraleigh's cage. "Please…don't hurt me."

Although I understood him because Fraleigh did, his vowels were rounder and his consonants sharp as spears—he was speaking Old Tongue.

Fraleigh held her breath and did not move.

The boy's hands curled into trembling fists. "Don't kill me, I'm trying to help you."

Fraleigh's eyes darted to Alastar, who glared at her from the other side of the cage. "How do you speak his tongue?"

I knew the answer to that—Alastar's father and Marcus Janus had conquered the other provinces before they ever set foot on Nordingaard. We must have been in the town that would later become Hyton.

The boy's mouth formed a fine line. "I had to learn the language quickly. If the Latimans think you're useful, you get to stay unchained."

Fraleigh swallowed. "What does he want with me?"

The boy let out a breath. "He wanted me to tell you that unless you want to spend the rest of your days in a hole underground, you will make him gold. Lots of it."

"Gold?" Fraleigh's eyes watered. "I cannot make gold! My magic doesn't work that way!"

The boy swallowed. "Sorceress, don't cry."

"If he finds out I can't make gold, he's going to…he's going to…"

The boy stepped toward the cage and Fraleigh scampered back into the bars like he had struck her. His eyes widened as Fraleigh started to sob.

What…what had Alastar the Conqueror done to her?

The boy cut a glance over his shoulder and then scooped some pebbles off the ground.

"*Aurum, lamia!*" He shook the pebbles in his palm. "*Aurum!*"

I wish I had a body so I could knock the idiot boy away from the cage. How was screaming about gold going to help?

Fraleigh shook as she cried, but then the boy dropped to his knees in the grass and held his hand through the bars of Fraleigh's cage.

His voice fell to a soft whisper. "I'm an alchemist's apprentice—my power is the art of illusion." He shook the pebbles again. "We're going to make him believe you turn stone to gold."

Wait…

I focused closer on the boy's dark eyes, finding flecks of violet within. The boy was not a mere meddlesome annoyance, he was *the* meddlesome annoyance.

Daigen.

Darkness swallowed me as if I had been forced underground. A trapdoor opened above me and light from a full moon flooded into a small stone chamber.

Fraleigh stood beside me and looked up at the light. Stacks of gold coins glittered on a small table—the only piece of furniture in the dungeon.

Alastar the Conqueror had not even given her a bed.

Daigen dropped from the ladder into the dungeon and Fraleigh quickly clawed a hole in the dirt floor with her hands. As my gaze followed Fraleigh's hands, I could not help but notice a stake in the ground that held an iron chain around her ankles.

Daigen tipped the sack in his hands and pebbles poured into the hole Fraleigh had just dug. As soon as the sack was empty, Daigen pulled a few gold coins out of his vest and shoes and handed them to Fraleigh.

Fraleigh conjured a tiny golden flame with green edges on her fingertip. She burned the Sudrian double eagle off the sides of the first coin as Daigen buried the pebbles.

Fraleigh had just burned the Austlandian cross off the last coin when she frowned. "There's blood on this one."

Daigen stomped on the covered hole to flatten the earth. "Don't worry about it."

Fraleigh's head snapped up as a dark shadow cast over the opening of the trap door. Alastar the Conqueror leaped into the dungeon instead of climbing down the ladder.

His deep blue eyes glittered as he scanned the stacks of coins. He turned to Daigen and a few smooth Latiman words rolled off his tongue like rainwater on stone.

Daigen glanced at Fraleigh and spoke in Old Tongue. "He compliments you on your work and has a gift for you."

Alastar flashed Fraleigh a nearly charming smile as he reached for the satchel against his hip. He unbuckled the satchel as he talked, low but fast.

Daigen's eyes widened. "Fraleigh, say no."

Alastar flashed him a deadly look. "You think I have not learned your barbarian tongue, boy?"

Fraleigh froze. Daigen's eyes were wide, but he did not answer.

Alastar turned his eyes to Fraleigh. "Darling Fraleigh, your power is so great that men from nearby nations will try to steal you. I will offer you my protection, on one condition."

He pulled a golden collar out of his satchel and set it on the table. "Use your magic to bind yourself to the House of Hyton for eternity, swear to never use your power against us, and I will unlock your chains."

This was the bad deal with the Hytons. Why would she have taken it?

Fraleigh stared at the golden collar, speechless.

Daigen stepped forward. "Fraleigh, don't—!"

With a quick swing of his arm, Alastar grabbed Daigen and pressed his forearm into his neck. Daigen struggled but could not get free.

Alastar's eyes gleamed. "I will make the decision easier—agree or he dies *tonight*."

Daigen's eyes bulged and his face turned scarlet, but he shook his head over and over.

"Darling Fraleigh, have I been so horrible to you?" Alastar's voice was impossibly kind as he strangled Daigen. "Other kings and conquerors would be *much worse* if they took you. I am just trying to keep you safe."

I was not foolish enough to believe anyone named "the Conqueror" was kind, but I had never imagined the revered legend of the Dukedom could be such a…such a monster.

Fraleigh's hands covered her mouth as her eyes watered. Even though I knew that collar was going onto her neck, I still held onto hope that she would resist.

Daigen's face turned purple and his head lolled forward.

Fraleigh threw down her hands. "Stop! I'll do it!"

The air in the dungeon shifted, growing heavy like Fraleigh was burying herself alive. Alastar dropped Daigen and walked to the table.

When the golden teeth of the collar shut around Fraleigh's neck, the bargain was made—Fraleigh's life for Daigen's.

A life for a life given in love. How could I have ever thought I could just manipulate Duke Hyton into releasing Fraleigh when *nothing* was more powerful than that kind of agreement?

Alastar lifted Fraleigh's chin and examined the collar. "You belong to the House of Hyton and its sons forever." He dropped her chin. "But the boy still dies."

"What?" Fraleigh cried. "But you said—!"

"I agreed that the boy would live tonight." Alastar swept the stacks of gold coins into the open mouth of his satchel. He held up the sack of gold. "Robbing the port will still cost him his head."

His Hyton Blue eyes flicked down to Daigen, who gasped as he pushed himself up from the dirt floor. "See you at sunrise."

The trap door slammed shut behind Alastar and the click of a lock echoed through the small dungeon. Only thin strips of moonlight crept through the gaps in the wooden door. Even in near darkness, Fraleigh pulled at the end of her chains to lift Daigen up.

He coughed. "You should have let him kill me."

Fraleigh's golden eyes scanned Daigen's face. "Do you have a knife?"

Daigen shakily reached for the scabbard at his hip and pulled out a knife with a curved blade—*Reginbani.*

Fraleigh took the knife from him, running the tip of the blade against her left palm. "You helped me, so I'll help you. I earned my power through a sacrifice, and maybe…maybe I can give you my power too. You can be deathless too."

He shook his head. "Are you talking about the old legend from the mountain? It's not going to work."

Her brow went hard. "Yes it will. The moon is full and everything that needed to happen did."

Daigen's brow furrowed. "No, that would mean—"

They looked at each other in a moment of silent understanding. He shook his head. "No, Fraleigh, you can't. I'm a criminal. I don't deserve your lo—"

"Do you love me too?"

Daigen took in a shuddering breath, but then looked into Fraleigh's eyes. "Yes."

"Then stay with me," Fraleigh pleaded. "Forever."

Daigen blinked out a single tear and offered her his right palm.

With the slice of a blade and a few whispered words, the dungeon filled with golden light.

It was not the same enchantment I had known. It was bright as a dandelion, warm as a night by the fire, and pure as fresh driven snow.

And with the might of a bond made from true love and sacrifice, two hearts became one.

Brilliant golden light flooded my vision and morphed into Fraleigh's gold irises as I gently left her memory. My hand trembled in her grip as I returned to the misty morning and the calls of the sea birds.

My eyes dropped to her golden collar. The words "*Ipse Dixit*" were still clearly etched, even after four hundred and fifty-one years.

"I know the choice I made," Fraleigh said as she released my hand. "Even after centuries of chains and cages, even when my power diminished little by little…it was worth it."

She swallowed and traced the scar on her palm. "*He* was worth it."

All this time, I had thought Daigen had a rivalry with Fraleigh. His disdain was not for her, but for the noble marriage enchantment.

The bond that originated from sacrifice had cheapened into chattel, became its own golden chain, and made every noble marriage a question of what was even real.

Daigen was angry enough to rip the corrupted blood bond out of my veins because it was a mockery of what Fraleigh had given, of what was supposed to just be *theirs.*

My heart ached, but I finally understood Daigen. He tore out my bond to make me a blank slate, uncorrupted by another Hyton lie. He wanted Riyan and I to have a chance at true, pure love because…that's what he and Fraleigh had.

And all he wanted was to get back the person he lost.

"But I *will* get you out of this," I said as I looked into Fraleigh's sad golden eyes. "A life for a life is an unbreakable bargain but…your sister has Riyan. She is going to doom him to an eternity in the place West of the Moon and East of the Sun if I do not free you by the full moon."

Fraleigh's long dark hair gently danced in the breeze. "Riyan knew the sacrifice he made, and he made it gladly. Why not just leave him be?"

My hands tightened into fists at my sides. "Because he does not deserve oblivion! I still…I still may not know how I feel, but who cares about my feelings when his life is on the line?" Tears pricked the backs of my eyes. "I will not turn my back on him, not after I have seen *exactly* what that kind of sacrifice does."

My eyes dropped from her face to that horrible golden collar around her neck.

Fraleigh responded with a calm smile. "Riyan's sacrifice was a gift… but it is still incomplete. A life for a life given in love—the Man of the Mountain will fight death for you."

I held my breath, listening to the soft pounding of my heart in my ears to ground me to the earth. Did she mean…immortality?

Fraleigh swallowed. "The Man of the Mountain wanted someone to walk the earth in the place of his lost bride, carrying her gifts so that she may live on…but he knows what I am doing is not living. He has searched for someone to replace me." She let out a breath. "When I saw you at that chastity examination, the Man of the Mountain spoke in my mind."

A chill ran up my arms.

I see you, Serafina Ravenwood.

I was seen, wanted, chosen…but it all seemed too perfect of a coincidence. I only had the gift of sorcery in the first place because Riyan took me to the healing spring after I had been poisoned. I was only poisoned because Rosaline told us to seek out Daigen…

I set my jaw. If Fraleigh could not refuse direct questions, then I was going to get some answers. "Did you tell Rosaline to instruct me to find Daigen?"

She swallowed and faced north. "The Man of the Mountain gave me an order…and one does not refuse orders from him."

I did not like that answer. "Did you poison me?"

"No." She turned to face me and her golden eyes were shining. "I never wanted you to get hurt, Serafina. Ever."

Her plea of assurance made the truth of a promised eternity sink into my skin. The Man of the Mountain wanted me to be the next Great Sorceress—ageless, deathless, and powerful beyond my comprehension.

I looked around at the headstones around us, my eyes falling on the open graves. An immortal life would mean I would have to watch *everyone* I knew die. Would I drop a handkerchief on Annalisa's coffin? Would I lay flowers at Brietta's headstone?

And Derrick…

I refused to picture myself sobbing at his graveside as my mother had.

"But though the path is laid out for you," Fraleigh said, "you don't have to take it."

I turned away from the headstones and looked back at Fraleigh, whose golden eyes were the softest I had ever seen.

"You can tell the Man of the Mountain no," she said. "You can keep your magic until you meet Death's black wings. I can hold on longer."

I furrowed my brows. "Does that mean…if I choose eternity, you lose your power?"

Fraleigh gave me a wan smile. "What little there is left, and I become mortal once more."

I swallowed. Eternity on earth was merely an option, though that option did not give me what I needed. "You cannot tempt me with eternity and expect me to forget about the man who allowed me to have it." I stepped forward in the grass with my arms folded. "What about your freedom? The bargain might be unbreakable, but every agreement has a back door."

Fraleigh let out a long breath, as if she wished I had never asked the question. She tapped the front of her collar with her sharp fingernail. "Only the Duke can speak these words and release the collar. Then my servitude is over."

I eyed the words "*Ipse Dixit,*" as if each letter spelled our salvation.

My white flame warmed my heart. Getting into Anders's head to force him to say the curse-breaking phrase would have been impossible, but he was no longer the Duke.

Derrick was. *My* Derrick.

That was why my magic drew me to him two nights ago. That was why my heart's desire pushed me to look for him and heal him.

"Derrick is the answer." A smile broke through my lips. "I have already connected with his mind once. I just have to get into his head, make him say the words to free you, and it is all over. You can be with Daigen again, I can save Riyan…"

The crease between her eyebrows, pinched with a mixture of worry and pity, made me stop.

Fraleigh's smile stayed calm, even as I felt the slight pull of the magic in the air around her.

"Again," she said with glassy eyes, "I am restricted on what I can say."

She stepped backward and dissolved into the air.

My chest rose and fell as she left me in the silence. Not even the seabirds sang. Even the waves at the shoreline were still.

Fraleigh might have been infuriatingly vague as usual, but for once she had given me enough information to get what I want.

Two little words spelled out Riyan's freedom, and I would force Derrick to say them.

Once Derrick got the crown at the next sunrise, his mind was *mine*.

Chapter Twenty Seven
Crown and Veil

The sun's glow lit the horizon on the morning of Derrick's coronation. Blue and white banners fluttered above the city square. Two thrones adorned with golden bull's horns stood at the center of the scaffold.

Brietta stood in front of her smaller throne, a sheer white veil covering her face. Baron Elvar was beside Derrick's empty throne, holding the crown of Lycaster. The other five Barons stood in a line behind him.

Annalisa and I gripped each other's hands as we stood at the front of the crowd. A line of soldiers in gleaming brass separated the Hyton women from the throngs of cheering townspeople.

Amethyst put her hand on my shoulder for balance. Her brown hair was neatly braided around her tiara, but her legs shook under the weight of her pregnant belly. Garnet stood on her other side, her eyes vacant as Amethyst's arm wrapped around her shoulders.

"We should have the soldiers fetch you a stool," I whispered.

Amethyst smirked, even as sweat beaded on her temples. "Mama stood through the whole coronation while in labor with *twins*. I can make it."

Trumpets blared and the crowd cheered. War drums pounded and the Lycaster soldiers forced the crowd to part so they formed an aisle.

The crowd of peasants and nobility alike rippled as they all dropped to their knees.

The hooves of a lone horse clacked on the cobblestones. General Hyton appeared, wearing the famous Taurus shield on his arm. I tried not to imagine the barbarian blood that had once stained the now-polished shield.

General Hyton's eyes shone brightly as he led a white horse through the aisle.

I kept my mouth clamped shut, but some of the Hyton sisters gasped as soon as we caught sight of Derrick on top of the horse. His curls hung limply around his hollow cheeks and his mouth was dry and tight. His Hyton Blue cape and brilliant gems adorning his hands and chest did nothing to brighten his pallor.

My stomach plummeted. In his hand was Alastar the Conqueror's spear. It looked *exactly* the same as in Fraleigh's memory.

Like the Taurus shield, the Conqueror's spear was a Hyton relic, passed down with each new Duke. I knew the spear played a role in the coronation, but I had always thought they used a ceremonial replica and not *the* spear.

The cheers of the crowd hushed as Fraleigh dutifully followed behind the horse wearing the same blue and white robes she wore to the funeral. Her chin was high, exposing that horrible collar.

The horse reached the front steps of the scaffold and Derrick jumped from the saddle. He looked nowhere but the steps as he ascended the platform. General Hyton handed the reins to another soldier and followed Derrick. Once Fraleigh had glided up the steps, General Hyton addressed the crowd.

"Vengeance!" he boomed. "A son's vengeance for his father built our Dukedom!"

I held my breath and shifted my legs, ensuring my Nordingaard crystal was securely tied to my thigh. Even though General Hyton was merely regaling the story of Marcus Janus's treachery, my stomach turned.

He knew I was a sorceress and had still not dragged me away in chains. He had to have something planned.

I tried not to stare at Traitor's Bane in its sheath across the General's back.

General Hyton armed Derrick with the Taurus shield, symbolizing how a son takes up the legacy of his fallen father, and turned back to the crowd.

"And just as Marcus Janus pretended to be our Conqueror's ally," he said, "a traitor is in our midst!"

The crowd jeered and my blood ran cold.

Although the crystal on my skin kept my heart from flying out of my chest, I squeezed Annalisa's hand.

Alastar the Conqueror had gored Marcus Janus with his spear as soon as he came down from Nordingaard mountain, taking the throne of the newly formed Lycaster for himself. To keep the tradition, every Duke had slain a traitor at his coronation. Was that General Hyton's plan for me? Reveal me as a sorceress and then drag me up on the scaffold?

I closed my eyes and let my white flame brighten. My crystal warmed against my skin and a cool calmness ran down my shoulders.

General Hyton would not take me without a fight.

The crowd hissed. I opened my eyes just as Hyton guards dragged a hooded prisoner up the scaffold steps.

I let out a relieved breath. No blade would kiss my neck.

But then General Hyton tore off the prisoner's hood and my heart stopped.

It was Brandt.

Brandt's round face was white and his eyes were the size of saucers as he faced the vicious crowd.

What had he told the General? Maybe I could stop this.

I shifted my weight forward but Amethyst kept her hand on my shoulder.

"Stay still," she whispered. "Everything we do affects how they see him."

I frowned. Regardless of the delicacies of the ritual, I still had to try to save Brandt.

I called out to the magic in the air, fanning out my power as much as I could.

"This man used his knowledge from our military academy to form his own militia in Bloodstone!" General Hyton boomed. "He snuck into the palace using a noble woman as his cover. He was found consorting with a raven, bringing Death into our walls!"

A raven—Erik. General Hyton had found Erik.

But the General said *militia,* not army. Brandt had kept some of the truth back.

As my magic searched for an opening, the crowd jeered.

"Northern filth!"

"Traitor!"

"Kill him!"

The magic swept around the scaffold, but none of the soldiers opened up. The light did not shine behind Brietta's veil. Derrick was all iron as he gripped his ancestor's spear.

Finally, my eyes met Brandt's watering ones.

"He used the raven to send secret communications to his conspirator!" the General shouted.

My lip trembled as my mouth fell open. General Hyton found my message to him, maybe even the one I penned to Evereon.

Brandt was captured because of *me.* Riyan had trusted me to protect the North, protect Bloodstone Fortress and its soldiers…and I failed.

Because of my carelessness, I failed them *all.*

"But he *refused* to reveal the other traitor!"

I choked on a sob as the corner of Brandt's mouth flicked up. He had still protected me.

Tears stung my eyes, but suddenly the white pinhole of light appeared between Brandt's brows and the bouncing tune of a flute echoed in the back of my mind. I desperately threw out the invisible tether and sent a message into Brandt's head:

"I can get you out of this. I am going to try everything I can."

Brandt took a shallow breath and shook his head once, only enough for me to see.

I bit my tongue so I would not cry. Brandt had called me the North's last hope. He would rather die rather than risk exposing me as a sorceress.

General Hyton gestured to Derrick. "Will you, the spirit of the Conqueror, defend this land? Will you protect its people?"

I nearly dropped the hold over my magic when the realization hit me—General Hyton was not supposed to kill Brandt. Derrick was.

My chest rattled with a sob, but still a spot of warmth from the crystal kept me still. I wrapped my magic around that warmth and sent it into Brandt's mind— carrying a memory of a young man and his fellow soldiers playing music beneath torchlight as Riyan danced with the woman he loved.

I sent a command as tears distorted my vision: *"Listen to the music until the end."*

Brandt blinked slowly, accepting the command.

Then that sweet memory of Riyan sent a different tune to my mind— it was lower and slower, but it was calming me too.

The magical tether broke as the soldiers forced Brandt to face Derrick. Derrick's arm trembled.

Sapphira leapt forward. "Kill him! Defend our House!"

Rubia, Pearl, and Emeralda followed, growing more vicious with every heartbeat as they shouted up at the scaffold.

Brandt's lip quivered only once before he spoke, his words cold steel. "I die for the North."

The voices of the crowd rose like a tidal wave behind us.

"The giants missed one!"

"Kill the snow-eater!"

"Feed his corpse to the ravens!"

Tears wet my lashes. Derrick was no killer, he would ask General Hyton to do it. A quick death from Traitor's Bane would be the mercy Derrick would give.

"Just close your eyes," Amethyst whispered. "We all did when we were girls."

But my eyes stayed on Brandt. I could not abandon him in his last moments.

"Vincere aut mori," General Hyton shouted. "Conquer or die!"

Then Derrick plunged his spear into Brandt's chest.

My hand flew to my mouth as I held back a scream. Brandt let out a pained cry. The tip of the Conqueror's spear was crimson and gleaming in the morning sun as it stuck out of Brandt's back.

Derrick's whole body shook but his brow was hard. With a hiss through his teeth, he pulled out the spear and Brandt's body hung limply between the arms of the soldiers as his blood cascaded onto the scaffold.

I held my breath as the soldiers let go of Brandt's arms. Before his body could crumple forward, Traitor's Bane sliced through the air and severed his neck in a single cut.

General Hyton gripped Brandt's blonde hair and held his head up to the crowd. "Hail Alastar XII!"

I used all my will to not vomit. In the corner of my vision, Baron Elvar placed the Lycaster crown on Derrick's head.

My hand pressed against my mouth so hard I nearly cut my lips on my teeth, but still the mysterious calming song played in the back of my mind.

General Hyton stuck Brandt's head on the tip of the Conqueror's spear as the crowd echoed, "Hail Alastar XII!"

Derrick stood in front of his throne as blood from Brandt's neck dripped down the spear onto his arm. He did not look at me, nor his sisters, nor Brietta—his blank eyes were bolted forward over the heads of the crowd.

Fraleigh dropped to her knees on the scaffold, just barely avoiding the trail of fresh blood, and bowed deeply in reverence to her new owner.

The crowd erupted into cheers. Soldiers appeared next to Derrick to remove the spear, but he would not release his grip.

After a few tugs and soldiers whispering in his ear, Derrick slowly uncurled his red-stained fist.

The entire right side of my body shook as Annalisa clutched my hand and silently sobbed.

"He is supposed to remove the Duchess's veil with his clean hand," Amethyst hissed. "The bloodshed is over. The people need to see their new Duchess. Why is he not moving?"

My heart pounded in my throat as I looked from Derrick to Brietta. Brietta's hands slowly pushed the veil up to reveal her rosy face and the crowd gasped.

Brietta pushed her shoulders back and dropped the veil on the scaffold, blood consuming the crumpling white gossamer.

General Hyton pushed down on Derrick's shoulder to get his knees to buckle and Derrick finally sat on the throne of Lycaster. Brietta gracefully followed suit.

The crowd was adoring, but Annalisa kept sobbing. "He is gone…he is gone…"

Derrick was gone—only Alastar XII remained.

I wrapped my arms around Annalisa and buried my face in her curls. I gritted my teeth and choked down a sob.

No matter what I had to do, I would force Alastar XII to release Fraleigh's collar. Not just for Fraleigh, or Brietta, or Riyan, or Freya's memory, or the women of Lycaster…but for Brandt.

No more blood would spill because of my failure.

Tears rolled onto my cheeks as the song in the back of my mind got louder, its low notes weaving themselves into words:

"Still with me somehow."

Part Four

Thread
and
Glass

Chapter Twenty Eight
Answer for an Answer

I drowned my turmoil the Hyton way—with a drink in my hand.

The celebratory coronation ball lacked any real celebration, and not just because the guilt from Brandt's death weighed on me. The Barons and other nobility spoke amongst themselves with hushed voices and darting eyes. Hissed questions of the new ruler cut through the bright music no one danced to.

"He would not let go of the spear. What does that mean?"

"I overheard the servants say he screamed in the tower all night."

"He can howl at the moon like a dog so long as he keeps the Darkest Night going every year."

I ignored the gossips and quietly sipped from my glass—at least I did not have to worry about anyone poisoning me.

Derrick, however, paid no notice to the worrying dissent. He was little more than a grim statue as he sat on his throne with a shadow over his eyes. A servant offered him a golden goblet, but Derrick's deadly glare sent the poor man scurrying away.

Brietta was quelling the fog of uncertainty, flitting from Baron to Baron and charming them with her glittering jewels and a wide smile. She kept her mask of genteel grace even though we all felt the ground cracking beneath us.

Annalisa nudged my elbow. "Stop looking so sour! Everyone is watching us."

My sip of wine turned into Brandt's blood on my tongue. I froze, but I forced myself to swallow it.

"He was my soldier, Anna," I whispered. "He died because of *me.*"

Annalisa raised her goblet and her low voice echoed off the metal. "He was the one who talked, not you." She took a sip and lowered her cup. "No one is more paranoid than Uncle Ragnar. As soon as he caught him talking to Erik, Uncle Ragnar would spare *nothing* to wring the treason out of him."

And yet Brandt had still withheld the truth and kept my secret safe.

I stared at General Hyton across the ballroom. He stood next to Baron Elvar amongst a flock of purple capes and dresses and flashed a smile that made my blood run cold.

General Hyton knew I was a sorceress. He had every right under the law to drag me up on the scaffold instead of Brandt, so why did he stay his hand?

The uncertainty clawed at my stomach. If "answer for an answer" was our game, I had to keep playing just to know what I was dealing with.

I tossed back the rest of my liquid courage and faced Annalisa. "What do you say we do some charming on behalf of His Excellency?"

Annalisa laced her fingers with mine. "*There* is the Hyton spirit."

The heels of our slippers clicked on the tile as we crossed the empty dance floor to the Elvars.

I glanced up at Derrick. He had his eyes fixed out the windows into the garden, his chin resting on his fist, and the crown of Lycaster resting heavily on his brow.

A little pull tugged beneath my ribs. I wanted to check on him to see if he was all right, but I had to see where I stood with the General.

I put on my best smile as we invaded the circle of Elvars. Baron Elvar's chest glittered with sapphires as he shot me a suspicious glance.

Vivian Elvar placed her hand on Brietta's shoulder as we joined the circle, breaking the conversation to dote on her only daughter. "We never dreamed she could be Duchess, but I suppose even the Duke's heir could not resist our darling Brietta."

Brietta took a drink from her goblet instead of rolling her eyes like she usually would.

"Ah, Serafina! Lovely to see you, dear!" Vivian's bejeweled hands flashed as she placed a showy kiss on my cheek. Her amber perfume was so strong I had to hold back a cough.

I glanced at General Hyton, hoping he would read the greasy lip stain on my cheek as a stamp of approval from the wealthiest and most influential people in the Dukedom.

Vivian cast a glance down at Annalisa as if she were vermin. "And greetings, Madame Thornebow."

"Pleasure to see the House of Elvar making an appearance for *my brother's* coronation," Annalisa sweetly replied.

"Your brother?" Baron Elvar replied with a barking laugh. "Damn, how many daughters did Anders have?"

General Hyton's smirk mirrored Baron Elvar's. "Some say one too many."

The rest of the Elvar circle threw their heads back and laughed as Brietta glared at her family.

"Oh, but you remember this one, Tyreon," Vivian said with a feline smile. "This is little Annalisa, she used to tease your niece back at Ashmore."

Brietta put a hand on her mother's arm and parted her lips to deflect, but Baron Elvar's scoff came first.

"I do not care about schoolgirl nonsense!" he said. "My brother might listen to you prattle on about the meaningless business of women, but I have more important things to give my attention to."

Baron Elvar looked at General Hyton and gestured to Derrick with his goblet. "For instance, the hell is wrong with our new Duke? He looks like an emaciated gargoyle! Has he even blinked?"

I opened my mouth to gently defend him, but Brietta beat me to it.

"His parents just died, Uncle!" she said. "He killed a man today!"

"And?" Baron Elvar replied, speaking to Brietta as if she were a child instead of the Duchess. "Business does not care, continental markets do not care—the neighboring kingdoms and empires are all looking to how that boy is going to handle things over the next few months. If he does not snap out of whatever trance he is in, all of Lycaster is in jeopardy!"

"Well deduced, Tyreon," General Hyton said with a smile.

"Brother, is that not a tad dramatic?" said Brietta's father. His purple doublet and round belly made him look like a grape.

"Spoken like a true second son, Vidaar," Baron Elvar said with a crooked smile. "You do not understand the damage Alastar the Bold did. Ravenwood and Bloodstone have had nearly zero output over the past seven years and Thornebow's markets never recovered after people stopped trusting their trade twenty years ago. If you never figured out that he kept most of court drunk and confused so they never realized how much he royally fucked our economy, then I pity you."

I kept my face schooled as he ranted. I did not know much about the economy, but I at least understood how much Ravenwood suffered after Anders sent most of its sons to die. What place did the richest man in the Dukedom have lecturing about the damage of an empty belly?

"Oh my, is Tyreon spinning a thread about the ledgers again?"

I turned toward the familiar voice. Mother had worked her small body into the circle of towering Elvars, squeezing in on General Hyton's left side. She smiled at Baron Elvar as she held a goblet in her hands. "The numbers are all so dizzying, your mind must truly be a marvel to keep track of it all!"

Baron Elvar's eyes narrowed. "What are you doing here, Adalia? No one here wants to sleep with you."

My stomach clenched and Annalisa gripped my hand. She squeezed it once, quieting all the scathing words that lashed up at my throat.

Mother laughed it off. "Oh, I am just bringing the General his refreshment."

General Hyton glanced at the goblet and raised an eyebrow.

"Ragnar, careful as always." Mother took a sip, her emerald eyes glittering. "See? Safe and sound."

General Hyton smiled and took the goblet from Mother's hands. "At least she is still good for something."

If I were not in danger of being imprisoned for sorcery, I would have boiled that wine right before it touched his lips.

My eyes flitted to the throne—empty. I searched around the room for any sign of Derrick, but I could not find him.

A missing Duke was certainly a problem. Solving that problem would make me look quite useful to the paranoid General—like a *benevolent* sorceress, even.

I squeezed Annalisa's hand and sent a gentle command into her mind. *"I have to find your brother. Entertain these snobs, will you?"*

Annalisa blinked and then a wide smile spread across her face. "Did any of you notice His Excellency has a scar on the back of his right hand?"

A small smirk flicked up Brietta's cheek, but her father and uncle raised their eyebrows.

Annalisa held up her right hand. "He tried to take my dessert when we were little, so I stabbed him with a fork. Nearly pinned him to the dining table!"

Baron Elvar barked out a laugh as I made a show of draining my goblet. I smacked my lips. "So vicious, Annalisa! But it looks like I am out of wine, I need to find more."

I maneuvered my skirt around the Elvars as they implored Annalisa to share more stories.

Whispers hissed past my ears as I crossed the ballroom.

"So much for our new Duke!"

"Looks like he *hopped* away!"

I glanced out the windows and found Derrick. He was standing in the garden and looking up at the bull statue.

I had not even spoken to Derrick since the Darkest Night. How could I face him again?

I closed my eyes and leaned into the soft song the Nordingaard crystal pushed into my skin. I was calm and I was brave—I could do something as simple as speak to a friend.

Even if he had just killed my soldier.

I let out a breath before I stepped out into the starry night. Even the tapping of my slippers against the steps did not catch his attention.

Maybe the sound of my voice would wake him. "Derrick?"

No answer. His face was still gaunt, but his chest rose and fell rapidly with shallow breath.

I wrapped my hand around his. "Derrick?"

His hand trembled. "Why is there still blood?"

I looked up at the statue. Servants had cleaned all of his father's blood off the stone and polished the golden horns clean.

"Derrick, there is no—"

"There *is* blood!" Derrick shouted. The muscles in his arm jolted harder. The veins in his neck bulged. "I still see it. I feel it on my hands. I smell it. Fuck, I taste it. I *taste* it!"

I grabbed his arms and pulled him toward me. "Derrick, look at me!"

His eyes met mine, but it was like he could not see me. The left side of his face twitched.

Shit, what was happening to him?

I stood on my toes and held his face. I stroked his sunken cheeks with my thumbs as he shook. He was little more than a skeleton wearing skin.

"When was the last time you ate?" I demanded.

He shook like a leaf in autumn, but stayed silent.

"Please, Derrick," I cried. "Please let me help you. I will call the servants and get you food—"

His eyes rolled back and his knees buckled. My arms quickly wrapped around him as his head lolled against my back. The crown of Lycaster fell from his head with a clatter.

I braced myself as I held him, but I could not help the smile that bloomed when three gentle notes from a harp played in my mind.

Alastar XII had let me in.

"What in the high halls of hell is going on?"

General Hyton's footsteps sprinted down the patio steps. Derrick's weight lifted off my body as the General heaved him over his shoulder.

Shit, this did not look good. In the General's eyes, I could have put Derrick under a spell and caused him to faint.

I tried not to sound defensive. "He has not eaten in days, General. We should get him—"

"I know," General Hyton huffed. "He refused anything we gave him in the Western tower—threw the bread right back at the guards like it was full of maggots."

The Western tower? Derrick had been locked in a cell all day? Is *that* how far the General went to keep Derrick safe?

Two guards appeared at the General's side and each one balanced the weight of their Duke's limp body between them.

"Take him to his chambers," the General ordered.

The soldiers obeyed, taking Derrick in the opposite direction of the ballroom doors.

"Not the passages!" he barked. "Someone could be waiting with a knife. Take him through the ballroom so everyone can have eyes on him."

The soldiers turned on their heels. My heart ached at the sight of Derrick's feet dragging lifelessly against the cobblestones.

I kneaded the fabric of my skirt. Derrick had lost his parents, killed a man, and was starving. No wonder he was starting to go...

No, I refused to even think of the word. Derrick always had a sharp mind and a dazzling wit. He just needed some comfort. Anyone in his situation would.

"Forbidden to lie, and yet you kept so many secrets."

I turned and General Hyton's shadow washed over me. I could have played meek and helpless, but that would do me no good. He knew I was a sorceress and therefore dangerous. Leaning into that assumption might keep my head on my shoulders.

Besides, he merely held the crown of Lycaster in his hand, not a sword.

I set my jaw and looked up. "You executed Brandt Olson."

His eyes were hard as he stepped forward. "I am the enforcer of laws, not the arbiter of mercy. He committed high treason."

"As have I, yet here I stand."

He caught my chin and my eyes met his. My neck was so bare and exposed, I nearly felt the edge of Traitor's Bane on my skin.

His finger traced my jaw as he kept me in his hold. "An answer for an answer, let's see if you will give me the whole truth this time."

A chill pricked my skin, but I held firm.

"Nikkolas Bloodstone was not hiring cadets from my academy to be mere fortress guards or to repopulate the province," he said. "That 'militia' Olson confessed to is a real army, isn't it?"

I could have spat in his face.

"Yes," I hissed.

He smiled. "Are you afraid of me?"

My eyes flicked down to the crown in his hand. "Only of the power you hold. But of *you?* No."

General Hyton's eyes gleamed. "Good." He released my chin and stepped back. "What can you do, sorceress?"

I chewed on my tongue and glanced around. No one would hear me unless the rose bushes suddenly grew ears. "I…I can heal. See memories. Set water ablaze." I swallowed, hoping I could quell the truth of the last trick I had learned, but my white fire forced it out. "A-and…control men…but only if they let me."

As soon as I thought I had doomed myself, he chuckled in his throat and smiled. "You do not need sorcery to control men." He turned. "Come. I owe you three answers and I wager that you would want to ask them in private."

Reluctantly, I picked up my skirt and followed him through the garden. He had every motive to make a death threat—I was a powerful sorceress, committing high treason, and my life was no longer bonded to his son's. What did he want with me?

He led us to the side of the palace and pressed on a brick. A low click filled the air and a stack of bricks creaked open—a door to the inner walls.

Right where General Hyton had just said someone could be waiting with a knife.

He chuckled at my incredulous look. "Between the General of the Lycaster army and a sorceress, nothing could hurt us in here."

I held onto my suspicions but stepped into the darkness. Maybe Daigen would be lurking around in case General Hyton tried to pull anything nefarious.

Or the General could *really* find out what the sorceress was capable of.

He sealed the passage behind us and held the crown as he walked in front of me in the narrow hallway.

The paranoid General left his back exposed to a sorceress?

My first question was the only one that burned at the front of my mind. "Why have you not executed me yet?"

"I am not a wasteful man." His voice was nearly as soft as his footsteps. "You are a powerful being in a world that is crumbling. My skills can only…do so much. The House of Hyton needs someone like you to keep it secure in these fragile times."

He knew Fraleigh was weak. After Baron Elvar's tirade about our failing economy in a war-hungry world, General Hyton needed a pillar to prop up Derrick's new reign.

A sorceress like me was just what he needed if the surrounding nations decided to invade…but I had no collar binding me into their service.

I did not need to appease the General, *he* needed to appease *me.*

I had already suspected the answer to my next question, but I wanted confirmation. "How do you know so much about sorcery?"

General Hyton suddenly turned a corner and I nearly tripped over my ankles to keep up. "My mother grew up in a manor on the base of Nordingaard. She told me tales of those who wish in wells and pray for the Man of the Mountain's gift. She was fascinated by the mysticism of it all—the agelessness, the inability to lie, the magic tears."

His voice hitched and he cleared his throat. "Forgive me, I cannot remember the last time I was able to talk about her."

Was the General actually getting emotional? Maybe I could use that to my advantage and get more information out of him.

I smiled. "Your secret is safe with me."

He looked over his shoulder and I briefly saw a glimpse of the boy who was once his mother's "Little Diamond."

"I miss her," he said. The crown shifted in his hands. "I wish I could have done more for her."

The pain beneath his quiet words made my heart ache. Despite looking almost identical to him, General Hyton had never been more like Riyan until that moment.

He was just a boy who missed his mother.

I could have had a dozen questions that could have been better than the one I had chosen as my final one. I could have asked him anything about Ilsa, or why he had been so cruel to Riyan at the military academy, but only one question felt right.

"Why did you never go back for Astrid?"

His eyes widened only slightly before he swallowed. "I went back right after my son was born, but the Bloodstone Fortress gates never opened for a Hyton again."

The silence that followed weighed on my chest. I was about to open my mouth and risk owing the General another answer when he suddenly turned down a dark hallway.

"Despite how it looks, I do quite like your mother." His pace was so brisk that I had to pick up my skirt and run to keep up with him. "We have an…alliance of sorts. Unfortunately, I have to keep Tyreon Elvar happy. We all have roles to play to keep the Dukedom secure."

Between him laying on flattery like sheets on a mattress and the coil of red hair on his night table, he sent the message loud and clear.

Of course the richest man in Lycaster wanted the beautiful Little Diamond all to himself.

The General opened a panel in the wall and a soft, warm light filled the narrow hallway. The smell of soot and burnt fat filled my nose.

The kitchen—I had to get Derrick some food.

"I will ensure this goes to its rightful place," General Hyton said, gesturing to the crown in his hand, "but if anyone is going to get my nephew to eat, it will be you. If you do not enter his chambers tonight, he might starve to death."

Chapter Twenty Nine
Castle of Dreams

My finger traced the bulls on the door of the Duke's chambers. Why did the bulls always have to be rearing? Could they not have a nibble of grass or a nice walk with a friendly cow? Seemed exhausting to always be fighting.

I let out a breath. I needed to quit stalling. The cup of hunter's root cream would get cold if I stayed out in the hall.

Derrick needed to eat. I needed to get into his mind and command him to free Fraleigh and sign a reformation for Brietta.

I had taken on the role of the Duke's mistress to get close to him. Everyone expected me to, no, *wanted* me to go past those doors, but after what had happened between Derrick and I on the Darkest Night…I was still afraid to.

The sound of muffled sniffles crept through the hallway. A door flung open.

"Damn it, Pearl, stop crying!" Sapphira yelled from her room. "None of us are going to get any fucking sleep!"

The frame shook as she slammed it shut. And *there* was my signal to quit stalling.

I stared down the largest, meanest bull carved in the center of the door. That pull that had tugged at my ribs the minute I caught sight of those carved doors intensified, beckoning me in.

I let out a breath. Whatever happened behind those doors would be for our freedom.

I gently knocked on the door. "Derrick?"

The door did not click open, but soft notes of a harp floated into my mind like dandelion seeds.

My white flame danced to the slow tune. Letting the music guide me, I slowly pushed open the door as I answered the call of Derrick's inner self.

Even in the dark, I marveled at the starlit splendor of the Duke's bedroom. The room was even larger than I expected, with multiple clusters of couches and chairs, but the gigantic canopied bed on the far wall stole my attention.

My feet whispered across the floor as I moved to the bed. The sheets and pillows were undisturbed.

"So, you found me."

My heart nearly jumped out of my throat. My braid swished over my shoulder as I turned to find Derrick sitting on the floor in the shadow of a large wardrobe.

I furrowed my brows, but quickly smoothed my face. If he was spooked, I needed to calm him down.

Careful not to spill my cup, I squeezed between him and the wardrobe and joined him on the floor. I was in my nightgown, but he was still in his splendid outfit from the ball.

"What are you doing down here?" I asked softly.

He chewed on his chapped lip. "Uncle Ragnar said this is the safest place for me, but he is a liar. This is the room where my father and grandfather were murdered, and I am next. I *know* it."

His inner self had beckoned me through the bedroom door, but his frightened delusions kept me out of his mind. Maybe a gentle correction was all he needed to quell the paranoia.

I placed my hand on his arm. "Your father was not murdered. He lost his balance and fell off the balcony."

His throat trembled. "Even still, I want to be as far away from that damn balcony as possible."

I looked across the room at the thin doors with panes of blue and green glass that must have led to the balcony. "Are the doors locked?"

His arm tensed beneath my hand. "Not sure."

I rose from the floor and carefully dodged furniture on my way to the balcony doors. I found the lock and turned it closed.

"There," I said with a gentle smile that I hoped Derrick could see through the darkness. "You will not fall off the balcony tonight."

Silence was the only response. Maybe securing the room even more would help.

I crossed to the bedroom door. The gleam of a silver tray on a low table caught my eye—a loaf of bread sat on it, not a single crumb touched.

I pressed on the door and glanced at the wardrobe. "You are afraid of being murdered but you left the door unlocked?"

Derrick peered around the wardrobe and then the gleam of a blade caught the blue and green light from the balcony doors. "I was going to kill the murderer before he could kill me."

I bit my tongue. "Derrick, no one is going to—"

"I already killed a man today. What is one more?"

My throat trembled as the image of Derrick plunging the Conqueror's spear through Brandt's chest flashed in my mind.

I could not drown in my failure. I was the North's last hope. I *had* to get into Derrick's mind so he would free Fraleigh.

I let out a slow breath and turned the lock closed. I joined Derrick in the shadow of the wardrobe and offered him the cup. "Here, while it is still warm."

Derrick backed away. "What is that?"

"Your mother's recipe." I pushed the cup forward. "You have to put something in your stomach."

His eyes went wide and he shook his head.

He must have thought it was poisoned. I lifted the cup to my lips. "Look, it is fine—"

"No!" Derrick leaped forward, but I held the cup in the air so none of the drink spilled. "I will not let you poison yourself for me!"

I grabbed his face with my free hand. "Derrick, it is not poisoned! Your father is gone! No one is left to poison you anymore!"

He looked at me like he had just fallen backward. The left side of his face twitched again and the knife fell with a clatter as he uncurled his white-knuckled fist.

Damn it, I lost my patience. Maybe I could fix it.

I shifted the drink to my left hand and put my right arm around Derrick's back.

I gave him a soft kiss on his sharp cheek. "Do you trust me?"

"I trust no one but you, Serafina."

Out of all the people in the Dukedom, *I* was the only person the new Duke trusted?

I thought I would be excited to use that trust to my advantage, but instead my heart sank like lead.

The irony was nearly as cruel as I was. He trusted no one but me and I was only there to manipulate him.

I glanced at the knife on the floor—a bread knife. "Then please let me take care of you. I know you have not eaten or drank since…since you were last poisoned, but you will die if you keep this up."

His mouth formed a tight line as he stared at the floor.

I had to push him further. "If you die, you kill Brietta. Do you want that?"

He finally accepted the cup with shaking hands and lifted it to his mouth. He sipped cautiously at first but then desperately tipped the goblet back, gulping down the cream like it was nothing but air.

He stared into the empty cup and licked his lips. "Reminds me of Mama."

And he never even got to tell her goodbye.

I leaned against his shoulder. The melancholy harpsong played again as soon as my forehead touched the side of his neck.

Suddenly Derrick was not a killer, but instead the scared teenage boy I had met at Ravenwood Manor. Even though I had only seen him as ripe fruit on a low branch back then…I just could not coldly flail him open and control him. He was too vulnerable, it…it felt wrong.

Damn my heart's desire! Why did my emotions have to drive my magic?

I gritted my teeth and held my breath. Regardless of how I felt, I needed to get through to him. Getting him off the floor would be a good start.

I rose to my feet and held out my hands. Derrick looked up at me with heavy eyes before glancing at the knife on the rug.

"Leave it," I gently ordered. "You are safe with me."

His face softened but he did not smile. His hands, tight and dry like he had spent hours scrubbing them raw, wrapped around mine and I pulled him off the floor.

His heartbeat pulsed in his wrist—a sign of life.

Derrick was getting better, but he needed to rest. "We need to get you to bed."

His thumbs ran over the backs of my hands. "Does that mean you are staying?"

It was a question, not a demand. Even still, the obligation of a Duke's mistress weighed on my chest.

But I chose this. I *chose* this.

As my answer, I stood on my toes and unclasped his cape from his left shoulder. Then his right.

I had already been with Derrick once. I could do it again if it meant Riyan got to walk the earth again, if Fraleigh could be free, if Brietta got her reformation…

The Hyton Blue cape fluttered down, pooling at his ankles. I held in a breath as I moved to unfasten the collar of his doublet.

He gently grabbed my hands before I could touch him. His shadowed eyes looked into mine. "I know what my new title means. What it means for us."

That he owned me…and my mother. He could do whatever he wanted to either of us, regardless of whatever role I called myself.

He released my hands and unfastened his collar, not taking his eyes off me. "But I expect nothing of you. I could not even *want* that after last time when we were interrupted…" He glanced to the side and let out a breath. "I just do not want to sleep alone. I hate admitting this but...I fear what I will see once I close my eyes."

Riyan had told me something similar about the giants coming back in his nightmares. Derrick may have not slain actual giants, but maybe his giants were different.

Maybe they were even bigger than I could even imagine.

I crawled to the center of the massive bed and sat on my knees. I pulled on the thread at the edge of my sleeve and listened to the rustling of fabric as Derrick undressed.

A weight dropped in the bottom of my stomach. How many times had Mother done the exact same thing? In the exact bed?

But this was different. We were just sleeping—nothing like the Darkest Night.

My mind quieted when Derrick pulled the curtains of the canopy closed, casting us in complete darkness. The mattress shifting with his weight and the sound of his breath were the only evidence that he was even there.

I slipped under the blankets. He wrapped his arm around my waist and linen brushed against linen as my nightclothes rustled against his. He laid his cheek against my head and let out a low, slow breath.

I had left my Nordingaard crystal in my room, not wanting to risk Derrick finding it in case we had gotten...close with one another. Still, even though my reliable trinket was no longer on my skin, my heartbeat slowed down and my mind stopped spinning.

Derrick and I had clung to each other through sheets of parchment for seven years, what made sheets of a bed any different?

The notes of a harp brightened the darkness. The door into Derrick's mind was wide open.

My eyelashes fluttered down as I followed each vibration of the magical harp strings like they were each a small tether. The vibrations wrapped around me and pulled me into Derrick's mind.

I opened my eyes to rolling fluffy clouds as far as the eye could see. Over my shoulder was a tall castle made of ink and paper with bright red turrets and blue banners, like it had been lifted straight out of a faerie book.

The drawbridge over the inky moat lowered into the clouds. Derrick was on the other side, standing in front of the massive castle doors.

That castle was not mere decoration. Whatever was past those doors had to be the inner workings of Derrick's mind.

I had to get inside to issue my command to free Fraleigh.

I crossed the bridge—it wrinkled like paper with every step—until I stood in front of Derrick on the castle stairs.

Well, not Derrick, but Derrick's inner self. He wore simple black from collar to toe, his curls were loose, and flecks of stardust glittered on his cheeks and forehead.

He was not Alastar XII, he was…

"Hello, Midnight." I glanced at the sweeping iron chains fortifying the castle doors.

He crossed his arms. "No! I have to keep the monster in."

The monster?

Suddenly he grabbed my face. "Your radiant light is so rare and devine, what shall I do if the stars never align?"

I searched his face for an answer as he squished my cheeks. What was he talking about?

His eyes shone with urgency. "A midnight sky is bleak, but your light can shine, though what if our two stars never align?'

He was little more than a faerie speaking in riddles, one who lived in his own world.

But…Derrick's mind *was* his own world.

This was the type of reality Brietta could bend with her poetry, or Annalisa with her paint. I only thrived in a reality that was logical and tangible, with a grip on the fabric of simple truths.

Although…maybe I did not need a paintbrush or a pen to work magic here.

I pinched the air and pulled down—a beautiful silver needle appeared between my fingers. With a wave of my hand, a glowing white thread appeared in the eye. The thread trailed into the tumbling fluff of the clouds farther than I could see. It never ended.

A crackling noise shook the air. Midnight jumped and turned toward the castle. A crack zig-zagged out of the doors and crept toward us like a bolt of lighting, cutting through the clouds as if they were stone.

"Oh no!" he cried. "The monster is coming!"

The crack raced for me and I dropped to my knees out of instinct. I gripped the cloud beneath me like a sponge and drove my needle through right as the crack reached my hand. The damage stopped.

I quickly stitched the cloud back together, weaving the thread of infinity until the foundation of the castle was completely repaired.

My fingers released the needle and it disappeared. Midnight helped me to my feet with a smile. "I wish I could let you in—all the way in." He glanced toward the chained doors. "I just have to keep you safe from the monster."

I pinched my magical silver needle. I could slay any monster if I got access to Derrick's mind, but frightened Midnight would have to open the doors.

Maybe I could somehow make Midnight less frightened of the monster.

What if I healed a fresh wound in his mind?

I wrapped the tail of the thread around my finger until it formed a loose coil. Then another, and another, until I crafted a head of curls bleached by thousands of sunrises. I sent the thread soaring through the air, weaving a dress that smelled of lavender and powder, then clear eyes that saw a bright future, and finally hands that had planted the seed of a new world.

The luminescent outline of Freya Hyton stood on top of the mended fracture in the clouds. She opened her arms to her son. "I love you too, Midnight."

His eyes glistened brighter than his cheeks as he wrapped his arms around his mother. "I love you, Mama. Goodbye."

I glanced over my shoulder—one of the chains over the doors had dissolved into dust.

I smiled, but I was fading. Making an illusion of Freya had exhausted my magic and I had no energy to loosen the remaining chains.

I floated out of the dream as easily as I had entered it and opened my eyes to the dark nest of the Duke's bed.

Derrick was vulnerable and broken, but as his breath slowed against my hair and his heart thumped steadily against my back, I let myself smile.

I still had a castle to invade and a monster to slay before I secured Riyan's freedom, but at least Derrick would spend one night in a dream.

Chapter Thirty
Viper's Venom

I ran my fingertips along the spines of the books, not even knowing what I was looking for.

Brietta wanted to read as many books as possible to look for any historical accounts that contradicted what Ashmore had fed us. She and Annalisa were holed up in the main library, but they sent me to the conservatory to investigate. Annalisa had said the conservatory was where the Hytons put all the books they did not care about preserving and maybe I would find a hidden treasure.

I doubted any treasure was in the conservatory, but I needed something to do until nightfall. I had needles under my skin as I fought the urge to try to access Derrick's mind again, but I had to wait for him to fall asleep for the best chance.

I had to slay the monster of Midnight's nightmares if I had any hope of getting control of Derrick's mind.

I scanned the spines for anything remotely interesting when a sad little pull tugged on my heart. I had hidden behind that same bookshelf on Riyan and I's wedding night.

What would our eight days together have been like had I not wasted that first night being afraid of him? He might have ended the lives of countless men, but he would have never hurt me.

I swallowed my guilt and looked around. Mother had helped me out of my Presentation dress that night but we abandoned it since Riyan's blood had stained it during the marriage ceremony. Where did it even go? A few ambitious maids had probably taken the dress and picked all the pearls off.

What a fortuitous treasure for them—those pearls were the last of the House of Ravenwood's wealth. I hoped they at least bought some good bread with their find.

A loud clipping noise echoed through the room followed by the rustle of leaves. Who else was in the conservatory?

I silently peered around the bookshelf. Mother stood at the edge of the curved line of plant boxes in front of the large sunny windows. She had her back to me, fussing with the sharp leaves of some plant.

I did not want to face my mother after stepping into her old role. I would rather just live my days parallel with hers until the full moon.

"You knew I was going to find you eventually." Mother said, not even turning around. "Are you brave enough to speak with me yet?"

Damn it, Mother!

Reluctantly, I stepped out from behind the bookshelf. The invisible pull of a lifetime as an obedient daughter guided my footsteps over to the plants.

I had almost forgotten what my mother looked like without her dark, seductive makeup. She wore her hair swept up and held in place with a silver comb. Her sleeves were rolled above her elbows and her black bodice was embroidered with red poisonous mushrooms.

"*Not poisonous,*" her gentle scold echoed in my memory. "*Harmless if left alone.*"

I stood next to her, eyeing the sweat that beaded on her temples and the flush of her cheeks from working in the sunlight.

She held her shears at the base of a green leaf. "We have much to talk about."

Clip.

Mother held the severed leaf out to me. "Here."

I wrinkled my nose but cautiously wrapped my fingers around the turgid leaf. The skin of the leaf was smooth like leather, but the inside was squishy like flesh. The severed edge wept with a clear nectar that smelled sweet and somehow familiar.

Mother clipped another leaf and placed it in her wicker basket. "Selene succulent. But I assume you have a burning curiosity for the more powerful plants?"

Not really. I never gave much thought to herbalism, but I was never foolish enough to reject information. "Knowing one's enemy is better than being in the dark."

She looked at me over her shoulder. "The dark is the best place to be when your enemies shine in the light."

My eyes darted from the leaves in her basket to her wicked smile. How had I never seen it before?

"You are the Viper," I said. "*You* made all the potions."

Her mouth formed a fine line. "Like I said…we do what we can to survive."

She walked a few paces until she stood in front of a plant with heart-shaped leaves with thick stems. I followed her, eyeing the beautiful fuchsia flowers that grew in small clusters at the top.

"For example," Mother tapped on one of the shining leaves with the tip of her shears. "When the Duchess came to me needing to make an heir, I offered her a mixture from the milk of the Venus heart. That secret granted me access to the Hytons' inner circle…but I never thought my little potion would create a high demand."

My stomach twisted into a knot—she invented Cupid's Blood. The hazy memory, the blood-speckled thighs, and the violet sickness all came from her hands. *She* ruined my chances at being Duchess. *She* had a hand in the invasion of my body. My own damn mother.

My nails bit into the leaf. "Then you could have made it wrong. You could have made it less effective."

"I could have. Once." The wicker handle of the basket crinkled in her grip as she looked at the pink flowers. "If I made the poison, I controlled what was in it. I knew the smell. The taste. The way it changed the way wine sloshes around the goblet. That knowledge was *power*. Your father never faced the axe for high treason because Anders needed me."

What she had done was disgusting…but I was not sure if I could blame her. Her wrists were bound the moment my father inked that agreement with Duke Hyton. Crafting potions might have been the only back door of that horrible deal.

Ravenwoods survive, she had always told me. Was that not all she had done?

Was that not all *I* had done?

I loosened my grip. "So that is why you were the Duke's mistress. It was just a cover for potion making."

A forlorn smile grew on her face as she eyed the pink petals. "No, though Anders did believe having the Viper in his bed made the outside world much less frightening."

I nearly retched.

She lifted one of the leaves of the Venus heart. "Get a closer look, these little ones like to hide in the shade."

I leaned over and spied a small plant with jagged, spiked leaves and black flowers like fangs shooting out of its bulbous top.

"Thornebow thistle," Mother said in a dark voice. "The nectar from this creates the deadliest poison known to man. Normally people poison their victims over time, little by little. Once there is enough poison in the body, the victim's blood turns black, the muscles spasm out of control, and they die within minutes."

My hand crawled to the side of my bodice, right over where my wound had been. My eyes danced from thistle to thistle as my blood ran cold.

That was what had poisoned me on Nordingaard.

But how? Erik and Endre certainly would not have poisoned me, Ganora would not have worked with anything like poison with how much power she wielded, and Daigen needed me and would have never risked my life.

So where had it come from? Who could have even gotten the Thornebow thistle into my body while I was sitting on Riyan's shoulder more than ten feet in the air?

And that dangerous little plant was just sitting in the middle of the palace conservatory where *anyone* could have access to it.

My mouth was almost too dry to speak. "Why grow it at all? If you destroy it, it cannot poison anyone."

"A viper needs her venom." She picked up her basket. "But now that you mention it, being the Duke's mistress was an excellent cover for my potion making. No one thinks a whore can be good at anything."

She turned and walked toward the bookshelves. Mother was being odd, as usual, but maybe she could help me on my original quest for knowledge. "I am looking for a book for Brietta—something enlightening."

Mother reached up and grabbed a blue book that read "*Secrets of Alastar the Wise*" on the spine. "How about this one?"

She tugged on the book and a loud click rang in my ears. Mother pushed the bookcase open like a door. An earthy smell wafted out of the dark space behind the bookcase.

She stepped through the narrow opening and I followed her. Inside was a small room lit only by a narrow window with stained glass panes of purple thistles. Bunches of dried herbs hung upside-down from the ceiling. Glass tinctures lined the wooden shelves on the walls.

Mother set her basket on a work table and laid one of the leaves in front of her. She used a small rolling pin to flatten the succulent leaf and squeeze the gooey nectar out.

"Close the door, Serafina," she grunted as she rolled.

I gently pushed the bookcase closed. The herb-filled room darkened but felt somehow safer.

Mother's arms shook as she rolled the pin. "Did Freya tell you why Anders sent all the sons of Bloodstone and Ravenwood to fight the giants seven years ago?"

I swallowed. "To show the Dukedom he was in control."

"No." Mother chuckled darkly as she scooped up the nectar and put it in a mortar. "Because there was a certain Bloodstone son he wanted dead."

Riyan was fifteen during that battle. Anders only sent a dozen soldiers to fight the giants while thousands of Bloodstone and Ravenwood boys died.

I knew Anders would have done anything to ensure his line of succession did not have competition, but I never thought he would have massacred thousands of his own people—thousands of *children*.

Mother held out her hand and I shakily gave her the leaf.

"He wanted to get rid of the Hyton heir that badly?" I asked.

She rolled the life out of the new leaf. "Ever since he was born. Nikkolas kept him safe in Bloodstone Fortress, then Ragnar kept him under lock-and-key at the military academy. The only way Anders could get him out of the academy was to send him to war, something his General could not refuse. Anders did not want his brother to suspect that he wanted his son dead, so *all* the Bloodstone and Ravenwood sons went up the mountain for plausible deniability."

Her voice dropped and became more hollow than the husk of the leaf. "It was a failed assassination attempt that murdered my boys."

My mouth went dry. I could not shatter her by telling her that her precious sons were alive and…I had failed to turn them back into men.

But why was Mother telling me all this? Why was she confessing…?

My heart stopped. My voice was soft as a suspicion turned into a question. "Anders did not fall off his balcony, did he?"

Mother's face revealed nothing as she scooped the nectar into the mortar again. "He had pushed me for so many years, but when I saw him poison you…it was time I finally pushed back."

I pictured it clearly in my mind—terrified Hyton Blue eyes with starry robes rippling in the night as Mother shoved Anders over the balcony railing.

And that meant she killed Freya too.

My throat tightened. "Freya did not deserve—!"

"Freya knew." She did not even look up. "After I undressed you on Selection Night, I met with her in secret and told her our plan. Anders would die before the next full moon. All the blood bonds would be sealed so the line of succession would be secure—"

"Our plan? Who are you talking about?"

Mother added a few drops from a tincture into the mortar. "Ragnar's allegiance is to his *House.* He was not going to let his brother destroy it."

The irony of the wielder of Traitor's Bane plotting to murder his Duke was chilling, but Anders sent Riyan to die. I would not have acted any differently if someone tried to hurt *my* son.

My hands crept over my bodice and rested over my lower abdomen. Without a blood bond, would I ever have a son? My chest ached at the thought of never having children, but without Riyan—

Mother's hands suddenly spasmed and her stirring stick clattered the floor. Her eyes widened as she grabbed her wrist. "Oh…damn my old age!"

I rolled my eyes. Mother had not even reached fifty years. Why was she being so dramatic?

"Here," I said as I picked up the stick.

She sheepishly looked down and massaged her wrist. "Could you help your geriatric mother? The mixture just needs to stir for another five minutes."

I was already taking up her old role as the Duke's mistress, did she want me to replace her as the Viper too?

I might have been a sorceress, but Mother had mastered the real magic of being pathetic enough to manipulate me. I began slowly stirring the clear, syrupy potion in the mortar.

Before I could ask what the potion even was, Mother cleared her throat. "I did not regale my sordid history for mere entertainment. I-I made a promise, and I need you to help me keep it."

I paused my stirring. I had never heard Mother's voice break before.

I looked over my shoulder into her shining emerald eyes. The tip of her nose was pink—she was barely holding back tears. "Freya agreed to let us usher in a new world without her so long as I kept Derrick safe."

I held my breath. Freya…gave her life for her dream of liberation?

Mother stepped forward until she was close enough to grip the edge of the work table. "I know I have asked so much of you, but if you do nothing else in life, protect that sweet boy. I owe Freya. We owe Freya for what she sacrificed."

I came to the palace to save Riyan's life. I only took on Brietta's dream of reformation because I thought it would free Fraleigh, but now Mother was asking me to shoulder yet another burden? For *Freya?*

I swallowed the question I nearly asked. Mother was normally as affectionate as a table knife and just as sentimental as one. I had never seen her show so much emotion for anyone outside our House.

The way she sobbed at the funeral was not just an act put on for Anders. Maybe my mother knew what real love was after all.

I looked back down at the potion and slowly dragged the stirring stick along the edge of the mortar. "At least you had someone other than Father."

She grabbed my wrist and forced me to face her. Her eyes were suddenly hard. "Serafina Helia, do not speak ill of him."

I yanked my arm out of her trembling grip. "He sold you."

"Because I *asked* him to. He hated it, but Ravenwood was doomed and you could not marry Derrick for another seven years—"

"But that was not fair!"

"None of this is fair!" Her voice echoed around the small potion room. "It was not fair that Freya and I could not be together after Ashmore. Nor was it fair that I could easily have boys while she choked down Cupid's Blood *desperate* for a son. Or that I had your father while she was stuck with Anders."

I folded my arms and stepped back. "Father is no prize. You have no idea how much that blood bond manipulated you—"

"Fuck the blood bond." She hardened back into the woman I knew, but a burning passion flared behind her eyes. "I love your father because he is a *good man.*"

She made no sense. "How can you pretend to love Father when you just said all that about Freya?"

Her voice softened, but her brow stayed hard. "Love is not a token that you pass from one person to another. It does not abide by the laws of time. Or logical sense. Or reality."

She let out a breath. "It took time…but he was *so* good to me and to your brothers…" She looked up at me and smiled. "Erik was made from duty. Endre was made…well, because it was fun. But *you,* our Little Ember, were made from love."

The herb-scented air somehow felt heavier on my shoulders. Mother's confessions made little sense. How could she have affectionate feelings for

Freya and Father at one time? How could she still respect him after he lost control of the Baronage of Ravenwood?

How could she love him just because he was a good man?

More conflicting questions screamed through my mind, but instead of letting them out, I tightened my grip on my arms and looked at my shoes. "The potion is stirred enough."

Mother let out a tense breath and replaced me at the work table. She reached into a small pewter casket and scooped out a tiny spoonful of fine white powder. She sprinkled the powder into the mortar and combined it with the nectar inside.

I eyed the pewter casket. "What is that?"

"Crushed *lethe* mushrooms." She transferred the potion into a tiny glass vial. "Or as it is known at parties, faerie dust."

I examined the small mound of white powder inside the casket. The familiar musty smell crept into my nose and I stepped away.

Mother put a stopper on the glass vial and handed it to me. "Here, a sleeping draught for Derrick. Added a little faerie dust for pleasant dreams."

The jar felt cold in my fingers. "He is wary of potions, you know."

"He is familiar with my sleeping potions." She let out a long breath but kept her mouth tight. "They are not exactly rare…Anders dosed all the wine he gave you and Sir Bloodstone. He wanted to give his son at least a couple nights of solace that you would be untouched."

My eyes dropped to the clear potion. *That* was why the succulent leaf smelled familiar. I thought it was mere exhaustion when I passed out after the wedding night, or when Riyan collapsed on the cobblestones after drinking three barrels of wine, but no. It was poison *again.*

How many fucking times had I been poisoned? How much damage had the Viper truly done not just to me, but to everyone else in the palace?

"Did you say you needed a book for Her Excellency?" Mother asked.

The oddness of Brietta being referred to by her new title pulled me out of my thoughts. "Yes, something interesting. Preferably something written by a woman…if that is even possible."

Mother smiled. "I will be right back."

She pushed the back of the bookshelf and slipped into the conservatory.

Light from the sunny conservatory filled the potion room, exposing the secrets like upturning a bowl and finding a worm underneath.

I rolled the vial of sleeping draught in my fingers. Giving Derrick a sleeping draught to help him cope with his new role could be a merciful gift.

Was it not better to let someone live in a dream instead of facing the horrors of life? It was kind, it was…

My white flame lit up my chest, scorching every bit of reasoning I had behind that little glass vial.

No. *Every* poisoning was a violation. My body had been invaded so many times that I could never do it to someone else. Especially not Derrick.

Mother wanted me to keep Derrick safe? Fine. I would make sure no one ever poisoned him again.

Even her.

I smashed the vial on the stone floor and stormed to the work table. I held the tin of faerie dust in my hands, sending out my magic and finding only a few twinkles of tears that had been inside the living mushrooms. The dust sparkled like a tiny hill of snow. So beautiful. So pristine.

And then I lit it all on fire.

Chapter Thirty One
God of Music

My mother was a more sentimental creature than I ever gave her credit for.

Brietta was delighted when I handed her Freya's diary, a treasure that my mother had kept hidden away. She said she would pore over it after she convinced Derrick to sit for his coronation portrait.

Since I had to wait for Derrick to return from his portrait sitting, I had changed into my nightgown early and lounged on a couch in the Duke's chambers. I stitched a leaf pattern into the cuffs of one of his shirts, finally having some peace at the end of the day.

Just as I was finishing off a stitch, a couple of sharp taps rang through the glass behind me. I looked over my shoulder and spied a large black blur on the other side of the stained glass doors.

One of my brothers was on the balcony.

I set down my embroidery hoop and rushed to the doors. I pushed the doors open and my heart sank.

No pink beak—it was Endre. Erik was still missing and there was no parchment on Endre's leg. Evereon must have decided further communication was not worth the risk.

A decision made much too late.

"Have you seen Erik?" I whispered.

Endre shook his head and flapped his wings to perch on the balcony railing—*exactly* where our mother had sent Anders Hyton to his death.

My breath caught in my throat as I stood between the doors, too haunted by Mother's confession of murder to step onto the balcony's surface.

"A certain Ravenwood sure was naughty, but at least she lived up to the House reputation."

I turned to the voice at my left—Daigen leaned on the edge of the balcony with a dark cloak hanging around his shoulders, seemingly having appeared out of thin air.

I wanted to bite back at him for slinking around the palace yet doing nothing to help me, but I could not find anger for him. Not when he and I were just trying to save someone who had saved us.

I let out a breath and forced myself to look at him. "Fraleigh still does not want you to save her. I hope she can forgive you once we succeed."

Daigen's brow softened slightly, but his mouth formed a thin line and he looked away. "She has not spoken to me since the day your Riyan was born. She should have known better than to think cursing me and shunning me for twenty-two years would stop the will of the Man of the Mountain. You were getting the gift of sorcery whether she liked it or not."

After witnessing the purity of their love for one another, the continued antagonism between Fraleigh and Daigen made little sense. What else was happening that Daigen refused to tell me?

If only I could *ask.*

I would just have to mask a question as an observation. "I saw Rosaline around the palace. How strange to see her away from Fraleigh."

Daigen chuckled. "Ah, so you realized that there are more cogs in my machination than just you and I." He lifted himself off the balcony's edge and faced me fully. "Never mind about Rosaline. Seems like you have enough to…handle as is."

His gaze flicked into the bedroom.

My nails pinched my arms as his barb lodged under my skin. "I have less than two weeks to get into Derrick's mind and force him to release Fraleigh. I thought you of all people would understand the need to do *anything* to help someone you lost."

"Oh, I understand." Daigen flashed a smile that was anything but friendly. "In fact, I am only here to give you some…validation. Following your heart's desire has worked, hasn't it?

I blinked in disbelief. The last thing I ever thought Daigen would give me was validation.

Daigen turned to Endre. "Your parents did not praise you often did they?"

Endre shook his head.

Daigen muttered something in Old Tongue and then turned back to me. "You know what you have to do?"

I gripped my arms. "I slay the monster in Derrick's mind, then I get him to release the collar."

A satisfied smile crawled up his lips. "Good, keep getting close to him."

He leaned against the railing and cocked an eyebrow. "Your other bird-brother is fine, by the way. Just focus on the new Alastar." He waved his hand toward the darkened bedchamber. "The answers are all around you, *Litlnadr.*"

He casually leaned back over the railing, his dark cloak enveloping him so he disappeared into the night. Endre flew off his perch and followed him.

The faint sound of footsteps pounding toward the doorway hit my ears. I stepped inside and locked the balcony doors just as Derrick burst into the room, the crown of Lycaster on his head and his Hyton Blue cape flying behind him.

I quickly stepped away from the doors. "How was your portrait sitting?"

His mouth hardened into a fine line as he removed his crown. "Never happened."

He flung the crown on a nearby table before unclasping his cape.

I eyed him with suspicion as he undressed. "But Derrick, you have to sit for your coronation portrait!"

He released his cape and started to unbutton his doublet. "That is what Brietta said. She argued with me for *two hours*."

Derrick threw off his doublet and crossed over to the northern side of the room.

"I looked too much like *him*." He stopped in front of the wall and ran his fingers through the roots of his hair. "Fuck, I need to cool down."

Derrick twisted an iron sconce on the wall and a panel opened. He pulled off his linen shirt as he crossed the doorway into the darkness.

No…it was not just darkness. The cerulean glow emitting from the chamber was too familiar.

Splash.

Curiosity overtook me and I stepped into the darkened chamber. My bare feet met tile. My eyes adjusted to the low light and then they widened—the secret chamber held nothing but a rectangular pool. The subtle glow came from rocks that were submerged beneath the water and embedded into the pool's walls. No…not rocks, Nordingaard crystals.

Derrick emerged from the surface of the water and rested on the side of the pool. "This is the one good part of having to stay in this awful bedchamber. Incredible, right?"

Incredible was not the word I would have chosen for a secret trove of dozens of illegal crystals. I could lose my head just for owning one, but the Hytons bathed in them.

Derrick dragged his wet curls out of his face. "This pool has water from the legendary healing spring on Nordingaard. Not sure if it actually does any healing, but it stops me from wanting to light something on fire."

I held my breath. Derrick was swimming in thousands of the Man of the Mountain's tears. If the healing spring had taken me into Riyan's worst memories before I even had the gift of sorcery, all that magic could certainly break down the doors of a paper castle.

Daigen was right again. The answers were *indeed* all around me.

I stepped toward the edge of the pool. "How interesting…mind if I join?"

Derrick's eyebrows furrowed. "Serafina, you cannot swim."

I sat down at the edge and eased my feet in. The magic tingled around my skin as I dipped my legs into the glowing water.

I curled my fingers around the stone edge of the pool. I would not drown, my magic would protect me…hopefully. I could at least see the bottom of the pool, but that did not mean my toes would touch.

My eyes found Derrick's discarded pants and shoes in the corner of the room but I quickly glanced away.

I needed to be in the water with him, skin to skin, just as I had been with Riyan in the real healing spring.

I pulled off my nightgown and tossed it in the corner of the room. I had already seen him nude and he had seen me. We were just humans in bodies.

This was *nothing* like the Darkest Night.

Just as I was about to shove myself off the edge, Derrick held out his hand. "Here, hold onto me."

I banished my reservations and took Derrick's hands as he eased me into the water. Magic swirled around my belly and then my chest as I dipped into the pool. Derrick locked his arms around my waist and pulled me in so my back was securely against his chest. My legs kicked limply in the water, but Derrick was tall enough to stand on the bottom of the pool. He was still too thin, but he had enough muscle in his arms and chest that I was not afraid of him collapsing again.

I let out a breath. My face was above the water. I was fine.

"Just imagine if we could relax like this all the time." Derrick sighed.

I lifted an eyebrow. "Does anyone get to relax all the time?"

"Fraleigh does." He chuckled. "Oh, to be the Great Sorceress, living in a palace of gold with every need provided for and only being called to work once a year. She surely got the better end of her arrangement with us."

Arrangement? Is *that* what he thought Fraleigh's forced servitude was?

I tried to keep my voice pleasantly inquisitive instead of disgusted. "What do you mean?"

One of Derrick's fingers swirled around a strand of my hair in the water. "We protect her, she protects us. You can imagine what the other kingdoms and empires would try to get their hands on her magic, but they *pay* thousands of marks for the blood bond enchantments instead of stealing the magic for themselves because the entire continent fears her."

I swallowed. It was exactly as Fraleigh had said, but sounded different coming from Derrick's mouth—like spreading balm over a festering wound.

"A good portion of Lycaster's treasury comes from selling those blood bonds—more than you would want to think." His muscles stiffened behind me. "But that is only one side of it. Everyone fearing Fraleigh means we do not have to spend what little money we have on armies or weapons of siege."

Did Derrick just admit the entire Lycaster economy relied on selling brides to other countries? How much did the Hytons get just from selling off his sisters?

A tremor in Derrick's left arm disturbed the water. "You have seen a map of the continent. The Sudrian empire is ten times our size and it is about to collapse. Rokuhama boasts a thousand ships in its navy and is ready to pick up the pieces the Sudrian rebels leave behind. The o-only thing keeping us out of all that c-conflict and from t-total financial collapse…is Fraleigh."

The weight of his words sank into my chest as his back muscles twitched. His voice broke. "And all s-she has t-to do…is s-sit in her…golden palace."

He was breaking down. I turned and wrapped my arms around him, pressing my cheek in the center of his chest. "Derrick, stop. Stop. I am here."

His chin dropped to the top of my head. His jaw trembled. His throat vibrated against my forehead, like his words were stuck and fighting to get out. "I…fuck…I am s-so….fuck!" His hold on me tightened. "I am fucking scared! I am s-scared and weak a-and…!"

He started to shake. I needed to calm him down, but using my magic would make the crystals glow.

"Close your eyes," I whispered. "Just close your eyes and breathe."

As soon as his face was buried in my hair, I sent out a wave of magic, waking up the thousands of tears in the pool.

The tears thrummed with power as I sent them swirling into Derrick's skin, each one a kiss of calmness. He let out a shaking breath over my forehead and the harp music sang in my mind again.

I could hear those chains over those paper castle doors slipping down, one by one. Yes, it was working! Just like with Riyan, the magic in the water was healing him.

The invisible doors to Derrick's mind slowly creaked open as harp music flooded out of the entrance. The power of the magic around me heated up the water as my magic pushed me toward Derrick's mind. I traveled down the tether my magic created and entered the space between Derrick's mind and mine—the dark gap between worlds.

"Sera?"

I knew that voice.

I looked around the dark chasm as the harp in Derrick's mind played its low melody. I was only ever in that place—that strange in-between— for a blink before entering someone's mind, but I was frozen as I searched for him.

The tiny Serafina who was suspended mid-travel cried out, where Derrick in the pool could not hear her, "Riyan?"

"Sera?" The voice rich as satin got louder. "Sera! I hear you! SERA!"

The vibrations of the harp swelled until they twisted themselves into a glowing rope in the dark chasm.

Then a horrible voice, layered like eleven men were speaking all at once, filled the darkness. *"You are mine, sorceress."*

Before I could scream for Riyan, the rope wrapped around my throat and yanked me through Derrick's open door.

And darkness suddenly became flame.

A crackling hearth appeared in the forefront of the memory. A large portrait of Alastar the Conqueror wearing his steel armor and brandishing his spear hung above the mantle.

The fire from the hearth spread throughout the memory, lighting up portraits and crossed swords on the walls and a large oak desk.

I must have been in the Duke's study…but what brought me here? The voice that yanked me into the memory was not Riyan's, nor was it Derrick's, but I somehow still recognized it.

Was it the monster?

I looked around, trying to find a monster, but instead I found a young Derrick—maybe nine or ten years old—sitting in an overly large armchair in front of the fire.

His cheeks were splattered with freckles as he sheepishly looked at the floor. A wreath of twisted ivy circled his head and a crudely-made lyre sat in his hands.

He looked just like the God of Music from the faerie stories. The God of Music was a little imp, but nothing if not romantic.

Anders stormed into the study. Derrick flinched as Anders ripped the lyre and wreath of ivy away and flung the costume into the fire. Sorrow gleamed in Derrick's eyes as the flames ate his trinkets.

Anders faced his son. "I swear, had your Uncle Ragnar caught you prancing around the garden like a little girl—"

Derrick looked up. "We were just playing, Father."

"Playing?" Anders roared. "You are on the cusp of manhood! No more playing with your sisters."

Sadness filled Derrick's eyes, but he nodded.

"Your mother made you weak, boy." Anders crossed to a wooden cabinet and pulled out a glass bottle of spirits. "She filled your head with lies about love and all that Midnight nonsense."

Derrick looked down at his hands. "Mama does not lie to me."

"Of course she does, all women do."

Despite me not having a corporeal form, I still burned with guilt.

Anders poured two goblets of spirits and handed Derrick a glass. Derrick looked down at the cup like it was filled with sewage.

"Drink it," Anders ordered. He knocked back his own cup and drained it in one gulp.

I knew I could not change what was happening, but I still wanted to yank that goblet out of that poor child's hands.

Derrick tentatively put the cup to his lips and wrinkled his nose at the strength of the drink inside. He grimaced as he swallowed. "It burns!"

"Get used to it." Anders poured himself another cup. "You are in for a lonely life, boy, and you will find that your only friends come in bottles."

Derrick looked into his cup. "My…sisters are my friends."

"And in a few years, you will never see your sisters again." Anders swirled his goblet. "They will be off in neighboring kingdoms manipulating their own men soon enough."

Derrick's brows furrowed. "My…s-sisters w-would not—"

Anders smacked Derrick on the side of his face so hard that he nearly knocked him out of his chair.

If Anders Hyton were not already dead, I would have killed him.

A red handprint burned on Derrick's cheek and ear. His eyes brimmed with tears and his mouth was frozen in shock.

Anders leaned over him, his face purple with rage. "What did I tell you about that damn stutter? You cannot be weak, *ever,* do you understand?"

Derrick blinked out a tear and nodded as his body trembled.

I wanted to hold him. He was just a boy!

"Oh, do not even cry," Anders growled. "Your grandfather once beat me with a leather strap so hard I could not use a chair for *three days.* Do you know why?"

Derrick shook his head.

Anders pointed to the portrait of Alastar the Conqueror. "Because we are always compared to him. We cannot show weakness or lack of discipline *ever.* If we are weak, they will destroy us."

"Who?" Derrick squeaked.

Anders gripped the arms of Derrick's chair. "Everyone. You are going to be the Duke of Lycaster. You will not have friends or anyone you can trust. Everyone will try to gain power over you, to use you for their own motives, and you need to know this now…"

He leaned in so his furious Hyton Blue eyes were right in front of his son's crying ones. "Conquer or die. No weakness."

Though I wanted to stay with frightened Derrick, the portrait of Alastar the Conqueror pulled my attention away. I stared at his painted Hyton Blue eyes as he stared back at me.

"*You are mine, sorceress.*"

The strange voice was back. An invisible force coiled around my consciousness and squeezed like a vise grip.

I was not alone in the memory.

I quickly released my hold over my magic. The study disappeared into a sea of darkness as I escaped Derrick's mind.

My mind settled back into my body. Water lapped at my shoulder blades as I opened my eyes to Derrick's collarbone. He was still, but his chest slowly rose and fell.

Even if he had fallen asleep, his arms stayed locked around me like a vault, keeping my head above the surface of the water.

I clenched my teeth. I wanted to dig up Anders Hyton and burn his corpse for what he had done to poor Derrick, but I had to focus on the monster in his mind.

Whatever was tormenting Derrick presented itself through Alastar the Conqueror's portrait, but the Conqueror was long-dead.

But I had to get Derrick calm and stable before I could investigate further.

Magic pulsed around my fingers and his blood vessels lit up at my command: "*Derrick, wake up.*"

He inhaled sharply and lifted his face from the top of my head. His heart thudded against my chest and he crushed me against him.

"Serafina!" he gasped. "I…I have no idea what happened. Oh…you could have drowned!"

I shook my head. "I am all right. But you need to go to bed."

Derrick pulled me out of the pool and we retreated into the bedchamber. He put on his night clothes as I combed my hair at the dressing table. After I had tied off my braid, I turned to find Derrick gripping the back of a chair and staring out the stained glass windows into the night.

His voice was hollow. "You should never see me like that, no one should."

I turned on my cushioned stool to face him. "Derrick, with everything you have been through—"

"That does not matter." He closed his eyes and hissed out a breath. "I c-cannot be weak or…"

He slammed his fist against the back of the chair as soon as his sentence failed.

The memory of his father's harsh words screamed in my mind. I flew across the room and wrapped my hands around his. "You do not have to finish, I understand you. You do not have to—"

"Yes…I…do," he gritted out.

After a few thudding heartbeats, I rested my forehead against his arm. I had to get him calm. "Everything will be better in the morning, we can just…go to bed."

Derrick ran a hand through the roots of his hair. "I usually will not find sleep after I…get like this, unless I have a sleeping draught."

Shit! I should have kept the sleeping potion Mother made. Now I had nothing to get him to sleep.

Nothing except magic.

I chewed on my tongue. My magic was not an invasion, it was an acceptance of an invitation. I was just trying to get Derrick to sleep…but no one was more vulnerable than when they were sleeping.

How convenient for a little serpent like me.

I swallowed. "Do you trust me to get you to sleep?"

He raised his face to meet my eyes and nodded.

I held my breath and pulled him into bed. Bitterness coated the back of my throat, but I glanced at the panel in the northern wall where the shining pool was hiding. Riyan was looking for me, even in the place West of the Moon and East of the Sun.

And if I wanted to ever hear Riyan's voice again, I needed to slay the monster that tormented Midnight.

My hips rested on the mattress as my hand softly stroked Derrick's hair. His eyes fluttered closed as I sent bits of magic through my fingertips, giving him peace and weaving him a dream.

The light between his eyes sparkled and the castle doors swung wide open.

I held my breath and dove into Derrick's mind.

Chapter Thirty Two
Alastar

With a flash of white light from my magic, I weaved into the deepest recesses of Derrick's mind.

My feet hit solid ground—I had feet? I looked down at my hands and smiled. My magic must have been getting stronger if I could create a body to walk through memories.

I stood in the middle of what looked similar to the palace ballroom. The black and white tile of the dance floor stretched all the way to the circular curves of the walls.

I looked up. The ceiling of painted bulls was gone and a dome of shimmering stars in a black sky stood in its place.

Arms wrapped around me and pulled me into a tall chest. Even Derrick's inner self smelled like oak and vanilla.

Now was my chance. I pushed away from him and looked into his eyes. "Midnight, you have to free Fraleigh. Summon her and say the words '*Ipse Dix—*'"

Boom. The floor shook.

Midnight gripped me so tightly I thought he was going to crush me. Damn it! He was not going to listen

Boom. The floor shook again, sending cracks through the perfect black and white tile. I jumped—the pressure was like the impact of a boulder crashing right under my toes.

The monster was trying to escape beneath us.

Midnight scooped me up in his arms and ran for a door that had just appeared on the other side of the ballroom.

BOOM.

He flung the door open. "Hide in here!"

As soon as he set me on my feet and slammed the door closed, darkness fell over me like a blanket. Wait…it was an actual blanket.

I sat up in a bed—*my* bed. I was tightly tucked into the sheets and my quilt weighed on my legs. Green wallpaper patterned with willow leaves surrounded me. He had shoved me into an exact replica of my bedroom.

With a grunt, I shoved the heavy blankets off my legs and headed for the door. I had to slay the monster.

I wrapped my hand around the iron handle only to find the door was locked. I rolled my eyes and pinched the air to retrieve my magic silver needle. I stuck the tip of the needle into the keyhole and wiggled the lock open.

The door creaked open and I stepped into darkness. My needle had disappeared. The faint sound of cheering echoed behind me.

I turned around, finding an archway lit up with sunlight at the end of a long hallway. Derrick stood in the shadow of the arch, twirling the hilt of a narrow dueling sword in his hand. He looked no older than eighteen and he wore a streamlined version of his black school uniform with a Hyton Blue band around his right arm.

I peered outside the archway—we were in the Hyton arena. A rainbow of colors of the noble Houses lined the upper boxes. Screaming peasants filled the lower rows.

The memory was the Heaston Spring Exhibition.

A loud voice boomed amongst the sand-filled arena floor. "Announcing first in his class, Grigory Orion Thornebow!"

Most jeered and hissed. The cluster of grey-backed nobles cheered and waved the banners of the Thornebow silver fox as Grigory stepped into the sun at the opposite end of the arena. He beamed in the noon light, effortlessly stepping away from the refuse thrown at him, and entered the white inner circle in the center of the sand.

I spotted Anders Hyton wearing the gleaming Lycaster crown. He sat in his throne beneath his Hyton Blue canopy with, not Freya, but my mother at his side.

Anders's brows were furrowed as he watched Grigory deftly swish his sword.

The Alastar trials might have ended, but the implication of the match went far beyond a schoolboy competition. The grandson of the treasonous Baron was facing off against the sole heir to Lycaster in the exact location where most of the heirs had fought and died for their title.

All the eyes of Lycaster were on Derrick. He could *not* lose the first of the endless trials if he was going to prove himself worthy of the name Alastar.

Especially not to a Thornebow.

"Announcing the sole heir to the House of Hyton…"

The cheering swelled.

"…*and* the Dukedom of Lycaster…"

Derrick let out a breath and his brow hardened.

"Lord Alastar Derrick Pervale Hyton!"

He stepped into the sun and the crowd went wild. I followed his footprints in the sand to get a closer look.

As soon as he entered the white inner circle, Derrick and Grigory crossed swords and waited for the duel to begin. From across the arena, Anders leaned on the golden armrests of his throne. Mother held her hand over her heart.

The boys so focused their chests barely rose with their breath, but then Grigory's voice was low enough to slip beneath the roar of the crowd. "I wonder what that sweet twin sister of yours will think when I beat your ass."

Derrick bared his teeth and sliced his sword. *Clink.* Grigory blocked him.

The crowd erupted with screams of delight—their heir had struck first.

The swords flashed in the sunlight as they dueled. Derrick moved with the genteel of a sportsman and had the advantage of height, but

Grigory had a ferocious edge, fighting with the tenacity of someone with everything to lose. He was a desperate boy with his family's honor on the line, a jaded noble son seeking revenge…

…or, some could whisper, a man with the spirit of the Conqueror.

Grigory pushed Derrick to the edge of the white line, nearly throwing him off balance to win the duel.

The entire arena held their breath as Derrick teetered on his heel, Grigory's blade crossed with his over his chest. Grigory hissed out a breath as he pushed his blade further, making Derrick's arms tremble…

"*You cannot be weak, ever!*"

Derrick suddenly pushed back and unlocked his sword from Grigory's force. The crowd thrummed with energy.

I looked around. The monster had spoken again, but I could not find him. My sight locked on Derrick as he escaped…and only because I was an invisible woman in a memory was I close enough to see the unthinkable happen.

Derrick spun around Grigory, catching him off guard…and then hooked his foot around Grigory's ankle.

He knocked Grigory into the sand as he completed his spin. Before Grigory could even blink, Derrick had the tip of his blade over Grigory's heart.

"Duel goes to Lord Hyton!" cried the announcer.

The crowd erupted into applause. Derrick turned and gave the arena a sweeping showman's bow.

Even though I could not affect the memory, I still tried to scream in warning as Grigory rose from the sand with a white-knuckled grip on his hilt.

"You damn cheat!" he shouted.

Derrick turned around right as Grigory sliced his face open.

The ribbon of blood that burst from Derrick's cheek blanketed my vision in crimson. I flailed my arms as I tried to swim through the vast expanse of red.

Maybe I could find a door into another memory.

I pushed with my magic, knocking on all the invisible doors around me…

"You cannot escape me, sorceress."

A claw wrapped around my ankle and pulled. I looked around, but saw nothing but red. How could I slay the monster if I could not even see him?

A blast of magic burst from my fist and the claws released my ankle. A sparkle of light glimmered above me as the door to another memory opened.

I reached toward the door and pulled with my magic, making my escape…

I crashed on a wooden floor and shoved myself up. I stood in the middle of what looked like a boys' dormitory room. No sign of the monster, but I needed to stay aware in case he was lurking beneath the fabric of the memory.

Derrick sat in a wooden chair at a desk, keeping his eyes down. Mother bent at the waist and lovingly applied balm over the fresh stitches on his wounded cheek.

The setting sun peeked through the window panes. It was merely a few hours after the exhibition and Derrick seemed all right, but I held back a wince as my eyes ran down the wound. Grigory had sliced him ear to lip.

The strong aroma of warm herbs filled the air. Mother closed the lid to her balm and dampened the smell only a little.

She gently brought Derrick's chin up so his eyes met hers. "You are not going to have a scar." She placed the round pot of balm in his hand. "Just apply this every morning when you wake up and every night before you go to bed."

Derrick's left cheek twitched slightly as he looked up with doe-eyes at my mother.

"Come on, show me that handsome smile," Mother said with a smile of her own.

He stretched his cheek muscle with a smile—it stopped twitching.

Mother patted him on the shoulder. "You are going to be just fine, sweet boy."

"I doubt that."

I turned away from Derrick to find Anders leaning against a bedpost on the other side of the room.

He glared at his son. "The Thornebow rat is going to your Uncle Ragnar so he can…discipline him. Although I should charge him with high treason for what he did."

Mother looked over her shoulder. "Oh, *Andie,* he is only eighteen. Besides, everyone goes into the Spring Exhibition expecting a few cuts and scrapes—is that not the fun of being a boy?"

Anders narrowed his eyes at Mother. "That is not the issue, *Dolly.*"

Dolly? I wanted to vomit.

He returned his sharp glare to sheepish Derrick. "The issue is that a *Thornebow* spilled your blood and you just laid there in the sand like a little worm. You should have run him through!"

"*No weakness!*" the monster roared.

I jumped and I swiveled my head, looking for the monster, but Derrick stood up and stole my attention.

"You wanted me to just kill a Thornebow to solve all of our problems?" he shouted "That did not work for you the first time!"

Anders launched across the room and his meaty fists gripped Derrick by the collar.

"Anders!" Mother cried as she grabbed Anders by the arm. "Leave him al—!"

Anders shoved my mother so hard she cracked the back of her head against Derrick's bedpost.

"Adalia!" Derrick cried before Anders choked him into silence.

I knelt beside my mother on the floor. She blinked, dazed, as her hand floated to the back of her head. Her fingertips returned stained with blood.

Anders's eyes widened but then narrowed into a glare. "He is *my* son, Adalia. Not yours."

He returned his ire to Derrick, who was red as a berry as his father choked him. "Your weakness will be the death of you—the death of all of us! The Thornebow rat was just the beginning. Soon, everyone will flock to pick you clean like ravens on a corpse. Toughen up, or you are going to face the consequences."

Anders released his grip and Derrick crashed to the floor with a gasp. His watering eyes looked up at my mother, but she did not look at him.

Mother glared with a poisonous malice at Anders as he dragged a silver flask out of his pocket.

I only wished Mother could have pushed back sooner.

"*I am only trying to protect you, sorceress.*"

I whipped around but found nothing but an empty bed. That damn monster was lurking beneath the fabric of the memory, I had to find him.

I turned back around. Derrick sat at his writing desk and stared at a sheet of parchment. His cheek only bore a bright pink line that was shining with fresh medicine. Mother and Anders were gone.

At least a day had passed between memories. I walked to the desk for more clues of where I was, but instead I smiled at the blank parchment. It was the beginning of one of Midnight's letters to Birdie.

Which letter was it? Was he going to tell me about a new song he learned? Or was I about to see him craft a new poem?

Derrick's head turned as two other boys entered the room.

"Damn, Derrick, are you still sulking?" Myles asked.

Gerond elbowed Myles in the ribs. "Careful not to upset the precious heir, lest he call for his father and ruin your life too."

Derrick furrowed his brows. "I d-did not c-call for my…my father…"

Myles and Gerond roared with laughter. Derrick's hand curled into a white-knuckled fist on top of his writing desk and his eyes shined.

"Oh look, the *s-s-stutter* is back!" Myles laughed.

"Is Der-bear going to cry?" Gerond shouted through his laughter. "Are you going to cry and get us sent to the military academy?"

Those pricks!

I wrapped my arms around Derrick's shoulders. He could not feel me, I could not change anything, but…he needed someone.

"*Toughen up,*" the monster growled.

Before I could look for the monster, the quill in Derrick's hand snapped in half. Then, with an underlying growl, he said, "Get out."

Gerond and Myles stopped laughing and their eyes went wide. The boys quickly retreated, slamming the dormitory door shut behind them.

Derrick threw the broken quill aside and yanked open his desk drawer. As soon as a new quill was in his hand, Derrick let out a long breath and melted back into the person I knew.

He dipped the quill in a pot of ink and wrote: "*Dearest Birdie, I won the Spring Exhibition. Life has never been better.*"

My fingers traced the parchment. We had wasted so many years trying to impress one another…what would our lives be like had we just been honest from the beginning?

Suddenly the ink on the parchment morphed into new letters, spelling out the message: "*You will never escape your bargain, sorceress.*"

What bargain?

I turned around, ready to confront the monster, but stardust-flecked Midnight had replaced the memory of Derrick at the writing desk.

"Serafina, get away from him!" He wrapped his arms around me and pulled me into the darkness of his embrace.

I pushed against him. Light entered my vision and suddenly I was tucked in my bed again.

"Stop protecting me, Midnight!" I yelled as I shoved off the blankets. "I am trying to help you!"

Boom. Hairline cracks appeared in the floor beneath the bedroom door.

The monster was coming for me. I sprung from the bed and retrieved my silver needle from the air. The thread of infinity tied itself through the eye and coiled in an endless loop near my feet.

I threw open my bedroom door and stepped into the ballroom of the castle of dreams.

With a wave of my hand, the shattered black and white tiles flipped back and exposed a wide pit. I stood on the edge and looked down—no bottom in sight.

I let out a shaking breath and steeled myself. I had slayed a giant, how difficult could the monster in Derrick's mind be?

My needle flew in the air, weaving the glowing white thread of infinity into a ladder that dropped into the pit.

The silver needle floated dutifully at my side while I descended the ladder.

Down, down, down, I climbed, my feet dropping into the darkness one after the other. Suddenly, my left foot did not hit the thread of the next rung of the ladder, but pressed against solid ground. I silently released the ladder but it still glowed, the only light in the pit.

My needle quickly stitched a lantern from the thread. I gripped the knotted handle and held it up—I could only see a few inches in front of me.

"Hello, sorceress."

My heart jumped and my hair stood on end. The monster was near. I swung my arm. The light of my glowing lantern blanketed the area around me, but I found no sign of…

Then its hot breath skated across my shoulders.

I spun around and my eyes dragged up. Head of a bull. Muscled arms of a man. Steel armor on its shoulders. A mouth that was too wide.

Worst of all, it had big, very human, Hyton Blue eyes.

A chill ran through me but my neck burned, where its teeth had once left bruises. My ears pricked with the memory of every promise of possession it had whispered.

I knew Derrick, but I knew the monster too.

His name was Alastar.

A huge claw pricked me underneath my chin and pulled my face up. Alastar took in a deep breath through his wide nose and his pupils dilated.

He opened his mouth in something like a smirk, showing off rows and rows of sharp teeth. "Are you mine, sorceress? Or are you a threat?"

I gritted my teeth behind closed lips as I quietly summoned my silver needle. If my timing was just right, I could drive my needle through his eye and end him…

Alastar dropped his claw and a growl reverberated through his chest. "I have my answer, then."

He opened his wide mouth and lunged for me. I dove out of the way, crashing against the wall of the pit near my rope ladder.

Alastar dug its claws in the ground and roared. With a flick of my hand, my silver needle speared his eye, sending the infinite thread through his skull. Alastar shook his heavy head and the thread snapped. I sent the needle through his heart, but he kept coming for me.

My heart thundered. I could not kill him.

I scrambled for the ladder. I had just pulled myself up the first rung when Alastar caught up to me.

Just as he was about to wrap his claws around my ankle, my needle wrapped the infinite thread around and around his thick wrist. The needle dove into the ground, yanking the monster back and stitching him to the bottom of the pit.

Alastar snapped the threads around his wrist, but the needle flew through the air at the same pace of my pounding heart as I pulled myself up the ladder. The needle weaved through the walls of the pit until it created what looked like a glowing spider web.

I heaved myself out of the darkness but commanded the needle to dart back and forth over the pit. Alastar roared and tried to climb through the web of threads, but its horns and claws got caught in my trap.

The needle shot out over the top of the pit and quickly stitched a tight basketweave over the opening. Right before I closed the pit, Alastar looked up at me through the threads.

"Mine," he growled. "Mine. Mine. Mi—"

And then I sealed him in.

I stared at the glowing blanket of thread over the pit. It was not as secure as iron bars, but it was all I had. I waved my hand and the black and white tile of the ballroom reappeared over my stitches.

I was tired…so tired.

I closed my eyes and let out a breath as I released myself from Derrick's mind.

The smell of the Duke's chambers filled my nose and I crumpled forward onto Derrick's mattress. I used my last bit of strength to brush the curls out of Derrick's face. He slept peacefully, blissfully unaware of the battle I had just fought.

I crashed next to Derrick on his pillow. I let out a breath and softly traced the invisible line on his cheek where Grigory's sword had slashed him.

If only Derrick's mental wounds could have healed so easily.

The monster that prowled in the darkest parts of Derrick's consciousness did not just come from the pain inflicted by his father. Alastar was also his grandfather, his great-grandfather, and all the way back until even pieces of Alastar the Conqueror had stared back at me with a covetous lust in its eyes.

As long as Alastar roamed inside Derrick, there was no way I could convince his trembling inner self to free Fraleigh—not when she was his, and the Dukedom's, only security.

I could not kill Alastar, but maybe I could banish him. I could stitch all the cracks in Derrick's mind together, make Alastar's pit deeper, and make that monster so small that Derrick was no longer beholden to him.

I only had eleven days left until the full moon. I had to heal every part of Midnight's domain until he felt safe enough to accept my commands rather than lock me in my bedroom.

If I made Midnight strong, Riyan would walk the earth again.

Chapter Thirty Three

Always There

I wished being the Duke's mistress just meant I lived on my back like I had first thought. That at least would have given me some rest.

I started my mornings draped in Hyton Blue and glimmering with a new gift from Derrick. An emerald pendant. An onyx ring. His great-grandmother's tiara.

He kept me sparkling and I kept him fed. I sat next to him at every meal, sampling each and every dish to check for poison. Just because the Viper held affection for Derrick did not mean others could not slip a potion into his food.

As the days passed, Derrick's cheeks had started to fill out again…and so had mine. I matched him bite for bite at each meal to keep him eating, fighting through the pain in my stretching stomach. My calves were rounder every time I tied my garters. My Nordingaard crystal had chafed against my soft thighs before, but it grew so unbearable I hid it away in a drawer.

Derrick was always too close for me to risk him finding the crystal, anyway. I missed the calmness flowing into my skin, but I just had to wait until the next full moon before I could wear it again.

Though I had used my magic every day, I had not heard Riyan's voice even once.

Every night, I asked Midnight to free Fraleigh from her servitude. Each time, Alastar roared from the bottom of his pit and created a new crack in Derrick's foundation.

As soon as Alastar shook the floor, Midnight would whisk me away to the safety of my bedroom in the paper castle before he disappeared.

My nights were sleepless and my days were no reprieve. Brietta sometimes called meetings with Annalisa and I to discuss a new detail in Freya's diary, only for Annalisa to snap that Brietta had interpreted her mother's scrawl wrong.

General Hyton sometimes gave me a break from the bickering and we would play a round of "answer for answer" over a cup of honeyed tea. In our visits, I learned he met Astrid the summer before his Junior year when he accompanied his mother to visit Hilda. Riyan was conceived when Ragnar snuck Astrid into a tavern during Winter Solstice. I also learned the General had to be cold and cruel to his son to keep him safe—anyone suspecting Riyan was a Hyton heir would have put him in more danger than he was already in.

In exchange, he asked me if I could learn to perform a blood bond enchantment.

My white flame surprised me with the truth—I could.

Though I was unsure if I could create a blood bond as strong as Fraleigh's, my magic was strengthened with every night I mended Derrick's wounds.

We had the same nightly routine. He locked his arms around my waist, I greeted Midnight, and I found a new door that led to a memory where Alastar had roared through his mind.

The memories grew heavier on my heart. He saw Freya draped limply on a couch and did not know if she was dead or alive. He shed lonely tears on his sixteenth birthday. He escorted each of his older sisters at their Presentations before they were torn away from him. He even refused to let go of Sapphira's arm the instant he saw Emperor Orlon's grey hair.

As the moon waxed in the sky, the walls in the paper castle got narrower and narrower until I was crawling on my belly to make my repairs.

But I pressed on. I was only able to mend the cracks in the walls because Derrick was always fighting Alastar, though he did not even know he was doing it. With everything I had seen in Derrick's memories, a weaker man would have succumbed to that voracious need for control.

Made me wonder what he was fighting for.

Regardless of the reason, his resilience gave me hope. After eleven Dukes, he could finally be the one to prevail over Alastar and release Fraleigh.

So if Derrick was going to fight, I would fight too.

At every party, Derrick gripped the arm of his throne while I sat in his lap, my Hyton Blue skirt draping over his legs. Though my eyelids were heavy as bricks, I forced myself to keep vigil over the ballroom, tasting each goblet the servants brought before letting Derrick have a sip.

Mother seemed to be acting in a similar role. She followed General Hyton around the ballroom like a dark shadow, her full lips always on the rim of his goblet before she handed it to him.

Annalisa usually only made a brief appearance at the parties before the crowd overwhelmed her, but Brietta swept through the ballroom with a dazzling smile. She mingled with men and women in every House color, occasionally throwing an approving glance to my place on the dais.

If I stayed glued to Derrick's lap, she did not have to worry about becoming pregnant.

But she did not always approve of my methods.

"You are cutting his meat for him?" she had asked one morning.

I folded my arms. "He gets very tense when he sees blood. I cannot risk him falling into another convulsing fit."

She pursed her lips and returned to reading Freya's diary. "Just feed him haddock from now on."

After a week of restlessness, the parties ceased and the season of business had begun.

I clung to Derrick's arm as we walked through the palace halls. His first official meeting with the Barons was in mere minutes.

Derrick wore the crown of Lycaster, his cape billowing from his shoulders and his chest gleaming with chains of gems.

He glanced down at his chest. "I hate wearing these." He twisted one of the heavy chains before releasing it with a *thunk* against his chest. "They were *his.*"

I smirked. "Well, with how inheritance works, the jewels were always yours. Your father just held onto them for a while."

He kissed my forehead. "Will you ever stop dazzling me with your brilliance?" He slowed his stride and pulled me closer to the wall. "I want you at the meeting with me."

I knitted my brows. "But I am a woman. The Barons would take it as a grave insult."

Even though I was a Baron. The thought tasted sour—what good was power if it relied on the acceptance of others?

Derrick's eyes twinkled. "No one denies the Duke what he wants."

He gripped the frame of a portrait of a beautiful fair-haired woman and swung it open like a door. A small set of steps greeted me through the portrait hole.

He helped me up the small ledge and followed me. At the top was a tiny room that fit only a plush pink chair, a footstool, and a small table with parchment atop it. The chair faced a large portrait of Alastar the Faithful, the fifth Duke of Lycaster.

Derrick placed his hand on my shoulder and dropped his voice. "You should see the whole meeting through the portrait."

I turned, reaching high to take his face in my hands. "You will do just fine."

I lifted onto my toes to give him a kiss on the jaw.

He wrapped his arms around my waist and smiled. "You do not have to always get on your toes for me. I can meet you at your height."

I lowered my heels to the ground and shrugged. "I never notice when it happens. When you are small, you spend your whole life on your toes."

He kissed my hair and turned to leave, but then looked over his shoulder. I gave him a reassuring smile and lifted the hem of my skirt, revealing the Hyton dagger tied to my garter.

I had to replace the Nordingaard crystal with the damn dagger. Derrick rarely let me out of his sight, but wanted me to have protection when I did. If all I had to do was don the familiar weapon to keep him calm, it was worth the minor discomfort.

He gave me an approving smile as soon as he saw the bull-headed hilt and disappeared down the dark steps.

I sank into the pink chair and looked at the large portrait. Though my eyelids were heavy from exhaustion, I focused on the light filtering through the other side of the thin canvas. After a few seconds, I could make out a large table with eight chairs on the sides and a large throne at the end closest to me. The afternoon sun lit up the eight banners of the provinces of Lycaster hanging on either side of the table.

The portrait was just another one of Daigen's tricks.

I shifted in the chair and thin markings on the wall caught my eye. A list of five women's names were carved into the wood paneling. A weight dropped in my stomach as my fingertips traced the most recent addition to the list: *Freya.*

The name was carved in her own writing. Had she sat in the pink chair before me, watching Anders—or more likely, Alastar the Wise—conduct business with the Barons?

My fingers ran up the list, recognizing the next three names as Duchesses of the past, but the first name carved in the wall did not belong to any Duchess. The name in jagged script was not written in any history book, but was special all the same: *Annalisa.*

I had no idea who the ancient Annalisa was, but I traced her name in the wood, feeling the weight of her unknown history with every stroke of the knife she used to make her mark on the palace itself. What else had she contributed to the Dukedom that no one knew about? Did the Annalisa I knew have any idea the name she carried could have more value than any gemstone?

I knelt on the chair cushion. I felt a little unworthy as I untied the Hyton dagger from the garter, but I tossed the feeling aside.

If I had to hide my magic, my power as a Baron, and even my very presence in the room, I was not going to hide my name too. I slowly and deliberately scraped the blade against the wood underneath Freya's name.

I was still her lioness, after all.

I pulled back the dagger and smiled. *Serafina*—the sixth strong, yet invisible, thread in the tapestry of Lycaster history.

The door to the meeting room creaked open and I sat down. The red-haired Baron Mydina walked in and had a seat underneath the light green banner bearing a great black wolf.

Baron Pebblebrooke came in next, seating himself beneath the light blue banner with a white swan. Baron Meadowshyre quietly followed, sitting next to him beneath the pink banner with a lark. Baron Amberfield sulked in and plopped in the seat under the yellow banner with the deer. Baron Thornebow slipped around the door and sat beneath the grey banner with the silver fox.

Finally, Baron Elvar strutted into the room and sat at the right-hand side of the Duke's throne. The purple Elvar banner bearing the sea serpent eating its own tail was the perfect backdrop for his proud face.

I looked to the left side of the throne—the seats under the crimson Bloodstone banner and dark green Ravenwood banner were empty. I folded my arms across my chest. Those seats were supposed to be *mine.*

The door swung open and Evereon walked in. His coppery hair was neatly combed and his Bloodstone cape fell from his shoulders. The Bloodstone and Ravenwood pins gleamed on his chest.

At least Evereon was keeping up appearances that he was running the North.

He sat beneath the snarling Bloodstone bear and rested his left leg on the Ravenwood chair. He tossed a vulpine glance to his father. "How disappointing, old man. You put in all that effort to make sure I never ended up in this room and yet…"

Baron Thornebow glanced at Baron Mydina. He had the same dark eyes as his nephew. "What the hell is *he* doing here?"

Baron Mydina straightened his spine. "Do not look at me, I have no son."

Evereon laughed. "I am Baron Bloodstone's proxy. Old Nikkolas would not come when he ran one province, but with *two*…he needed someone trustworthy to handle the North in his stead."

Baron Mydina snapped his head toward his son. "There is nothing trustworthy about you—!"

The doors swung open. All six Barons and Evereon stood. Derrick entered the room, keeping his shoulders strong and his head high. He crossed the room and sat on his throne. The Duke himself was sitting at my feet.

I threw out my magic and created a tether between his mind and mine. If anything were to go awry, maybe I could calm him down.

"Hail Alastar XII," Baron Elvar recited dryly.

"Hail Alastar XII," the other five Barons grumbled in reply.

Evereon kept silent.

Derrick's voice was deceptively strong. "First order of business."

Baron Elvar shifted his shoulders. "You have held the crown for a little more than a week. How do you intend on fixing our failing economy?"

If Baron Elvar had brought up finances at the coronation, surely he had a plan he was just waiting for the blessing to use. I slid the suggestion down the tether: "*Ask him what he thinks is best.*"

Derrick blinked, accepting it. "You control all of our sea and river mercantile, Baron Elvar. Certainly you have a few ideas."

Baron Elvar smiled. He turned his shoulders so he addressed the other Barons more than his Duke. "General Hyton gave me intelligence that the surrounding kingdoms and empires are failing."

Derrick kept his face schooled, but Midnight scoffed and echoed down our tether: "*Acting as a mouthpiece for his lover? His poor rich heart is going to crumble when he finds out Uncle Ragnar only fucks the most useful person he can find.*"

My heart tugged at the thought, but the Barons listened with intrigue.

"We should take advantage," Baron Elvar said. "Starting with the Sudrian empire."

Baron Thornebow leaned on the table. "You want us to invade Sudria? The Southern provinces share a border with them. Any war would be in *our* lands!"

Baron Mydina nodded in agreement.

Baron Elvar waved his hand. "I am suggesting *expanding* Thornebow into the territory of a crumbling empire. We can use the spoils of war to restore Thornebow's economy to what it was before Alastar the Bold executed your father."

Baron Thornebow narrowed his eyes and smiled. Even Barons Pebblebrooke and Meadowshyre exchanged looks of consideration.

"No," Derrick's voice cut through the air like a blade. "I will not wage war against my sister."

The Barons raised their eyebrows. Evereon smirked.

Alastar's growl shook the tether. As inflammatory as the suggestion of war was, I could not risk Derrick breaking and letting Alastar wreak havoc in his mind.

I issued a gentle command: "*Stay calm, Derrick. Just listen.*"

He blinked and his shoulders dropped only enough for me to notice.

Baron Elvar chuckled without a single note of warmth. "I forgot you have relations in every kingdom, but I would hope that our Duke would not let that weakness ruin an important opportunity for us."

The word "weakness" made Alastar roar from the bottom of his pit.

I quickly sent another whisper into his mind: "*You are not weak. Stay calm.*"

But Derrick did not accept the command. He tightened his grip on the arms of his throne. "A reluctance to pillage like vultures is not weakness, Tyreon."

The other Barons shifted, each tossing a look to Baron Elvar.

Baron Elvar stared at Derrick with a hard brow. "Our markets have no output. People are starving in the North. Just think of what the Sudrian rebels would pay for their empress's head."

Derrick leaned onto the edge of the table, his voice low and dangerous. "You would do well to hold your tongue before talking of spilling Hyton blood."

I gritted my teeth and desperately pushed down another command: "*Derrick, stop!*"

Baron Elvar scoffed. "Hyton blood? That woman stopped being a Lycastrian once she bonded to Emperor Orlon." He waved his hand to the rest of the table, as if beckoning their support. "The one good thing Alastar the Bold did was sell off a daughter to each of the neighboring kingdoms. Their lines of succession depend on blood bonds to the brats that are in the palace *right now.* Think of the leverage we could have—!"

Derrick slammed his fist on the table as Alastar tore at the threads of his prison. "My family is *not* your leverage!"

I gathered the strength for a forceful blast of magic to try to pull him back, but Evereon scoffed and broke my focus. All the eyes in the room turned to him as he relaxed in the Bloodstone chair.

"A war with Sudria would be a terrible idea," he said.

Baron Elvar turned his ire to Evereon. "Of course you would protest, *half Sudrian.*"

Baron Mydina cut a glare to Baron Elvar, but Evereon flashed a smile. "You talk of what you can gain from war, but you have never borne scars from a General."

Suddenly every eye was on the line that cut across Evereon's face, even mine.

He had said Riyan gave him that scar. Had he lied?

"Our lands still bear the scars of the first battle against the giants of Nordingaard." He turned to Derrick. "How are you going to heal them, *Your Excellency?*"

The tether on Derrick's mind thinned—I was losing him.

"I had nothing to do with that," Derrick responded, low and clipped. "You cannot blame me for—"

"I do not blame you," Evereon snapped back. He swung his foot off the Ravenwood chair. "But I *demand* that you take responsibility now that you have the power to do something. Ravenwood and Bloodstone are still starving. What are you going to do about it?"

The tether snapped and Derrick threw me out of his mind.

No, damn it! *No!*

I pressed my hands against the thin canvas of the portrait, casting out my magic to try to reach him again, but I could not get in.

The Barons glared at Derrick, each waiting for him to rise to Evereon's challenge. Even after a few pounding heartbeats, Derrick still refused to answer.

Evereon shook his head and smiled wryly, not taking his eyes off Derrick. "Just what I thought—nothing. Just like your old man."

Derrick got up so quickly that the throne flew back and slammed against the wall beneath my feet. Evereon jumped up and he and Derrick stood toe-to-toe.

I wanted to claw through the portrait and drag Derrick back by his collar. Derrick's neck was tense and rage burned in his eyes—Alastar was rising.

All my efforts were about to go up in smoke.

Evereon merely chuckled in the face of the monster. "The North trusts *nothing* from Hyton Palace."

Evereon turned, his boots thudding harshly on the floor as he walked past the Barons and shoved the door open.

My blood boiled. Alastar was tearing through its prison because of him.

I tore out of the secret room and stormed through the halls, hunting Evereon down. A flash of crimson rounded a corner and I followed it.

I turned the corner and found Evereon with Rosaline in a darkened alcove.

"Why in the high halls of hell did you pick a fight with him?" I bit out.

Rosaline's eyes went wide, but Evereon casually turned to face me. "Someone needed to speak for the North." His yellow eyes flicked down to my skirt. "Especially since its Baron changed colors."

I gripped my Hyton Blue skirt so tightly I thought I would tear a hole in the satin. "I am doing everything I can to bring Riyan back from the mountain. You have *no idea* what I have been through to get to this point—"

"I have a pretty clear picture, actually," Evereon snapped. Rosaline tugged on his arm and whispered at him to stop, but he shrugged her off. "All I've heard since arriving in this cursed city is how the new Duke will never sire an heir because he can't keep his hands off his mistress for even a moment."

My mouth went dry, but flames raged in my stomach and behind my eyes. "How dare you think you know anything—?"

"You got lost." Evereon dropped his voice and squared his shoulders. "I warned you, but you still got lost."

He glanced toward the white box with pink ribbon I just noticed was in Rosaline's hands. "No point in any of this now, Rosaline. Not when she already has everything she ever wanted."

His crimson cape swished behind him as walked down the hall.

Did he think I wanted to be owned? Trapped under watching eyes? Working to the point of exhaustion?

Did he really think that having the Duke under my control was what I had always wanted?

I opened my mouth to tell Evereon he was wrong, but no words left my lips.

My heart dropped to my stomach. I tried again, but I produced nothing but silence. My hands slowly wrapped around my throat as I braced myself to accept the cold truth that coursed through my veins.

I could not tell Evereon he was wrong because I could not lie.

No…I could not have gotten lost. I only had three days left to save Riyan. I just had to work harder, I just had to…

I turned to Rosaline, who looked at me with wide eyes as she clutched the gift in her hands.

"Tell me why you came to Hyton Palace," I ordered.

Rosaline shook her head and tried to back out of the alcove. "The timing isn't right. I was under strict orders to—"

"Fuck what Fraleigh told you." I raised my hand as my throat tightened. "Fuck whatever Daigen's plan was. I will get an answer even if I have to rip it out of you."

Magic trembled in the air, but Rosaline did not cower. She gripped the sides of the gift box and her voice was soft as the beginning of an avalanche.

"Fine, Serafina. I just hope you are ready for what I have to show you."

Chapter Thirty Four
Pearls

Rosaline sat beside me on a couch in a room far away from any listening ears.

I looked at my Hyton Blue skirt pooled around my feet. *That* was all I had ever wanted—to be a Hyton, to have Derrick's heart and mind in my hands, and to have real power.

Riyan gave *his life* for me and how had I repaid him? By getting lost in my own desires!

Rosaline wrung her hands. "Daigen was very specific about timing. If you didn't get this gift at the right time, everything could go wrong."

I glanced at the box with the pink ribbon in Rosaline's lap. "Is that the gift?"

She shook her head. "Captain Mydina said this arrived at the Fortress a few days after you left. He brought it because he never got a response to his message and was worried."

"Because that was the message that got Brandt killed." I dug my nails into the couch cushion and bit down on my shame. "I am a failure. And a disappointment."

Rosaline let out a quiet breath. "He used to say that too."

I looked up at her. I had forgotten that Rosaline was Riyan's childhood friend. She knew him.

Her full lips turned up in a smile and suddenly a white light appeared between her eyes. The sound of a gentle wind through flower stems traced my ears.

She held out her hand. "*This* is the gift."

I stared at her palm and my stomach twisted. Was I really ready for what I was going to face?

But Riyan once said I was the bravest person in the Dukedom. I had failed so many times over the past three weeks, but I could at least try to prove him right.

I closed my eyes, my magic forming the connection between Rosaline's mind and mine as I took her hand.

A flurry of blue and yellow flower petals swept my mind down the tether and placed me in the middle of a field of wildflowers outside of a hovel. A young girl, no more than eight and thin as a twig, picked flowers beside me.

The girl's mother stood on the side of the road. Her lips were painted bright red and she bared her calf to the road, her draped skirts failing to hide her pregnant belly.

"Rosaline!" called a boy.

I turned to see a large blonde boy running toward us.

Riyan. He was so *young*.

Rosaline smiled, but then her eyes widened with fear when Riyan ran up to her. His hair was past his shoulders, his sleeves were in shreds around his arms, and he was barefoot like he had burst out of his shoes.

His face looked nine years old, but he was over six feet tall.

Riyan's eyes were full of tears. "Rosie, I…I grew."

Rosaline gripped the flower stems. "What happened?"

"There was an accident with Grandmother and…" Riyan ran a hand through his long golden hair. "No time to explain. Grandfather is sending me away. To Hyton."

He handed her a small leather pouch that clinked as it moved. "Here, ten marks. That should be enough to get your family to Hyton Palace. Grandmother says they're always looking for maids."

Rosaline's eyebrows flew to her hairline as she weighed the pouch in her hand. "Ten whole marks…are you coming with us?"

A tear rolled down Riyan's cheek. "No. I have to…I have to go, but I want you to be all right. Thank you for being my friend when no one else would."

And then he leaned down and kissed her.

The memory ended as the two children said goodbye. I pushed out of Rosaline's memory. I left Rosaline's mind behind and returned to the feeling of my palm in hers.

I opened my eyes to find her crystal blue ones shining back at me.

"Bloodstone had the coldest winter in a generation that year," she said. "My family wouldn't have survived it. He…he saved our lives."

A chill crept along my shoulders. Riyan's selflessness and caring was never just a push from a corrupted blood bond…that was just who he was.

Beneath the blood on his hands and the magic in his veins, there was always a good man.

Regardless of what anyone had tried to make him—a beast, a monster, an heir, a rival, or a threat—Riyan was *good*. He was good, and kind, and…and…

…and what did that make me?

I pulled my hand from hers and my throat trembled. "Should I even know what is in the box?"

Rosaline's fingernails tapped on the edge of the white box. "I can't see into someone's mind like you, but I was with Fraleigh long enough to learn how to read what is never written down."

Her eyes met mine. She could see me.

But somehow I did not mind it.

She smiled and gently pushed the box into my lap. "You don't need this but…maybe it will finally put a real smile on your face."

I swallowed the lump in my throat. My fingers pulled at the pink ribbon and I lifted the lid of the box. On top of rippling black satin was a large and slightly crumpled note. The handwriting was nearly illegible, but I was still able to make out the message.

Serafina,

*I know I'm not what you wanted. I know none of this is
what you wanted.*

*I made a mess of your Presentation dress, but I can fix
it. Hopefully I can fix everything and give you the life
you deserve.*

I'm glad I chose you. I hope one day you will choose me too.

—Riyan

The tip of my nose stung as tears lined my eyes. My hands shook as I set the note aside and lifted the black satin.

A soft gasp escaped my lips. Inside the box was a golden headband with two rows of shining pearls.

Did Riyan even have the gold all those pearls must have cost? Father had drained the Ravenwood treasury just buying the pearls on my Presentation dress!

But if the pink ribbon on the box meant the gift came from Hyton square, Riyan had to have ordered the piece during the two days we were in Hyton. And why would Riyan try to fix my Presentation dress? Unless…

My heart stilled as my thumbs ran over the cool pearls—the pearls from my Presentation dress.

Riyan had saved them.

Tears dripped onto my cheeks. I thought my precious dress was ruined, but no, Riyan was thoughtful enough to save it. He was also thoughtful enough to feed me, care for me, and love me with every part of his mind and body.

But was that enough for a monster like me?

I blinked back tears as guilt coated my stomach like pitch. I did not deserve Riyan, or his love, and *especially* not his sacrifice.

I did not even deserve the magical gift in my heart. What was I even good for? Why did I even have it in the first place?

And *fuck* was I tired of asking questions with no answers to satisfy me.

I hissed out a breath and gently placed the note and the pearls safely in the box.

"Thank you Rosaline." I slowly shut the lid on the box as my heart pounded, the diamond in my heart sparkling with the need for the truth. "If you will excuse me, I need to have a word with a very old man at the bottom of a very dark pit."

Chapter Thirty Five
A Thousand Choices

I pushed past the doors with the carved bulls and went to my wardrobe. I rifled amongst my linens until my hand found the Nordingaard crystal. The magic from the crystal sang into my palm as I retrieved it.

The crystal was not enough, so I searched further in the drawer. Like a whisper, the scrap of linen that held my embroidered flowers met my fingertips.

Once, I had told Riyan to find his flowers instead of his fear. As my own hands traced the stitches, I searched for something I could not find—proof I had ever deserved the man who had worn the flowers in the first place.

I grounded myself in the woven threads as my heart sank. Stitching Derrick's mind had consumed so much of me that I had not stitched with real thread in days.

I had spent so much time in dreams that I forgot what something real even felt like.

The box with the pearl headband slid into my drawer as I buried it beneath my linens. As much as I wanted to put the headband on and admire it, I did not deserve the gift just yet.

I needed answers first.

My clothes slid off my skin and the Hyton dagger clattered to the floor as I released my garters. I pulled the satin ribbon of the choker around my neck and my lungs filled with cool air as the gentle warmth of the crystal flowed into my throat.

I wore nothing but the crystal as I crossed the room and twisted the sconce on the northern wall. I trembled as I crossed the tiles, but then I gritted my teeth and sat at the edge of the pool.

The threads of the flowers rubbed against my fingers as I wrung the scrap of linen in my palm—my turn to find my flowers instead of my fear.

I slid my toes into the water, then my legs. With a final breath of courage, I pushed the rest of my body in. I kept a tight grip on the edge of the pool as my legs limply floated in the water.

I was not even sure if I could reach the Man of the Mountain through the false healing spring, but I had to try.

I closed my eyes and channeled the white flame in my heart that smoldered with the desire I had since the beginning.

The desire for what was real.

A low vibration hummed through the water. The ancient voice that was warm as flame but cutting as frost reverberated in my mind. "*Serafina, I have been waiting for us to talk again.*"

I swallowed. "So you can ask me to walk the earth in place of your lost bride?"

"*Later, Little Ember. You have to come to the place West of the Moon and East of the Sun before we can finish what we started.*"

"Why did we start it?" I hissed. "Your bride sacrificed herself for you and you think I can take her place? I am a damn snake. What in the high halls of hell makes *me* worthy of this gift?"

The water lapped around my shoulders, the magic within thrumming with energy.

"*I never asked my bride to give up everything for me. I wished she hadn't.*"

A flicker of light stirred in my chest. Never had the Man of the Mountain sounded more like…a man. Not a legend, but a human.

"*But Death does not listen to matters of the heart, her only justice is balance.*"

I had heard of Death being like a woman before, but it was odd to hear the Man of the Mountain speak of her like she was merely on the other side of a negotiation.

"When my bride gave me her powers, giving her life for mine, I became eternal. But for what? My grief had pulled me down to a place between the living world and the halls of hell so I could be as close to my beloved as possible. I could no longer walk the earth and use the power she gave me, so I searched for someone to shine with her light—never to replace her, but to let her live again. So, I chose Fraleigh and invited her to drink from the well of my tears. Her soul was not ripped from her body and thrown into the chasm with me like the others, but instead she was filled with magic, ready to receive the gift. But as soon as her father sacrificed himself for her and she chose eternity…I saw her future. I knew then that she would never walk freely like my bride. I saw a new path and let everything fall into place."

A new path…that led to me.

I always thought my resemblance to the bride in the old song was a fun coincidence. Riyan blood-bonding with me had already filled my body with magic so I could receive the flaming diamond in my heart. Riyan having that magic inside him in the first place was because of Ganora.

Did the Man of the Mountain really bend centuries of history just to let the circumstances end up as they were?

"I only fight Death and arbitrate bargains and the twists of reality as people make them. Though I may interfere through a whisper to those who carry my gifts, I cannot dictate the will of a mortal heart. Each choice made in love or sacrifice was a stepping stone in the path that led to you. From Ganora and Daigen all the way down to the young Duke and Riyan… everything was a choice."

The magnitude of carrying a gift made from the sacrifices of so many souls weighed in my stomach.

"Over a millennium, thousands of young women carried my bride's likeness, hundreds carried her spirit, and dozens could have walked the earth in her stead, but very few had the opportunities of circumstance that fell into place like footsteps leading to where you stand now—ready to receive her power of deathless wonder in its entirety."

I kicked my legs limply in the water. "So it was all based on circumstance—hapless luck?"

"*Is it not always hapless luck when we meet a person our soul sings for? You can manipulate the circumstances all you like, but you cannot force an ember to awaken.*"

In response, the tiny ember within my heart burned bright red.

I ignored the ember and hissed out a breath. "And I am still a monster, remember? You knew I wanted power above all else, and you still gave me your gift?"

"*Your winter has passed yet you still prefer the cold,*" he said with what sounded like a sneer. "*The love you still deny is more powerful than any gift I ever gave you.*"

When my brothers left, I had thrown stones at the innocence of love until it shattered within me. I hardened my skin into scales. I manipulated everyone I could.

After cutting my tongue with so many lies it became forked, why would anyone ever love me?

Both my white flame and my red ember went quiet. I could not even feel the linen beneath my palm as I gripped the edge of the pool. A tear dripped off my lashes.

I deny love because I do not deserve it.

I deny love because I *still* have not earned it.

"*A lie so heinous you cannot even speak it!*" The Man of the Mountain was angrier than I had ever heard him. "*Do you think I earned my bride's sacrifice? You have the gift of sorcery because I knew Riyan Bloodstone's heart. When I kept you with me in the place West of the Moon and East of the Sun for two days, all he did was wish that you would awaken…*"

Suddenly the crystal on my neck warmed. The white light from my neck grew brighter and brighter until I had to slam my eyes shut.

Even though my eyes were closed, darkness could not touch me.

"Please wake up, Serafina! It's been two days! Wake up, please!"

Riyan.

A gentle warmth filled my whole body. Was I connecting with him through my magic? Was a bath in the imitation healing spring all I needed to find him?

"A week," Riyan said. "We've been married for a week. I couldn't even make it seven days without breaking you too."

No…I was hearing a memory. Riyan had said he cared for me in the crystal cave while I was asleep and talked to me until his throat was sore…

My heart jumped. The Nordingaard crystals in the cave had captured Riyan's memories of him caring for me. But if that were true, that would mean his emotions were so intense that…

"I love you, is that what you need to hear? Is that how I wake you?" Riyan cried. "I *love* you, Serafina Helia. I love you. I would give *anything* to see you open those hazel eyes."

My fingertips traced the facets of the heart-shaped crystal as my chest shook with a sob. The crystal did not just capture the intensity of Riyan's despair or his fear of losing his bride, it captured his love for me.

That is why the crystal kept me calm—Riyan's love was flowing into my skin the entire time.

And I had accepted it. Savored it. Craved it.

"Is this the world punishing me for all the bad things I have done?" Riyan's voice broke. He was crying. "Why must you shoulder the consequences of my mistakes? I'm sorry, Serafina. I'm so sorry."

My chest glowed with gentle white fire. I wanted to reach through the memories and hold him, to show him I was alive and hale not in spite of him, but *because of* him.

White light spread across my collarbone into my arms, filling up my fingertips with power. I parted my lips and my voice shook. "I cannot deny him any longer."

The Man of the Mountain's voice filled my mind. "*Then follow my one command—seek your heart's desire, my monster.*"

I set my jaw and let my magic flow into the pool of tears. The water warmed around my legs. The intensity of the glow of each Nordingaard crystal in the pool passed through my eyelids.

I did not care what I was risking by using every bit of my power in the Duke's chambers, not even the fold between worlds could keep Riyan from me.

"Sera?"

His voice caressed my ears and I slowly opened my eyes. I did not see the edge of the secret pool in Derrick's chambers. Nor the edge of the glowing water.

All I saw was Riyan.

Chapter Thirty Six
Worthy

Eight days married. Eighteen days apart.

No matter how many times the sun had risen and fallen since I last saw him, it was like no time had passed at all.

Riyan floated in the dark abyss in the place West of the Moon and East of the Sun as if he were suspended in the middle of the sea. Somehow he did not look fifteen feet tall, but instead the same size as his father.

Though he was little more than an apparition in the blackness, I still knew him. What was trapped in the place between worlds was not just Riyan's mind, it was his barest, truest soul.

And he was *exactly* as I had always known him.

His golden hair swept across his collarbone. His chest rippled with waves of muscle. A peaceful smile rested on his strong jaw.

I nearly pushed through the blackness to wrap my arms around his bicep when a small ribbon of white light slowly coiled in the dark space around Riyan.

His twilight blue eyes followed the light and he smiled wide enough that the precious dimple on his right cheek appeared. "There you are, Sera. Getting brighter every time."

I furrowed my brows but then my heart swelled. He was not seeing me, he was seeing my magic.

I knew the Man of the Mountain arbitrated my twists of reality from the bottom of his pit, but I had no idea I created a spectacle when I channeled my power.

Riyan's eyes followed the dancing ribbon of light. "Let's see if you can hear me this time."

He pushed himself through the chasm until he was right next to the ribbon of magic. My magic burned brighter, casting its glow on his chiseled face. His smile widened and he sang:

> *"Just as blossoms bloom and wither,*
> *But still grow upon the bough,*
> *Even though I am not with her,*
> *She is still with me somehow."*

My lip trembled as a smile stretched across my face. The tune I had heard in my mind and in my dreams was his song. It was him all along.

It was *always* him.

The white fire inside me swayed to the music and the ribbon of magic around Riyan brightened. He let out an exuberant laugh and kept singing.

> *"Untouched by the endless winter,*
> *I'm still warm even now,*
> *For even though I am not with her,*
> *She is still with me somehow."*

I needed him. *Needed* him.

Magic tingled against my skin, pulling my body further into the water. Slowly, my fingertips left the edge of the pool as the swirls of magic carried me away.

I could not be afraid. Riyan was there.

My chest was alight with white fire. My limbs shivered from thousands of tears of lost love pulling me into that space between worlds.

Just as I stretched out my arms to embrace him, my hands hit an invisible barrier. I scowled and pushed again, but the barrier would not budge.

Damn it! My magic still was not strong enough to transport me! Was I not worthy enough to let the magic take me to him?

No, I could not admit defeat. I had to be more to Riyan than just white light in a dark chasm. He had to see me.

The ribbon of light around Riyan perked up like a serpent and rushed toward me.

Suddenly every part of my body was aglow.

Riyan's head swiveled around as he followed the tail of the ribbon. When his eyes met mine, he froze.

My heart dropped into my stomach. I had not thought this through. How was I supposed to face him again after the Darkest Night? Or after I became Derrick's mistress? Or failed to save Brandt?

Though I tried to dim my own light, Riyan's smile was incandescent.

"You heard me?" he asked. His eyes sparkled even in the abyss.

I gave him a tight smile and nodded. I swallowed my shame and forced myself to speak. "Riyan, I am sorry."

His brows knitted. "What could you be sorry for?"

How could I tell him? "So much has changed since you saw me last…"

"I know." He moved closer through the darkness. His head was slightly above mine, even though I still felt so far away. "I've seen it in your magic. Every time you reached for your power when you were scared, or panicked, or angry…I knew."

My stomach knotted. "Do you know everything?"

He frowned. "No. I forced my way down to that old man at the bottom of the pit and demanded he tell me, but the only answers I got were the patterns in your magic."

My mouth suddenly went dry. I had to tell him. "Riyan I—"

"You don't have to tell me." He shook his head and gave me a half smile. "Each time you were in distress, you got stronger. Your magic, it… it kept getting brighter so I knew you were okay."

My magic might have been stronger, but my soul still felt weak. I had to free the ugly truth. "But Riyan—"

"But nothing, Sera," he said with a laugh. "I know you. Everything you could have done was for your own survival and that is all I want—all I have *ever* wanted."

Why was he not letting me confess to the evils I had committed?

"Really?" I said. "I got Brandt Olson killed. I wasted myself on faerie dust and revealed the North's weakness." Tears threatened the backs of my eyes and my voice broke. "Anders Hyton slipped me a lust potion and Derrick…did not know. Anders is dead, but the slimy taste of that potion has *never* left my throat."

Riyan's face softened. "Sera, don't you dare blame yourself—"

"And then I became Derrick's mistress so I could get access to him." I folded my arms. "I am in his bed every night, manipulating his mind while he sleeps."

A muscle ticked in his jaw. "Don't do this. I'm already in a damn gap between life and death and you still think you can push me away?"

Push him away? I was only pushing him to see the truth!

"I am a monster and a failure." My nails bit into my forearms and my body shook. "And even though I have everything I had ever wanted in Hyton Palace, I am still trying every damn day to save you."

His face hardened. "The hell you are!"

My heart jumped into my throat. Maybe he never wanted to see me again after what I had just admitted, but saving him was not about me.

"But you do not understand!" I pleaded. "The Hytons kept Fraleigh enslaved since the beginning and Ganora will trade her freedom for yours. I am so close to getting Derrick to unshackle her—"

"No, *you* do not understand." Even the chasm between worlds trembled at the depth of the power in his voice. "You are *not* a monster or a failure and you are not supposed to save me."

Why was he being so damn dense? "But if I do not free Fraleigh by the full moon, Ganora will blood bond with your body to use as a weapon against the Hytons! You will be trapped in the place West of the Moon and East of the Sun forever!"

"Then let her." His face was hard as stone. "That was my bargain, remember? My life for yours."

He sounded just like Fraleigh. "But—"

"The bargain was that you live your life." He leaned forward, matching my obstination with his own. "So be with Derrick. Swim in luxury. Have your faerie-story happy ending."

Fire flared through my veins. "You think this is my happy ending?"

"It should be. We had an agreement too, remember? You promised me you would try to be happy."

My chest rattled with a sob. Although I was always following my heart's desire, I still could not say I was happy. No matter how hard I tried, that is where I had constantly failed him.

I looked away and let my heart thud against my ribs for a couple of moments before Riyan's soft voice filled the chasm. "I fell in love with you because of your laugh, you know."

I knitted my brows and looked up at him. "How is it even possible to fall in love because of something so small?"

He smiled. "You were already so impressive, but that laugh of yours?" His smile widened and warmed his voice. "The flush in your cheeks, the unbridled joy in your voice, the sparkle in your eyes…if I could have bottled your laughter and carried it with me, I would have never felt afraid again. And on my birthday, when you rolled around in the Bloodstone lilies and laughed so beautifully the flowers opened up even more just to hear it?"

My lip trembled, but Riyan's smile only got brighter. "That was it—I loved you. Nothing you ever said or did was going to change that my heart beat in time to the beautiful melody of your laughter. If I was going to do anything worthwhile with my life, it was to make sure you kept laughing."

My heart sank into my stomach as if it were made of lead.

When was the last time I laughed?

"Serafina Helia…just please tell me you're still laughing."

My hand floated through the water to press over my aching heart.

I had not laughed *once* since he left me.

Hurt flashed across his face as my silence became the answer he dreaded. "You promised me, Sera! You promised you would try to be happy!"

I threw my hand down through the water. "I tried, Riyan! This whole time, I tried!"

"Try harder. Eat something decadent. Go sit by yourself and sew. Wrap yourself in all the Hyton jewels!"

"You think that will make me happy? Isolation and riches?"

"No!"

"Seeing the Bloodstone lilies made me happy." My chest shook even as my magic held me steady. "Reading faerie stories with you made me happy. Or when we shared meals. Or when you laughed in the face of darkness over and over."

Riyan's shoulders dropped. "Serafina, don't—"

"You." Though my white flame was bright as the sun within my chest, my lungs tightened. I took a tiny sip of air as I fought a sob. "*You* made me happy. At first I could not untangle what was magic and what was real between us. Then I convinced myself nothing was ever there because I could not bear the thought that I had lost you."

"Serafina, please—"

"I buried myself in lies until I choked." My heart raced and my chest tightened. "I told myself that I never knew you, or that you never could have loved me, but the problem was never you, it was *me.*"

Riyan's eyes watered. "Sera, stop."

"I have everything I ever wanted in this damn palace, but I am suffocating without you. I only breathe when I am with you!"

His stunned silence was deafening. My throat trembled, but I forced out the words. "How can you expect me to be happy when I cannot even breathe?"

The weight of the past eighteen days crashed down on me all at once. The poison. The violation. The failed plans. The burden of Derrick's fragile state.

My heart thudded against my ribs as I sobbed. I ran my thumb over the scrap of linen fabric as an invisible fist gripped my lungs tighter and tighter.

"Sera!" Riyan raised his hands to try to hold my face, but his fingers hit the invisible barrier between worlds.

He snarled in frustration and pushed. The barrier gave a little under his immense strength, but would not break.

The magic weakened in the water around me and my heart pounded faster. My magic was failing me. I was going to drown.

Riyan's palms flattened against the invisible barrier. "Breathe, sweetheart. Breathe."

My eyes clouded with tears as I struggled to get in air, but my hands slowly floated up to meet Riyan's on the side of the living world.

I could not be afraid. Riyan was there.

I let out a cool, shaking breath as my heartbeat started to calm down. His soft words of encouragement traced my ears and my chest filled up with life again. I blinked away my tears and looked into his eyes that were beautiful as the open sky.

My white flame spun, pushing out the warmest truth I could tell. "I love you, Riyan."

He smiled, showing off his sweet dimple. "I know—I've known since I got here." He laughed softly. "You said it in my mind before I left."

My heart swelled. He *did* hear me on Nordingaard.

My eyes dropped to the bits of white fabric peeking out from behind my palm. I was not yet powerful enough to transport myself, but what about a tiny scrap of linen?

I closed my eyes, focusing on the magic within the fabric. The tears sparkled back at me and my white flame spilled my love into them, twisting the warmth of the water around my hands until nothing was left in my fingertips.

Go to Riyan. Show him I love him.

I opened my eyes and the fabric was in Riyan's right hand.

I smiled. "Until you see me again, you have a piece of my heart to hold on to."

He closed his fist around the fabric, but his face fell. "Serafina, I mean it. Do not come for me."

I pressed against the perimeter and opened my mouth to argue, but he silenced me with a smile. "Mother is here. She's young, so it's more like having a younger sister, but she finally knows me. And…" He swallowed and glanced away for only a moment. "...and I don't have to face my father either. So, I'm fine here. Don't risk anything for me."

My hands curled into fists against the barrier. "You cannot stop me."

Riyan smiled despite himself. "I know." He pushed against the barrier again and his smile turned wicked. "You're still my little ball of fire."

I leaned closer to the barrier, my lips flush and full. The separation between worlds had not yielded to brute force, but maybe if I pushed, I could be close enough for a kiss…

The bedchamber door crashed open, jolting me upright. The chasm started to fade around me.

"Serafina! Where are you?"

Derrick's voice sounded far away, but in reality he was mere steps from the bathing chamber.

I could *not* let him find me using sorcery.

I snuffed out my magic and Riyan disappeared. The pool stopped glowing. The crystal cooled against my neck and the tears quieted against my skin.

Derrick raced through his chambers and gripped the frame of the open panel. "What are you doing?"

I took one look at his wide eyes before I crashed through the surface of the water.

The water was cold and dark, but I held my breath and ripped the choker from my neck. I released the crystal from my hand. Just as it started to sink, a big splash disturbed the water. My lungs burned as my limbs flailed in the water, trying to find the surface.

Bubbles surged past me and then a chill washed over my skin. My hands pressed against tile as I coughed.

Derrick crushed me to his chest and water dripped from his cheek onto my temple. The cold gems across his ribs pressed into my skin. He had jumped into the pool fully clothed to pull me out.

We were both shivering, but he would not let go of me.

"You nearly drowned!" he cried into my wet hair. "I cannot lose you. I cannot, I c-cannot…"

I held my breath as all the warmth in my chest disappeared. Guilt seeped down my spine as Derrick shook around me.

The moment I left Hyton Palace to save Riyan, I was going to destroy Derrick.

Chapter Thirty Seven
Shatter

Derrick might have pulled me out of the pool and saved me, but my thudding heartbeat against his did not give him any reprieve.

He was completely shutting down.

I pressed my hand against his trembling chest, but he did not respond to my magic. My shivering fingers unlocked the clasps of his cape and jewels as I kept repeating that I was right in front of him. I grabbed his cheeks, pressed my forehead to his, and whispered reassurances and apologies.

Half an hour passed before his hammering heartbeat finally slowed.

Derrick and I sat on one of the couches in his chambers, curled up underneath blankets as a tray of warm tea sat in front of us. He stared at the carpet and dryly explained that the Barons disbanded shortly after Evereon walked out. They were all furious that Derrick had lost control of the meeting.

I held my cup as my stomach twisted. I had needed to go to the imitation healing spring and find the truth of my power, but Derrick still needed me. I should not have just abandoned him.

"And the Barons were not the only ones making demands of me," he grumbled. "Annalisa wants dinner tonight. Just the four of us."

Maybe Annalisa could even be there to hold him up once I left to save Riyan. Then it would not hurt him…as much.

I took a sip from the cup and tried not to spit it out. Rosaline was apparently still in charge of the tea. "Some time with your sister is just what you need."

Derrick sneered and took the cup from me. "Doubt that."

He threw tea back, not wincing once at the barbed taste.

The room with dark green walls felt like it was closing in on us as we picked at our plates. I sat on Derrick's right-hand side at the round dining table, wearing the violet dress he had selected for me.

Brietta sat across from Derrick, proudly dressed in a deep green and wearing the same emerald tiara she wore for the Presentation. She glanced up at her husband as we ate, clearly waiting for him to share about the Baron meeting, but Derrick just stabbed at his haddock, silent.

Her brown eyes flicked over to me. The flipping of worn pages tickled the back of my mind as the door between Brietta's eyes opened.

"*It went poorly,*" I sent into her mind.

Brietta let out a slow, yet frustrated breath.

The only person not steeping in the tension was Annalisa. Her cheeks were pink and her curls bounced around her shoulders as she ate.

"Grigory wrote that he would be back for me soon," Annalisa said with a smile and a glance at her brother. "Since I will move to Thornebow province right after he returns, I think it would be a great opportunity for a farewell ball so—"

"No." Derrick took another stab at his fish. "I cannot think of a worse use of what little time I have than to attend another ridiculous ball."

Annalisa blinked and looked down at her plate. I tried to throw a magical tether her way, just to explain that Derrick was in poor spirits because of my swimming attempt, but her deflated mood kept me out.

She let out a determined breath and looked squarely at her brother. "Derrick, this is my last chance to—"

Derrick glared at her so fiercely that Annalisa visibly shrunk in her chair. Her eyes darted down and her fingernails clicked as she picked them underneath the table.

Brietta glanced at dejected Annalisa and then her gaze settled on her husband. "Your father used to do that too."

Annalisa looked up from across the table with fearful eyes. We both dared to glance down the table at Derrick, whose brow turned hard.

I could just picture Alastar pacing at the bottom of his pit.

Derrick gripped his fork. "What did you just say?"

Brietta put down her fork and straightened her spine. "Fight for dominance at every possible moment. Right after the coronation, he started restricting everything Freya did."

I sent a command into her mind: "*Damn it, Brietta! Not now!*"

She cut me a glance and broke the tether between our minds.

Derrick's hands curled into white-knuckled fists on top of the table. "Leave my mother out of this."

Brietta did not even blink at his rising anger. "Would you rather me lie to you for the rest of your life? If you are acting like an ass, I am going to tell you."

Time to end this. I reached for Derrick's wrist, but he stood up and slammed his palms on the table. The cutlery rattled. Annalisa flinched.

"Do not lecture me on what you know *nothing* about," he bit out.

"You cannot intimidate me." Brietta folded her arms. "If you wanted a meek and obedient Duchess, you should have chosen someone else."

I did not know who to reach for first—Brietta to get her to shut the hell up or Derrick to get him to calm the hell down.

"I *wanted* to choose someone else," Derrick said darkly.

"And do you think that gives you any excuse to act exactly like your father?"

My heart jumped to my throat and Annalisa gasped. Too far. Too fucking far.

Before I could act, Derrick picked up his plate and threw it against the wall by Annalisa's head. She screamed as the porcelain shattered mere inches from her ear.

I stood up to grab Derrick, but he had already stormed out of the room. He slammed the door behind him so hard that the frame rattled.

I turned to Brietta. "What could you possibly gain from agitating him like that?"

Brietta stood and gripped the back of her chair. "He is getting worse, just like Freya's diary said Anders did. I have to stop him from turning into a monster."

She had to stop him? She had never faced Alastar. "That is what *I* am doing. Every night, without rest. And if you do not want him to shatter when I leave—"

"Sera, you coddle him!" She released the back of her chair and her brows knitted. "I thought I understood how you felt about him, but now you are compromised!"

"Compromised? All I am doing is fixing—"

"You cannot fix him, Sera!"

Fire filled my throat and I nearly opened my lips to fight back when Annalisa's trembling voice broke the tension. "This is all my fault. I should not have said anything. I should not have made him angry."

I unclenched my fists as soon as I heard her voice. "Anna, no—"

She let out a sob and Brietta and I were instantly at her side. We both rubbed her back and soothed her, trying to convince her that she held no blame.

Rain pattered in my mind as my thumb stroked the back of Annalisa's hand. Just as I was about to lean into the raindrops and answer the call for help, Brietta looked across Annalisa's trembling curls at me.

I did not need to throw out a tether to read Brietta's eyes. She needed me to find Derrick before he destroyed anything else.

With a soft breath, I rose to my feet and started my search.

The music room was empty. So was his bedchamber. I even tried the kitchen with no luck.

At last, flickering firelight from a door on the first floor caught my eye—the portrait room of the Dukes and Duchesses past.

I silently pushed the door open to find Derrick staring up at the portrait of his grandfather. He gripped his hands behind his back and his chest was still.

I let out a rueful breath. After weeks of searching, we still had no idea who murdered Alastar the Wise or why.

Though whose fate was more necessary to unlock—the Alastar Derrick Pervale of the past or the Alastar Derrick Pervale of the present?

The soft light of the ember in my heart gave me the answer.

I shut the door and clicked the lock behind me. Derrick must have recognized my soft footsteps as his low voice rumbled over the popping of the fireplace. "I need to apologize to Lis. And Brie. I need to…I-I hate…"

His words failed him again. I passed under the wrathful eyes of Alastar the Conqueror as I joined Derrick on the other side of the room. He still did not turn from the portrait, so I wrapped my arms around his middle and pressed my cheek between his shoulder blades.

The eyes of the Conqueror, the Good, the Terrible, the Beguiling, the Gentle, the Faithful, the Brave, the Cunning, the Steadfast, the Wise, and—horrifyingly—the Bold all weighed on us. Each one of them was just a piece of the monster in Derrick's mind, tearing him at the seams.

And what was going to happen when I left him to save Riyan?

Derrick's voice rumbled against my cheek. "What legacy will I leave when I die? Will I just be 'Alastar the Weak?' or 'Alastar the Tongue-tied?'"

I smiled softly against his spine. "You will have a much better name than that if I have anything to say about it."

He let out a long, shaking breath. "It hurts how much Brietta hates me."

I pushed on his ribs to turn him around, but he would not look at me.

"She does not hate you," I said.

Not a lie.

I canted my head, trying to catch his downcast eyes. "She is merely angry about…the state of the world."

Still not a lie.

Derrick stepped away from me. "I was so excited to meet her. After everything you had said about her in your letters and what I had heard from her brother…"

He raked his fingers through the roots of his hair and headed for the fireplace. "Well-read. Witty. Imaginative. Trustworthy. She was such a good friend to you and I thought once you and I were married…she would be my friend too."

In a blink, his gaze turned wrathful and speared the portrait above the mantle. "But *he* ruined it!"

Anders's coronation portrait had replaced Alastar the Wise above the fireplace. The Anders Hyton in the portrait was thirty years old, handsome, and confident—completely unrecognizable from the man I had known and feared.

When did Alastar finally consume Anders?

I shook away the thought and focused on the present. Maybe reconciling Derrick and Brietta would be what would save him. I could prime him to sign Brietta's planned reformation and she would be so happy that she would want to be Derrick's friend. She could halt Alastar's destruction while I saved Riyan.

I took a step toward Derrick and forced a smile. "I think if you just heard her out—"

"He ruined us, Serafina!" Derrick turned around and his pained blue eyes met mine. "He *ruined* us!"

I gripped my hands and held my breath. The fire crackled behind Derrick as his scream echoed around the room.

Derrick's face softened. "I am so sorry, Serafina." He dipped his head and pressed the heels of his palms into his eyes. "Everything is slipping and I do not know why."

Because he was waging war against the monster in his mind…and he had no idea.

I placed my hand on his arm. "Derrick, it is all right to admit that being the Duke is hard."

He barked out a laugh so loud that I jumped back. "Hard? Serafina, this is my life!" His eyes gleamed with something between madness and anguish. "Being an Alastar is my *life!*"

He gestured to the portraits around us. "Every Hyton son has been the same way. You are either the Duke of Lycaster or you are dead!"

My eyes danced along the cold faces of the Dukes' portraits—each of them the winners of the Alastar trials, each one with blood staining their hands.

Derrick sank onto the nearby couch. "I cannot change it. I cannot sulk about it. This is just my life."

The defeat that spread across his face pained my heart. Even if my affinity was healing, I had no idea what I could really fix.

At the very least, I could make my friend feel better about the life he never got to choose.

I sat next to him on the couch and rested my cheek against his shoulder. "Remember when I wrote to you that I loved roasted hazelnuts? And then suddenly Annalisa got tins of roasted hazelnuts in her parcels even though she hated them?"

I looked up through my lashes and caught his smile. "I told her the sweet shop included the tins for free so she would keep tossing them onto your bed."

My smile grew bigger. "Remember when I used to tell you all the Ashmore gossip because you were bored?"

His nose wrinkled as he let out a quiet laugh. "It was better than any theatre."

I wrapped my hands around his arm. In the silence, we said more than we ever could on parchment. He was there for me and I was there for him, regardless if we were two schools apart or two provinces apart.

If he knew that, maybe he would not shatter.

"No matter what happens, we are still Midnight and Birdie," I said. "Remember that when the burden of your life is so heavy."

I let go of his arm so he could turn toward me. His eyes were soft—even Alastar was quiet within him.

I gently brushed a stray curl out of his face. "Think of girlish gossip instead of sneers at court. Feel the threaded stars under your fingers instead of the weight of the crown. Taste roasted hazelnuts instead of the bitter tang of Cupid's Blood."

Derrick's brow suddenly hardened. "How do you know what Cupid's Blood tastes like?"

My stomach dropped. No…*no!* How could I have let that slip? He could not, *could not* know the truth of the Darkest Night.

I would tell the truth how it benefited me—how it would benefit all of us. "I…remember when Brietta was poisoned at Annalisa's ball. She grimaced right after tasting that oddly purple wine—"

"Serafina." His eyes were dark. "When did he poison you?"

A direct question. I swallowed, keeping my teeth clamped shut as the truth tried to force its way out of my throat. I held my breath and my chest burned.

Derrick turned his shoulders to me, his chest rising and falling with his furious breath, but his voice broke. "When?"

I closed my eyes as my breath escaped me—and so did the truth. "The Darkest Night."

The log in the fireplace cracked with a sickening pop. I peeled my eyes open—Derrick's face was completely white.

I reached for his hand. "Derrick, you had no way of knowing."

He jerked his hand away like his touch would burn me. The muscle under his left eye feathered.

"Derrick, no!" I tried to grab his arm but he rose from the couch. "Your father hurt me, not you!"

He walked to stand in front of the fireplace and I leaped to my feet.

"I cannot lie!" I pleaded. "Listen to me, *you* did nothing wrong."

"But my body did." He glanced over his shoulder, the orange firelight dancing in his watering eyes. "Just like with Brietta, right?"

My hand pressed against my heart and I thought my chest might cave in. Tears stung my eyes. "Derrick, how could you think—?" No point in explaining. If I got into his head, I could fix the cracks in his castle walls. Regardless of what either of us felt, he still had to release Fraleigh from servitude.

I might have already lost Derrick, I could *not* lose Riyan too.

My hand shot out, beckoning him to take it. "Come on, we need to go to bed."

His eyes dragged up from the fire and settled on his father's portrait. His jaw clenched. He did not move an inch.

Only after convincing him that someone might attack me if I went upstairs alone did he leave the portrait room. He silently escorted me to the Hyton bedchambers with his eyes bolted forward and his jaw set tight.

I nearly tripped over my feet when he stopped abruptly in the middle of the blue-carpeted hallway.

"Stay in your room tonight," he said, low and clipped.

I glanced at the familiar door, but I did not dare move. I *had* to get into his mind and fix what I broke. "Derrick, do not do this—"

"That is an order." He would not even look at me. "And lock your door."

His shoes thudded on the carpet as he retreated to the carved wooden doors at the end of the hallway. I wanted to chase after him and try to get him to see sense, but my feet were glued to the rug.

He…he had never ordered me to do anything before.

After Derrick's chamber doors slammed shut, I resigned myself to bed. I had not even bothered to take the Hyton dagger off my garter, I just fell on my back and crushed a pillow to my chest.

I refused to admit defeat. The full moon was only three nights away, but I could still save him *and* Riyan.

Even though sadness weighed on my chest like a damp, musty cloud, my eyes fluttered closed.

I could free us. I could fix him. Everyone would be happy…

Then the sting of smoke filled my nose and my eyes popped open.

Chapter Thirty Eight
The Mad

If there was smoke, there was fire.

I leaped out of bed as the rest of my limbs caught up to my pounding heart. I had no idea how long I had been asleep.

I flung open my door and the stench of smoke was even stronger.

More doors clicked open in the hallway. Amethyst rushed out of her bedroom and opened a nearby door. "Emie! Did you overturn a candle again?"

Bleary-eyed Emeralda emerged from her bedroom, her dark curls mussed. "Why do you have to blame me? Maybe Garnet is *experimenting* again!"

Another door across the hall opened and Garnet's hand entered the hallway, flashing Emeralda a poignant middle finger.

One by one, the doors of the Hyton family chambers opened…except the doors with the carved bulls.

My feet were moving before I could think. I raced down the hallway and pushed open the familiar carved doors.

"Derrick!" I shouted.

No answer. The blankets on the bed were undisturbed. The couches and chairs were empty.

I stood in the center of the dark room as my heart thundered. Where was he?

A warm hand rested on my shoulder. Brietta.

"Sera, Pearl overheard shouting," she said. "A fire started in the ballroom. We need to get out of the palace."

The ballroom, where poison flowed as freely as wine.

A shiver rattled my chest—Derrick set the fire.

I looked up at Brietta and my voice sounded hollow as it reached my ears. "He found out about the Darkest Night."

Her face blanched. Her free hand flew up to the center of her chest, where the magical bond that connected her life to Derrick's must have twisted and turned beneath her ribs.

If he burned, she burned with him.

Without saying another word, I raced down the hallway, weaving through the princesses in their nightgowns. My feet carried me through the halls and down the stairs as quickly as my heart pounded. The horrible sting of char filled my nose as I got closer to the ballroom.

Some of the fleeing maids and servants tried to stop me, some even pulling on my arms, but I tore away from them.

I had to find Derrick.

Smoke curled from the seams of the ballroom doors. Heat flashed through my skin as I grabbed the handle, but I hissed through the pain and flung the door open.

I might as well have opened the door to an oven.

Thin smoke filled my chest and I coughed. The door slammed shut behind me. I opened my eyes to a tall shadow snapping a violin bow in half.

"Derrick," I called, my voice stifled through the sickly sweet smoke.

My eyes burned as I approached the flames that raged from shattered bottles of liquor on the floor. Blazing streaks of syrupy Cupid's Blood burned holes in Anders's coronation portrait. The gilded frame cracked under the heat.

The dark wood of Derrick's harp splintered as it smoldered. Each string that Derrick had lovingly plucked writhed in the flames like dying snakes. His crushed violin sang one last time as it sizzled at the bottom of the kindling.

His music…his song and his voice…was all turning to ash.

He looked over his shoulder at me, his face an unrecognizable shadow. "Is this how I finally kill him?"

I glanced down at the burning instruments—the "him" did not just mean his dead father. He was fighting Alastar…even if that meant destroying parts of himself.

I grabbed his hand and tried to pull him away. His arm was limp—he did not resist, but he did not yield to me. His eyes were fixed on the fire, watching every part of his guilt die in front of him.

"Come on!" I cried, pulling him toward the ballroom doors. My magical commands pushed through his skin, but nothing responded. I was banging on the door of a paper castle engulfed in flames.

I let go of his hand and swept through the ballroom with my magic. Only a couple of tears in the air sparkled—the intense heat had banished all of the moisture from the air.

I coughed as my eyes stung. I could not breathe, but I still had to try to get to him. "Derrick, we have to go!"

He still did not move. Was he even aware of what was happening?

Maybe Midnight could still hear me. Midnight spoke romance and not sense, but he was terrified of one thing more than Alastar.

"Do you want me to become ash with you, Midnight?" I fought through the smoke in my throat as embers swirled around us. "Fine. Hold me in your rage. Reduce me to cinders." I coughed out smoke. "Keep *suffocating* me!"

Light flashed in Derrick's eyes and he picked me up in his arms. My arms locked around his neck as he broke into a sprint. My face took shelter in his smoke-stained curls.

He kicked the garden doors open and I gulped in the cool, damp air of the night. He kept running, his feet crunching in the gravel.

My stomach lurched as we tumbled forward.

I laid on my back on the garden path for a moment, stunned. I rolled onto my hands and knees and tried to find my breath. The night breeze kissed my cheeks as I looked up, my eyes finding the rearing bull statue.

Derrick coughed as he kneeled in front of that deadly statue. He looked at me, his wide eyes searching for an answer as they watered.

But then he collapsed into the grass.

I ran to him, falling to my knees as I scooped up his limp body. My hand splayed over his slow-rolling heartbeat. Smoke stung my eyes as I cried.

I was losing him. He was losing himself. Was he too far gone even for me to heal?

I stroked his hair as his slow breath skated across my collarbone. He was fragile as glass in my hands. He would not let me into his mind. There was nothing I could do except…

"Help," I cried softly. "Help! I have the Duke! Help us!"

Footsteps pounded through the dewy grass. Palace guards kneeled beside me, each trying to take Derrick, but my arms stayed locked around him as my tears wet his hair. Heavier footsteps broke apart the crowd of guards.

"Does he breathe?" General Hyton asked.

I nodded with my cheek pressed to Derrick's temple. I was going to keep Derrick safe. I was going to make him well again. I was—

General Hyton grabbed me by the waist and tore me away.

"No!" I screamed through my sore throat. I only had enough time to see the palace guards pick up Derrick before the General's deep blue eyes were right in front of me.

His thumb tugged on my cheeks as he checked my eyes. My head fell into his palm as he looked at the underside of my jaw and my neck. "Are you hurt?"

"No," I said softly. "But Derrick—"

General Hyton glanced over his shoulder. "Take him to Baron Elvar's house in the city! Make sure everyone standing at the palace gates sees him—they need to know their Duke is alive!"

He turned back to me and held my jaw again. "Is the fire contained?"

I coughed. "It was just in the ballroom. Doors shut."

He let out a small breath. "Good. We will just wait until the fire has nothing else to eat."

General Hyton picked me up and my head flopped onto his shoulder. My body swayed a little as he carried me through the garden. He patted my arm and I let out a ragged breath.

The General might have kept me safe, but I still needed to fix Derrick…somehow.

He took a few more steps before voices began to murmur around me. Then his voice smoothed and brightened. "I trust you can keep her safe for me while I take care of the palace."

I lifted my head as the General lowered me to my feet. Brietta's hands wrapped around my shoulders and pulled me to her side.

While she and the General argued in hushed tones about the state of the palace, my eyes searched for Annalisa. I found her alone, holding her arms near some tall shrubs.

If anyone knew who could make Derrick whole again, it was the other half of his soul.

I broke away from Brietta and pushed through the crowd as panicked whispers hit my ears.

"Did you see them carry away His Excellency? He looked so weak!"

"He set fire to his own palace!"

"He's going to be Alastar the Mad!"

My stomach churned as the gossip spread like a disease. I fought the urge to throw my magic over the crowd like a net and burn their tongues.

Annalisa's watering eyes flicked up to meet mine as I called her name. She threw her arms around me before I could say anything.

The fight between Midnight and Alastar was destroying Derrick's mind. There had to be a way to kill Alastar. Of all the twelve Dukes, someone must have done it.

I thought back to Alastar the Wise's portrait. The stern and cold-eyed man that was painted shortly after his coronation did not match the same man from Freya's stories—a man who listened to her, respected her, and nurtured her ideas.

Had he slayed his generations-old monster before anyone had realized he had done it?

"Anna," I whispered, "I know we do not have much time…but if we find out more about your grandfather, we might save Derrick."

Annalisa's face steeled. She grabbed my hand and pulled me through the crowd until we came upon a group of whispering maids. All the maids backed away with downcast eyes except for one.

Merri looked softly at Annalisa even though her face was creased with worry. "Madame Thornebow, what can I—"

"Take me to the vault," Annalisa commanded.

The maids nearest us gasped softly. Merri's eyes went wide as she scanned the courtyard to see if anyone else overheard.

I furrowed my brows. I had abandoned the plan to uncover the truth about Ilsa long ago, why was Annalisa bringing it up again?

Merri leaned forward and lowered her voice to the barest whisper. "Anna, I know I promised to take you there one day, but now is not the time."

"Now is the perfect time," Annalisa said, not bothering to keep her voice low. "Everyone is so distracted with the fire that no one will see us."

Merri's throat trembled as she swallowed. Before any of the other maids could protest, she turned on her heel and weaved through the crowd. Annalisa followed, pulling me along with a brightness in her step.

Merri looked over her shoulder before she opened up a door on the side of the palace and quickly led us up a tight staircase. The smell of char filled our noses as we walked down the dark hallways within the palace walls.

A whisper skated across my teeth as I followed Annalisa. "Why are we going to the vault?"

"I already know everything about my grandfather," she replied. "If you are looking for a missing piece, it would have to be where all her treasures were. Grandfather doted on his Duchess more than any of my other ancestors did."

Merri stopped in front of a large rectangle in the middle of the dark hallway that must have been the back of a portrait.

She folded her arms and refused to look at us. "Push through. And hurry."

Annalisa shoved the back of the portrait so hard she momentarily became a battering ram.

The secret door swung open to a world of cold blue.

I looked up, a window in the ceiling stained with fractals of cerulean and indigo glass poured moonlight over the small room. Dazzling dresses on large mannequins sparkled in the icy light. Exquisite furs lay over carved wooden chairs. Gleaming gemstones sat in open pewter caskets.

And I thought *my* Derrick was generous.

Even though the room was filled with glittering treasures, my eyes fixed on a large portrait of Duchess Ilsa that rested on the floor. She looked through the portrait with a countenance of cold steel with a large blue diamond hanging from a long chain around her neck.

The Diamond of the North in all her glory.

Annalisa said nothing as she walked to the portrait. Her eyes watered as she gently touched the canvas, her fingertips tracing her grandmother's young and flawless face, then her mythically-long hair.

She turned to me and the familiar hardness in her eyes had returned. "Do you see any answers?"

I scanned the portrait and my eyes settled on the large diamond around her neck. Just as Brietta had said, a diamond that large and colorful would have been abhorrently expensive, even for such a prized bride.

Maybe because it was not actually a diamond…

I swept the room with my magic and a flash of white caught my eye. White light flowed out of the thin seams of a black box on one of the tables.

The velvety box caressed my palms as I opened it and I finally let myself smile—Ilsa's necklace was a Nordingaard crystal.

My magic poured into the crystal as I searched for memories trapped inside the facets. A sweet humming echoed in my mind and my palms tingled where they touched the crystal.

I was almost in…

"People are coming!" Merri hissed through the portrait hole.

I quieted the light from the crystal and dropped the heavy necklace beneath my bodice.

Annalisa and I hurried back through the portrait. We quietly snuck through the walls, following Merri's lead.

I chewed on my thumb until I broke skin, leaving little drops of blood on the stone walls as we walked.

I should have been marking the inner labyrinth more, but at least I had a way to get back to Ilsa's vault if I needed more clues.

The sky was a light periwinkle as we stepped out into the courtyard. Even the fresh dew on the grass could not mask the smoky smell that hung in the air.

"Where is she?" an angry voice shouted.

If I had not been looking at Annalisa, I would have missed the flinch that preceded the wide smile. "Grigory!"

I furrowed my brows. Why would she flinch?

Golden-haired Grigory shoved through the crowd, but his dark eyes lit up when he saw Annalisa. His grey traveling cloak fluttered as he spread his arms wide. "There you are, precious!"

Annalisa crashed into his embrace harder than Grigory expected and threw off his balance.

"Watch it," Grigory snapped as he caught himself. "You know that's my bad leg."

Annalisa drew up her shoulders sheepishly. "Sorry, sorry. I just missed you."

He gave her a half smile and then kissed her cheek. "I hear we are clear to go back into the palace." He tugged her waist tightly against his chest. "After I am done with you, I need to find that brother of yours for a little conversation."

Annalisa's cheeks flushed and she did not argue. He turned with her and they joined the crowd of maids and servants who sleepily walked back into the palace.

I quietly kept a few paces behind them as they ascended the palace steps. Grigory missed a step and lost his balance. He caught himself by bracing against Annalisa, but his quiver tipped and a single arrow slid out onto the palace steps.

I was not familiar with too many arrows, but I had never seen one that was black as Death on the sharp tip.

Before I could pick up the arrow, it snapped under the lead foot of a sleepy servant. The black-stained arrowhead skidded down the stairs and was lost in the crowd.

The question of where Grigory had been weighed on my mind, but Ilsa's crystal weighed heavier on the center of my chest.

The full moon was in two nights—whatever memories were inside Ilsa's crystal would be my last chance at healing Derrick so I could free Fraleigh.

The fate of Derrick's mind and Riyan's life weighed on my shoulders. I could not fail.

Chapter Thirty Nine
Thunderstorm

Murdered in his bed is what I had grown up hearing.

So that is where I sat.

I folded my legs beneath me in the middle of the Duke's bed, careful not to let the Hyton dagger cut my leg. The pearl headband from Riyan kept my hair from falling into my face. Even while in a fold between worlds, he still took care of me with his gifts.

I held Ilsa's Nordingaard crystal in my hands. Gentle humming pulsed into my palms, beckoning me to see the Diamond of the North's secrets.

Just as I was about to dive into the memory that whispered into my mind, my eyes suddenly pulled to an empty spot on the floor near the door. My heart tugged near that spot, but I had no idea why.

I shut my eyes and focused on the dozens of memories the crystal held.

Show me your husband, Ilsa. Show me the man he was.

A whisper of feathers carried me into the memory and deposited me in a chair in the palace library. Derrick lounged in a chair opposite me, the firelight casting a warm glow on his face.

What was Derrick doing in the memory? I thought I was seeing Ilsa's life not…

I got a closer look…it was not my Derrick, it was Alastar the Wise. He had the same square edge to his jaw like Riyan and General Hyton, but his resemblance to the Derrick I knew was uncanny. From the dark curls to the sad eyes, he looked nearly identical.

Ilsa appeared next to me as quietly as a whisper. The crystal around her neck glittered in the orange firelight.

She turned her face to the light of the fire. "Derrick, you have your son. Now I want mine."

The chill of her voice could have dampened the fire. Just as she had pledged on her wedding day, she held no love for her doting husband.

Alastar the Wise looked up from his book. "What do you mean, my darling Ilsa?"

Ilsa tightened her grip on the back of her chair. "You raise your heir the way you want—with logic and discipline. I raise my child the way I want—with love and tales of the North."

Alastar the Wise let out a low sigh and snapped his book shut. "Anything you wish for is yours."

A raised voice behind a veil pulled on my consciousness. Was something happening in the physical world? I dropped my magic as the memory dissolved around me.

I grounded myself on the Duke's mattress and listened again.

"Do you not have ears, Thornebow rat?" an irate voice snapped. "I asked you where my sister was!"

Had Annalisa gone missing?

I quickly shoved Ilsa's crystal pendant beneath the blankets and jumped to my feet. A chill rushed through my body as I passed the spot on the floor that had taken my attention moments before.

I reached the door just as Grigory replied, "Can you dogs not let her rest? She needs time to pack before we escape from this tastelessly opulent brothel disguised as a palace."

I opened the Duke's chamber doors. Grigory and Sapphira were standing toe-to-toe in the hallway.

Sapphira glowered down at him. "Not Anna, I meant Rubia! I cannot find her or Pearl."

Grigory sneered. "Not my problem. If you will excuse me, *Empress,* I have an urgent appointment in the Duke's study."

Sapphira rolled her eyes and disappeared through the nearest door in the hallway, but my eyes followed Grigory as he went down the hall.

Was Derrick back in the palace already? Why did Grigory want to speak with him?

The flame around my heart sparked to life and tugged me forward. I glanced over my shoulder at the abandoned crystal in the bed. I needed to see Ilsa's memories so I could find a way to kill the monster in Derrick's mind…

…but leaving Grigory alone with Derrick could provoke the monster to cause even more damage.

I shut the door behind me and crept down the hall. I counted three doors down from Annalisa's bedroom and pulled the sconce on the wall.

I was within the walls in a heartbeat.

My magic swept through the dark narrow halls. The small droplets of my blood stains on the walls sparkled in my mind's eye like a tiny path of glowing moonstones.

The paths would lead me either outside or to Ilsa's vault. Ilsa's vault might be near the Duke's study, so maybe if I followed that…

Then my magic picked up a glimmer of a new path…and it seemed fresh. I inched closer to a smear of blood on a brick—the blood was darker than mine, but still sparkled with magic.

I smiled—Daigen.

With the white light in my chest guiding me, I followed Daigen's trail through the halls until I found a small "X" in smeared blood on the back of a large portrait.

I held my breath and placed my fingertips on the portrait, only pushing slightly forward…

"You got what you wanted, now I want the rest of it."

Grigory's voice made my arms freeze. I had only opened the portrait enough so that I saw a sliver of the Duke's study on the other side.

A low chuckle echoed through the study and a shiver crawled down my spine. I did not need to see him to know it was Derrick but his voice sounded…rougher. "And what exactly did I pay you to do?"

My brows furrowed. Derrick had made a deal with Grigory?

I dared to push the portrait open only a sliver more. Grigory's strong, folded arms were in view and I caught the corner of his sneer. "You wanted Bloodstone dead before he could seal that blood bond and you got it. Hand over the rest of the eight thousand marks."

I held my breath so I would not gasp. No, Derrick would never—

Derrick slammed something that sounded like a goblet onto the desk. "The deal was one thousand up front to agree, then seven thousand when Riyan Bloodstone was eliminated and Serafina was safe at the palace."

No. I could not, *could not,* believe my Derrick would have done it.

Boots thudded against the floor.

"And still," Derrick said in a low growl, "I just overheard my uncle tell Baron Elvar that Riyan is still alive."

Grigory shifted on his feet. "The Queen of the Giants took him, I saw it. He is as good as dead."

"Not the same as dead."

The cold truth sunk in and I could not deny it for a moment longer. I had patched up the wounds in his mind, stayed with him, and cherished him…

…and he paid Grigory Thornebow eight-thousand marks to murder my Riyan.

"I spent weeks hunting him!" Grigory shouted. "I shot at him in the lily field. I set off an avalanche on the mountain. I was even attacked by two birds, but everywhere I tracked him, he used your girl like a human shield!"

Every strange noise in the trees back in Bloodstone, every unsettling feeling…I had just written off Riyan's heightened awareness as mere paranoia, or the strange feelings as magic, but no—it was Grigory Thornebow the whole time. He followed us through the mountain. His bootprints were in the snow at the peak of Nordingaard. He was the one who—

"I almost landed an arrow in his eye," Grigory said, "but he moved at the last second and I got her instead!"

He had poisoned me. His arrows were tipped with Thornebow thistle.

A clatter echoed through the room and suddenly Derrick slammed Grigory into the wall. His white-knuckled fists gripped Grigory's collar and his face was ruddy with drunkenness.

Had I not seen his corpse, I would have thought Anders had Grigory by the collar.

Alastar was taking over.

Derrick bared his teeth. "You shot my Serafina?"

Grigory threw Derrick off, twisting him against the wall, and slammed his forearm against Derrick's throat. A flash of a blade appeared in Grigory's hand and he stabbed the wall next to Derrick's cheek.

My heart raced but my blood ran cold.

Derrick's chest rose and fell as he stared Grigory down. Derrick bested Grigory in height, but he must have been too drunk to resist his hold.

"The whole Dukedom knows you have no honor, so I'm not surprised you are trying to cheat me again." The edge of the blade kissed Derrick's cheek, leaving a bead of blood on his skin. "But let me make myself clear…"

He dug the blade deeper. "I'm a fucking Thornebow. We don't stay down after you Hytons step on us. I'm not handed what I deserve like the rest of you pampered dogs, I *take* it." Grigory leaned closer. "So give me what I'm owed, or I'll make sure you *never* see Annalisa again."

Derrick's eyes flashed. He shoved Grigory and cracked his fist against his jaw.

I held my breath. The portrait stayed open as I backed away.

Grigory fell back, but quickly rose to his knees as Derrick stood over him.

Blood dripped from Derrick's cheek, but his eyes were murderous. "I will rip your tongue out of your mouth. I will break every one of your fingers. A quick death on the scaffold is more than you deserve—"

"Death?" Grigory flicked his knife to his own neck and shot Derrick a mocking glare. "You kill me, you kill your twin sister."

Derrick's brow stayed hard, but he took a step back as Grigory shakily rose to his feet. "You cannot threaten me, Derrick, so give me my fucking marks."

I could have helped Derrick, but he had given me a dagger with a loving smile and then turned around and hired an assassin.

Alastar XII would never get the benefit of my magic again. I had wasted my days and nights trying to heal him so he would release Fraleigh, but I was done. I would burn him from the inside until "*Ipse Dixit*" sprang from his throat.

He offered eight thousand marks to kill Riyan? I would make him pay for it *tenfold.*

Then the raging flames in my heart turned a different direction. Those bastards had brought Annalisa into their plans. Grigory was threatening her safety and using her as a bargaining tool.

I had to warn her. I had to get her away from him.

My feet pounded down the hallway until I stared at the river of blue carpet on the other side of the wall.

I flung open the door of Annalisa's room. She stood near a trunk bearing the Thornebow silver fox as she rolled up the canvas of her completed painting.

I slammed the door shut and clicked the lock. "Anna, I have to hide you."

"Why?" Her voice was hollow and her eyes were downcast.

I crossed the room. "Grigory is angry."

Annalisa shrugged. "Men get angry. Not much we can do about it."

Damn it, why was she acting so strange?

I gripped her wrists and her eyes shot up. "He hurt Derrick and threatened him with hurting you too."

The light between her eyes opened up. Thunder rolled in my mind.

Annalisa's voice was distant as grey storm clouds moved into the edges of my vision. "But Grigory said he and Derrick were friends in school…"

Darkness blanketed my vision and the rumbles of thunder turned into claps of a sky's rage. The rainstorm crashed into the surface of my mind, completely drowning out Annalisa's voice.

I leaned into the storm, the sheets of cold rain barrelling down as I walked beneath the dark clouds.

A strike of white lightning lit up a memory in the clouds—Annalisa's bedroom lock clicking shut.

"All right, Annalisa. Let's get this over with."

The thunder rolled. The raindrops hit my face in hundreds of tiny punches.

Second lightning strike—sharp hands picking at fingernails.

"Grigory, no…I am not ready yet. Just give me one night to rest and—"

The rain fell harder. Faster.

Third lightning strike—dark eyes flashing with primal rage.

"You're my wife. You don't get to tell me no."

A deafening clap of thunder threw me onto my back. The weight of the storm pressed on my chest. The rain turned into shards of icy hail that stabbed me over and over.

"Please, stop! Please—"

A hand squeezed the sides of my neck and the echoes of Annalisa's voice turned into nothing more than a squeak. My hands flew to my neck as I coughed, drowning in the rain, but I felt nothing on my skin but the pain of burning fingerprints.

Shallow gasps and cries echoed through the raging clouds.

Fourth lightning strike—the violet and orange leaves of the tree above Annalisa's bed. Then the two ravens flying away. Then black painted wings warped through frightened tears.

I gritted my teeth, fighting through the downpour, and shoved myself out of the memory.

Pastel shades flooded into my vision. My body trembled and shivered, the hairs on my skin standing pin-straight. My eyes snapped to Annalisa's bed, then the ravens above it.

He…he violated her.

Annalisa dropped her canvas and gripped my forearms. Her voice broke. "What did you see?"

I tore my eyes from the painted ravens to her white face. I examined her neck—where Grigory's hands had bruised her weeks ago.

But she had covered it up. She covered it *all* up.

My voice shook as my white flame incinerated my chest. "He hurt you."

"No, Sera, he loves me!" Annalisa pleaded. "You do not understand, he just made a mistake!"

Twin flames burned behind my eyes. I could not see anything other than the glow of my outrage. My hands slid around her wrists.

Even though Annalisa begged me to forget what I saw, her door was still wide open. Her blood was glowing in her veins. Her inner self cried out, "*Help me. Help me. Help me.*"

So I answered her call.

Invisible fire hissed through my teeth. "My magic smolders in your veins. His hands shall sear if he touches your skin."

Lightning from Annalisa's mind struck against my magic. I did not fight it, but leaned into it—pushing my love for Annalisa to overpower what Grigory had done.

My body shook, but my voice was strong. "And should he ever try to take you again…he will *burn*."

The power surged from my heart, through my arms, and then to my hands where it passed into Annalisa's body.

My curse wrapped around her veins like a ribbon, sealing my enchantment in her very blood. As soon as that ribbon was tied, I released my grip on Annalisa's wrists and collapsed to the floor with a gasp.

I blinked through my blurry vision. Annalisa examined her arms with wide and fearful eyes. "You…you cursed me?"

"I protected you." I let out a shaking breath and pushed myself off the floor. "He will never—"

"He is my husband and now he cannot even touch me?" she screamed. "I could be carrying his child right now!"

I furrowed my brows. I helped her and she was screaming at me? Was she just worried about a possible baby?

I stood up and held out my hand. "Here, maybe I can check to see if you really are—"

She shoved my hand away. "Just because you are never getting Riyan back did not mean you had to take me away from *my* husband!"

She pushed past me, but I matched her fire with my own. "Annalisa, I *will* get him back, but why are you angry—?"

Annalisa was nearly at the door before she turned and threw down her fists at her sides. "No! No matter what you and Brietta do, Derrick will never let go of Fraleigh, he will never sign a reformation, and nothing will *ever* change!"

My white flame blazed. "I will force him, I am powerful enough to—!"

But her watering eyes quieted the flame around my heart. She shook her head, as if no power in the world could chase away the storm in her mind. "We were never lionesses…we were just crazy like my mother."

She opened her door but paused for a heartbeat. "And we were doomed like my grandmother."

She slammed the door. My white flame intensified with every pound of my heart.

I could have found Derrick and forced him to bend to my will, but my heart's desire did not lead me toward wrath.

Though the pull around the diamond in my heart went against all logic and sense, I chose to trust it.

I left Annalisa's room and pushed open the doors with the carved bulls. The panel in the northern wall was already open.

Riyan was my reason for starting this journey, maybe that was where my heart's desire was leading me.

I walked toward the northern wall when the air tightened around my neck and stopped me. I looked down as the magic in the air strangled me. I was in the same spot on the floor that had pulled my eyes earlier.

My white flame flared around my heart, pouring power in my veins. What about this spot was so important that my magic directed me to it?

Then I caught a sparkle of white light in the corner of my eye. On the Duke's bed, Ilsa's Nordingaard crystal flared white light through the blankets. The air around me was sticky, saturated with magic and memories.

I swallowed as I stared, and every question I had led to one answer.

Ilsa.

Chapter Forty
Truth of the Diamond

I turned toward the Duke's bed, ready to unlock the truth beneath Ilsa's Nordingaard crystal, when the sight of a maid holding a silver tray made me freeze.

My heart pounded in my ears as our eyes met. Her eyes widened as she gripped the tea tray in her hands.

"Pardon me, Miss Hyton," she said with a dip of her head. "This is for His Excellency's afternoon tea."

I held my breath. She was looking at me, not the bed—she did not see the glowing crystal beneath the blankets.

I gave her a tight smile and took the tray from her, trying not to appear too eager for her to leave. Derrick would be back to his chambers for tea soon. I did not have much time to search through Ilsa's memories.

The silver tray rattled as I set it on a low table. Steam softly curled out of the teapot's spout and tickled my nose.

Smelled perfectly brewed…and I had not refreshed myself in a while.

I poured myself half a cup and tasted it. The sweet taste coated my tongue and I hummed in delight as it ran down my throat. Rosaline definitely did not brew it.

I set the cup on its saucer with a clatter and jumped back into the large bed. I fished Ilsa's crystal out from under the blankets and poured my magic into it.

Show me how I can fix what is broken.

The soft beating of white wings carried me into a memory of the Duchess's bedroom and placed me on a couch next to Ilsa. The pleasant scent of freshly-cut flowers filled the room. Ilsa's Nordingaard crystal dangled from her neck as she traced the leather cover of the book in her lap.

A young maid with curly chestnut hair opened the bedroom door. Her eyes were wide as tea saucers. Ilsa's eyebrows raised at the rhythm of her footsteps.

"Oh, Merri, Baron Thornebow sent me another book!" Ilsa said with a smile. "The cover has the most delicious design worked into the leather, but could you read it to me?"

Merri took the book and flipped open the cover and her face went white. I stood and looked over Merri's shoulder. On the front page read: "*Run away with me, Ilsa. I understand you like he never did.*"

Merri snapped the book shut with a tense breath.

"What did the front cover say?" Ilsa kneaded her skirt. "I heard he was going to write me a sweet note!"

"It was a joke about a cow, Your Excellency," Merri lied. She hid the book behind her back and took Ilsa by the hand. "Come with me, your son is in trouble."

I followed Ilsa and Merri down the palace halls until we reached the wooden door of the Duke's study.

Ilsa's hands hurriedly felt around the door until she found the handle. She pushed the door to reveal Alastar the Wise at his desk with young Ragnar and Anders standing in front of him. Alastar the Wise had grey streaks in his curls and Anders was the handsome man I recognized from his coronation portrait.

"My darling Ilsa," Alastar the Wise said in a tense voice, "leave us. This matter is none of your concern."

"If it involves *my* son, it concerns me." Ilsa reached out and Ragnar took her hand. He was about the same age as he was in Astrid's memory, with his long white hair flowing down his back.

I settled near the wall and got a clear view of Anders rolling his eyes at Ilsa lovingly clutching Ragnar's hand.

Ragnar smiled. "Mama, I have wonderful news—I have a son. The House of Hyton finally has an heir!"

Ilsa's white eyebrows lifted only for a moment before her face softened. She splayed her hand over Ragnar's heart.

Anders glared at his younger brother. "Freya is actually in labor this time. The twins will be here soon and—"

"And you have a weakness within you that makes you only have girls," Ragnar said smoothly.

Anders set his jaw and cut a glance to his father, who did not so much as blink.

Ragnar ignored his brother and held his mother's hand over his heart. "Astrid Bloodstone had my son, Mama. I fell in love with the North, just like you wanted!"

Alastar the Wise leaned on his fists. "The House of Hyton will have an heir."

Ragnar's eyes flashed with triumph.

"We will have a strong lineage."

Ragnar squeezed his mother's hands.

"But it will *not* be because of you."

Ragnar's face fell. "But I am the only one with a male—"

"And I have six granddaughters perfectly capable of ruling," Alastar the Wise interjected, his voice hard.

Anders's eyes widened.

Alastar the Wise was going to make his granddaughters eligible for the throne? Did that mean he had listened to Freya all those years ago? Was he about to sign the reformation making Lycaster women citizens like Freya had dreamed of?

I walked over to Alastar the Wise and examined his hard face. Maybe he had not killed the Alastar in his mind yet, but he was close.

There was something in his eyes…something clear and pure…

Anders stepped forward. "Father, my daughters were not raised to—"

"Then we can change that," Alastar the Wise cut in. "Just as Freya said, what has chasing after the perfect male heir gotten the Hytons? Bloodshed and betrayal!"

Anders shook his head. "Freya—"

"Is right." Alastar the Wise glared at his son. "If you had not spent so much time filling her with Cupid's Blood and instead *listened* to her, you might know that too."

The fierce protection…the reverence in his voice…the respect…

…Alastar the Wise *loved* Freya. It was not romantic, but it was pure and powerful.

Was it powerful enough to kill the centuries-old monster in his head?

Anders's eyes darkened. "*You* pressed me for an heir, Father. All you ever told me growing up was the importance of our line—"

"Then let that be my greatest regret of my reign." Alastar the Wise turned his ire to Ragnar. "Second only to this—I let your mother raise you. You ruined a young girl's life, but now you will finally reap the consequences of your actions. You will not marry *anyone*."

Ilsa gasped. "Derrick, no! You cannot do that!"

Alastar the Wise cut a glance to his eldest son. Anders bit down his thinly-veiled frustration and ushered a wide-eyed Ragnar out of the study.

I crossed to the closed door, the very edge of the memory, where Ilsa heard her eldest son whisper, "I will not put my daughters through this hell. I stand with you, brother. If I have no son, yours *will* have the throne."

Anders *wanted* Riyan to inherit the crown?

Alastar the Wise rose from his desk and took both of Ilsa's hands. She clutched his fingers and her brows knitted in a plea. "Derrick, we agreed that he was my son. Let him have his love! You know Fraleigh would still—"

"I do not trust his intentions," Alastar the Wise replied gently yet firmly. "What was he doing going after a girl who was not in his selection year?"

He had a point. Why had Ragnar pursued Astrid knowing they would never marry?

"Maybe because he wanted a real choice in who he married!" Ilsa cried. "Do you really think people fall in love with whomever they pick out of that pen of women?"

Alastar the Wise swallowed, his eyes filling with the heartbreak that Ilsa would never see. "He will answer for his irresponsibility. That is my final word on the matter."

Ilsa threw down her husband's hands and walked with a scowl out of the study. I followed her into the darkness right before the door slammed shut.

I had reached the edge of the memory, so I pulled myself out of that fractal of the crystal. I took a breath as the smell of the Duke's bedchamber filled my nose.

Suddenly my chest was tight and the air felt like syrup. The memories of decades of tears shed in that bedroom had flooded into my body all at once.

Different magical signals screamed in the back of my mind. My white flame flared at the many cries for help, filling my arms and legs with righteous heat.

Then one cry dominated over the others—it was rough, demanding, and desperate. The fabric between worlds stretched as the cry from somewhere beyond got louder and harsher.

My eyes snapped to that empty spot on the floor and I could not even blink. I gave in, letting the tears in the air push on my back, beckoning me to leave the bed. I put one plodding foot in front of the other as my body tingled with energy.

I fell to my knees on the floor and my hands splayed over the rug. The tears below me were bitter and cold. Regret. Lies. Disdain.

Then I closed my eyes and my magic let the memory take me away.

A sharp gasp clawed through the darkness. Thin strips of moonlight entered the memory, illuminating Ilsa folding out of her bed as she clutched her throat.

My stomach turned. This was it. This was the night she died.

Her Nordingaard crystal swung from her neck as Ilsa choked on nothing. She stumbled through her room and out the door. I had no choice but to follow her as she raced down the hall to the door with the carved bulls. She found the handle immediately and shoved open the door.

"Derrick!" she cried through her hoarse voice. "Derrick, help!"

I followed Ilsa as she ran into the bedroom. The curtains around the Duke's bed flew back and Ragnar emerged from the mattress. His chest heaved as he unwound two crimson ribbons from his wrists.

Alastar the Wise's body was lying on top of the mattress. His eyes were bulging, his face was purple, and a thin red line marked his neck.

Ragnar had killed his father—strangled him with the hair ribbons Astrid left outside Bloodstone Fortress.

Ragnar ran for his mother. "Mama!"

Ilsa's eyes widened. She could not see her husband's body in the bed, but her fading blood bond revealed *exactly* what her Little Diamond had done.

He put his hands on her shoulders as his mother gasped. The red ribbons dangled from his wrists. "I did it for love. You told me love was the most powerful magic there is, and now my love is going to save you."

I scowled. Just as my mother knew the taste of poison, I knew the taste of a lie.

Love had *nothing* to do with Ragnar's motivations.

"Rag—" Ilsa choked.

Ragnar held Ilsa's crystal in his hand and he sang. "No girl, can't be undone. I won't stop 'till your life is won."

The crystal glowed weakly. *He* was praying to the Man of the Mountain to fight Death. He was trying to sever his mother's blood bond with sorcery.

Ragnar's face lit up. "Don't you sleep until we've run to the West—"

But only a plea of true, pure love can persuade the Man of the Mountain to listen. And because Ragnar was lying…

The light of the crystal went out. Ilsa's gasping stopped and she fell out of her son's grip to the floor—the *exact* spot where I was kneeling in the living world.

"No!" Ragnar cried, falling down with his mother as her face turned as violet as her eyes. "Please, Mama, no! Astrid told me this would work! I thought I could spare you…I thought I was powerful enough…"

But Ilsa did not answer. Ragnar cried bitter tears alone.

The Diamond of the North would shine no more, so there were no more memories left for me to see.

I pushed out of the tragic past and opened my eyes. I mentally traced the twisted fibers of the carpet below my hands and the tears from Ilsa's last breath and Ragnar's failure sang back at me.

The General's lies stained the memory. If he had not murdered his father for his love of Astrid, why had he done it?

The Nordingaard crystal still glowed white as it dangled from my neck. The magic forced a prickling sensation up my shoulders as I tried to hold myself upright.

Another memory was desperate to show itself, but I thought I was done?

I glanced up at the teapot. The steam had stopped curling out of the spout. Derrick would be back soon. I had no time to—

The sound of splintering glass pricked my ears. I gritted my teeth as the grating noise echoed in my mind. The same force from before pushed me to keep searching the memories.

My mind started to fog. My eyelids were heavy. My body might have been exhausted from the intensity of the memories, but the spirit behind the memory would not yield.

The insistence was all too familiar, like a cup forced into my hands.

I glared at the glowing crystal as it dangled. My white flame burned with disdain but twisted through my limbs as I connected with the force that beckoned for my magic.

Show me, Anders.

With a crash through my mind, the Duke's study materialized in my vision. Starlight streamed through the windows. Young Anders was at the oak desk, the crown of Lycaster resting on his head. His eyes were bloodshot. An empty bottle of spirits was next to one hand as he pushed Ilsa's crystal around the surface of the desk with the other.

His hands were dry and cracked like he had washed them a dozen times.

The door clicked open and Ragnar walked in. Anders did not even look up.

"We did it." Ragnar said with a rueful smile. "The Dukedom believes that Baron Thornebow killed Father. Your plan was masterful."

Anders still scowled as he stared down at the fractals of the crystal.

Ragnar cleared his throat. "He committed high treason anyway, with what he wrote in that book. What a moron. He knew Mama could not even read it herself."

Anders rose from the desk. "Do you think this is fucking amusing? In the past twelve hours, I was crowned, we executed a Baron, and Nikkolas Bloodstone accosted me about what you did to his daughter!"

Ragnar smiled. "He will calm down once I marry Astrid and his new grandson is named heir."

Anders steeled himself. "I already took care of Nikkolas. You are to marry *no one else* but Astrid Bloodstone, I gave Fraleigh the order."

Ragnar's smile fell only slightly, as if he had suddenly grown suspicious. "Then let us marry right away. Lycaster needs an heir and the sooner we legitimize our union—"

Ragnar stopped, his eyebrows knitting in confusion as his brother's low laughter filled the study.

"You really thought this would work?" Anders said. "You thought you could take Mother's bedtime legends as fact, trap a hapless girl into bearing you an heir, and come for my throne?"

Anders was just as paranoid as Derrick had been.

I waited for Ragnar to offer another explanation, but his silence made me weary.

Finally, he put on a smooth smile and spoke up. "You cannot just assume the worst of me, brother."

"Oh, I will not assume. In fact, I will give you everything you want." Anders waved his hand toward the door. "Marry her. Prove your intentions were pure."

I knew from Ilsa's memory that Ragnar's intentions were not pure, but I still hoped that he would deny his brother's accusation, or offer another explanation, or change his mind.

I held onto hope for the girl in the wheeled chair who painted him on her walls and was certain that he would come back for her.

But for all my hoping, Ragnar's face hardened. "What are you not telling me?"

Anders laughed again. "Your bastard son is a giant." He laughed louder as he stepped around his desk. "Try getting Lycaster to rally around you with an abomination for an heir and a *madwoman* as Duchess!"

Ragnar's smooth veneer dissolved and he was white with shock. He did not even move as the flash of a blade appeared in his brother's hand.

"Just as I thought," Anders said. "I do not need you to keep the House of Hyton strong."

Quick as lightning, Anders grabbed Ragnar's long hair and sliced it off with one swing of the knife. Ragnar's eyes fell to his beautiful white hair as it tumbled to the floor.

Anders pointed the knife to his brother's chin. "You wanted to be a killer, now you get to be one—for *me*. You go to the military academy, your mistake stays in that fortress, and the truth of what you did dies with us."

Ragnar's face turned cold. "You said you stood with me."

Anders smiled. "That was before *my* son was born mere hours ago." He pressed the very tip of the blade into his brother's chin. "That was before you k-killed o-our…"

Anders clamped his mouth shut. His grip on the knife weakened. Now *his* face was white.

Ragnar's eyes gleamed. "Oh, Andie. Is the stutter back? What would the Barons think?"

Even I could feel the power shift in the room. Somehow, Ragnar's towering height became even more obvious.

Before Anders could even blink, Ragnar grabbed his brother's wrist and twisted the knife free. He snatched the hilt and weighed it, looking down at the blade in consideration as it cut through the gentle starlight from the window. Anders was frozen in horror.

His cold eyes slowly looked up from the blade to his older brother. "Actually, Andie, I think you need me after all."

What was before me was not mere sibling rivalry, but an Alastar trial that no one else in the Dukedom got to witness. One Hyton brother was made of glass, the other from cold steel. One wore the crown, but the other would have to keep him from shattering.

Especially when the eyes of the Dukedom would never look away.

Suddenly an invisible force pushed on my chest, shoving me toward the door. The spirit behind the memory was insistent that I leave, ashamed of his failure.

Anders had much more than that to be ashamed of.

With a final glare at the two brothers, I shot out of the memory with a crash.

As soon as my mind was back in my body, I sucked in a gasp and collapsed to the floor. I rolled onto my back and my eyes fixed on the ceiling. Ilsa's Nordingaard crystal weighed heavily on the center of my heaving chest, its white light still shining at the edge of my vision.

The truth of Ilsa was not what would damn the Hytons, it was the truth of her *son*.

Ragnar was the murderer, the monster, the…

I needed to think, but my mind was slow. My arms felt like they were filled with bricks. My eyelids drooped, threatening to crash closed at any minute.

This was not the magical exhaustion I had experienced before…this was…

I forced my head to roll back until I caught sight of the teapot.

The *tea*.

I pushed against the thick blanket of fatigue that was smothering me. My magic weakly fought the potion within me, but even my white flame was quieting.

A door clicked open. I pushed my head up just in time to see the toes of Derrick's boots.

Then everything went dark.

Chapter Forty One
Taste of Iron

Even within the void, darkness is never eternal.

Only my reprieve from the abyss was not so pleasant.

The sharp taste of iron weighed on my tongue. No, not just the taste of iron…an actual weight.

I opened my eyes but still could not see. Something heavy covered my eyes and scratched my face. I shifted my shoulders—I was lying on a floor made of steel plates. Iron chains manacled my wrists and ankles.

I tried to slow my breathing, even though I could only breathe through my nose. My mouth was sealed shut with an iron gag. I shook my head and both the chains of my gag and my chainmail blindfold rattled.

I had been captured—imprisoned for sorcery.

No time to panic, I had to figure out where I was.

Everything smelled metallic. I could not hear anything—not the rustling of wind, or the din of conversation, or even footsteps against the floor. I had never heard such loud silence before.

I must have been underground.

I writhed on the floor, the sharp rattling of my chains bouncing off the metal walls and floor. I pulled at my restraints and tested for a weakness, but I found none. My blindfold would catch all my tears. Steel mitts encased my hands so I could not scratch blood from my skin. The iron gag stopped me from biting my tongue or opening my mouth.

Every way I could think of using the moisture in my body to get a sparkle of magical tears, the Hytons had prevented it.

Though they would be useless for my escape, tears stung the backs of my eyes. The restraints were not made for me—they were Fraleigh's. If this is how far the Hytons would go to keep a fist over Fraleigh…how did I ever think I could convince Derrick to release her?

Even with all my struggling, the Hyton dagger stayed securely against my calf. I supposed Derrick did not bother to frisk a sorceress for weapons.

My heart ached. Had Derrick really imprisoned me and chained me?

A familiar voice echoed outside, like it filtered through a thick metal door. "Relax, Jonson, the little serpent is just waking up."

I smiled around my gag. Daigen was there, probably disguised as a mortal soldier, and he had spoken up loud enough that he wanted me to know it.

Though his presence was a strange comfort, he was not there to rescue me. Time was running out, but he had made it clear that my heart's desire would lead me to the right answers.

I focused on what little magic responded within my body. Seeing Ilsa's and Anders's memories had left me exhausted, but I could not give up. The magic drew my attention to the hint of familiar sweetness that lingered on the back of my tongue beneath the tang of iron. Although Derrick had hired an assassin behind my back, I could not believe he could ever bring himself to slip a sleeping potion into anyone's drinks.

And that tea was too good for Rosaline to have made it, in fact, it was…perfectly brewed.

General Hyton.

I screamed a curse around my gag. I had thought he was appeasing me because I was powerful, but no, he was coveting me. I had the magic of the North—I could bring down armies and defeat Death.

I had, no, I *was,* everything he had ever wanted.

I bit down on my gag. Fuck him, he was a monster. He had tricked Astrid into falling for him. He had used her love for him to get the crown of Lycaster. He…

…he sounded exactly like me.

I unclenched my jaw as my white flame gently fanned truth through my veins.

He was a monster, but so was I. Had I not seen his betrayal coming because he was merely my mirror?

As much as I wanted to deny it, I could not condemn the General for doing what I had done to Derrick for years. I had made him love me, want me, and need me because I had thought that was the only way I could have control.

Even for the past few weeks, what had I done? Entered his mind night after night to get him to free me. I had cared for Derrick and wanted to heal him, but my motivations were not entirely pure either. The result was still the same.

Ragnar's actions had broken Astrid…and I was going to break Derrick.

I shifted on the floor and rolled onto my back, letting the chains fully weigh on the center of my chest. I could not just wallow in failure. If I did not release Fraleigh by the full moon, Riyan's body belonged to Ganora.

Ganora had made her terms for Riyan's freedom clear, but there had to be another way. Something had to be more powerful than…

My eyes widened beneath the chainmail. The white flame gently danced around my heart, filling my body with white light from my chest down to my toes.

Every agreement had a back door except one—one that not even Ganora, nor anyone else, could interfere with.

I channeled what little magical energy I had and sent out a call to Daigen. I felt a little tickle between my eyes as he made the tether connecting his mind to mine. The connection was weak, but I still sent out: "*I know what I need to do. Can you get me to Nordingaard?*"

Daigen's answer filtered into my mind. "*I will free the corpse reaver. You run, and run fast.*"

Heavy footsteps slammed into metallic stairs outside of my prison and then two bodies snapped to attention.

Keys jingled. A heavy lock clicked open. Then another. Then another.

A frightened voice whispered outside the door, "General, are you sure—?"

"I fear nothing, Jonson," General Hyton replied. A heavy door groaned on its hinges. The General's voice was louder as he stood over me. "Especially not a girl who just needs a firm hand."

He grabbed my manacled wrists and hauled me to my feet. The chains slithered off my ankles and my legs were free.

The General's voice rumbled against my chest. "I will escort her to His Excellency myself."

My heart dropped. I needed to run, not face Derrick.

General Hyton pushed me forward and I blindly followed his lead. He kept his hand around my chains as we walked up a set of stairs.

His voice brushed against my ear. "Apologies for the preventative measures, but the palace is in chaos. The maids found you in the Duke's chambers and word spread like wildfire. Everyone from the peasantry to the nobility is calling for your head."

Even with a chainmail blindfold, I could see right through his lies. He had timed everything just right so Derrick would find me unconscious.

The General's voice dropped to a whisper only I could hear. "Our Duke is descending into madness. We cannot predict what he will do with you now, but I do know one thing for certain—he is so unstable, he needs his General now more than ever."

A muscle in his arm shivered as his thumb stroked my wrist. "And even a mad Duke would not kill a sorceress if she was blood-bonded to his General."

I nearly jumped up the next step but found nothing but air. My heart leaped as I fell, but General Hyton caught me.

He did not just want me as a sorceress, he wanted me…as a woman. I was the only noble woman free of a blood bond, making me able to bear children…*heirs*…oh, I was going to vomit.

I was no different than a teenage Astrid to him, an available womb.

General Hyton hauled me to my feet. "Your pink-beaked raven is caged in the guardhouse. Your Bloodstone allies have abandoned you.

Your mother has no sway over the Duke any longer. Your little friends are too wrapped up in themselves to help you."

He thought he could back me into a corner to agree to his horrid proposal?

A thought even more bitter than the iron on my tongue seeped through my mind. My white flame gently danced, spreading not anger through my veins…but pity.

General Hyton might have been the brother made of steel, but he was transparent as glass. If the gag had not forced me into silence, I would say…

I see you, Ragnar Hyton. I *am* you.

We clung to towers and then battlements like creeping vines. We carried the burden of a birthright that was never ours. We feasted on the greatness of our achievements yet we were always starving.

Always starving.

But just as I had learned to crumble, so could he. He did not need to seize the North like the Conqueror had. He did not have to plot, and kill, and fuck to finally have the satisfaction he craved.

The owner of the crimson ribbons in his night table drawer was still waiting for him. And if she was anything like her son, she would forgive him for coming to his senses nearly too late.

But he would not release my gag, so he could go through the rest of his life pretending he was not a monster too.

General Hyton halted me. I tried to figure out my surroundings—smell of gentle perfume, carpet beneath my feet, and the slow rhythm of the General's breath behind me.

He swept my hair from my back and over my shoulder. I scowled behind my gag as his breath caressed the shell of my ear. "You deserve mercy for everything you did for my son. As the General of His Excellency's army, I can give you that mercy in one of two ways: a blood bond on the full moon or a blindfold on the scaffold."

I held my breath as he wrapped a ribbon around my neck and suddenly the familiar surface of my Nordingaard crystal was flush against my throat.

He pulled the ribbon into a tight knot. "Think on it, Serafina. I would hate to see you go to waste."

A smile tugged on my lips that he could not see. General Hyton wanted my power, my magic, and my blood bond. He thought he could put me in a vulnerable position like he had with Astrid's pregnancy and force me to go along with his plan?

Little did the traitorous General know, I was not afraid of any axe on the scaffold.

The final stepping stone to finish what the Man of the Mountain had started had laid in front of me while I was chained and manacled. I was finally going to choose eternity. I would become ageless, deathless, and more powerful than ever.

I would make a bargain that not even the Queen of the Giants could refuse.

A life for a life given in love. Ganora wanted a weapon to free her sister? She could have *me*.

A door creaked on its hinges and the General's voice lifted to a deceptively reverential tone. "Your Excellency, I bring you the sorceress."

He pushed me through a doorway. I did not resist.

Once the General left, all I would have to do was manipulate Derrick one more time into letting me run. I would take Annalisa and Brietta, flee to Bloodstone Fortress, and trade my life for Riyan's.

Just as he had done for me.

Carpet beneath my feet turned into wood. The General's boots thudded across the floor until he retreated through the doorway.

The low ebb and flow of Derrick's breath reached my ears. It was slow, but strained and ragged, like a bull ready to charge.

All I had to do was face Alastar one more time, then we would all be free.

Chapter Forty Two
Consumed

My heart pounded in time with each of Derrick's footsteps as he approached me. Derrick would let me in again, and once he released my chains, I was going to run straight for Nordingaard.

I might not have freed Fraleigh, or the women of Lycaster, but at least I was going to free Riyan.

Derrick stepped behind me. Oak and vanilla mixed with the sting of spirits filled my nose.

He was drunk again? That would make this even easier.

He unwove the chains around my wrists and they dropped to the floor in a heavy heap. He unclasped the lock at the back of my head and I gasped as he pulled the iron gag out of my mouth. The gag landed on the floor with a loud thud.

Just as I thought, Derrick would not have kept the woman he loved in chains for long. I still had his heart. I still had his mind.

I counted his footsteps as he circled around to face me.

His hands floated up to either side of my face, his thumbs caressing the line of my jaw. Slowly, the chainmail clinked as he lifted my blindfold like a veil.

I opened my eyes—Derrick's face was hollow, his brow was hard, and his eyes were bloodshot. A slight red line was visible on his cheek from where Grigory's knife had nicked him, but otherwise he looked unharmed.

At least on the outside.

He let out a ragged breath through his nose. Even though his voice was dry, sadness soaked his words. "Did you use sorcery on me?"

My white flame seeped up my throat, carrying the truth with it, but I kept my voice cool. "You wanted to dream and I made it happen."

And if he let me get a little closer, I would let him dream again…

Derrick's eyes softened, but then snapped up as a loud knock pounded on the door.

I took the brief opportunity to scan the room. We were in the Duke's study. A golden sunset soaked the blue curtains and oak furniture.

"Your Excellency," a guard warned from the other side of the door, "you cannot just—"

"Derrick!" Brietta shouted. She pounded on the door again. "What are you doing to her? If you hurt her, I swear—!"

A guard grunted like he had just taken an elbow to the clavicle. Derrick stomped toward the door.

I kept my eyes on the far wall as the portrait of Alastar the Conqueror stared down at me. My arms shivered as I pictured him putting the golden collar around my neck as he did with Fraleigh.

Derrick yanked the door open. "You always think the worst of me! Does she look harmed to you?"

Brietta ran into the room and took my face in her hands. "Did anyone hurt you?"

Pages flipped in the back of my mind and the light between her eyes twinkled. I sent her a quick message: *"New plan. We run, now."*

Her brown eyes went wide, but the tether between us broke as Derrick slammed the door shut.

He tossed a glare at Brietta as he flipped the lock. "You knew about her. Of course you did!"

Brietta matched Derrick's glare. He walked to a cabinet against the wall and pulled out a bottle of spirits.

"Has anyone in this palace *not* committed treason?" His eyes flared as he uncorked the bottle. He took a swig and yanked the bottle from his lips. "Do I need to interrogate my sisters next? Find out who else is plotting against me?"

I shot Brietta a look, beckoning her to take my lead. "I never plotted to hurt you, Derrick."

Calm him one more time. That was all I had to do…

Derrick's darkened eyes flicked over to me and Brietta's hand slipped over mine.

A warm smile suddenly spread across Derrick's face. "Of course not, darling. Not you. Never you."

Derrick gestured to Brietta with his bottle. "*You,* however, have been plotting with my uncle to depose me."

I kept my face schooled but gritted my teeth. How could Derrick be so paranoid and still wrong?

Luckily, Brietta's voice was calmer than I expected. "Derrick, that is not true. I only spoke with the man to clean up your mess from last night."

Last night? Not even a full day had passed since Ragnar slipped the sleeping potion into my tea. I had more time to get to Nordingaard than I thought.

Derrick set down his bottle and spread his hands on top of his desk. "And sneaking around the library with Annalisa? The only use my twin has for books is to turn them into weapons."

Brietta stayed calm. "We found your mother's diary."

He scoffed. "And what did you find in those wine-stained pages? Inventive ways to manipulate your husband? Incoherent babble about my dead grandfather? Or perhaps a detailed list of every way to destroy me?"

I squeezed Brietta's hand. Derrick's paranoia had spiraled to an incomprehensible level. Maybe if he just let me touch him, I could put him to sleep one last time and give us a chance to escape.

Before I could take a step forward, Brietta straightened her spine and spoke up. "Our plans of freedom, Derrick. That was what was in the diary."

I looked from Brietta to Derrick. His brow creased and his shoulders stiffened.

Brietta took a step forward. "Full citizenship for the women of Lycaster. Property ownership. Access to inheritance. No more bride auctions."

I bit my tongue. Revealing our plans was not going to make Derrick any less paranoid, but it would at least give me time to look for a way out.

Derrick's voice was low. "You know I cannot do that."

Of course he would deny her—Alastar would never allow it.

My eyes darted toward the study door. There was at least one guard outside and likely the General too. Not ideal.

Brietta stepped forward until she was right in front of the desk. Her spine was straight. "It is time. Your mother knew it, your grandfather knew it—"

"The Barons would stop it." Derrick rose to his full height, but Brietta's eyes were still higher than his. "They are already looking for a reason to dethrone me and behead me. The only liberation you will *ever* see is when your head is liberated from your shoulders."

My eyes swept the walls, searching for the portrait I had looked through earlier.

Brietta gestured to me. "You fear the Barons when a sorceress has been by your side this whole time?"

Derrick barked out a laugh and shoved away from the desk. "I see what you are doing now. You are trying to use my love for Serafina against me."

He stepped in front of me and held my shoulders. Even though he looked at me with glassy eyes and a smile, the door into his mind was bolted shut.

I still had no way in *and* no way out.

He kept his eyes on me. "But you do not understand what Serafina and I have, Brietta. She demands nothing of me."

Brietta's voice had a deadly edge. "Because she has no choice—you own her."

He shot a glare at Brietta. "I never made that happen."

My white flame raged and I could not hold back. "You *liar.*"

Derrick's eyes widened. Even Brietta held her breath.

I stepped out of Derrick's embrace and glared up at him. "You gave me that dagger saying you just wanted to keep me safe, but then you hired Grigory Thornebow to kill Riyan before my blood bond was sealed."

His chest rose and fell as he silently looked at me. I tightened my hands into fists at my sides. "Eight thousand marks was quite a bargain— eliminate the Hyton heir *and* own me."

The air was tight as a noose. I barely reined in the flames inside me, ready to counter when Alastar finally broke free. If Derrick took a single step forward, I would choke him on his own tears.

But instead of fighting back, his face softened. "He was going to kill you, Serafina."

The ember in the center of my heart warmed and my fire cooled only slightly. He was still wrong. "Riyan would have never—"

"Not him." He shook his head slightly. "My father."

Brietta looked at me as I held my breath. Duke Hyton was a horrible man, but would he have really killed me?

Derrick grabbed the bottle of spirits by the neck. He took a long drink before leaning against the edge of the desk and staring at the sunset through the window. "He never even wanted that monster in Selection Night, but my damn uncle had backed Father into a corner. Uncle Ragnar led a surprise siege of Nordingaard without my father knowing—the prime opportunity to show off his bastard to the entire Dukedom." Derrick swirled the bottle. "He gave Father a choice—either Uncle Ragnar would reveal that *he* conquered Nordingaard where their Duke had failed…or his monster would get the first selection of a bride. Father had to choose stability of the Dukedom, even if that meant giving the dangerous heir his own line."

My eyes darted to Brietta and her face turned white—she was supposed to be Riyan's choice. *She* was the price of the Dukedom's stability.

Derrick turned to me and his voice broke. "Nothing was going to stop my father from trying to kill him…not even a blood bond with the woman I loved."

I could not breathe. My chest was tight, but my heart was warm.

He put down the bottle and stepped closer to me. His beautiful blue eyes swam. "So, yes, I paid Grigory to kill him. I gave you that dagger and promised you a marriage to another man if you protected yourself."

Derrick took my hands in his and suddenly I was trapped in the pools of his eyes. "Riyan was always going to die. If you had sealed that blood bond…I could not let you die with him."

My throat trembled with a fledgling sob. I wanted to scream at him and curse his blood for trying to murder Riyan. And for deceiving me. And for plotting behind my back.

But I could not deny that his intentions were anything but pure. Every ribbon of logic and sense in my mind twisted into an endless knot. Why could I not just hate him? Why could I not just put him to sleep and run like I had planned?

Derrick's thumbs stroked the backs of my hands and he smiled. "I would turn the world upside down for you, Serafina."

"You *ass!*"

We both turned. Brietta's white face had flared red.

"You only paid Grigory to save *her!*" she yelled. "If Riyan had chosen me like your father planned, you were just going to let me die with him?"

I yanked my hands out of Derrick's grip. He squared his shoulders and his lips opened to reply, but Brietta cut him off.

"Was I just the sacrificial Hyton lamb?" she shouted. "Big enough to breed but not valuable enough to save?"

His brows furrowed. "Brietta—"

"I wrote those damn poems!" Her eyes watered, but she still bared her teeth. "For years, it was *me!* And you would have just let me die!"

The situation was spiraling out of control. We had to get out, even if we just had to outrun Derrick without using magic.

Then Derrick turned to me and I froze. "That was you, Birdie. She is just lying—"

Brietta pushed herself between us. "How much longer are you going to stay in your damn dream, Derrick? There was no Birdie, there was Serafina and me trying to make you fall in love with her!"

Brietta was backing Derrick against the wall, so I scanned the portraits. Each one was too small, too high, or too round to be the one I needed…

"We were foolish schoolgirls, grasping for control wherever we could." Brietta stepped forward as Derrick stepped back. "But now *you* get to be the fool…"

My eyes settled on a portrait of three pink roses that was the right size…

"Serafina and I are leaving you…forever. Your line dies with you, you stubborn bull."

I quickly cast out my magic, sensing the faint twinkle of an "X" on the other side of the portrait.

Daigen had made both a window and a door.

"She is not leaving me!" Derrick cried.

I whipped my head around. Derrick's chest rose and fell as he barely contained his outrage.

My stomach knotted—Alastar was rising.

His voice was low and deadly as he faced Brietta. "You can lie to me all you want." He took a small step forward and Brietta took one back, then again. "I might not always know what day it is. Or how to speak properly. Or whether blood truly coats my hands. But one thing I know for certain is that Serafina *loves* me."

I nearly choked on my tongue as guilt consumed me whole. Derrick stepped over and held my face. My breath froze as tears pricked the backs of my eyes, but my white flame spread through my body, warming my throat as the truth that I had held back for years threatened to escape.

Soon, my life would no longer be mine. Soon, I would never have the opportunity to release the truth on my own terms.

So I finally let the truth out.

"Derrick, Brietta is not lying," I whispered. "I…I lied."

His brows knitted. "No, Serafina—"

"She wrote the poems." Tears wet my lashes. "I used her so you would fall in love with me. I used you to get the crown."

"But I do love you." He gripped my face and stole the air from my lungs. "And you love me…"

No music entered my mind, but the light between his eyes opened. He was begging, *begging,* for me to come in. To soothe his inner self. To stitch up his broken mind like I had done so many times.

"And you will not leave me." His voice shook. "You c-cannot leave me."

I stood on my toes and placed both my hands on his jaw. The ember in my heart was warm and pulsing. Midnight cried out to me as I made the thin tether between his mind and mine.

I closed my eyes and entered his mind. Midnight stared back at me in the center of the ballroom. All the stitches I had made every night glowed and strained under the widening cracks in the castle walls and floor.

I did not want to hurt him, but the flames around my heart raged with the truth, pushing me to my one true desire.

I needed Riyan to breathe again.

I pushed forward, my lips brushing his. "Sleep, Derrick."

My Nordingaard crystal warmed against my neck. The white light reflected in Derrick's wide eyes as I broke his heart.

I held back a sob as I gently quieted Derrick's mind, putting every bit of him to sleep, and I commanded: "*Let him dream.*"

But as soon as Midnight accepted the command, the words "I lied" echoed through the starlit ballroom. The glowing white threads disappeared. The cracks in his mind split wider. The castle foundation crumbled. Alastar's prison vanished.

With a low growl, Alastar slowly climbed out of the pit. Midnight only had enough time to look over his shoulder before the monster unhinged its wide jaw.

And Alastar ate him.

Part Five

Ice
and
Gold

Chapter Forty Three
Raven's Flight

The twelfth Duke of Lycaster laid at my feet on the floor of his study.

I shut my eyes and used every bit of my concentration to keep Derrick asleep, but the monster in his mind was running free.

Alastar rammed his horns into the magical barrier of dreams I placed in Derrick's mind. My tether over him shook.

"Brietta," I bit out as I struggled to keep my hold over Derrick's mind. "There is a portrait of three pink roses on the far wall…that is our way out."

Brietta's footsteps pattered to the wall then hinges creaked.

"How long will he be asleep?" she asked.

My muscles ached as my power drained little by little, but I gritted my teeth and held on. "Not long. We have to get Anna."

She quickly grabbed my hands and guided me through the portrait hole into the inner walls of the palace. I could only focus on maintaining the fading light of my magical tether as Alastar rammed into my magic over and over.

We had *minutes* before I lost control.

Brietta popped open a panel in the wall and low light from sconces filtered through my eyelids. The smell of perfume and old wood of the royal family's chambers filled my nose. My feet stepped onto the plush carpet as I followed Brietta's lead.

"Why are you avoiding me?"

My eyes snapped open as soon as Grigory's voice hit my ears. My white flame roared, filling every inch of my body with a furious heat—enough to incinerate a giant again.

The power was too great to ignore. I had to make a choice.

In a heartbeat, I let Alastar loose and focused on a different monster.

"Grigory, *please,*" Annalisa cried. "I am trying to protect you."

I yanked out of Brietta's grip and flung open Annalisa's bedroom door just as an agonized scream filled the air.

Grigory stared with wide eyes at his trembling hand. His palm flared red like he had just grabbed molten iron. Annalisa had her back to the wall and her arm in front of her like a shield—frozen in place from when Grigory had grabbed her wrist.

Grigory looked from his burned palm to Annalisa. "What did you do?"

My arms were shaking with rage as I lifted my hands. "Not enough."

His wide eyes met mine and my power flared. The tears in the water bowl on Annalisa's dressing table braided themselves into a rope of fire.

Grigory was a different kind of giant, but he would suffer just the same.

"*Burn.*"

The rope wrapped around his neck and he screamed. His hands flew up to his throat but he tore them away when they touched my flames.

My heart pounded. I could not kill him without killing Annalisa, but I would make him pay for what he did to her.

Annalisa's palms pressed into the wall behind her. She looked down at Grigory speechless, her eyes brimming with fear and pity.

"Come on, Anna!" Brietta cried. "The lionesses run together!"

Annalisa closed her eyes and pushed off the wall. She ran past Brietta and I, screaming her sisters' names in the hallway.

Grigory was on his knees and screaming when I released the rope.

Brietta pulled me out of the doorway and slammed the bedroom door shut with both hands. "How do we run? Where do we go?"

I took her hand and pulled her along the hallway. "Through the walls. Follow my lead."

Annalisa burst out of a bedroom door. "I cannot find any of my sisters!"

Brietta snagged Annalisa's hand as we ran past her. "We cannot wait! We have to go now!"

I had just turned the iron sconce to open the panel in the wall when a scream filled the halls. It was not the pained groans of Grigory as he nursed his wounds, but the broken, anguished cry of a man who had lost everything.

Derrick had just awoken into his worst nightmare…and now Alastar was fully in control.

I gritted my teeth and pulled Brietta and Annalisa through the wall. I led us through the dark halls, following the sparkles of magic I had left on the bricks until we saw moonlight.

Annalisa tore through the tight wooden door first, sprinting through the grass faster than I had ever seen her run. Brietta and I huffed as we struggled to keep up with her.

Tears streamed down Annalisa's face as she panted, her blonde curls flying out behind her as she ran into the night.

She ran so fast I swore she grew wings.

Annalisa ran right to the stables. I followed and the strong scent of hay hit my nose. Brietta caught up to me as soon as we were in the darkness of the stable.

"I…hate…running," Brietta panted.

"I hope you are ready to ride then," Annalisa said. She led a white horse out of its stall, it had already been reined and saddled.

"Sera, ride with me." She pointed to Brietta. "Brie, take Derrick's horse."

Merri led another white horse out of its stall. Her eyes glistened as she held out her hand.

"Here, Your Excellency," she whispered. "Let me help you up."

A warm hand pushed on my shoulder. "You too, Serafina."

I turned. Rosaline was waiting with an outstretched hand.

I accepted her help and seated myself on the back of the horse. I wanted to tell Rosaline where I was going and what I was about to do… but I could not let Annalisa and Brietta hear me.

I could not poison their first sip of freedom with the knowledge I was about to give mine away.

"In case I may never see you again…" I said. "Thank you for everything you showed me."

Rosaline's eyes shone and her soft cheeks rose with a somber smile. "Thank *you,* for saving him."

I swallowed all else I wanted to say, letting her read the truth I would never write down.

Rosaline nodded toward Merri, who guided Brietta onto the other horse. "Daigen is going to get us out, but he will be at the fortress when you arrive."

Why would Merri help us commit treason? Before I could ask, I had my answer as Annalisa ran into Merri's waiting arms. Merri stroked her curls before kissing her on the cheek.

"Run," Merri said, a single tear rolling down her face. "Run because your mother couldn't. Run because Ilsa couldn't."

Annalisa set her jaw and raced back to her horse. She had tied her garters around her skirt to form makeshift pants. She leaped onto the saddle behind me and swung her leg on the other side of her horse.

She grabbed the reins and flicked them. "Go, Diana!"

The horse trotted out of the stable. Annalisa's heartbeat pounded against my back as she shouted, "His name is Apollo, Brie! Just kick him and follow us!"

I gripped the horn of the saddle with both hands as Diana galloped through the palace courtyard toward the gate.

Guards shouted around us. I looked back—Brietta had a white-knuckled grip on Apollo's reins as he caught up to us.

An arrow whizzed past my face.

"Not near the Duchess, moron!" a guard shouted. "Don't let them leave!"

The iron palace gates started to swing closed.

I reached out my hand and only the smallest sparkles of magic in the air responded. My power was nearly exhausted and the iron held no water, no magic tears. They were going to trap us.

Suddenly the gates froze in place, leaving a wide gap between them, as a pained cry echoed from the gatehouse. "My eyes! It got my eyes!"

A flash of black flew out of the gatehouse. The sheen of dark feathers rippled in the moonlight. Only when we were a second away from the gates did I see the spot of pink on a beak.

Erik.

I counted the pounding of hooves against the gravel until we raced through the gap in the iron.

I let out a breath and smiled. Brietta laughed behind us.

We were free.

Erik dipped through the dark sky, flying in front of Annalisa and I as our horses raced through the city. His pink beak pointed the way through the streets of Hyton, past all the brick houses and shops, until we met the stillness of the countryside.

The moonlight sparkled on the waves of Odeneye lake and the river below as we approached the bridge into Bloodstone province.

More hooves thundered behind us. I dared to look past Annalisa to see the Lycaster cavalry chasing us down the hill to the bridge.

Derrick had sent the army to drag his Duchess back.

Diana's and Apollo's hooves clapped on the stone bridge as we raced across. I had to stop the cavalry somehow. I could destroy the bridge, but my magic could do nothing against stone.

I needed something with life. Something with water.

Diana galloped into the dirt on the Bloodstone side of the bridge.

"Stop!" I shouted. Annalisa pulled on the reins. "I have to take out the bridge!"

As soon as Diana was still, I slid off the horse and clumsily landed in the grass. My heart pounded as I scanned the moonlit bridge for any weakness, or maybe a tree I could enchant to fall and block the cavalry's path.

But…what if trees had already fallen in their path?

Riyan had once told me he had used tree trunks to support the bridge as part of his punishment for snapping Grigory's leg. My eyes went straight for the first two wooden pillars near the Hyton side of the river.

I threw out my magic. The tree trunks sparkled with tears and so did the river beneath them.

My Nordingaard crystal lit up as my feet tried to keep steady on the steep incline of the riverbank. I tried to focus on sparkling tears in the river, but the water was moving too fast. The tears passed by me before I could command them.

I had to get into the river.

I looked down at the rushing water. It was no magical healing spring nor a pool with defined limits. If I lost control over my magic, I was going to drown.

But if I let the cavalry cross the bridge, Riyan would be stuck in the place West of the Moon and East of the Sun forever.

I swallowed my fear and lowered my foot in the river. The cold water soaked my shoe and my stocking, the magic in the water kissing my skin like gentle embers.

Annalisa and Brietta gripped the back of my dress as I entered the river. I was up to my waist in the water, but magic was all around me.

As soon as the first horse came down the hill toward the bridge, I plunged my hands into the water, connecting with the last dreg of my power.

"Burn!"

The surface of the water was ablaze. I shielded my eyes from the blinding light and heat flashed across my cheeks.

A scream tore out of my throat as Brietta and Annalisa yanked me out of the water and onto the grassy riverbank.

Annalisa hit me in the stomach and I huffed out a breath. She screamed and cursed as she hit me and rolled me in the dirt.

Smoke singed my nose.

"She is good!" Brietta cried. "The fire is out."

I coughed up dirt and grass, but then a loud rumbling sound made me snap my head toward the river. The stone bridge was crumbling into the flaming river—my fire had eaten the wooden supports.

The cavalry's horses reared up and whinnied at the flames that danced on the surface of the water.

I let out a breath, the air from my lips cooling my smoldering body, and looked down—my skirt was soaked and my waist was singed.

The cavalrymen shouted on the other side of the river and I looked up. Pain filled my body, and not from the kiss of flames against my skin.

But I could not look south and grieve what I had left behind. My heart's desire was north, where Riyan would soon walk the earth again.

Annalisa's curls bounced as her head snapped toward Hyton. "I have to go back." She raced toward the river as the flames were dying down. "I left Magnus! I have to go back for Magnus!"

Brietta shot me a look. We both knew she was not worried about the damn cat.

I picked up my sopping skirt and sprinted toward her before she could take a swim. She sat down at the riverbank and started to take off her shoes.

"Anna!" I shouted. "Do *not* go back to Grigory after what he did!"

She shot me a glare over her shoulder. "Your curse cannot stop true love."

What was she saying? How could anyone love someone who had hurt them?

Before I could open my mouth, the rustle of wings swept past my ear and Erik flew to Annalisa. He pinched one of her curls with his beak and tugged her back.

She tried to shoo him away, but he dodged her hand and flew back to yank another curl. Annalisa screamed and picked up a nearby branch. She leaped to her feet and chased after Erik as he flew inland.

"I will knock you out of the sky, you rat with wings!" Annalisa shouted.

Erik flew right in front of her, *just* out of her reach, as she swung that branch over and over in her blind rage. He led her further down the path to Bloodstone Fortress until she was out of sight.

Safe and sound.

Chapter Forty Four
Unbroken

I never thought saving someone would make them hate me.

Annalisa and I rode on the back of her horse all night, but she refused to speak to me. Even though her chest was against my spine and I could feel her breath on the back of my head, I was not too keen to speak to her either. If I did, I just *knew* she would start with excuses for what Grigory had done.

No sweet little talks or shining gifts could make up for the bruises he left on her neck and the deeper wounds he placed in her soul.

I was *glad* I had burned him and cursed her to keep him from touching her, but arguing with her would accomplish nothing. I just had to get her safely past the Bloodstone Fortress gates and *then* get her to see sense.

The sun greeted us as the sky turned pink and we stopped to rest beneath the Bloodstone apple trees.

Brietta and I sat together in the shade of a large tree, catching the falling apples that Erik clipped from the branches with his beak.

I caught an apple in my lap and looked up at my brother. "Maybe you should stay a bird—you are just too useful."

Erik looked down with an expression that I could only read as annoyance before flying away.

My eyes followed Erik as he flew to a tree deeper into the grove, right above where Annalisa was feeding Diana apples. She had her eyes downcast and her thumb was tracing the bottom of her golden Thornebow pendant.

I was going to throw that damn pendant in a river the instant I got the chance.

Brietta's apple crunched as she took a bite. "Should I ask why you lit Grigory on fire?"

I fought back a scowl as I carved a piece of apple with the Hyton dagger. Annalisa was too far away to hear us, but I kept my voice low anyway. "He hurt Anna."

Cold rain ran down my shoulders as I remembered the terror in Annalisa's memories. How could I have been so foolish? Riyan had told me Grigory had hurt women, but I was so eager to believe he had changed just because he had made my friend smile.

Riyan had been too merciful. He should have broken *both* of Grigory's legs and forced him to crawl like a slug the rest of his life.

Brietta let out a pensive breath as she held her half-eaten apple. "Do you think the blood bond is making her…act that way?"

Annalisa turned from her horse and walked deeper into the grove, screaming at Erik to fuck off when he tried to follow her.

"Maybe." I cut off another piece of my apple and slipped it past my lips. The blood bond interfering with her mind was the only logical explanation. "The bonding enchantment was designed to push you toward your husband…whether he was a good man or not."

The golden bonds flowing through the veins of every Lycaster noble had Alastar's essence corrupting them—conquest regardless of cost. I scowled and cut off another piece of the apple.

Brietta eyed my dagger as I ate. "Could you take it out?"

I stopped chewing and looked at her.

"Your blood bond was removed, why not mine?" Her fingernails pierced the skin of her apple. "Even though I *know* Derrick will have to yield to my demands eventually…what if something happens where he…?"

I swallowed my apple and my stomach twisted into a knot. Derrick had already sent the cavalry after us and the rest of the army was sure to follow. I could not imagine a situation where the inevitable confrontation was bloodless. Still, just picturing a battle with Derrick dead…

A sudden pang speared my chest. No, he *would not* die. I would make sure of it.

"Could you try?" Brietta asked with big eyes.

She was so desperate, I had to help her. I bit my tongue and rose to my feet. Brietta stayed kneeling in the grass, her heart and mind open as I splayed my fingers toward her.

The golden blood bond from Fraleigh's magic twisted around Brietta's heart like a halo, its light shining in every one of her veins.

Brietta closed her eyes and the bond loosened, like she had let go of her end of a rope. I closed my fist, feeling the tautness of that golden rope of light instead of air against my skin.

Even though her blood bond was sealed, I could pull it out of her throat just like Daigen had done with me. In theory, anyway.

If my magic let me do it, the bond would shred out of her body with the intensity of the sun. It would hurt her…and it would hurt Derrick too.

Before I could even tug on that bond, anguish radiated into my hand and up my arm. Everything I had done to Derrick blared back at me like a trumpet, announcing my guilt loud and clear.

I released my fist as my eyes stung with tears. Brietta opened her eyes.

The little red ember beneath the diamond in my heart glowed red. As much as I wanted to protect Brietta, my magic could not remove her blood bond.

My heart might have been bathed in flames, but it would never desire to hurt Derrick again.

The afternoon sunlight lit up the battlements of the towers of Bloodstone Fortress as we finished our ascent of the mountainside.

Daigen stood with his arms folded at the open gate, his cloak fluttering around him in the soft breeze as he waited for us.

Annalisa stopped her horse at the gate and I dismounted. My legs ached from the long ride, but I wanted to get to Daigen before Annalisa or Brietta could ask any questions.

His violet eyes glanced past my shoulder. "Do they know?"

"No." I held my arms. "They would try to stop me if they did."

He looked up at the bright blue sky, where the waxing moon hid behind the treeline. "You have until tomorrow night. I suggest you rest now."

I avoided the eyes of the soldiers as I escorted Annalisa and Brietta through the courtyard. A couple of maids came to our aid as soon as we entered the fortress keep, helping Annalisa and Brietta find refreshment and accommodations.

For once, I did not bother with food. I silently dragged up the set of spiral stairs in the corner of the dining room until my feet found the hall with the crimson carpet runners. I could have turned left in the hallway to where my bedroom door had been, but instead I turned right.

The oak door creaked as I pushed it open. A shiver skittered across my shoulders as the mountain air crept in through the cracks of the broken window. Someone had boarded up the window and removed the fragments of glass from the floor, but Riyan's huge mattress still sat atop of a shattered bedframe.

Despite the chill in the room, I peeled off my singed clothes. I crawled into Riyan's broken bed and pulled his heavy blankets over my shoulders. His scent of nectar and wheat filled my nose as I hugged his pillow.

Only one more night until he was back in our world again.

The Nordingaard crystal pulsed heat against my throat as I finally let myself rest.

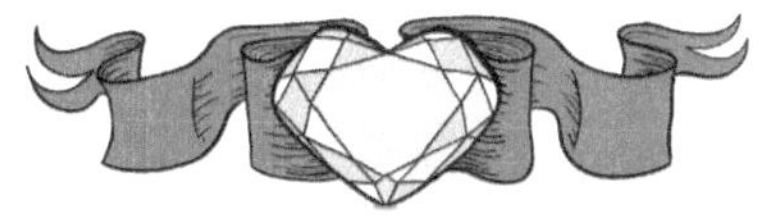

I slept for sixteen hours.

My last meal as a mortal was a crust of bread that I nibbled in the corner of the kitchen. Every bite of the bread turned to ash in my mouth, but I needed energy for the journey up the mountain.

I had dressed myself comfortably from my old wardrobe and pinned the crimson cape that was once Riyan's around my shoulders.

I had successfully avoided everyone else in the fortress, including nosy Erik, but I still allowed myself one goodbye.

The sunset cast an orange glow on all of Astrid's paintings in her bedroom as I knelt before her wheeled chair.

Her hands were delicate as parchment as they rested in mine. Her grey eyes stared at the wall, but I knew whatever shards of her mind floated around in her head could still understand me.

I smiled at her. "I am bringing him back, just like I said."

Astrid's eyes slid to the wall above her bed. "Ragnar."

I turned, following her gaze to the portraits of Ragnar she had painted. She still held out hope for him, but he had used her and abandoned her.

It was so unjust.

The flutter of butterfly wings caressed the back of my mind. Astrid's door was open.

I had tried not to hurt her in the past…but she deserved the truth.

As gently as I could, I sent an image of the Ragnar I knew into Astrid's mind. Astrid blinked only once.

Her face was still.

"I thought lionesses did not keep secrets?"

I looked over my shoulder. Annalisa leaned on the doorframe with her arms crossed.

Her deadly eyes flicked down to my cape. "After the hell you put us through, you are just leaving?"

I rose to my feet. "I told you I was going to bring Riyan back."

"And what happens then?" Annalisa lifted off the doorframe and stalked forward. "Brietta has been talking with the soldiers all night about the defenses for when Derrick comes. Do we revolutionize the Dukedom while you come back to your happily ever after?"

"I might not come back at all." My throat tightened, but my Nordingaard crystal kept me calm.

Her brow hardened. "Why?"

Damn it, a direct question. I could not bite it down, so I let it out. "I am taking Riyan's place, giving the Queen of the Giants my eternal servitude."

Annalisa's chest deflated, but I had to take care of my obligations before she could try to talk me out of my plan.

"No matter what happens after midnight," I said, "someone *has* to look after Astrid."

Her eyes softened as they moved from Astrid to her paintings on the wall. Her face tensed as soon as she recognized her uncle. "I could never do much to right my family's wrongs…but I can start here."

I let out a relieved breath. "Thank you, Anna."

She pursed her lips and kept her arms folded. She was too angry with me to beg me to stay, or to even tell me goodbye, but it was better for the both of us that she stayed silent.

She could hate me all she wanted as long as she was safe.

Annalisa stared at the portrait a moment longer before turning back to me, keeping her eyes down. "My cycle came. I was never with child, I was just…I think I was just distressed…"

Before I could stop myself, I wrapped my arms around her. Her scent of rose petals and paint filled my nose. She circled her arms around me and rested her cheek on top of my head.

Even though I listened closely, no rain fell in Annalisa's mind.

I held my breath and forced myself to pull out of her embrace. I looked from Annalisa to Astrid as the three of us stood in the dying sunlight from the window.

I had no idea what Ganora would do with me at midnight, or the next day, or until I met the edge of oblivion, but I held one certainty in my heart.

The ones I loved were still unbroken.

Chapter Forty Five

Freedom

The sky had darkened into a rich blue as Daigen and I stepped outside the stone walls of Bloodstone Fortress.

I held out my hand. "Shall we finish this the way we started it?"

Daigen raised an eyebrow but took my hand. "What are we finishing? If anything, we're starting something new."

I supposed his beloved's impending freedom made him optimistic, a feeling I shared.

A rustle of feathers disrupted the air before Daigen could pull me through it with his magic.

Erik landed on a low tree branch above us, giving me a pointed look with his small black eyes.

Damn it! Why could he not have just stayed in the fortress keep with Annalisa?

I pursed my lips and shook my head as tears threatened to appear. What a sick twist of fate—now *I* was going up the mountain to face the last giant without knowing if I would ever return.

"I will not tell you goodbye, Erik." My throat shook as I fought a sob. "Not when Endre is not here. Not when it might be forever this time. Not…"

I forced myself quiet before I could finish my thought—not when I also failed to turn them back into men.

Erik turned his gaze from me to Daigen. A chill coasted through the breeze and cut across my shoulders.

Daigen kept his violet eyes on Erik and slowly lifted his arm. Erik took the invitation and perched on his forearm. For a heartbeat, Daigen and my oldest brother simply looked at each other.

Then Daigen said in little more than a whisper, "I will keep my promise."

What had he promised my brother?

After a moment, Erik spread his wings and gently flew to my shoulder. He preened a hair close to my face and then took off for the gate.

My heart ached as my eldest brother left me again, but Daigen's voice pulled me out of my sorrow. "Your brothers will be men by sunrise."

I turned. Daigen's face was softer than I had ever seen it. Did he know what Ganora planned to do with my eternal servitude?

He gently took my hand. Bits of magic dragged against my skin and Daigen pulled me through the air. We left the Bloodstone Fortress gate behind as a frosty wind whipped across my cheeks.

I opened my eyes. Two towering boulders stood in front of me, a rolling fog pouring out between them.

My heart pounded. My fate was on the other side of those boulders.

The moon was rising in the inky sky. Snowflakes stung my cheeks as I turned to face Daigen for the last time as a free person.

He closed his cloak around him, though he did not look cold, and gave me a small smile. "I will be here when you come out."

His words loosened the knot in my chest. I hated how vague he was, but at least he was sure that I *would* come back from the place West of the Moon and the East of the Sun.

I gripped the Hyton dagger from its place on my belt. I needed it to slice my palm just as Fraleigh had to make my final bargain, but the familiar bronze hilt was a comfort all the same.

"Tell Astrid hello for me, would you?" Daigen called.

I smiled. "I will."

I turned back around and took the first step, feeling the weight of my impending bargain like iron in my toes.

The fog blurred my vision and filled my lungs, but I kept going. Everything went dark, like I was treading between reality and a nightmare, but I kept going.

At last, a tiny pinhole of rainbow light reached out through the fog like an old friend. Like a moon in a starless sky, the light grew bigger and bigger until it was all I could see.

I blinked, and then I faced the familiar tall runes surrounding the wall of churning water. The water threw off rainbow light like little stars.

My blood buzzed with energy. I stepped forward as if my heart were pulled on an invisible tether, only stopping when I was at the edge of the swirling water.

The door to eternity was at my feet.

"So, where is my sister?" asked a voice cold as a frost.

Quiet but heavy footfalls filled the air. The Queen of the Giants appeared behind a rune depicting a crying man, directly across from me on the other side of the well.

I held my breath. She was fifteen feet tall, wearing the same necklace of bones and tunic of blackened animal hides that I last saw her in.

I held out my dagger as I met her icy gaze. "Fraleigh will have to just wait a little longer. Now *I* have a bargain for *you*."

The weight of the air crashed around me. Ganora's eyes flicked down as water of the well swirled faster. My white flame flared around my heart, rattling my ribs and bringing tears to my eyes.

My hand shook around the dagger, but the moon was crawling toward the center of the sky. I had no time to waste.

I swallowed and let my conviction bleed through each word. "All my life I fought for power, whether it came in the form of security, or sorcery, or a crown." I tightened my grip on the bronze hilt. "But love is the greatest power in the world. It is more powerful than any bargain, any title, and more powerful than *you*."

Ganora's eyes went wide as I sliced my left palm. Blood dripped from my wrist into the well of tears. My eyes raised to Ganora's icy ones and the white light from the well nearly blinded me, but I remained firm.

"A life for a life given in love," I said. "You take my eternity and Riyan goes free."

I could have choked on the weight of the air around us. She could do nothing to stop my bargain, but a smile still crawled across Ganora's face. "Your eternity on my terms? Done."

My stomach turned at that smile, but the warm white light in my veins kept me calm.

It was done, no going back. I had saved him.

Ganora waved her hand over a mound of snow and the white powder disappeared into a flurry. I choked on a gasp—Riyan's body was on the ground. He was still fifteen feet tall, his limbs stiff and frozen, and a mask of ice was over his eyes.

With a slow turn of her hand, Ganora's magic lifted Riyan's body from the snow and lowered him into the churning well of tears. His body disappeared into a thousand years of sorrow without so much as a splash.

I gripped the hilt of the Hyton dagger. I held my breath for the last time I would need to and took my bravest step forward.

White light engulfed my vision and a low voice of frost and flame wrapped through the white void.

"*Welcome back, Little Ember.*"

Chapter Forty Six
Horizon of Eternity

My feet hit solid ground and I opened my eyes to darkness. Water gently swirled around my body, but my heart did not beat.

I was in the place West of the Moon and East of the Sun.

Suddenly Ganora parted through the dark waters as if she were stepping through gossamer curtains. Somehow we were the same size.

"A thousand choices through the centuries led you to accept the Man of the Mountain's gift in its entirety." She tilted her head. "And so you have completely surrendered to me."

Trails of crimson swirled from the cut on my palm like ink blots on a contract. "Name your terms, Queen of the Giants."

"For your sacrifice, your beloved shall walk free." Her voice was low and powerful, adding to the weight of the water with each word. "Though you have not laid down your life to take *his* place…"

What was she saying? Was she not using me as a weapon to free her sister?

"…you will take mine," she said. "You will take my power and my eternity. And Daigen's. And Fraleigh's."

I slowly shook my head. This was no bargain. "There must be more."

Ganora's mouth formed a tight line. "When the Alastar comes to Nordingaard, surrender yourself. *You* will go under the collar in Fraleigh's place."

My hand flew up to my neck. I was prepared to face eternal servitude to the Queen of the Giants, *not* the man I destroyed. "No, I can still free Fraleigh without it. With all the power you promise, I can convince—"

"No you can't!" Ganora snapped her teeth. "You know an Alastar would never let her go unless he had something more powerful to take! If the Man of the Mountain takes her power back and makes her mortal, the Hytons will keep her enslaved until she dies!"

I shook my head. I could not chain myself to the monster I could not slay. I could not face General Hyton after what he proposed, nor Derrick after I had broken his heart.

"You *cannot* back out now, Serafina," Ganora said. "This was the Man of the Mountain's plan from the beginning. I listened to his whispers and forced *just* the right circumstances to poise you to make this bargain."

The chill of her power prickled my neck again, just like when she had strangled me in front of desperate Riyan. She was never taking revenge for her fallen giants, or waiting for her perfect weapon to return to her...

"I never cared about the boy," Ganora said with a hollow laugh that crackled with desperation. "He was just the only way to get to you—the only way to free my sister, to free all of us!"

Ribbons of color swirled around me in the darkness, each an image of a choice made that led me to the bottom of the thousand-year-old grave. Riyan falling to his knees as Ganora choked me. Grigory Thornebow's poison arrow that led me to the healing spring. The Man of the Mountain ordering Fraleigh to refuse to help me at her golden palace. Riyan brushing a hair away from my face as I slept next to him. A voice like satin saying "I choose Serafina Ravenwood" amongst a group of suitors.

My chest rattled with a sob, but the final vision that flashed before me sent a chill down my spine.

It was Daigen, his violet eyes twinkling as he led Astrid by the hand through the foggy mountain pass to the well.

If my heart were beating, it would have broken.

The Man of the Mountain had said a series of choices made before I was even born led me to eternity. He never said those choices were for my benefit.

I knew I should have never trusted Daigen. He helped me, he *trained* me, but I never realized he was just feeding a lamb to lead it to slaughter.

I was so desperate to get Riyan back that I had fallen right into the trap they had all laid.

"And I am tired." Ganora's voice broke as she clutched her chest. Suddenly she was not a queen, but a child. "It's been centuries and…I just want to go home."

I bit my tongue and looked up, finding the pinhole of light at the top of the chasm—the moon at midnight. Memories of Riyan's laughter filled my ears. I remembered his strong arms wrapping around my body. I smelled nectar and wheat in the crook of his neck.

I smiled despite myself. As long as Riyan was breathing, darkness would never touch me…even if I knelt before Alastar XII as his slave.

A calm wave of finality washed over me. My white flame twisted, weaving my words into the infinite threads of eternity as I spoke. "What is done is done. I will take what you give and give what you must take."

Ganora gave me a grim nod and held out her left hand. A matching gash appeared on her own palm and released a delicate swirl of blood into the dark water.

She grasped my palm. Cobalt flames surged through my veins. My stomach dropped like I had just fallen and the coldest fear I had ever experienced dragged through me.

My left arm vibrated as I gripped Ganora's hand and all the fear twisted into icy rage. Her power lit me up with blue light that burned the clothes from my skin. Though I was naked and vulnerable, I felt like I could crack the earth, tear down the heavens, and fold a storm in my hands.

On the other end of that thread of eternity, Ganora's hair brightened from cold white to warm blonde and her grey skin blossomed into pink.

Suddenly I was no longer holding the hand of the Queen of the Giants, but instead a young teenage girl. Had I not known any better, I would have thought she was just a first-year student at Ashmore.

"The bargain is in your blood," Ganora said, her voice sweet and childlike. "Free my sister as you have freed me."

My veins glowed with the bond of the bargain. Ganora looked up and raised her small arm, pressing against some kind of perimeter.

A male voice I did not recognize broke through the fabric between worlds. He spoke in Old Tongue, but the confines of language did not hinder understanding in the place West of the Moon and East of the Sun.

He was calling his daughter home.

A woman's hand reached through the invisible barrier. Ganora's pink cheeks rose with her smile as she grasped the hand.

Slowly, the hand pulled Ganora through the perimeter until she disappeared in the darkness.

A shiver crawled down my spine. That was her…*Death*.

My chest shook with the weight of Ganora's eternity coming to an end, but then I heard a familiar tune in my ears.

"Still with me somehow."

The voice was not Riyan's, but a feminine voice I had heard before. I took a step through the darkness, following the song in my blood, until I found a girl with twin braids kneeling next to the body of a giant sleeping man with golden hair.

Astrid's body was more transparent than Riyan's. We were all nude, but no embarrassment plunged through me. The mortal rules of modesty could not reach us.

"Astrid," I said gently, "I am going to bring him home."

Even though I was talking to her mind, frozen in place from when she was seventeen, Astrid looked up at me with two-decades worth of heartbreak. "He never came back."

I gave Astrid a soft smile. "No, but *I* will. I promised Riyan I would take care of you."

Astrid's brows knitted. "A promise…" She looked down at Riyan's sleeping body. "I climbed the mountain for Ragnar. He *promised me* we would be a family."

I knelt beside her. "You can still be a family. Once Riyan enters the world of the living, I will make sure you can join him."

If I could not be with Riyan once I went under the collar, he at least deserved to have his mother with him.

Astrid's lip trembled only once. "I never got to hold my baby, and even now…"

She tried to wrap her arms around Riyan's massive chest, but her limbs passed through—completely transparent.

She sat on her knees and looked down at Riyan. "But as much as my heart sang for Ragnar, I loved my baby since the first punch in my womb. I would have climbed a dozen more mountains if it led him to a love like yours."

The image of Daigen leading her to the Man of the Mountain's grave flashed through my mind. He *destroyed* her to get Fraleigh back.

If I were Fraleigh…I would have done much worse to him than merely curse him with a hideous face.

My mouth formed a fine line. "Even after Daigen tricked you?"

She looked past Riyan into the vast darkness. "I am not even angry with him anymore. Each time he visits, he promises me it will all work out…but I am tired of promises."

Bitterness coated my tongue, but I at least would keep true to my word. "Daigen sends his regards."

Astrid smiled. "Tell that monster to eat shit."

Then the spirit of her mind faded into the swirling darkness.

Riyan and I were alone, together at last.

I ran my hand down the side of his sleeping face, tracing the contours of his temple and his cheekbone. My power and Ganora's twisted in my veins as I kissed his forehead. "Please, wake up."

The darkness of the well swirled with ribbons of white light.

I knelt by his arm and placed my hands over his heart. I closed my eyes. The flames around the diamond in my heart danced, filling every part of my body with the white light of truth.

"Riyan." My voice thrummed with power as the magic in his body answered my call. "You were always more than a beast or a monster. You are a man—the fastest, strongest, and most wonderful man alive, worth more to me than any power I could ever hold."

Riyan's heartbeat awakened underneath my hands. Each of his veins lit up like its own line in a love song.

"No longer shall fear overtake you," I said with a smile. "No more shall your body betray you. Return to the flesh that was always yours. Become the man you were supposed to be."

My magic flowed from my hands and into his heart. His heart pumped white light with each beat, erasing Ganora's curse from his blood. My hands sank lower as his body compressed.

I opened my eyes. The Riyan that slept below me was no longer giant…but instead the size of his father. He was still tall, but no one would ever again mistake him for anything but what he was—a man. A *good* man.

His chest rose with a deep breath. His eyelashes fluttered, and the moment his twilight eyes met mine, sunspots danced in my chest.

"Sera?" He sat up, his right hand finding my left.

I nodded as my smile stretched my cheeks. The sunspots grew bigger until they tickled my ribs.

Riyan looked down at me and shook his head. "You are not supposed to be here. You were supposed to find happiness without me. You were supposed to—"

"I chose *you*." I smiled, feeling light and powerful all at once. "I finally got to choose you."

My chest shook and I could not contain the sunlight any longer. A laugh bounced with my breath. Then it grew, louder and happier, until Riyan smiled wide enough that his dimple appeared.

He raised his hands, examining them, and then his eyes flicked back up to my face. His palms rested against my jaw. He had never held my face before—finally he was a perfect fit.

Riyan laughed, just once, before lifting my face. His eyes were luminous with my white light as I gently brushed a strand of hair from the middle of his forehead. The heartbeat in his wrists gently pulsed against my neck. My eyes fell to the curved lines of his lips and my heart pounded.

He was real. *We* were real.

Then his lips met mine and I was whole again.

I kissed him back, drinking him in as I wrapped my arms around his neck. My chest pressed into his. Our hearts pounded against each other, crying to join together again.

I pulled away with a small gasp. For a few heartbeats, we held each other with our lips a breath apart.

"*Forge a new blood bond,*" the Man of the Mountain whispered in my mind, "*the eternal bargain must be in his blood too.*"

A shiver of ancient power passed through my body and I suddenly understood why we could not refuse a direct order from the Man of the Mountain.

But just as Fraleigh once said, my sacrifice was a gift. After his father had ordered him to walk at the hem of Death's robes for years, I could give Riyan an eternity away from her black shroud.

I dragged my eyes up to Riyan's. "Ganora is gone. I took her power and reversed her curse on you." I swallowed. "I am just like Fraleigh now. Ageless. Deathless."

He smiled. "You will never die?"

How could I tell him the terms of my bargain? He would never forgive me when he found out. "Yes, but there are…conditions. I can marry you again, make my own blood bond enchantment, and you can be deathless too. But you do not have to be with me. As soon as we get out of here, you can live your own eternal life—"

Riyan grabbed my chin and lifted it so my eyes met his. "I do not care what the conditions are. Whether it's for an eternity or just one day, I want you."

My heart swelled. His lips said, "I want you," but the way his voice broke said, "*I need you.*"

And I would be with him as much as I could.

I kissed him. The fingers of his right hand laced with my left. The scar on his palm opened up to meet mine.

Our blood mixed. Power surged through my veins into his. Our hearts lit up with white light as they raced.

My blood bond was not painful, it was pure. The sun and moon joined in an eclipse of eternal devotion. There was no Serafina and Riyan, there was only us.

Our tears had fallen, our blood had flowed…

"*And when Alastar comes to the fortress,*" the Man of the Mountain whispered in my mind. "*You both shall become Death's greatest foe.*"

I broke our kiss as my stomach dropped. Our blood bond glowed in both our chests, bright as a new day.

A life for a life given in love—as soon as I knelt before Derrick, Riyan would greet the horizon of eternity.

The water rumbled and swirled around us as we rose through the well. I looked up—the moon in the center of the sky grew closer.

Riyan's arm hooked under my legs and he held me close. My arms wrapped around his neck as we pushed through the surface of the well.

We rose from the churning rainbow water like we were floating. His hair and face were soaked and so were mine. The cold mountain air whipped around our bare bodies, but my magic kept me warm.

He took his first step out of the well. He stood in the snow, holding me tightly against him like he would never let me go again.

My heart thudded as I looked up at him. The light of the full moon blanketed every ridge and contour of his body in a soft glow.

A slight flush spread across his cheeks and the strong bridge of his nose. I pressed my hand in the center of his chest and sent a soft push of magic to keep him warm.

Riyan turned his head and his breath stilled as his eyes met mine. Whatever haze in the dark chasm between worlds that had erased the concept of modesty was gone. Riyan's gaze roved down every curve and dip of my body that my wet hair had not clung to.

His fingertips grazed the side of my breast and my cheeks heated. My hand curled over his chest as his heart began to pound. He gripped the soft flesh of my thigh but then loosened his hold like he thought better of it.

"We, uh…" His voice broke as his gaze dropped from my eyes to the curve of my hip. His throat bobbed as he swallowed. "We need to get off this mountain before you freeze."

I looked up at him through my eyelashes. "Do I look cold to you?"

He glanced at my breasts but then closed his eyes and shook his head. "Come on, sweetheart, let's get you some clothes."

He stepped through the snow, but desire still built within me, the pressure raging against the power I had inherited from Ganora. Anger, lust, and fear of the unknown all clashed in my body, begging for a release.

Traitorous Daigen had said he would wait for me on the other side of the pass. The peak of the mountain was our only sanctuary before my bargain demanded payment.

I did not want to corrupt what Riyan and I had with that bargain, not yet. For the small amount of time I was still free, still completely his, I wanted to surrender every bit of myself to him.

I kissed Riyan's neck and he stopped in his tracks. His pulse quickened underneath my lips as he shivered.

"Serafina Helia," he tried to tease, but his voice was tense, "still so damn impatient."

A low-burning fire warmed the bottom of my stomach. I did not care if we were on top of a mountain with nothing around us but snow and rocks, I wanted something pure, something *ours*.

I pulled away from his throat and looked into his eyes. "Could we?"

He scanned our sparse surroundings until his eyes settled on a tall rune ahead of us.

Heat spread through my body. Yes, the rune would do.

But a crease formed between Riyan's brows. "Sera, you deserve a bed—"

I grabbed his strong jaw so his eyes met mine. "You told me before we separated that you would have me the *instant* you were the size of a normal man." My eyes flicked down to his chest. "And here you are."

His cheek pitted like he bit it. He sighed. "I want you…so badly, but I want to make this easy."

"I never wanted *easy*." My heart pounded against his. The white, pure light of our bond flared, aching to join together. "I wanted what was real. I wanted *you*."

I kissed him—tasting him, *savoring* him. He kissed me back for a heartbeat before pulling away.

His breath warmed my flushed lips. "Are you sure? After what happened on the Darkest Night?"

"Please." I sounded vulnerable, but I did not care. I was vulnerable. I was hurt. I was confused. All that was certain was that I loved him and he loved me. "I…I need you too."

His mouth formed a fine line and he let out a tense breath. His eyes flicked up toward the pass and he leaned forward, about to take a step, when his eyes met mine again.

"Fuck it." His lips crashed into mine and all my worry melted away. He broke the kiss only to press his forehead against mine. "Anything you want, sweetheart. Today and always."

Chapter Forty Seven
Control

I could have said a thousand words to fill the small gap of air between us, but one unspoken word weighed on my tongue.

Finally.

Riyan held me close to his chest as he stepped through the snow. My heartbeat quickened as the heat in my hips intensified.

His warm body against mine shielded me from the sting of the wind. My eyes flitted from the strained muscles in his neck, the focus of his eyes, and the light from the full moon filtering through his eyelashes.

"I hope this will work," Riyan said with a soft smile. He released my legs and pressed my back against a wall of ice.

I gasped and jumped forward. My legs wrapped around his waist and my arms locked around his neck.

"Riyan!" My back must have grazed one of the tall runes. "Cold!"

"Sorry." He laughed and the hard muscles of his abdomen shook against me. The sensation sent heat to my core—the friction felt *good*.

Riyan's eyes flicked down, like he also felt that sudden rush of heat against him. Suddenly I felt a nudge against my thigh. My cheeks blazed and my heart pounded. Even though Riyan was no longer a horrifying size, he still felt *very* large.

Would I even be able to wrap my hand around it?

His eyes dragged from my heaving chest to glance over my shoulder. "You think you could…?"

"Oh," I breathed, forgetting what words were. I activated my magic in every ice crystal on the rune. I matched the heat of the magical tears to the heat within me, and within a heartbeat, every bit of frost melted away.

Riyan slowly rested my shoulders against the ancient stone. The muscles in his arms were stiff but his eyes were soft as they traveled up and down my body.

He leaned in and his words were warm against my lips. "I can't decide where to touch you."

I smiled. "Then touch me everywhere."

His lips met mine and he groaned low in his throat. He kissed me tantalizingly softly, but I surrendered to his lead, letting him take his time.

He could take all eternity, if he wanted.

My legs stayed locked around him, so he freed one hand from my thigh. His fingertips left a trail of prickling gooseflesh on my skin as he caressed the curve of my hip, the edge of my stomach, and then finally my breast.

He palmed the side of my breast, his thumb tracing a circle around my nipple. I tilted my head back as pleasure spread through my chest at his touch.

"So pretty," he said softly. He dropped his hand to grip my thigh again, his fingers digging into the soft flesh. "But these were always my favorite. And now you've given me even *more* to squeeze. Can't even wrap my hands around them anymore."

My laugh skated across his smile. "Your hands are just smaller—but I did eat a lot of pies at the palace."

"I'll get you more pies." His voice was barely more than a rasp before he kissed me again. "A dozen." Another kiss. "For breakfast." Another. "Every morning."

He hungrily kissed where my neck met my shoulder and I let out a throaty whimper. Pleasure wicked into my hips, but my belly stayed relaxed. With each kiss he pressed to my skin, my moans turned into exhales. Each heartbeat was a stamp, marking a joyous moment on a timeline with no end.

Riyan's hands kneaded upward as he kissed me, his fingers gently caressing the creases between my thighs. With each little sweeping touch, his fingers moved closer and closer to my center.

Pressure built within me, winding around my spine as tightly as thread on a bobbin. I wiggled against him, desperate for friction to relieve the tension, but Riyan nipped my earlobe instead of focusing his attention lower.

His low rasp caressed the shell of my ear. "You writhing little thing…" He bit my ear again.

I wiggled against him hard enough that he groaned against my neck. His calloused palm dragged down my lower belly and his fingers gently swept across my pulsing desire. Each feathered touch brought a needy whimper to my throat.

"I didn't forget." His voice was breathy and ragged against my lips. "I didn't forget how much you liked this…"

His fingers gently dipped inside me and I moaned through my clenched teeth. He stroked me from within, drawing my pleasure out, but I clenched around him.

His fingers were not enough. I *needed* him inside me.

"Riyan," I begged in a soft whine.

He picked up his pace and smirked. "You're close, sweetheart. You're dripping onto my wrist…"

"No, I want to finish with you!"

He slowed down and looked into my eyes. "What was that?"

I bit my lip. The pressure inside me was so intense, I thought I was going to burst. "*Please* fuck me, Riyan."

His throat tensed and he let out a long breath. "You are not making this easy for me."

I shuddered as Riyan slowly withdrew his hand. He met my half-lidded gaze and sucked every bit of me off his fingers before lowering his hand back to my hips.

Riyan's voice was low with warning. "I don't want to hurt you. I might be the size of a man, but I'm still a lot bigger than—"

"But I *want* it."

His mouth formed a hard line and his throat bobbed as he swallowed. "Same rules as last time. If anything hurts, we stop."

A naughty thought tugged at my mind. "Well, it can hurt a little…"

"*Sera.*"

"*Riyan.*" I mocked his dark tone with a smirk. "I am the most powerful sorceress in the world. You cannot break me."

His eyes darkened. He adjusted himself, the tip nudging at my opening. I whimpered as just that feathered touch sent a shot of pleasure into my hips.

And then he started to push.

I gasped, gripping his shoulders to brace myself. He paused and I settled into the stretch.

I let out a breath when I realized he was holding in his.

"Keep going," I whispered against his cheek.

He kept his eyes on the rune and slowly pushed again. My heart thudded as he alternated between pushing and giving me time to adjust. I hummed little noises of encouragement into his skin.

Riyan pulled back, just enough to feel him slide inside me, before pushing in again. He hit me in just the right place, sending sensation up my spine.

"Oh *fuck*," I gasped.

Riyan continued his easing rhythm, but his eyes were intently focused on the rune. His muscles were so tight they were vibrating.

He was holding back.

"Riyan," I huffed out, "look at me."

His fierce eyes met mine and every thread of control within him snapped.

His lips crashed against mine as he thrust into me. He bit my bottom lip and I arched my back, my breasts smashing into his chest.

Fuck yes.

His rhythm turned into a pulse, growing faster and faster.

"Yes…yes…," I whimpered into his neck.

Pressure built inside me, but my blood was glowing. My heart was screaming like a triumphant battle cry. The power of our bond surged through every vein, every heartbeat, and every heavy breath that escaped our lips.

After the moon had waned and waxed in the night sky, watching over us as we fell deeper in love, Riyan and I had finally sealed our blood bond.

But Riyan was not done and neither was I. He yanked my hair back and I screamed into the night. His hips slammed into mine over and over. Harder. Deeper.

"More," I cried. "*More.*"

"You want more?" he rasped. "I'll give you more. I'll give you *everything.*"

He pushed into me with his full force. The rough stone scraped against my shoulder blades. Every bite of pain instantly melted into pleasure.

So I cried out for more.

The stone shook behind me with every thrust. Any words he tried to say shredded into a growl against my forehead. My nails dragged across his shoulders as I screamed.

A crack echoed in my ears. My stomach dropped as I fell back.

Boom.

I hit the cold powder. The snow hissed under the magical heat of my body, melting under my back, then my knees, and then my feet as I shakily brought myself to stand.

Half of the rune lay in the snow. Riyan was on his back and panting.

His eyes examined the jagged edge of the broken rune. "Fuck, how hard was I—"

Snow melted away from my feet as I ran to him. A storm of ice and white fire raged in my chest along with the pressure between my legs. The words on his lips vanished the moment I sat on the hard wall of muscle on his lower abdomen.

"I need more," I panted. I wrapped my hand around him—my fingers did not even touch my thumb, but I would not stop. I lowered myself onto him and my eyes rolled back as he filled me up again.

I pressed my hands against his chest and slowly moved my hips.

My turn to have control.

I had practiced on my pillow enough times at Ashmore to know the motion, but Riyan's hands gripped my hips and helped me.

"You take me so well, Sera," he said with a wicked smile. "Keep going."

I pressed my fingertips into Riyan's chest as I grinded against him. The sensation was reaching its peak. My legs started to shake. His muscles tightened and shuddered in response.

"Sera," he breathed, "I'm about to—"

At last, I sailed into that sweet release. My legs trembled around him as I rode into it, higher and higher.

Riyan gripped my thighs hard enough to bruise and hissed out a breath, but I did not stop. I was about to explode. A second orgasm rolled through me and I lost control of my muscles.

With a gasp, I came out on the other side of my climax. The stars danced in my vision. I could only register the soft hair on Riyan's chest beneath my hands as I folded forward.

We panted, listening to each other's heartbeats slow down as I laid on his chest. Riyan's arms wrapped around my back, his fingers slowly drawing soft little circles on my skin. A quick sweep of my magic cleaned me off and I let myself rest.

No more cracking or rumbling stone. No echoes of screams. Even the wind was still.

My head was swimming and my body was limp, but I mustered the strength to speak. "I love you, Riyan."

"I…you…" he said with a thick tongue, too dazed to talk. He chuckled lightly and kissed the top of my head. Suddenly the sound of a wave washed into my mind, carrying his voice with it. "*I love you too.*"

I propped myself up on my elbows as I looked down at him. No light was shining between his eyes, but it did not need to.

We had a blood bond—a permanent tether into each other's minds.

I just hoped that would be enough to keep us together when my bargain would soon force us apart.

Chapter Forty Eight
Dark Flame

If I could have just stayed on Riyan's chest at the peak of Nordingaard mountain for the rest of my eternity, I would have been happy.

But my happiness was not part of the bargain I made.

Out of the corner of my eye, the swirling water in the Man of the Mountain's grave flared with white light. It was calling me.

I slowly pushed off Riyan and walked through the snow. I crossed my arms over my bare breasts as the chill raised the hairs on my skin. My toes stopped on the smooth stones at the edge of the well as the water gurgled, pushing something to the surface.

Bronze flashed through the rainbow light in the water and I could not help but laugh—the Hyton dagger had returned. I dipped my hand into the warm water and pulled it out by the hilt.

A dark lump followed it. I furrowed my brows as I pulled mounds of sopping fabric out of the well.

Riyan had followed me to the edge of the well and eyed the heavy fabric in my hands. "What is that?"

I commanded each tear dampening the fabric to dissipate into the air. The folds of grey, green, and brown dappled cloth were instantly dry. I picked through the cloth and held out a simple linen chemise and leather slippers that likely came from my wardrobe at Bloodstone Fortress.

I frowned at the familiar cloaks in my hands as I tossed them into the snow. Daigen could not earn back my trust with favors.

As I slipped on the chemise and the shoes, Riyan picked the green and brown cloak off the pile and let the thick fabric tumble down. "The Man of the Mountain is giving us presents?"

"No." My voice was pinched, but Riyan's hands throwing the cloak around my bare shoulders made me unclench.

"Ravenwood green." Riyan said with a smile as he tapped me on the nose. "Now you look just like—"

He stopped himself, but I knew he meant I looked like my brothers.

I needed to tell him they were alive, but he would see them soon if Daigen kept his word…which I now doubted.

I bit down a scowl. Daigen wanted us dressed before he met with us on the other side of the pass, but what could he possibly say after he had betrayed me? Whatever it was, I did not want Riyan to hear.

I handed Riyan the grey and green cloak. "Do you trust me?"

"Does a bear shit in the woods?"

Not the time for jokes. I shot him a look and his smirk softened into a loving smile. "Of course I do."

I turned my head toward the low-rolling fog in the rocks that led further down the mountain. "Daigen is here. Give me ten minutes to speak with him. Alone. I will call for you when we are done."

He raised an eyebrow. "Call for me?"

"Through our bond." I could not help but smile. "You will know when it happens."

Riyan shook out his cloak as I turned away. I passed by the destroyed rune, taking in the image on the bottom half and mentally stitching it together with the broken top half—a woman with an outstretched arm and blank eyes.

And only because I had seen her did I understand who the rune depicted. Even though the chill of the wind stung my cheeks, my chest was warm as I stared at the destroyed rune—reminding me of what my bargain was for.

The totem we had shattered with our love was Death.

I held that warmth around my heart like an unbreakable promise as I stepped into the fog.

The rolling fog was warmer. The snow beneath my feet was softer. The darkness was less suffocating.

Only when the fog parted and I met violet eyes and white hair did ice stab me between my ribs.

Daigen clasped his hands, his grey and white dappled cloak fluttering around his shoulders. For a moment, we merely exchanged looks as heavy as the towering boulders around us.

I would not break, so he spoke first. "If you want an apology, you won't get one."

The image of his purple face as Alastar the Conqueror strangled him flashed in my mind. He would have rather died than condemn Fraleigh, but he was more than willing to condemn me.

Blazing heat poured into my hands as they curled into fists at my side. The tears in the air and the snow quivered in fear as they waited for my orders.

My voice came out in a heavy whisper. "I trusted you."

"And you still need to. This is not over."

I held my breath as my heart punched my ribs. "I am through listening to you, you monster."

Daigen smirked and all the delicious ways to torture him ran through my mind. Rope of fire around the throat. Ice shards in his stomach. A scream of frost and flame that would linger in his ears until the end of time.

"A monster, am I?" he said. "Do you really think your Riyan would be any different?"

I let out my breath and the tears in the air stopped shimmering. How dare he think Riyan was ever capable of such a horrible betrayal?

Daigen walked through the snow, punctuating his words with every step. "I begged. Sold my skills. Built a fucking palace. *None* of it was enough to free her."

He stood in front of me, his eyes swimming with nearly five centuries of rage. "And then I switched tactics."

Metal gleamed in the moonlight. He held his ancient knife in front of his heart. The tears in the air whispered its name against my ears. *Reginbani. Reginbani.*

And only because I had heard that ancient barbarian tongue in Fraleigh's memories did my heart know the knife's true meaning.

Reginbani—Duke slayer.

The blade flashed in Daigen's hands and his gaze fell to the snow. "I started with the Conqueror's sons. No Hyton sons, no bargain—but eight dead heirs did not persuade the Conqueror to release the collar."

I stared down at the blade, picturing drops of blood rolling off its edge.

"Then when the fucker turned ninety, I thought drawing a quick line across his neck would have been the last of the Hytons…and that horrible deal would be over." He scowled. "Imagine my surprise when a son, young and spry, appeared out of nowhere and claimed both the crown *and* my wife."

The biting wind circled around him as he looked down at his blade. "Before I could strike, he stole our blood bond." The wind twisted faster as his voice dropped. "It was *ours,* and the Alastar you call 'the Good' turned it into a weapon against us. If I killed him, I took an innocent woman with him. I was stuck…"

His harsh voice broke through his teeth. "But I was still an ever-present threat. I haunted their days in their halls and then their nights in their dreams. The fifth Alastar bribed us with that damned golden palace to end the terror. I only stayed my hand because they tortured her less if she was away."

His voice broke and I held my breath. Torture. An iron box underground. Chainmail blindfold. A perfectly-fitted iron gag.

All of it would soon be mine.

The blue-tipped flame wrapped around my heart, encasing my chest in a shield of ice. My panic pacified, but still my vision fogged with cold tears.

Daigen's voice dropped but shook with rage. "This was the only way out. Hate me all you want, but you *have* to trust me. I can still kill that damn Alastar."

"Sera?" Riyan called. "Are you all right?"

I sucked up my tears and turned. Riyan had emerged from the fog, the gifted cloak wrapped around his hips. He must have sensed my panic through our bond.

Daigen's face smoothed into a smile. "Just taking you back to the fortress, big fellow. No need to break a boulder over my head or whatever it is your dear General taught you to do."

Riyan's brow hardened and his gaze turned deadly. I bit my tongue and turned to Daigen. He had hidden *Reginbani* away and held out his hand.

Even though I did not want to touch him, I could not change the terms of my bargain. I had to take his power too.

I leaned into the icy calmness of my blue flames and sent Riyan a message: "*Take Daigen's hand and I will explain later.*"

Riyan's eyes were still hard, but he stepped through the snow and grabbed Daigen's wrist.

Magic dragged against my skin, but instead of the normal white light, dark purple flooded my vision. Screams of men and animals filled my ears. Violet flames twisted around my veins and slithered into my chest. The dark flame wrapped around the diamond in my heart and danced with its blue and white counterparts.

Daigen had just given me all of his power.

My feet found grass. The air around me was warmer.

I let out a cool, easy breath and my vision returned. We were outside the Bloodstone Fortress gates, right where we had left. Daigen's hand released mine and I turned.

If I had not known the dark violet eyes and white hair so well, I would have thought a stranger stood in front of me. The lavender glow from his skin was gone. The sharpened edges of his face had rounded.

Nothing but a mere nineteen-year-old alchemist's apprentice stood before me.

Riyan jumped back as soon as he noticed Daigen's smoother, more pallid appearance. "The fuck was that?" He looked around. "How did we get here?"

"And to think I will never get that reaction again." Daigen may have looked younger, but his voice had the same seasoned edge.

"*Se-ra!*"

I turned my head and violet light from the dark flame coursed through my veins. A small black ripple burst through the trees, his outline barely visible against the night sky.

A smile tugged at my lips as I whispered, "Endre."

Endre flew closer. "*Se-ra!*"

Riyan appeared at my side. "What did you just say?"

I spread my arms. I pictured messy hair, burn marks on fingertips, and whispered giggles across a nursery. The magic within the approaching bird lit up with sparkling light. The darkness disappeared. Death's shroud lifted.

"Serafina, are you saying that raven is—?"

I closed my eyes. *Come back to me, brother.*

A chest crashed into mine, but arms wrapped around me before I could fall back. Laughter brighter than morning bells rang in my ears. Mint and fresh smoke filled my nose.

"Sera!" Not a croak, a voice.

He lifted me off my feet and spun me around. My laughter mixed with his. Only on the third rotation did he put me down.

I pushed off his chest and looked up. I met mossy eyes, black waves that fell to his shoulders, fewer freckles than I remembered, seven years of age added to his face, but…

Endre. It was Endre.

He gave me a big kiss on the cheek before breaking the hug. Riyan stood still, his face white.

"Riyan!" Endre called with a wide smile. "You shrank!"

Riyan's eyes watered. "You were a raven this whole time?"

The drop in Riyan's voice tugged on my heart, but Endre laughed. His dark green cape fluttered behind him as he ran up to Riyan and jabbed him in the neck with two fingers, pantomiming a bird's beak. "I tried to tell you! Not my fault you were too thick to take the hint!"

Riyan's smile banished his tears. He wrapped his strong arms around Endre and crushed him to his chest.

Endre laughed. "You could not bother to put on a shirt?"

Riyan chuckled back. "The cloak wouldn't fit around my shoulders."

"Show off."

Chains clinked behind me. The fortress gate was rising for its Baron.

Endre broke away from Riyan and ran for me. "Rosaline and Evereon are behind me." He grabbed my hand and we ran together toward the open gate. "Ev knows the way even in the dark, so I flew ahead as soon as I felt your magic at midnight."

I held my chemise as I struggled to keep his pace through the courtyard. "Does that mean you know about my—?"

"Erik!" Endre shouted. "Get your feathered ass out here!"

We stopped at the bottom of the keep's steps and soldiers flooded out of the keep to greet us. Then a woman taller than all the soldiers stepped into the moonlight. Brietta wore a crimson robe over her nightgown, her eyes shining as soon as she saw me.

My heart sank for only a moment—Annalisa had told her about my bargain.

But she did not know my eternal servitude was not with Ganora.

Brietta stood at the top of the steps and shouted back into the keep. Annalisa appeared, the hem of a lacy nightgown skating around her calves. A pink-beaked raven was perched on her shoulder.

Annalisa's eyes brightened when she spotted us. She sprinted down the keep's steps and Erik bobbed as she nudged her shoulder up. "Go, Bird Brain! Go!"

Erik quietly took to the air when Annalisa was in the middle of the steps. I extended a hand and lit up Erik from the inside.

I closed my eyes. The violet flames beneath my skin danced with the memories of a stern voice, charcoal-stained hands on top of drawing paper, and a soothing story during a storm.

I released the command with my breath.

"I do not approve of any of this," said a deeper voice than I remembered.

I opened my eyes. Erik's black eyes beneath his heavy brow stared down at me—eternally serious as always. I still smiled.

Endre shoved Erik's shoulder. "You grump!" He splayed all ten fingers in front of Erik's face. "We *finally* have hands! How can you be upset about this?"

Erik's stern expression did not change.

Annalisa ran to Erik and grabbed his arm. He nearly jumped out of his skin as she pulled him around to face her.

A shrieking cackle erupted from Annalisa's lips and she pointed up at Erik's face. His black eyes flashed with bewilderment, but my eyes followed Annalisa's finger and I laughed too.

Erik's large crooked nose was still bright pink.

Endre ran over to Annalisa and picked her up by the waist, even though they were the same height, and spun her while she giggled. "Seven years, and I can finally hold a beautiful girl again!"

Erik's brow hardened. Annalisa laughed and pointed at him as her feet returned to the ground. "Oh, he is a *mean* Bird Brain. Sera, change him back!"

Riyan joined Endre and Annalisa. They exchanged bright introductions and re-introductions as Annalisa measured the top of her head to Riyan's chin.

Brietta slowly descended the steps and joined us on the grass. Her brown eyes were still shining, but her smile had softened.

Erik turned to me. "Say nothing to Endre. This will go poorly if he believes the sorcerer tricked him when he said he was helping you."

Erik knew about my fate? Daigen must have told him before we went up the mountain, but the Erik I had known would have *never* let me leave if he knew what the bargain was really going to be.

How wicked was Daigen's mind that he could work around his inability to lie and trick all three of us?

Brietta pressed her hand over her heart. "What is he talking about, Serafina?"

A direct question I could not ignore. I let out a breath and looked only at Brietta. "The bargain for my eternal life was not with Ganora. When Derrick comes to the fortress, I have to go with him." I held back tears but my voice still broke. "I am his."

Brietta's face fell. The flicker of flipping pages tickled the back of my mind as she searched for a way out, but she would not find one.

A life for a life given in love. Nothing could ever break that bargain.

Daigen's voice cut through the night air. "If my calculations are correct—and if you're smart, you'll assume they are—, you have two sunrises left before the Alastar arrives at the fortress."

Hushed murmurs blanketed the courtyard. Derrick would arrive to take me that soon?

My vision pulled like I was falling backward. My knees buckled. Only Riyan's warm hand wrapping around mine kept me upright.

"Two sunrises left?" Riyan smiled. "Let's make this next one count."

Our new blood bond glowed around my heart as he took me in his arms and walked past the eyes of the crowd. His walk turned into a run as we crossed through the gate, then a sprint as he dodged the trees in the woods.

Even though I removed Ganora's curse, I left the power she gave him. He was still the fastest man alive.

The stars were quieting. The night was hazy with the impending dawn. Despite the weight of my bargain tightening its hold around my neck, I still laughed into Riyan's chest. He did not need to whisper into my mind for me to know where we were going.

He was taking me straight to the Bloodstone lilies.

Chapter Forty Nine
Consolation

Never before was I so eager for the sun to rise.

As Riyan held me in the center of the grassy meadow, I caught him up on all he had missed since we separated…except that Derrick was going to collar me.

I could not break his heart just yet.

The first break of golden sun over the rocky ridge sent red fire into the familiar meadow as the Bloodstone lilies opened their petals to greet the day.

The fragrant smell of the lilies shoved the image of Alastar's covetous glare out of my mind.

I gave Riyan a grateful kiss. He kissed me back and squeezed my thigh. Heat flooded my hips as my heart pounded.

We certainly made the first sunrise count.

I was on my hands and knees, the soft petals of the Bloodstone lilies tickling my breasts and belly as Riyan took me from behind. He held my hair in his fist and exhilaration from the pain flicked down my spine.

My arms shook from holding myself up. My legs shook from the building pleasure.

Right as I was at the edge, he slowed down. The glorious pinnacle of ecstasy slipped away and my insides wound into a frustrated knot.

"I was close, you fucking bastard!" I cried.

"And here I was thinking you'd be grateful that I was going easy on you." He chuckled and tugged on my hair. "But this could be fun—I'll go *nice and slow* to stretch you to the edge of your good-girl vocabulary. Let's see just how many bad words you know."

I dug my nails into the grass and closed my eyes as that knot in my hips pulled even tighter. "Come on, Riyan."

"Where are your manners?" He gave me a light smack on the ass before returning his hand to the curve of my hip. "Say please."

"Please," I whimpered.

Riyan picked up his pace and snapped that frustrated knot out of existence. Pleasure brighter than the sunlight flared behind my eyes as I cried out into the crisp morning air. As soon as my legs started quaking, he gripped my hips and finished with me.

Little by little, he slowed. My entire body trembled from both the ricochets of my climax and from fatigue, but I slowly tried to catch up with my racing heart.

With a satisfied sigh, he released my hair and tumbled onto his back in the lilies.

I let out a shaking breath and shot Riyan a look. "Whatever happened to—" I dropped my voice to imitate his, "'*Get on your hands and knees, Sera, I don't want to crush the flowers?*'"

Riyan gave me a dazed grin. "Eh, they'll grow back." He raised his hands to form a frame with his fingers. "I could commission a portrait of this—the flush on your cheeks, the 'freshly-fucked' glaze over your eyes, and on all fours in the middle of Bloodstone lilies. Gorgeous. I would hang it above the mantle in the dining hall."

I tucked some strands of hair behind my ear. Maybe he should commission a painting of me, it would be the only *me* he would get to have.

He wrapped his arm around my waist and gently pulled me onto his chest. I snuggled into his shoulder as our heartbeats calmed down.

I let out a soft sigh. "You might be smaller now, but you still make a great mattress."

He gently swept my hair off my back. "I'm glad you brought me down from the mountain just to be your furniture." He kissed the top of my head. "Although just imagine all the fun places you can sit."

Riyan's arms wrapped around me as I took a deep breath and his scent filled my lungs. Birds sang their morning melodies in the trees. The fresh sunlight smiled down on us.

Finally, a moment of paradise.

"So, when are you going to tell me what's bothering you?" he asked.

Shit.

I pushed up on my elbows and looked down at him. His face was still calm, but his voice was serious. "What I just said about you in the lilies…I thought you would laugh, but I heard the crackling of a fire burning instead."

Fuck, our bond worked both ways. He might not have the gift of sorcery, but he could still hear my inner self calling for help.

Not that he could do anything to sever my bargain.

"I know your immortality came with conditions," Riyan said, "and you don't want to talk about them because they're bad. I might be stupid, but I'm not that stupid."

"You are *not* stupid."

"My point is that I saw the panic in your eyes when I heard that burning." Riyan's arms wrapped more securely around me.

I bit my tongue. Had I really been that transparent?

"Just *tell me*, Serafina," he begged. "I want to make you feel better and I don't know how."

What could I even tell him?

I gripped his shoulders and looked him in the eyes. "You can do nothing to stop it. Just…hold on to the truth that we will both be alive in the end."

His brow hardened. "My immortality is not a consolation gift for your unhappiness."

I bit my tongue and glared at him, keeping my thoughts as quiet as possible in case he could hear them. The bargain was set, the last thing he should do is make me feel guilty about it.

I shoved out of his arms and walked across the lilies to where we had thrown my chemise. I slipped the chemise over my body and caught Riyan's eyes as he looked at me from across the meadow.

The gentle breeze ruffled his golden hair across his back. "It's okay to be scared, sweetheart. I…I'm scared too." His shoulders dipped forward as he looked at the lilies. "Not because the army is coming, I just…I don't want to see my father again."

The sound of a wave breaking on a rocky beach crashed through my mind. The diamond in my heart lit up.

Riyan was tugging on our bond. Despite the distance between us, I could not ignore the call for help.

I carefully stepped across the lilies and placed my hand on his shoulder. "Your father might be a monster, but that does not make you any less of a man."

His brow stayed hard but his lip twitched. He had looked the same way when he wanted to talk about his failed battle with the giants, but somehow could not bring himself to. I bent at the waist and kissed his temple, sending a little white flame of truth through his skin to give him the bravery to talk.

Riyan's throat bobbed as he swallowed. "He was tougher on me than anyone else. His command was the beginning and the end of my world. When he told me to fuck someone up, I just *did it*. Didn't matter if it was a piece of shit who murdered three women or…"

His voice broke. "…or Evereon Mydina for defying an order to fight me."

I wrapped my arms around his shoulders and tried not to think about that jagged line that split Evereon's face in two.

He took a long, deep breath. "I was only ten years old when I did it. Even after he was screaming and holding those bloody flaps of skin against his skull, I didn't feel bad. My General gave me an order and I wanted to make him proud."

I rested my chin on top of Riyan's head. Of all the rumors I had heard about the forsaken Mydina heir, none of them painted a picture of someone who refused to harm a child.

He was a better man than I gave him credit for.

"Let Evereon Mydina keep the House pins," Riyan said. "Let him rule the North. I owe him that much."

I let out a soft breath. "He does not want it, Riyan. He cannot have heirs."

"Then who should it be?" He twisted out of my hold to look up at me. "You said you can't have it because of your bargain and I sure as hell don't want to be Baron!"

His hair fell in his face and he angrily raked it back. "If I stay a Bloodstone, I have to face that I destroyed every member of my House. If I claim my Hyton blood, showing the whole Dukedom that I'm *his* son…"

He shook his head only slightly and then his eyes met mine. "I have to face that I want it. He's the only family I have left other than you and…"

I gritted my teeth to keep my lip from quivering. He did not need to finish his thought, I felt it, I *understood* it. His desire to be sheltered in Hyton Blue was different than mine, but it was still just as strong.

Where I had wanted power and security, Riyan just wanted a family.

Just as the monster inside Derrick was larger than any giant, so was Riyan's father in his own mind.

And just like Alastar, the General would be near impossible to overcome.

Strands of Riyan's hair fell into his face again and he tucked them behind his ear with a scowl. "Everything just feels so wrong, even my damn hair. General Hyton would always shear it every two weeks—"

I walked around to his back before he could say anything more and began combing through the tangles in his long golden hair with my fingers.

We only had one sunrise left, but I was making him something he could have even when we were apart. If I was not going to get a happy ending like in a faerie story, I could at least give Riyan one.

I pulled the pins and leather wraps out of my own hair and worked them into Riyan's, braiding back the front strands so they would stay out of his face.

"I told you before that I don't need to look pretty," Riyan said with a laugh.

I stuck my tongue out at him but kept braiding. When I finished, I ran my fingers through the ends of the shining golden hair that flowed freely down his back. "There! Just like Prince Haldar."

Riyan played with the tail of one of his braids. "Why Prince Haldar? There are no more giants to slay."

Suddenly Alastar's breath was on my neck again. I swallowed and shoved the thought of him away.

Alastar could take my eternity, but he would not take my last day of peace.

I sat in Riyan's lap and kissed his cheek. "There are always giants. Most of them just live in our heads."

Chapter Fifty
Smoke in the Sky

When Riyan and I returned to the Bloodstone Fortress keep, Evereon and Rosaline were waiting for us.

Riyan opened his arms to Rosaline as soon as he saw her sitting in the cavernous dining hall. Despite Riyan still wearing only Daigen's borrowed cloak around his hips, Rosaline ran across the room with no hesitation and crashed into a hug.

I smiled as the two friends reunited. At least Riyan would still have Rosaline when Derrick left the fortress with me.

Annalisa soon came over with a big lump of fur in her arms. With Hyton Palace erupting into chaos after we escaped, Rosaline and Evereon could not leave without Magnus the Bedwarmer.

The din of impatient soldiers filled the hall. The entire Bloodstone army was crammed along the sides of the hall, waiting for us to arrive.

Brietta parted through the soldiers to join us when Evereon stepped over with Erik at his side.

My brother gave me a look I instantly understood—he had told Evereon about my bargain.

Evereon gave Brietta a respectful nod. "Duchess." He turned to me. "Baron."

I looked him in the eyes and shook my head. I could not accept the title of Baron, not when the entire Bloodstone army would see me kneel before the Duke of Lycaster as soon as the next sunrise.

He would have to hold onto the House pins for a little longer.

Evereon's eyes flared for only a moment before Annalisa's voice cut through the tension. "Hello, it is I, *nothing,* with no title. Nice to meet you."

She glared at him with Magnus still in her arms. Instead of apologizing for not addressing her, Evereon flashed her a vulpine smile. "Lovely to meet you too, *nothing.*"

Her glare sharpened but Evereon turned back to me. "You might be deathless, but the rest of us aren't. We have to make a plan."

I swallowed the bitter guilt that I had again failed the North as Riyan took my hand. We sat on the bench of the long dining table and listened as Evereon stood in the center of the room and addressed the army.

He started with the story of their escape. He and Rosaline had taken a ferry across Odeneye lake before the Lycaster army gathered at its shores, but they passed beneath a soldier hanging from the gatehouse as they ran from the palace. Evereon said his eyes had been gouged out before he had been executed.

My blood ran cold. I never thought Derrick would go that far.

Rosaline leaned over to Annalisa and reassured her that they left Merri in a safe location in the city. Annalisa let out a relieved breath and scratched Magnus's ears.

Brietta sat next to me and listened intently, scribbling notes on parchment with a piece of charcoal.

We learned the caravan that I had sent to distribute food to the starving peasants of Ravenwood had returned, only my father had not come back to the fortress with them. The soldiers reported that as soon as Father heard the Lycaster army was approaching, he abandoned their party and disappeared.

I never thought my father would be such a coward.

From what Evereon reported, Derrick had horses, foot soldiers, and support of the Barons—all to bring the Duchess of Lycaster back to the palace.

Endre leaned on his knee with a dueling sword resting at his hip. "So what do we have to fight back? Weapons? Supplies?"

Evereon folded his arms. "That all depends if the wall is fixed."

"Give me and some men a few hours," Riyan grumbled at my side. His muscles tensed. "I can move stone bricks faster than you can blink."

"Then it becomes a waiting game," Evereon said. He scanned the soldiers gathered in the hall. "Horses and arrows do nothing against stone walls and the Lycaster army has no siege weapons. They'll block the gate for a few days and see if they can starve us out."

Brietta wrote "negotiation" on her parchment and underlined it.

"Nikkolas Bloodstone prepared me for this *exact* situation," Evereon said. "We will just have to rely on our food stores until Alastar the Mad gives up."

The Mad. My heart ached.

Brietta grimaced at the name, but she hissed out a breath and kept writing notes. I cut a glance at all her plans neatly lined out on the parchment—none of it was any use. She had never met Alastar, he would *never* allow Derrick to yield.

"What food stores?" Calder Anson shouted. "You mean the ones the fucking sorceress sent to Ravenwood?"

The bench jolted backward as Riyan leaped to his feet.

"Watch your fucking tone," he growled.

The whole room went quiet. Some of the soldiers clutched the hilts of their swords, but Calder did not let up.

"Nice to see where your loyalties lie, *for now*." He sneered. "Of course, when the General comes to the gate, you'll just roll over for him like always."

Riyan lunged toward Calder, but I wrapped a rope of magic around Riyan's wrist, yanking him back before he could jump over the table.

I sent a whisper into Riyan's mind, *"Calm down, Riyan."*

He set his jaw and sent a message back. *"I don't give a shit if you're Baron or not, no one runs their mouth about my family and lives."*

He held onto his fury and kept his eyes locked on Calder. Calder did not even flinch, but Endre stood between their death glares.

"Fire in the blood is what we need to stand against the Duke," Endre said with a confident smile. "If it comes to steel against steel, we will need that passion to win!"

Brietta's soft voice floated over the crowd, melting the tension in the room. "The Hytons do not fight with steel, but with false information." Every soldier turned their eyes from snarling Riyan to her. "Captain Mydina, what have the Hytons been saying?"

The air in the room shifted as the collective attention turned to Evereon. Endre walked to stand beside him, keeping his weight on his toes in case someone else lashed out. Erik stayed seated at the table, watching everyone over steepled fingers.

I released my magical hold over Riyan's wrist. He sat down at my side, rubbing his wrist where the tears must have tickled his skin.

Evereon cleared his throat. "The latest story Rosaline and I heard was that a sorceress absconded with the Duchess and is holding her prisoner.

Brietta rolled her eyes and scoffed. "Of course."

I bit my tongue. I was the villain in Derrick's narrative, not that I did not deserve it.

"And there's an archer going around saying the sorceress placed a curse on his bride—made her skin boiling to touch," Evereon said, his gaze jumping over my head as he addressed the crowd. "He's showing everyone the burn marks on his neck to prove it."

The soldiers murmured. Endre turned to me and I felt Erik's cold black eyes on me as well.

Although pride surged through my veins at having marked Grigory, I still turned to Annalisa. Her face had blanched. She had even stopped petting Magnus.

Evereon addressed the crowd, not me. "The army's plan is simple—kill the sorceress to reverse the curse and free the Duchess."

An invisible fist squeezed my heart. Derrick could not kill me, but he could make me wish I were dead. I could only hope Alastar merely hungered for conquest and not revenge.

The soldiers murmured, a few even shouting over the crowd.

"What will he do when he finds out she can't die?"

"This is ridiculous!"

"Just turn the bitches over once he gets here!"

"I'm not dying for any damn Hyton!"

Brietta stood up and threw her shoulders back, but Annalisa slipped off the bench and ran. Magnus gave a low meow, upset at having been abandoned.

She passed me and pouring rainfall clattered in my mind. I placed my hand on Riyan's shoulder, ready to send him a message to protect Brietta while I ran off for Annalisa, but a strong voice made me still.

"None of you will die for me!" Brietta shouted.

Every eye turned to Brietta as she stood at the table. She kept her brown eyes on Calder. "I may not know you, but I know your struggle. The Hytons have used you and abandoned you, leaving you to starve in the famine they created."

My brows knitted. I had thought Brietta only cared about Ravenwood's plight because she was my friend, but…she actually cared. She not only listened to me, she understood.

Brietta stepped away from the bench and walked into the center of the room, sweeping her eyes across the faces of every crimson-clad soldier. "The Hytons have taken so much. They took your sons and your brothers. They robbed you of your hope…and mine too. We will fight the Hytons not because of a mad Duke, but we will fight for us."

"Us?" Calder sneered. "What do you mean 'us?' You are just a spoiled noble girl."

Brietta reached down and grabbed the hilt of Calder's sword. Before he could stop her, she held out the blade to the crowd.

The iron must have been heavy, but her arm did not tremble and neither did her voice. "I am the Duchess of Lycaster. Alastar the Mad cannot kill me without destroying himself." She dropped the tip of the sword to the floor with a soft tap, punctuating her point, and turned to Evereon. "I am your greatest weapon. No steel or stone will dare cross the gate if I am standing atop it."

The soldiers around us murmured, but not with dissent.

"Never again," Brietta said. "Never again will the Hytons crush you underfoot. Never again will your cries go unheard. Never again will the lamentations of women go unpunished. If anyone should fall, it will not be for me—it will be for the freedom of everyone in the North."

Riyan cut me a look and sent a message into my mind: *"Is she sure she wants to be a Duchess and not a General? She is brilliant."*

I smiled as Endre rushed to Brietta's side, instantly rallying support for her cause. I had once thought her greatest talent was poetry on parchment, but with only a few words from her lips, she had shifted the entire battle. Instead of morale that would wither the moment I gave myself up to Derrick, the army now had something to fight for. She had braided her own ambitions of freedom with the North's desperate thirst for it.

Brietta had her own army…but Annalisa was still in pain.

I gave Riyan's back a quick pat and then I weaved through the crowd of cheering soldiers. My magic searched for Annalisa as I ascended the spiraling staircase, following the sound of sheets of rain.

Annalisa's voice echoed off the stone. "Get lost, Bird Brain!"

I rounded the corner and found them. Annalisa stood near a large window in the hallway, her cheeks shining with tears. Erik stood in front of her.

"Do not listen to those ruffians downstairs," Erik said calmly. "You are safe here."

"Oh, I already know what a Ravenwood's definition of 'safe' is," Annalisa snapped. Her watering eyes turned to me as I approached. "A curse in my blood. Separating me from my true love. Taking me away from my family!"

This again? "Anna, I already told you—"

"Justify it however you want." She clutched her arms so hard that her fingernails must have pinched through her sleeves. "You never gave me a choice. You got to choose Riyan, Brietta got to choose a war for her freedom, but *I* never got a choice."

I avoided Erik's judging eyes as my stomach knotted. I had just wanted to protect her, but she was right. Just as I was grieving the last hours of my autonomy, Annalisa was grieving the loss of hers.

And *I* had taken it away from her.

"I am sorry, Anna." I looked into her glassy eyes and her lip trembled. "You deserved a choice too."

Just as Annalisa's brow softened, I caught sight of a dark swirl in the clouds. I cut between Annalisa and Erik and gripped the windowsill, looking through the glass panes to the south.

Over the trees was a large cloud of smoke. Judging by the distance, it was coming from the Bloodstone apple grove.

"Derrick," Annalisa whispered. She pressed her hand against her heart. "Oh, Derrick."

The destruction was not just cruelty, it was a message. Derrick did not intend to wait us out like Evereon had predicted. He was an Alastar. He was a conqueror.

He was going to smoke us out.

Chapter Fifty One
Bonded

Pandemonium struck as soon as the dark wisps of smoke curled into the sky.

Riyan rushed to the courtyard to repair the fallen wall. Endre and Evereon inventoried weapons. Brietta focused on how to put out any incoming fire. The last I saw of Annalisa was her watering eyes as she shut Astrid's bedroom door in my face.

My last evening of freedom was in solitude.

I used to enjoy the peaceful embrace of a lonely night, but my heart raced as I paced across Riyan's bedroom. I chewed on my tongue as I walked back and forth, the flickering candlelight on the writing desk my only companion.

What was the point of all the defenses? Everyone but Riyan knew I was going to kneel before Derrick and give him the most powerful weapon he could possibly possess. How could Brietta still hold on to her plans of freedom knowing Derrick was just going to point me at her like a gilded sword?

What was the point of *any* of it? Of uncovering the lies, of fighting Alastar, or of trying to change the entire fabric of the Dukedom? We had just caused damage left and right, to what result? Nothing. We gained *nothing*.

My white flame flared between its blue and violet companions and I let out a shallow breath. Fine, I should not blame Annalisa and Brietta. *I* had gained nothing. Seven years of manipulating Derrick had sent him into madness.

I had made him want me, I had made him need me, but I had done my job too well.

Without realizing it, I had taken Derrick and I's mutual desperation for one another and weaved them together until I had forged our own bond. I had just wanted to make my own security, but instead of wrapping that threaded bond around Derrick's wrists like I had planned, I had circled it around my own neck.

And because of my bargain, that bond between us would never sever.

All the magical flames raged within me. Cold clashed against warm and light flared against dark, but deep within that diamond in my heart was that flickering red ember—that infuriating little ember that would not let me hate Derrick despite everything he had done.

Would I still be unable to hate him after he snapped that collar onto my neck?

The memory of three low notes on a harp and a warm laugh against my cheek gave me my answer.

I yanked back the chair at the writing desk and sat down. I slammed parchment on the desktop and my magic cut the quill sharper than a needle.

I hated myself for what I felt, but hating my own emotions is what sent me down the path to forge that bond with Derrick in the first place. Maybe if I faced my actions, the next eternity might be bearable.

I dunked the quill in the pot of murky ink and wrote:

Midnight,

I am so sorry. For everything.

—Birdie

I slammed my eyes shut, but a tear still trickled past my eyelashes. The red ember pulsed in my heart four times as I kissed the parchment right over where I had written "Midnight."

I had done it with every letter I had ever sent him. It was a bit of my own superstitious nonsense, a frivolous wish that maybe I could have won his heart.

I opened my eyes to see my teardrop had smeared the ink of the "M." The ink swirled in the teardrop before it dried into the parchment, leaving behind a ruined smudge.

What was I doing? We were not schoolchildren any longer. He was the Duke and I was his slave. Wishing would do me no good.

And neither would any worthless letter.

My flames twisted as I focused on the tear that had mixed with the ink, and then I incinerated the parchment.

The door creaked open. I turned from the mound of smoking ash to the door where Riyan stood. He had not bothered to put on a shirt after his bath. His hair was still slightly damp from him washing away all the masonry dust, but the style I had weaved earlier was still intact.

The wall was repaired, but what did it matter?

The light from the candle in his hand flickered across his soft smile. "Do you want to talk?"

Did I need to talk? Yes. Did I *want* to talk?

"No," I said softly.

"Me neither." He set the candle on the desk and slowly lowered to his knees in front of me. He rested his head on my lap and let out a long, heavy breath as his shoulders dipped.

I could not help but laugh. "Comfy?"

He looked up at me and smiled against my thighs. "I'm just glad I could at least fix something I broke…for once."

My eyes flicked up to the shattered bedframe. "No one can fix everything they break."

A slow, melancholy wave in the back of mind pushed his worry through our bond. I slid my hands through the roots of his hair, my thumbs tracing the braids above his earlobes. I responded to his tide of unease with my crackling fire.

Neither of us were all right, but we were only brave enough to say it through our magic. Riyan did not want to face his father. I did not want to face Alastar's jaws.

We were stuck, but at least for one night, we could be stuck together.

Through my burning anguish, the little red ember pulsed in my heart.

I held back a frown. I had acquired more power than any other being alive, and yet that damn little ember remained. Once my servitude suffocated my flames in a few centuries, would that ember still be there, glowing strong? Would it still mock me with its presence? Would that ember be all that was left once my spirit had died?

Ice from my blue flame pricked my ribs. My chest rattled with a sob and Riyan lifted off my lap. He wrapped his arms around me and I buried myself in his shoulder as I let the tears run into his hair.

He slipped something soft into my hand. I sniffed away tears as I traced my thumb over the bumps of threads—it was the scrap of linen with the embroidered flowers.

I pulled away and met his soft smile. "Came to me out of the well when you went to speak with Daigen. Figured I would give it to you when you needed it the most, just like you did with me."

I clutched the flowers and my worry began to wane. His thumb stroked my neck and I savored his touch. It was the last night that spot would ever be bare…

"Kiss my neck," I whispered.

He brushed away my hair and pressed his lips in a feather-light touch just below my ear.

My eyelashes fluttered closed. "Again."

He kissed me on my neck, then my jaw, then my lips. I wrapped my arms around his shoulders. He lifted me off the chair and laid me in the middle of the bed.

I sank down on the plush mattress. Riyan's arms bracketed me, his silken hair fell toward me, and the back of his hand gently caressed my cheekbone.

Riyan could not fix my bargain just as he could not fix the bed he had destroyed. Though there was nothing either of us could do about my eternal servitude…we could at least have a night that *earned* a broken bed.

I kissed Riyan with a whimper and locked my legs around his hips.

He pulled away softly and gave me a wicked look. "Really? Three times in one day?"

My body ached to be with him just one more time, but heat spread across my cheeks from embarrassment rather than desire. "Too much? I was just worried with the army coming tomorrow—"

Riyan silenced me with a kiss. "Stop talking." His calloused hands rounded my hips and he raised the hem of my nightgown. He planted a kiss in the center of my bare chest. "Stop worrying." He kissed my lower belly. "Just enjoy this moment of happiness…"

He settled between my legs but his eyes stayed locked on mine. My heart pounded with anticipation as his arms wrapped around my thighs and he dipped his head.

I held back a gasp as the first long, gentle sweep of his tongue threw me to the edge of ecstasy. I rolled my head back onto the pillow and gripped the sheets as he took me slowly, so agonizingly slowly. I grinded against his face and he tightened his grip with a scolding grunt.

He raised his head, looking at me over the slight swells of my belly and my breasts. He licked his lips and smirked. "I wonder at what point in your immortality you will finally learn some patience?"

I huffed out a breath as desire pulsed within my hips. "When you stop pissing me off."

His smirk softened into a smile. "I missed you."

Riyan lowered himself again and I whimpered as he tasted me. His hand slid up and caressed my breast, his thumb tracing circles around my peaked nipple that matched the circles he traced with his tongue.

Each delicate touch sent a shock of pleasure through me. My legs started to shake, but I did not merely want his mouth, I wanted *him.*

I raked my fingers through the roots of his hair and tilted his head up. My hand found his jaw and I brought his mouth to mine like I was starving. The taste of my arousal traced my tongue.

He held the back of my head, his fingers lacing with my hair, as he folded me in half.

"Right here," I whispered against his lips, "just like this."

Riyan shifted my legs to the right side of his chest as he loosened the laces of his pants. "See? Being patient is rewarding."

Though I desperately needed him inside me, I could not help but laugh.

I only caught a glimpse of his devious smile before he slowly entered me. I dropped my head on the pillow and closed my eyes. Soft moans escaped my lips with each thrust as I savored the feel of his rough edges against my soft curves.

The splintered edges of the bed creaked beneath us. Riyan quickened his pace and the rough motion bent and snapped more of the shattered supports. He slammed his hand into the headboard and it cracked, but my cries of pleasure nearly drowned out the noise.

"Not so mouthy now, are you?" he said with a wicked edge to his voice.

I almost shot back about him being "mouthy" when he was between my legs, but I could not find the words. White light filled my entire body as I enjoyed him, enjoyed *us.*

My head fell to the side and I felt the tickle of his calloused palm cupping my flushed cheek. He eased his rhythm but my body pulsed around him, wanting more. My eyes opened only slightly as I looked up at him through my heavy lashes.

His face was soft and his voice echoed through our bond. "*I take back what I said earlier about commissioning that portrait of you for the dining hall. No one else gets to see you like this. This is just ours.*"

I closed my eyes and smiled into his palm. Ours.

The word repeated through our bond as heat and light filled my body, slowly reaching its pinnacle. I gripped the planes of tight muscle on

Riyan's legs as pleasure built within me. His lips caressed the top of my head as he whispered that he loved me. My body started to shake, but my mind was calm and clear.

I was safe. I was warm. I was *his.*

We finished together and crashed beside each other on the mattress. Before I could even think to move, Riyan wiped the sweat from my brow and kissed me on the forehead. I rested my head on his chest and crossed my leg over his waist, clinging to as much of him as I could. His hand cupped the back of my thigh and his chin rested on top of my head as his heartbeat slowed to a quiet thump.

Although my body craved the bliss of sleep, I savored Riyan's smell too much to lose even a second to unconsciousness.

So I just breathed, long and deep, even though I never would have to breathe again.

I breathed because I *could.*

As I let out a long exhale against Riyan's skin, I finally understood why Fraleigh was willing to face the collar. Pain is temporary. Despair is finite. A cage can only get so small.

Alastar could drag me away into the sunrise, but Riyan and I were bonded—unbreakable. No matter how brief my moments of reprieve might be throughout eternity, Riyan would still be there.

My fingertips brushed the hair on his chest as my hand curled into a fist. Riyan and I might never end, but I still never wanted our time together to stop.

Golden light flared through my eyelids and I buried my face into his shoulder.

No, just a little longer.

The song of the birds filtered through the broken window and I gritted my teeth.

We were eternal. It would be all right...

Soldiers shouted outside as they formed ranks. "The Duke is coming!"

Riyan's chest stirred and he tightened his grip on my thigh. I opened my eyes to the sickly yellow light that leaked through the boards nailed to the shattered window.

Time had finally run out.

Chapter Fifty Two
The Last Sunrise

My heart pounded as I forced myself to sit up in bed. Strips of sunlight painted the mattress like the bars of a dungeon cell.

Alastar was near, ready to take my bargain in full.

Riyan took a deep breath and his beautiful eyes fluttered open. The weight of the fateful morning settled on our throats and silenced us. Even our bond was quiet.

He gave me a soft smile and a kiss between the eyes before he rose. I clutched the blankets and watched as he dressed—a simple shirt and pants with leather armor over his heart.

Very little protection, but that would not matter. Deathlessness would be my parting gift.

Riyan swept his crimson cape over his shoulders and I jumped off the mattress. His eyebrows raised as I rushed over and held out my hand. He gave me a knowing smile and placed the steel—not gold—Bloodstone pin in my palm.

I raised on my toes and poked the pin through the crimson wool. I was dressing him for a battle he had no idea he was going to lose.

I gritted my teeth behind closed lips. Riyan had sent men to Death to get justice for women he never even knew. "The Beast" would not let any man take his wife without spilling his blood.

My red ember flared in my chest but my mouth was dry as I spoke. "No matter what happens, do not hurt Derrick."

His mouth formed a hard line, but I responded with an even harder look.

"Swear to me that no harm comes to Derrick," I ordered.

He hissed out a breath. He was suspicious, but said nothing of it. "Fine, if nothing else but to keep Brietta safe."

A gentle knock rapped on the door and Riyan swallowed.

"I'll take that as my cue to head to the courtyard," he said.

I gripped his cape, begging him not to leave if only for one more heartbeat.

He smiled and slipped the embroidered fabric into my stiff hand. "Find your flowers instead of your fear, sweetheart."

His hand cupped my jaw and he kissed me one last time. The ice from my blue flame paralyzed me as I watched him walk to the door.

Riyan opened the door. "She is all yours."

Brietta and Annalisa walked in. Brietta dressed in splendid Hyton Blue, wearing glittering jewels she must have found around the fortress.

"My aim is to be as visible as possible." Brietta pushed her shoulders back and lifted her chin. "Once the people hear the truth of my escape, negotiations for my return shall begin. I will not surrender until we are all free."

Well, not all of us would be free.

I nodded anyway, though the familiar numbing fog crept behind my eyes. My feet moved on their own until I realized I was at the wardrobe. I pulled open a drawer until my hand curled around a familiar hilt.

I gently held the blade of the Hyton dagger flat against my palm as I walked over to Brietta.

"Here," I said, "hopefully you will find it as useful as I did."

Brietta gently accepted the blade while Annalisa picked through my wardrobe and selected billowing white linen. Simple and comfortable, she explained.

I let her dress me, my arms feeling like they were full of sand as I slipped them into the sleeves.

Annalisa slid my pearl headband behind my ears and told me I looked like a faerie princess.

But I was never a faerie princess. I was always just going to be a slave.

Three knocks echoed through the door. Annalisa furrowed her brows, but answered. Erik was on the other side.

He looked at me and held out his arm. His sleeves fell almost to his knuckles, but I spied flashes of black markings on his hands.

My toes were full of lead as I dragged myself over. I wrapped my arm around my brother's and he led me through the halls. Annalisa and Brietta followed solemnly behind.

As I leaned on Erik's arm, I sensed a low energy pulsing through his blood. Magic still coursed through his veins, but darkness stuck to his muscles like thorns.

Only when Erik stopped did I look up. A couple of Bloodstone soldiers pulled the keep's doors open and Endre bounded up the steps with a wide smile.

Brietta and Annalisa gasped softly behind me, and not just because Endre wore only his Ravenwood cape on his top half. He had black marks all over his skin that were shaped like feathers but pointed like blades. The feathers fanned out like a collar across his chest and decorated his arms like he still had wings.

"What are you doing?" Erik spat. "Cover *those* up!"

Endre's mossy eyes glimmered. "I am not ashamed of our past." He spread his arms and looked up at Annalisa. "Just little mementos from our time as ravens."

Erik's lip curled as he released my arm. "Try not to get yourself killed."

Endre shot him a look. "Go brew some tea and let a real swordsman handle things." He glanced at me. "Come along, ladies. We have a battle to win."

Brietta and I descended the steps with Endre's escort. I looked over my shoulder. Erik offered Annalisa his arm, but she blew past him to join us.

Sparkles of pink and gold light broke through the wispy clouds. Morning mist crawled over the grass. The magical tears in the heavy air tickled my cheeks.

Some rain would quell any weaponized fire.

I stopped in the center of the courtyard and spread my hands, forcing my magic to reach out for miles as I awakened thousands of tears in the air.

"What is she doing?" Annalisa hissed.

The tears trembled, ready to listen. I closed my fists and pulled inward.

"Look up!" Brietta cried.

I pulled and pulled, straining under a massive yet invisible weight. All the tears in the sky followed my command, moving over the fortress and pressing together to form heavy clouds.

The clouds were filling with tears, but I needed more. I reached out further, lower in the sky, grabbing every sparkle of magical moisture I could…

"*I feel you, sorceress.*"

Alastar found me, even through my magic. My stomach dropped, but I gritted my teeth and kept my hold over my power, dragging the tears to the fortress.

"*You are almost mine,*" he said with a growl. "*I can smell you. I can taste you.*"

I dropped my power with a gasp and fell into the grass. I looked up and the grey clouds above me were ready to burst open. Rain would fall with just a snap of my fingers.

"Sera!" Riyan rushed over and knelt beside me in the grass. "Are you all right?"

"She is brilliant!" Brietta said with a wide smile. "She just nullified Derrick's greatest weapon."

Riyan helped me up. He kissed me on the forehead, his hand lingering over the pearls on top of my head. "You look beautiful, sweetheart."

I could not help but smile, even as my fate approached.

"Archers, to your places!" Evereon ordered.

Footsteps scrambled to the wall. The rolling of the cavalry's hooves echoed up the mountainside.

The Lycaster army had arrived. Derrick was mere paces away.

The pull of my bargain flared through my blood. I could not run from my obligation any longer.

I broke out of Riyan's grip. My heart ached as he called for me, but I climbed the gate's steps, winding up and up until my face hit the heavy air.

Legions of cavalry lined up in front of the fortress gates. Grigory Thornebow with fresh burns on his neck led the rows of archers. Carts full of dry hay were positioned near the gate along with soldiers holding torches. The six Barons mounted their horses beneath their House banners. General Hyton wore gleaming brass atop his white horse, positioned right in front of the Barons. Fraleigh stood beside the General's horse, her golden eyes finding mine as a magical tether connected us.

"*I'm sorry, Serafina,*" she whispered. "*I tried to stop Daigen. I tried to stop them all.*"

My eyes traced the gleaming band around her neck that was about to be mine. She tried to defy the will of the Man of the Mountain and let herself suffer just to save me.

No one deserved a collar, but Fraleigh deserved rest.

A slow wave of calm washed through me as I sent a message back: "*I am a Ravenwood regardless of what color I wear. I will survive this too.*"

Fraleigh's mouth formed a tight line and suddenly that calmness in my body dissolved.

The moment my eyes found the glint of the golden Lycaster crown, I stopped breathing. He wore his Hyton Blue cape over Alastar the Conqueror's steel armor. The Taurus shield was on his arm and the Conqueror's spear was in his hand.

The Duke of Lycaster had come to conquer Nordingaard…and I found nothing recognizable in those beautiful Hyton Blue eyes.

Heartbreak had hardened him, from the harsh cut of his jaw to disdain burning on his brow.

And it was all my fault.

Then Alastar's voice invaded my mind, shredding at any sense of peace I had left.

"*Mine. Mine. Mine.*"

Chapter Fifty Three
Blood for Blood

My heart pounded in my ears, counting down the seconds of freedom I had left.

The morning wind ruffled my hair and I swore I could feel Alastar's claws around my neck. Riyan's footsteps thundered on the stone steps as he joined me at the top of the Bloodstone Fortress gate.

He looked down at the Lycaster army that had appeared out of the trees. Our bond strained with worry the moment he found his father, but then lit up with fury when he saw Derrick at the front line.

Riyan might not have known the terms of my bargain, but he must have pieced the fragments of my emotions together, just as he had when he was in the place West of the Moon and East of the Sun.

His hand wrapped around mine and his touch pushed the low heat of primal rage into my skin.

Though Derrick was merely in front of the gate, he matched Riyan's building disdain brick by brick.

"I will give you one hour to surrender what you have stolen, monster!" he shouted. His black horse shifted from the tension, but Derrick's glare remained firm. "If you fail, I will roast you alive!"

Brietta glided to the top of the gate. Her shoulders were back and her red hair was radiant amongst the dark sky. She positioned her body between two battlements and looked down at her husband.

"We will *never* surrender," she said. Low mumbles rippled through the army. "And I was not stolen. I *ran* from you."

Alastar's rage echoed in my mind.

"And you think you can threaten me?" Riyan shouted with a wicked gleam in his eyes. "You think you can threaten *her?*"

I nearly jumped out of my skin as he raised my arm, my fingers still laced with his.

"She is now more powerful than Fraleigh ever was," he yelled through the thick morning air. "And we have a *sealed* blood bond."

Derrick's eyes widened. Alastar roared and sent shivers down my spine.

I could not let Riyan antagonize him any more. I could not let anything get worse. "Riyan—"

"Behold!" General Hyton's voice boomed. "My son! The rightful heir to the House of Hyton!"

Warmth passed through Riyan's hand to mine as he lowered my arm. "*My son*" echoed through our bond. He held his breath and I held mine, but for a different reason.

General Hyton was not claiming a son at the edge of a battle for sentimental reasons.

My eyes flitted amongst the rows of soldiers. Swords were still sheathed. None of the archers had notched their arrows. Even from the top of the gate, I could still spy Grigory Thornebow's smirk.

The General was not going to siege the fortress, he was establishing a line of succession. He was about to depose Derrick.

Ice trickled down my spine as Derrick's eyes shifted to General Hyton. He gripped the Conqueror's spear.

Did he have enough sense left to know what was happening?

General Hyton turned his horse to the army, facing the line of Barons specifically. "He is the Hero of Lycaster and he blood-bonded with a sorceress even more powerful than Fraleigh!"

Fraleigh's eyes widened as she slowly stepped back from General Hyton's horse. The army rumbled with cheers but Riyan's face fell. Tension built in the mist. Thunder rolled in the distance.

Derrick turned his horse to General Hyton, but then a soldier ran up and sliced a sword at its back leg. The horse screamed and reared up, throwing Derrick off before it ran.

Derrick landed in the grass with a hard thud. He lifted his face off the grass with a wince and my heart ached.

He was hurt.

General Hyton's horse trotted over to him. He pointed Traitor's Bane down at Derrick. "This is where my brother's line ended up! Weak! Powerless!"

"Hear, hear!" Baron Elvar cried. The other Barons cheered in agreement.

Like a wolf in the bushes, Ragnar had waited decades for his perfect opportunity. The path to the Lycaster crown had fallen into place— support of the Barons, a sorceress bound to his blood heir, and Fraleigh ready to perform her famous bow, solidifying him as her owner.

I looked for Fraleigh amongst the crowd, but I could not find any sign of her Hyton Blue robes or golden eyes.

I had not seen Daigen all morning, either.

General Hyton pointed up at Brietta. "His Duchess ran from him. Even *she* sensed his weakness!"

His arm trembled and he quickly lowered Traitor's Bane. How was a man with his amount of strength struggling with the weight of his sword?

General Hyton dismounted his horse. He walked to the line of Barons just as two soldiers forced a struggling cloaked figure next to him.

"My brother had the same weakness, letting women run all over him...and it led to his downfall." His sneer smoothed into a cold smile as his eyes swept over the line of Barons. "A traitor is in our midst..."

General Hyton tore away the cloak and my heart dropped. Mother fell to her knees in the grass, bound and gagged while the other Barons jeered.

I held out my hands and awoke the magic in the air. Maybe I could pull myself through the air, maybe I could save her.

Just as I nearly stepped off the battlement, Mother's emerald eyes found me. White light gleamed between her furious eyebrows and the sound of pine needles on a forest floor rustled in my mind. I sent out a small tether and her mind screamed one word:

"*Wait.*"

Derrick pushed himself up from the grass with gritted teeth, but he still clung to his shield and spear. My heart nearly pounded out of my chest as I watched him struggle.

General Hyton glared at Derrick. "He may dress himself in our relics, but he never had the spirit of the Conqueror." His eyes flicked up to the Barons. "And neither did his father."

The crash of a wave breaking pulsed through my mind as Riyan's hand gripped mine. If Ragnar was claiming *he* had the spirit of the Conqueror all along, why had he not just taken the crown? He already had everything lined up…

General Hyton turned to a cart covered in canvas. "The impostor in the grass wasted his time with his lover, wasted his body with faerie dust and spirits, and nearly wasted our great Hyton Palace, but under my rule…"

He reached into the cart. "…we shall have the entire world on bended knee!"

He yanked out a brown-headed woman with her hands tied. Amethyst. "Austland!"

He threw her to the ground and pulled out another woman. Rubia. "Latimus!" Then Garnet. "Rokuhama!"

One by one, he threw each of the bound Hyton sisters to the ground in a heap. They cried behind their gags and tried to get to their knees.

A chill like snow ran down my back as I watched the princesses struggle. The Hyton sisters were mean, but they were *innocent.*

"And most importantly…" he yanked out Sapphira by her hair. "The Sudrian empire!"

The army cheered as Sapphira struggled under his hold like a feral cat.

Derrick inched closer to General Hyton in the grass and murder gleamed in his mad eyes. Mother's wide eyes followed him as she shook her head and curled her fists into a white-knuckled grip.

General Hyton dropped Sapphira into the heap. "We will hold each for ransom. If their countries do not give into our demands, we lop off their heads, sending their blood-bonded rulers to their graves!"

I nearly pulled myself out of my skin. Why did Mother want me to wait? Someone needed to help them!

Derrick shakily rose to his knees, using the Conqueror's spear for leverage. Mother cried through her gag. Horses screamed in the distance.

General Hyton turned to Derrick and gripped the hilt of Traitor's Bane.

This was not a staged deposition, it was an *execution*.

This was the final Alastar trial.

The little red ember in my heart blazed, sending a blast of warmth through my body. The blood in my veins twisted with a swirl of color and light.

I *had* to save him.

I reached out into the air. Magic sparkled around me.

Traitor's Bane gleamed in the torchlight as General Hyton shouted, "Time to end the madness!"

Magic dragged against my skin with a scream and then my arms wrapped around a breastplate.

Ragged breathing filled my ears. Then steel sang as it thudded in the grass.

I looked up. General Hyton stood over me, his eyes down at his fallen sword and his right arm twitching.

I had finally stepped through the air.

I was on my knees with my arms around Derrick. His eyes were squeezed shut—he must have thought he was already dead.

General Hyton looked from me to my mother. She smiled wickedly beneath her gag and uncurled her fists. The crescents her fingernails had dug into her palms leaked out beads of black blood.

She shared his food and drank from his cups—the Viper had struck the heel of the General. She had poisoned them both with Thornebow thistle.

The General was never going to harm Derrick. The poison made him unable to swing his sword and it was slowly killing him.

But would the magic of Mother's blood bond save her?

A cacophony of screams echoed in front of us and I looked up. The princesses were free of their bonds and hauling themselves onto horses. Lycaster soldiers with slit throats littered the ground. Sapphira had knives in both hands, slashing red ribbons into every soldier who came near them. Rubia leaned over from her horse and yanked Sapphira up to ride away.

A soldier ran amongst them. Though his uniform was stained with blood, he appeared unharmed. He must have freed the princesses.

General Hyton's shoulders trembled as he turned toward the chaos. "Do not let them get away!"

Arrows flew through the air, but the princesses broke through the ranks, their horses running into the forest around the fortress walls. The lone soldier did not follow them, but instead took his own horse and sped toward us. His helmet fell and his hair seemed too silver to belong to a normal soldier…

General Hyton's head spun back around and his black-lined eyes strained. "Hold formation!"

"Run, Little Ember!" cried the soldier.

That was no soldier…it was my father.

Mother screamed behind her gag as Father reached down and scooped her up onto his horse. Derrick shifted, as if he had just realized he was still alive, and turned to face me.

A chill washed through me as soon as my eyes met his furious ones. I had lost his mind *and* his heart.

My white flame surged as General Hyton approached. I flung my arms around Derrick again and pushed us through the air back to the fortress.

We both landed in the courtyard with a thud. Dozens of footsteps crunched in the grass.

My chest met the curve of the Taurus shield as Derrick shoved me off him. I gripped the grass and tried to catch my breath as he glared down at me.

"After everything…" he panted, "…you chose the monster?"

Red-uniformed soldiers crashed into him and he shouted in pain. They grabbed him by the arms and legs as he fought them off. They stripped him of his shield and spear and dragged him into the keep, but his furious eyes stayed on me.

"*Mine,*" Alastar growled in my mind.

"Serafina!" Riyan called. He ran over and grabbed my hand. "What did he do to you? I don't care what I promised, I'll break him into pieces!"

My lip trembled. The call of the bargain pulled within my blood. I could not keep it from him any longer. "Riyan…I have to go to him."

He gripped my hand and held the back of my head with the other. "What are you talking about? He is mad—!"

"Riyan, my bargain was to take Fraleigh's place as the Duke's slave." The words tasted bitter, but a weight lifted off my chest.

I tried to pull away, but Riyan held me in an iron grip. "The hell you are! I will destroy him. Raze his palace to the ground. Slice the neck of every soldier—"

I took the embroidered flowers out of my pocket and slipped them into his hand. "Find your flowers, Riyan." His blood lit up on my command and I raised onto my toes. "You will be deathless when you wake."

I kissed him, enchanting him with the loving touch of my lips to dream. He closed his eyes and his knees buckled as he fell into the grass. My chest shook with a sob.

As much as it hurt to leave him behind, I had to fulfill my bargain.

A life for a life exchanged in love. Nothing could ever break it. Nothing could ever save me.

Chapter Fifty Four
Ring of Gold

Riyan was lying on his stomach in the middle of the fortress courtyard, but his blood pulsed as he fought my enchantment to keep him asleep. I closed my eyes and focused as I tried to keep him under.

I was trying to give him mercy. He could not stop my bargain, so I was not going to force him to watch as I became the Hytons' eternal slave.

Mint and fresh smoke filled my nose. A warm hand laced with mine. "Come on, Sera. I am right beside you."

Charcoal and tea leaves followed. "As am I."

I cried as Erik and Endre led me up the steps. The keep's doors creaked open. The warmth of Bloodstone Fortress filled my nose, likely for the final time.

Daigen's voice filled my ears. "Let us take it from here, Reavers."

Us?

Erik and Endre released my arms. Two slender yet sharp hands took mine.

"Everything will be all right," Fraleigh whispered.

Daigen had taken her from the battlefield. I should have known he would not need sorcery to perform his tricks.

Her magic gently knocked against the door into my mind and I slowly let her in, ready to accept her power before I completed the terms of my bargain.

Warmth flooded my body. Gentle green and gold fire crawled up from my palms and into my heart. Ganora's blue flame of icy rage danced with Fraleigh's golden flame of loving heat. All of the flames swirled together around my heart until a rainbow of light burst through my chest.

I took in a breath, feeling every sparkle of magic in the air enter my lungs.

Daigen's muscled arm looped around my right arm and Fraleigh's thin arm linked with my left. They led me forward, but each step I took felt heavier and heavier. I squeezed my eyes shut tighter as Riyan fought harder against my magical veil that kept him asleep.

"It doesn't hurt," Fraleigh said in my left ear as we walked. "I promise, it doesn't hurt."

I counted my pounding heartbeats as I blindly followed Daigen and Fraleigh's lead. The sound of splintering wood and slamming iron echoed through a door.

"He's not taking captivity well," a soldier said.

"Let the immortal go first, then," Daigen said, "lest the mad Duke crack one of our skulls open."

I swallowed through my shaking throat. Daigen tucked a strand of hair behind my ear and whispered, "This is when the trust part comes in—this is what *all* my planning led to. I saw what you had hidden away the first time I entered your mind. All you have to do now is tell Midnight your truth."

He patted me on the shoulder as keys jingled. What was I supposed to tell Midnight the truth about?

The door creaked open and Daigen gently pushed me forward. My heart pounded in my ears as I stepped into the room.

I instantly hit a wall of saturated rage in the air. My skin shivered.

It was too late for Riyan to act, so I let out a slow breath and lifted my enchantment over him. I opened my eyes, but I could barely see the dark figure with a chest of shining steel and a halo of gold around his brow.

"Come to wound me again?" he said, the bitter sting of heartbreak staining his words.

I gripped my hands and shook my head. "I…I have a gift, Your Excellency."

The thick silence was deafening. I swallowed and leaned into the strength of my power. "I slayed Ganora and her giants are gone. Her power is mine. Fraleigh's power is mine."

Alastar growled with hunger in the back of my mind. I set my jaw and kept my chin up. "Release her from her servitude and take me. You will control the most powerful sorceress the world has ever seen. You can keep your crown. You can finally quiet the Barons…"

Derrick pushed off the wall and I took another breath.

"…and you can have all of me," I said. "I am eternally yours, Derrick."

He moved closer. The tiny song of the unbreakable bargain in my blood overcame every instinct of self-preservation that screamed in my muscles.

The memory of Daigen's voice pulled on my mind. "*Tell Midnight your truth.*"

I held my breath. Beneath the rainbow of flames around my heart, the little ember pulsed four times again. Four times for four words.

And I had the truth at last.

I had slammed brick after brick over that ember over the years, trying to snuff it out so its power could not affect me, yet it never grew cold. With a brush of lips under a waxing moon, the ember grew, destroying my stone defenses, and letting me laugh, and cry, and love like I never would have let myself before.

Because of that little ember, I had *life* again.

I closed my eyes, letting that ember sing with the truth I had denied myself over and over. The truth was too big, too frightening, to say aloud, so I pretended to turn my tongue into a quill and my words into ink.

Just a message to Midnight, like I had done hundreds of times.

With my last breath of freedom, I finally let the truth of those four words out. "I love you, Derrick."

A heartbeat of suffocating silence passed. I opened my eyes and the darkened figure of Alastar Derrick Pervale Hyton did not move.

Not that I expected him to. Nothing could change my bargain. Loving him could not stop the collar, but it still freed me in a way.

I loved Riyan with every fiber of my soul, but love did not just come in one color. It did not abide by the laws of time, or sense, or reality.

Riyan was my eternity of red, but Derrick was my blue. He was the yarn of a winter shawl, the sparkle of starlit tears, and the ever-changing sky.

I had loved him and yet I had earned his hatred. He never asked to be bound in the strife of the mortal and the deathless. Though his hands were not bloodless, he still did not deserve the cruelty of our circumstances.

If I could not change anything…I at least wanted him to be happy.

"This is how our stars align, Midnight," I said. "This is how we shine forever. It was always supposed to be us, right?"

My chest was warm and my breath was calm. If Daigen just wanted me to free the truth to finally have peace in my last moments of freedom, then I was grateful I had trusted him one last time.

Derrick trembled though his face stayed hard. He was fighting something, whether it was the pain in his body or the urge to exact revenge against me. His eyes were hollow and dark. Blood lined his lips.

Derrick's eyes swept to look behind me and his low voice cut through the air like a knife. "Come forward, Fraleigh."

The hem of Fraleigh's robes whispered along the floor. Her cerulean aura was gone and her features had softened. She looked exactly like the teenager I had seen in her memories.

The air shifted as she approached, getting heavier and heavier around my shoulders. The bargain in my blood sang.

He had accepted.

I swallowed, the muscles in my neck pulsing without the weight of the collar. The bargain dissipated out of my skin, satisfied.

A life for a life given in love.

Derrick's hands disappeared under the curtain of Fraleigh's black hair.

"*Ipse Dixit,*" he murmured. Fraleigh gasped as the collar released. "It means, 'it is what I say it is…'"

He stood in front of me, the ring of gold open toward me like gilded jaws ready to clamp down on my neck.

"…and I say it is over."

Snap.

My heart froze. I could not breathe. Derrick held the two broken pieces of the golden collar in his hands for just a moment before throwing them to the floor with a clatter.

Twelve generations of power was now in pieces at my feet.

Derrick's entire body shook. I was frozen in place as my eyes darted from the broken collar to Fraleigh. Her hands rubbed her bare neck as her eyes watered.

Derrick's hand shakily unclasped his steel breastplate as I stood speechless. My bargain was satisfied, but how? The collar did not go on. I was supposed to sacrifice my life for Riyan's—that was the deal.

Derrick's armor clattered to the floor along with his cape. He lifted his face and his beautiful blue eyes stole the breath from my lungs. A ghost of a smile traced his lips. The door between his eyes opened and three notes from a harp sang softly in my mind.

Midnight was always there for me, he had said. He kept me safe from Alastar.

My Derrick was back.

Fire sparked in my feet as I raced for him. I crashed into his chest, throwing my arms around his shaking body.

White light passed from my skin into his. My magic warmed his muscles until it banished the bruises forming under his skin. My thread of infinity wrapped around each of his fractured ribs and pulled them back together.

His body was healed, but I still soared across the magical tether into his mind and found Midnight himself standing amongst the smoldering ruins of a paper castle. He was covered in blood and his shining eyes flicked down Alastar's corpse—torn in half down the middle.

His love was pure enough to finally slay Alastar.

"It is over," Midnight said with a shaking laugh. "It is over."

"It is over," I heard against my hair.

I pulled out of Derrick's mind and looked up at his colorless face. Slowly, Derrick dropped to his knees.

His eyes glistened as he looked up at me. "They need power. I have none anymore. None." His trembling hands rose to his head. "And since there is no one alive more powerful than you, Serafina Helia…"

He lifted the crown of Lycaster from his brow and presented it to me.

My hands floated forward and took the crown from his hands. The crown of Lycaster was mine. After all this time…it was *mine.*

I could not believe it. I had the power of my magic, Riyan at my side, and the entire Dukedom at my disposal.

I had everything I ever wanted.

But the crown was cold against my fingertips. No power emanated from it. No promises of glory came from its spiked peaks.

It was just a ring of gold in my hands.

Though in someone else's hands, the crown could be a stepping stone to greatness. The laurels of a righteous champion. The promise of a breaking dawn.

I cast out my magic until I heard the flutter of flipping pages hiding in the hallway—listening in.

"Brietta," I called.

The guards moved away from the door. Brietta cautiously stepped past them, wringing her hands in front of her. Her eyes dropped from my bare neck to the crown in my hands.

Her face blanched. "Sera, how are you—?"

"Ready to finish what Freya started?" I lifted the crown a little higher.

Her eyes watered and her hand pressed against her lips. Her head shook once…

…but then she gracefully lowered to her knees.

A smile pulled at my lips as I placed the crown on Brietta's auburn brow.

Footsteps clicked in the doorway and we both looked up. Annalisa's hands pressed against the doorframe. Her mouth dropped the moment she saw the crown on Brietta's head.

Derrick's voice was low. "Am I still an ass?"

Brietta and I turned around to face him. He still knelt on the floor beside the broken collar and Alastar the Conqueror's discarded armor. His eyes were heavy as he looked at Brietta.

For the first time, Brietta was speechless. "I-I, you…" She took a deep breath and straightened her spine. "I suppose not."

Derrick hummed. "I assume you have no regnal name in mind? Unless you *did* plan to depose me all along?"

Brietta's cheeks turned pink as she shook her head. I could not help but smile.

Derrick rose and took a step toward Brietta. I took a step back, giving him enough space to hold out his hand. Brietta looked up, held her breath for only a moment, but accepted his help.

He smiled softly as he lifted her off the floor. "Brietta the first, then?"

She nodded and Annalisa and I exchanged glances. Derrick was building the bridge between them all on his own.

He straightened the crown on Brietta's head. "All hail Brietta."

"All hail Brietta," I repeated.

"Only if I have to," Annalisa said with a smirk.

Brietta's eyes glittered as she looked over her shoulder at Annalisa.

"Now we just have to figure out what to do about Uncle Ragnar." Derrick spat out the name like it stung his throat. He picked up the pieces of the steel breastplate off the ground.

I swallowed. "He is dying. Slowly. My mother poisoned him."

Derrick flashed a wicked smile. "Good. One less thing to worry about."

A weight pulled in my chest. General Ragnar Hyton would not go down quietly. If he had spent two decades crafting his plan, he had to have an escape route—one final trick to play.

Derrick walked back to Brietta and attached the two halves of armor around her chest.

Brietta's cheeks went as red as her hair as Derrick snapped the latches on the sides of her ribs. "You may hold the crown of Lycaster in your own right, but many outside these walls will not like it." He secured the latches on Brietta's other side.

"But you are the ruling Duchess," Annalisa said as she leaned against the door frame. "You are a *Hyton.* Make them accept it."

He snapped the final latch. Brietta's breath heaved, her breasts squished so they filled the chest of the armor.

Her eyes flicked up to Derrick's face and they both held their breath. Annalisa and I shot each other a quick glance, neither of us knowing what was to come from the stalemate between them.

Derrick dropped his gaze and cleared his throat. "You do not have to believe me now, but I will tell you every day for seventy years if I have to…" He finally looked up at her. "I *never* would have just let you die."

Brietta smiled. Through the power I inherited from Fraleigh, I sensed the golden ribbon twisting around Brietta's chest. The blood bond she shared with Derrick did not burn or ache, but instead shined—only a little, but enough to see that she had grabbed on to her end of the bond again.

Soft sobs trickled into the room from the hallway. I stepped around Brietta and looked past Annalisa through the door. Daigen clutched Fraleigh, his cheek mashed against hers, as she softly cried with a wide smile.

Daigen's thumb stroked her neck over and over. "I did it. I finally killed him."

After nearly five centuries, the Conqueror was gone.

I turned my head toward the sound of heavy panting. Endre sprinted down the hall and his eyes flared as soon as he saw Daigen. Fraleigh screamed as Endre grabbed Daigen by the shirt and slammed him into the wall.

"The hell did you do to my baby sister?" Endre growled. "You said you were helping her! How the fuck did you deceive me—?"

"Endre, no!" I pushed against his arms until he looked over at me. I lifted my chin to show him my bare neck. "Derrick snapped the collar and gave up his crown. I am fine!"

"I never deceived you, asshole," Daigen choked. "You know I couldn't."

A mixture of relief and panic flashed across Endre's face all at once. He released Daigen from the wall and raked his hand through his messy hair as he tried to find his breath. "He does not know…"

Ice spiked through my veins, knowing exactly who he was referring to. "What is happening with Riyan?"

Endre's eyes were wide. "He claimed the crown. He says he is the Duke of Lycaster."

My heart raced. I had told him I would be the slave to the Duke. The magic of the collar was bound to the *Duke,* not Derrick.

"He cannot do that!" Annalisa scoffed. "Just because he has Hyton blood does not mean he can—"

"He challenged his father over his claim, a trial by combat," Endre said with a knitted brow. "He opened the challenge to anyone in the Dukedom—whoever makes him fall has the crown."

Annalisa's eyebrows raised. "Uncle Ragnar still stands?"

Endre's face blanched as he looked at me. "He told me it was the only way he could free you."

My throat seized. I lifted on my toes and sprinted past Endre before he could stop me. Annalisa screamed at Derrick to follow her. Brietta shouted down the hall. I drowned them all out as blood pulsed through my body.

I never sacrificed my life to let Death balance the scale, so Riyan was not deathless like I had assured him he would be.

Still, he issued his own Alastar trial, a fight to the death to win the crown…

…and he did not know he was mortal.

I paused at the open door of the keep, wrapping my fingers around the frame as I froze.

The Bloodstone Fortress gate was wide open. Riyan stood alone in front of the gate, an axe in his hand.

General Hyton stood in front of him with a smile on his face.

Ready to make his final move.

Chapter Fifty Five
The Final Giant

The two Hyton bulls stood head-to-head at the fortress gate. Father against son.

The once great General Hyton looked sickly and weak, the veins in his neck stained black and his arms twitching. Riyan's muscles were tense. The turmoil in his blood bond raged, the waves in his mind crashing into the rocky beach with the force of an entire sea.

I splayed my fingers and our bond lit up.

"Riyan, Derrick let me go. I am free. Come back—"

"My son," General Hyton said, his voice lined with pride and admiration, "strong and unyielding—a true Hyton heir."

Riyan's grip on his axe loosened. The army rattled with cheers and exaltation.

Something rippled through Riyan's muscles, a different kind of magic, one that I had used to practice for years before acquiring the gift of sorcery.

General Hyton had moved all the pawns in place to take the crown. The only piece left was the one in front of him.

And the General knew *exactly* how to manipulate his best soldier.

"I had to hide the truth from you to keep you safe," his voice was smooth as honey with a break of false devastation carefully placed between words. The brass plates on his shoulders shook as his chest twitched. "My brother tried to kill you so many times. I had to be hard on you so no one else would suspect."

Riyan's shoulders sagged.

I threw out another command as I descended the stairs. "*Riyan, he is manipulating you! He is dying and just wants you to save him!*"

Riyan shook off my command. He was clinging to that hope of the family he always wanted. I could tell him that his father had attempted to coerce me into bearing his heir and snap him out of that fantasy…but I would devastate him.

I just had to keep trying to make him see sense.

My feet hit the grass. I picked up my skirt and threw out another command as I ran to the middle of the courtyard. "*Riyan, no! Brietta has the crown! She will heal Lycaster! Do not listen to him!*"

General Hyton's eyes glistened even though black lines creeped toward his irises. Riyan's entire body went still as his father placed a twitching hand on his shoulder.

"I wanted so badly to be your father all those years and now I can be," General Hyton promised. "We can be a new House of Hyton, son. You and Serafina can start our family."

Riyan took another breath. Our bond tingled in my veins as he sent me a message. "*I don't want him to die, Sera. I could have a second chance with my father. If you could just take the poison out—*"

"A new House of Hyton?" cried a voice from the sky.

I stopped just before I reached the gate and looked up. Derrick was at the top of the keep's most southern tower, standing between the battlements with a small figure in his arms. Annalisa stood behind him, her hands gripping the back of his shirt so he would not fall.

The small body in his arms shifted and looked out—Astrid.

No one could ignore the last Bloodstone daughter as Derrick held her out for the entire army to see.

Astrid stretched out her hand.

"Ragnar!" she cried, her voice ringing like a small bell through the heavy air. "Ragnar!"

I turned. Riyan looked up at his mother with watering eyes. General Hyton's body shook with tremors, but his face softened—like he just felt the caress of crimson ribbons against his skin again.

"You want a new House of Hyton?" Derrick roared. "A new, strong House of Hyton would not throw its daughters away." He held Astrid up a little higher. "*This* is what you did for the power you seek! You manipulated a school girl, you tricked her into a pregnancy, and you abandoned her!"

My heart swelled. Derrick had backed General Hyton into a corner. The Barons and the army would not accept that their strong, ruthless General would ever let feelings for a seemingly broken woman soften him.

If General Hyton chose Astrid, the following that he had built on blood and supremacy would topple. Even though I knew the monster he was, how the craven push for supremacy had destroyed him, he still had a heart left.

So I held my breath and hoped that he finally chose her.

The General's trembling face turned to ice. He turned on his heel and faced the Barons. "The mad Duke's last effort to secure his line is to use a mad woman. How fitting."

Astrid wilted in Derrick's arms as her hand curled back to her chest. Her weak sobs traveled through the air like blue butterflies.

Riyan's blood blazed as he turned from his crying mother to face his father.

The General chose poorly.

Even though I was a master of sorcery, I never abandoned my old talents. Like a serpent in the rocks, I still knew the best time to strike.

With a pounding yet heavy heart, I sent the message into Riyan's mind. "*He does not care about being a family. He tried to force me into a blood bond so I could bear him a new heir.*"

Vermillion rage surged through our bond. Riyan set his jaw and gave Derrick a knowing look. Derrick returned with a nod.

Riyan gripped his axe handle.

Derrick covered Astrid's eyes.

"Look at that pathetic sod on top of the tower," General Hyton shouted, "trying to sway you with the tears of a stupid—"

Chop.

I lifted my chin as I watched the black blood spill out of General Hyton's severed neck. The sky shimmered for a moment, revealing a white raven that only I could see. The raven descended to earth to take the son she loved to the other side.

Riyan's back muscles shook. Red waves churned and crashed in his mind. Slowly, Riyan's trembling arm raised as he held up the head of Ragnar Hyton, General of the Lycaster army, and the famed Little Diamond in front of the six Barons.

Riyan had slayed his final giant.

"Who is next?" Riyan roared. Even the mountain shook from the power of his fury. "Who dares to challenge the last Hyton heir—"

Riyan's head snapped back. The tail of an arrow stuck out of his right eye.

And the diamond in my heart exploded.

Chapter Fifty Six
Vengeance

I only registered the sound of Riyan's body hitting the ground as my body filled with light.

I did not know who had fired the deadly arrow…but they would pay.

They would *all* pay.

I screamed, holding the heat of a blazing star in my throat. Thunder cracked at my command and the clouds poured down on the fortress. My hands twisted around the magic in the rain. My feet left the ground.

Every one of the Man of the Mountain's tears in the rain, in the grass, and in the blood of the men outside of the Bloodstone Fortress gate lit up in burning barbs of pure pain. My blood was the sun. My scream was the terror of the night.

There was no sky or ground. There was no air.

There was only my hunger for vengeance.

Cries of anguish echoed in the distance. The soldiers of the Lycaster army dropped to their knees, pressing their faces into the mud as they screamed. All of their minds and hearts opened as they begged like worms for me to do *anything* to ease their torment.

The fabric between worlds stretched at the seams. Mere memories became monsters. Freya's laughter shrieked through the air. The agonized cries of brother slain by brother tore through the clouds. Barbarian iron clashed with Latiman steel. The Man of the Mountain's wails filled the sky and suddenly I was not alone.

Someone else was within me—someone I knew, but had never met.

Her power flowed within me. I was her hands and feet. I carried her heart.

The first sorceress.

Then the flames around my heart grew until there was no separation between my body and the magic. I was light. I was punishment. I was justice.

I was a fucking monster.

My bones bent and my skin hardened into scales. I pushed into the sky, using the raindrops like a path to crawl down each of the hundreds of trembling tethers. I slithered through the army's disgusting minds, my tongue flicking out as I smelled their evil deeds and my fangs glimmering as I hunted down the guilty.

Then I found him. The false hero. The gutter rat that preyed on the vulnerable.

Grigory Orion Thornebow.

He was hunched over on the ground, his bow near his left hand. I hissed through my fangs and his head snapped up in agony as I scorched him from within. His brown eyes popped open and widened when they saw me.

"What are you?" he asked with a trembling whisper.

My power dragged through the rain as I formed a dark and icy claw in the air. A guttural cry tore from my mouth as I forced the claw down Gigory's screaming throat. I curled the talons around the golden blood bond, the precious gift forged from selfless love.

A gift he did not fucking deserve.

My claw gripped the bond. The fabric between worlds strained.

"Grigory Thornebow," I hissed, my voice magnified on every drop of pouring rain. The voice of the first sorceress braided with my own, magnifying her ancient rage.

"You do not deserve the magic of my sacrifice." I yanked on the bond and the golden light leached from his veins and twisted into a rope. The faint glowing line arced through the sky toward the southernmost tower of the fortress, connecting with Annalisa.

I pulled, but Grigory stubbornly held on, even through the torture.

I bared my fangs and threw my power behind me. My vision cleared through the magic in the raindrops—Annalisa and Derrick curled behind the battlements and sheltered Astrid with their bodies.

I focused on Annalisa, letting my words echo in the air around her.

"Let go, Anna." My voice was warm as the golden fire of my power, but it was not a command. It was a choice.

Annalisa kept her eyes squeezed shut as she gripped the bond.

A gentle voice echoed through the rain. "Let go of him, Lis. I am here. I have not been…and I am sorry."

Annalisa gripped her twin brother.

"I want you back," Derrick said into her curls. "I miss you too."

The two halves of the same soul wove together.

So Annalisa took a deep breath and let go.

The blood bond shredded as I yanked it out of Grigory's body. It dissipated in the air, returning to the clouds like it was nothing more than a lightning strike. Both the bond and the curse in Annalisa's blood gently evaporated out of her skin.

She was free.

My heartbeat slowed. My power drew inward. The light emanating from me dimmed and panicked voices grew louder and louder amongst the calming rainfall.

"Sera!" Endre shouted. "Sera! Look down!"

My body returned to flesh and bone as I descended in the air, light as a feather. I blinked and my vision cleared.

A tall, golden-haired warrior rose to his feet at the gate with Grigory Thornebow's black-tipped arrow in his hand. He clenched his fist and the arrow snapped in half, each end falling on top of the discarded head of his father. His cheek was stained with trails of blood, but two twilight eyes looked back at me.

Warmth filled my body as my toes touched the earth.

Riyan was deathless, just like the Man of the Mountain had said. But I never went under the collar. I never sacrificed myself. Derrick…

My heart stopped. I looked up at the tower and caught a peek of Derrick's dark curls as he comforted his twin.

Derrick had broken the collar and killed Alastar. He gave up everything, his throne, his crown, his *life*. He gave up his life because he loved me.

A life for a life given in love—Derrick's sacrifice balanced the scale and made Riyan deathless.

Riyan's eyes twinkled as they glanced behind me. His voice rang out through the soft rain, strong and clear. "Only the one who can force me to kneel rules Lycaster."

Then the kiss of a blade pressed against my neck. Cold steel pressed against my back. I forced down a smile.

"I have your sorceress, beast!" Brietta shouted. "Kneel!"

A small smirk crept up on Riyan's face and we exchanged glances. The ruler of Lycaster could not be handed power, she had to *take* it.

Riyan slowly knelt and laid his axe in front of him. He lowered the crown of his head to the top of his knee.

The last Hyton heir had yielded.

Brietta lowered the blade from my neck and I turned. She gave Evereon the Hyton dagger as he handed her the Conqueror's spear. The Taurus shield was strapped to her arm. Daylight broke through the clouds and illuminated the crown on her brow as a gentle breeze fluttered the Hyton Blue cape around her shoulders.

Brietta made her demands without ever opening her lips. She was a Hyton—stubborn, unyielding, and fixated on problems that she intended to solve.

Most importantly, she would show all of Lycaster that she had the spirit of the Conqueror.

She was ready to play her role and I needed to play mine. I had just tortured the entire Lycaster army, seen their evils, resurrected the phantoms of history, and ripped a blood bond before their very eyes. Unlike Fraleigh, I truly was powerful, and unlike Fraleigh…

…I would submit to the crown of my own will.

I swept my arms, letting my white sleeves billow in the breeze. Slowly, I lowered to my knees and bowed, ensuring that everyone outside the gate could see me.

The most powerful sorceress on earth would not kneel before a tyrant, but she would serve and protect a friend.

Brietta held the spear firmly in her hands, but a tiny smile that only I could see rose on her face. "Do you, Great Sorceress of Nordingaard, pledge yourself to the House of Hyton?"

A flush spread across my cheeks. "My eternity is yours, Brietta."

A low rumble echoed outside the gate as the Lycaster army realized the auburn-haired woman wielded not only the Conqueror's spear, but every bit of my power as well.

Brietta turned to the open gate and held the Conqueror's spear in front of her. With a swift jerk of her arms, she snapped the spear over her knee.

The army and the Barons gasped as the pieces of one of Lycaster's oldest relics fell to the dirt.

Brietta held her head high. With a signal from Evereon, trails of red-uniformed soldiers bled from the stone walls and flanked her.

She stepped through the open gate and Riyan rose to let her pass. He walked toward me, each one of his steps getting heavier and his shoulders sagging with the weight of what he had just done.

The whinny of a horse made my head snap to the gate. As soon as Father's mare made it into the courtyard, Father slid from the horse's back with Mother in his arms.

Mother's small body convulsed and twisted. The Thornebow thistle had her.

Brietta addressed the crowd outside the gate as Mother and Father crumpled into a heap. Her voice was bright as the dawn, "People of Lycaster—"

A muscle in Father's cheek twitched, even though his eyes stayed clear of any poison. Their blood bond was taking them both into the black fire.

Not if I got there first.

I ran through the soaked grass and dropped to my knees next to Mother.

"You did it, dear," Father whispered. "Ragnar is gone. Anders is gone. You avenged our boys."

Mother's eyes were squeezed shut. Something between a grimace and a strained smile spread across her twitching face.

I grabbed Mother's shaking hand as my white light flowed into her skin.

"*Easy there, Viper,*" I whispered into her mind as my magic purged the poison from her veins. "*Freya wants you to stay and see the new Lycaster.*"

Mother's heartbeat slowed. Her blood bond with Father glowed brighter as my white light extinguished the black flames.

A tear leaked onto her cheek as she slowly fluttered her eyes open.

"They are here, Frederick," Mother said as she looked up. "They came to take us to the other side."

I followed her eyes. Erik and Endre stood above me. Endre shook his head as he barely held tears back. Erik's face was still stoic, but his eyes watered.

I swallowed my cowardice and clutched Mother's hand. "No, Mother. You are alive and so are they. They never left us."

Her dark eyebrows knitted and I held back a wince. Just when I thought she was going to scream at me for keeping the truth from her, she launched out of Father's lap and flung herself into Endre's waiting arms. She buried her face in his shoulder and her chest rattled with sobs.

"My boy!" Father cried as he crushed Erik to his chest.

A large hand appeared at my side. I took it as Riyan slowly helped me up.

Brietta's speech continued over my parents' joyous sobs. "No more shall brother turn against brother. No more shall the provinces fight with one another."

Riyan nearly folded in half as he wrapped his arms around me and rested his head on mine. I took in a breath of nectar and wheat as I stroked his hair.

"Breathe, Riyan," I whispered into his chest.

He let out a hollow chuckle. "Don't need to do that anymore."

I pressed my cheek against his heartbeat. "Then do it because it feels good."

"Nothing feels good right now."

I pulled away slightly, only so he could look me in the eyes. "It does not have to." I sent a sweep of magic over his skin, cleaning the trails of crimson blood from his cheek and the splatter of black blood from his hands. "Feel the grief and the pain and the sorrow. Let yourself feel everything because I will feel it all with you."

He kissed me on the forehead and the light of our bond sang, but his eyes drifted to the top of the southernmost tower. Derrick held both Annalisa and Astrid as they cried, their sobs barely audible amongst the triumphant celebration.

"What can we do?" Riyan said in a heavy sigh.

Brietta's voice rose over the fortress walls. "We shall progress! We shall fix what is broken!"

I eyed Astrid. "I made a promise and I intend to keep it."

"And tomorrow," Brietta said, "the dawn shall break on a new, better, glorious Lycaster!"

Chapter Fifty Seven
Eternally Yours

Not even an hour after the golden sunrise spilled onto Bloodstone Fortress, Brietta dipped her quill into the inkwell.

The Barons all gathered in the dining hall to sign the new Lycaster charter Brietta had drafted. Soldiers in both red and blue uniforms lined the walls to bear witness. Some of Lycaster's army, including Grigory Thornebow, had fled the moment I had released my power over them.

If I never saw Grigory again, it would be too soon.

Riyan and I stood on either side of Brietta as the Barons prepared to sign. We were her immortals, her shield and sword.

Baron Elvar was the first to sign the charter. He added his large signature with a flourish, but not before cutting Riyan an icy glare.

"*I don't trust him,*" Riyan said through our bond.

I kept my eyes on Baron Elvar's back as he walked away. "*Me neither. He is not going to just let go of his Little Diamond being taken away.*"

Baron Amberfield was next in line with the quill and the other Barons followed behind him. The Barons had agreed to grant every woman in Lycaster equal rights and privileges in exchange for a full pardon for their treasonous sedition. Evereon had suggested at least cutting off a finger to serve as a reminder, but Brietta stressed that her rule was based on progress and healing. To prove that point, Brietta reinstated the Baronage of Ravenwood.

The golden Ravenwood pin gleamed on Father's chest as he added his signature at the bottom of the charter. He gave Riyan an approving smile before returning to stand with Mother. Mother held both Erik's and Endre's hands, her smile rosy as a fresh blossom.

Only one more Baron needed to sign.

"*I hope this works,*" Riyan whispered through our bond.

Annalisa handed Magnus to Rosaline and she broke away from the crowd. The pack of Hyton sisters whispered to each other.

Derrick had decided to remain out of sight so he would not darken the occasion with the past. I was glad he was not there to react to what was about to happen.

Even though her eyes were downcast, Annalisa kept her spine pin-straight like a proper Ashmore student as she walked to the center of the room.

I sent a whisper of confidence into her mind, reminding her of what the three lionesses had discussed the night before. She clicked her nails together once before looking up.

"There was no such thing as an unmarried noble woman before today." Her voice was dry, but she swallowed and gathered her strength. "But a new Lycaster gave us choices."

Annalisa glanced at my parents. "I choose to join the House of Ravenwood, to honor my grandmother," she cleared her throat and then her voice rang out, "Ilsa Ravenwood."

The crowd murmured. Ilsa's name was no longer verboten.

Elation splashed across my parents' faces, and, just as I predicted, Endre unclasped his green cape.

Daigen was not the only one who could predict the choices of others with exact precision.

I suppressed a smile as Endre strode over to Annalisa and wrapped the cape around her shoulders. He gave her a soft smile and kissed her hand. "Welcome, Annalisa Ravenwood."

"*Go, Riyan,*" I prodded through our bond.

"And on the same…theme." Riyan's voice faded. He forgot his lines. I had no idea why Brietta had insisted on giving Riyan a script.

Riyan reached into his pocket and pulled out the golden Bloodstone pin. "We cannot choose how we are born…or who we are born to," he walked forward until he stood in front of Endre. Annalisa shot me a sly glance and backed up as she held the green cape around her shoulders.

Endre looked up at Riyan with a quizzical look. Riyan smiled back at him. "On the recommendation of Captain Mydina of the Bloodstone army, I pass the Baronage of Bloodstone to the fearless Endre Ravenwood."

Erik's face blanched as his younger brother slowly took the pin. Endre flashed Riyan a smile. "You really think a bird can be a Baron?" Riyan returned the smile. "Better than an immortal bastard like me."

Endre winked and fastened the golden pin of the snarling bear to his chest. He unsheathed the dueling sword at his hip with a quick flourish and gave the crowd a gentleman's bow. "An honor to serve the North."

The crowd returned Endre's bow with warm applause, even Annalisa clapped with fervor, but I could not help but notice Erik's ice-cold glare.

Just as I predicted Endre's acceptance of the Bloodstone baronage, I also knew our stuffy big brother would be furious about it.

Riyan and I both snuck out of the keep as the celebration feast began. Riyan left first, saying he was going to bury his father in a place so secret that not even the ravens would find him. When he disappeared, I headed for the door with the painted flowers.

Daigen held Astrid in his arms as the three of us stepped through the air to the snowy peak of Nordingaard. Slowly, I lowered her into the churning rainbow well with me.

In the darkness of the chasm, I summoned Astrid's mind. She appeared through the dark water, but the body I held in my arms was no longer hers, having aged twenty-two years without her.

None of it seemed fair…or balanced.

My power formed a ribbon of white light that slithered through the darkness and pressed against the veil into the next world. The cold hand that I had seen once before answered me.

Just as the first sorceress had fought Death over an injustice, so did I.

Astrid's life was stolen from her, I argued. Her life must be returned to her.

Appeased by my reasoning, the darkness in the chasm began to swirl around us. My healing light poured into Astrid's body as her mind returned to it. I erased wrinkles, strengthened her muscles, and returned the freckles to her face.

When I rose from the grave of millions of tears, the golden-haired girl in my arms was seventeen again.

We sheltered in Daigen's hovel for a few hours, taking turns to help Astrid navigate her body again. Despite me turning back the clock, her mind struggled to connect with flesh and bone. Wiggling her fingers was a triumph, taking steps would be near impossible.

But Astrid did not care if she never walked again, she just wanted to return to the fortress.

She had someone she was desperate to see.

I stepped through the air beneath a sky smeared with pink. We stood in the courtyard and Fraleigh had joined us, happy to see Astrid healed.

"Is he coming?" Astrid asked from Daigen's arms.

I pulled on my bond. "Soon, Astrid."

With a crunching footstep in the grass, we looked up. Riyan stepped out from behind the shadows of the tower, a bouquet of purple and white flowers in his hand.

His shoulders curved forward and he gave her a soft smile. "Mother, I—"

"Put me down!" Astrid cried as she pushed off Daigen's chest. Daigen gently dropped her legs and held onto her hand. I grabbed her other hand to keep her steady. She hissed out a determined breath and took her first step in the grass.

Her heartbeat pulsed in her wrist as she took another. She yanked her hands out of ours and sprinted for only a heartbeat before her knees buckled and she tumbled down.

Riyan ran for her. Daigen and I both lurched forward to help her, but Astrid snarled out a breath and crawled on her trembling forearms through the grass.

"Riyan!" She pulled forward as her body shook. "My baby! *Baby!*"

He dropped to his knees and pulled his mother into an embrace, pressing his cheek against hers. Astrid's trembling arms could not raise all the way, but a smile spread across her face as her fingers wrapped around Riyan's arm.

She *finally* held her baby.

I could not stop the tears that escaped. I looked over my shoulder for Daigen, but he was no longer in the courtyard.

The master of illusions had disappeared and he took Fraleigh with him. Free at last.

I stood against the wall as everyone danced—the ideal place to be. Evereon played his violin. Calder strummed the lute. Alastar the Conqueror's armor stood in the center of the feasting table. Annalisa and Astrid had painted a giant blue "B" in the center of the breastplate, surrounding it with thumbprint flower petals.

Mead poured freely as the new Baron of Bloodstone danced with every woman that he could get his hands on, as well as a few men.

I smiled as Endre picked Astrid up out of her wheeled chair as the music swelled. Astrid laughed as he held her in his arms and spun.

The door next to me clicked open and Annalisa stepped out. She brushed a tear from her eyes and folded her arms. "He did not take it well."

I leaned toward her so she could hear me over the music. "You are not leaving him, not really."

"That is what I told him—a dozen times." She pulled a familiar gleam of bronze from a belt around her waist. "Promising to keep this on me calmed him down."

The sight of the Hyton dagger in her hand warmed my heart.

"Love and protection?" I asked.

She smiled. "Something like that."

Annalisa looked out onto the crowd. Mother sat in Father's lap as they drank merrily. Erik stood with his shoulders against the opposite wall.

She sneered. "Do I have to stay with Bird Brain?"

I laughed. "Go find my mother—she always knows what to do." My eyes flicked to the closed door. "I will handle him."

Annalisa wrapped me into a hug as Endre bounded over.

"I have danced with most of your sisters already." He flashed Annalisa a charming smile and held out his hand. "I saved the best one for last."

Annalisa rolled her eyes, but accepted his hand as he pulled her into a dance. I turned around and let out a breath before I opened the door.

Derrick sat in front of the crackling fireplace, his arms folded over his knees. The room was surprisingly quiet despite the party outside.

I held my hands in front of my stomach. "She is going to be just fine, you know. We *all* will."

He turned to me. Alastar might have been dead, but his eyes were still hollow. "Some of us more than others."

I swallowed and tugged on my bond to beckon Riyan away from the mead barrels.

I took a few steps forward, erasing the distance between us. Derrick's eyes lingered on the Hyton Blue ribbons I had tied above my elbows.

I picked at the threads of my skirt as I found my voice. "I am sorry… for being so cruel to you."

He gave me a wan smile. "Truly I am the cruel one. I begged you to stay and yet I am the one who will leave in the end." His smile warmed. "Though whatever time I get on this earth, I am grateful to have a friend who will tolerate me."

I smiled back and gestured to the door. "You belong out there with us. You should be proud of what you have done."

He scoffed. "Proud? I am a stain on the Duchess's new reign. A burden of the past."

Before I could step in, a low voice filled the air. "Burden?"

Derrick and I turned our heads. Riyan held open the door as noise from the party flooded in. He clicked the door shut behind him and his brow creased as he stepped toward Derrick. "No man who gave what you did is ever a burden."

Derrick stiffly rose from his chair, but I took a step back. We had planned this meeting to be calmer, but I let Riyan handle it—man to man.

Riyan took a few steps forward but Derrick did not unclench.

"You freed Sera. And the girls. And my mother." Riyan's lip trembled only once. "And me."

Derrick's face softened.

"I remember thinking my life was nothing but bleak loneliness," Riyan said. "I thought I was broken, never to be fixed." His chest rose and fell as his eyes watered. "And if you think I am going to let the man who gave me an eternity of happiness go through the rest of his life alone in the dark, you are dead wrong."

Derrick's eyes widened as Riyan lowered to one knee. Riyan looked up at him and only a single heavy heartbeat passed before he spoke again. "Serafina gave her eternity to Brietta, but my eternity is *yours*. I will serve you, your line, and your legacy, though it will never be enough to repay what you have given me." His voice shook as tears gleamed in his eyes. "And I swear to you, so long as I walk this earth, you will be known to history as Alastar the Liberator."

Derrick's hard shell finally broke. He swallowed a trembling breath and his voice was low. "I…I have a few requests."

"Name them," Riyan said.

"First," Derrick said with a measured tone, "my Duchess needs a General."

My heart jumped as Riyan's eyebrows raised. After a thudding heartbeat, Riyan smoothed into steel. "Done."

"Then, I want you to swear to me, that even after I am dead…" Derrick's eyes swept to me. "Dance with her. Send her notes. Give her roasted hazelnuts just because. Never forget her birthday."

Tears lined my eyes. Warmth spread through my chest from that sweet ember that first showed me what love felt like.

Derrick gave me a soft smile and returned his attention to Riyan. "I will never see the end of eternity, but promise me that you will love her the entire way."

Riyan's eyes glistened. "Always."

Derrick lowered his arm and his smile grew. "Welcome to the new House of Hyton."

Riyan gripped Derrick's forearm and rose. He looked him in the eye for only a second before crushing him to his chest in an embrace.

My heart swelled, the rainbow flames twisted around my chest, and the red ember in my heart glowed as Derrick's beautiful blue eyes looked over Riyan's shoulder at me.

Even though Derrick would one day leave me, that little red ember would blaze in my heart as long as it was beating.

I would love him. I would protect his children and his grandchildren. I would be his friend as his skin wrinkled and his hair bleached. I would cry at his grave.

Even as thousands of midnights passed on the timeline, Riyan and I would stand beside him.

So I looked into his Hyton Blue eyes and sent a message into his mind. From Birdie to Midnight.

We were, and forever would be,

"*Eternally yours.*"

Epilogue

Annalisa

When I was young, I was Lady Hyton. When I married, I thought I would be Princess Annalisa.

But as I stood in Bloodstone Fortress with a goblet of mead in my hand, I had earned a new title I had never heard of before: Divorced.

The word only existed outside of Lycaster, but it had still crept through the party and strangled me like a vine.

Soldiers and maids danced to celebrate their new Baron in the cavernous dining hall, but a few eyes occasionally tossed me a look as I stood to the side. No one really knew what to make of me, the divorced woman.

And even though I had chosen to claim the House of Ravenwood as my new home, I was not sure what to make of myself either.

Without being a wife…who was I?

I drained my goblet and looked across the hall. Endre sat atop the feasting table, filling goblets of mead from the spout of a barrel and handing them to the starry-eyed women who gathered around him.

I licked my lips. His dancing was delightful…until the touch of his skin sent a screech through my body like nails on slate and I ran away.

Endre's wide smile as he chatted with the other women might have been evidence that I had not hurt his pride, but I knew better.

A calming breath blew over my lips as I tucked a curl behind my ear. I needed to talk to him again, at least to convince him that I never wanted to reject him.

I just…was scared of being touched.

I clutched my goblet and gathered my skirt to walk across the crowded hall.

"We need to talk," said a stern voice.

I yelped and dropped my goblet. I whipped around, my heart pounding against my ribs only to find Erik standing next to me. His hands were tightly folded behind his back as he looked at me expectantly.

The judging looks of the crowd pricked the back of my neck. Embarrassment from my sudden outburst flared across my cheeks, but I shoved it down.

"Why the fuck would you sneak up on me?" I hissed in a whisper.

His black eyes scanned the crowd behind me. "How can anyone sneak up on you at a party? I merely walked to you."

I quickly bent over and picked up my goblet, pretending I had never dropped it in the first place. "Fuck off, Erik. Can you not see that I am busy?"

"You can make a fool of yourself with the others later," he said dryly. "We have matters to discuss."

I furrowed my brows and scoffed. Make a *fool* of myself?

"Who are you to judge me?" I poked him in the center of the chest. "Maybe you did not hear me in the hall earlier, but I get to choose who I am and what I do with my life."

He looked down his crooked nose at me and did not even blink. "And all I am asking you to do is choose when you move into Ravenwood Manor."

Move into Ravenwood Manor? With *him?*

I folded my arms. "I am not moving into the manor."

A small crease appeared between his dark eyebrows. "You are a Ravenwood now, where else do you intend to stay?"

I was not going to let him win. I stood my ground, clawing through my deepest memories. "My grandmother had a house at the base of the mountain. I shall stay there and be the lady of my *own* house."

"You cannot manage an entire house alone," he countered.

"Oh, I will not be alone," I said with a confident smile. I quickly scanned the crowd of drunken faces. "I will have…only the best…"

My eyes settled on a curvy woman with chestnut braids speaking to Evereon Mydina.

"Rosaline!" I snapped my eyes back to Erik's and smiled. "Now that Fraleigh has disappeared, she needs someone to employ her. It is the *perfect* situation."

I thought Erik would accept defeat and finally leave me be, but no, he was a stone wall. He was worse than his damn sister!

His chin dipped slightly and his voice dropped. "That house has been abandoned for decades."

I held back a shudder at the thought of cobwebs stringing through my living space, but I could not back down now. "You doubt my ability as lady of the house?"

"Not in the summer." He leaned closer, as if invading my space was going to convince me of anything. "But in the winter, you will freeze."

I kept my smile on and leaned in. "Then I will just need to find someone to keep me warm." I pointedly flicked my gaze over his shoulder. "And if you will excuse me, I need to have a drink with your brother."

His face was all granite. I won.

I turned away, victorious, when he caught my arm.

My head snapped toward him. A scathing curse sat on my tongue, but the weight of his gaze silenced me.

Erik's voice dropped so low that only I could hear him. "When are you going to stop pretending you are all right?"

I tried to swallow, remembering the golden light that had poured out of my mouth and left me with nothing inside. My choice was supposed to be my freedom, but I was still chained to a deep craving, one that plagued my thoughts, my dreams, and each time I glanced in a mirror and found dark brown eyes glaring back at me.

But I would never admit that to a nosy, overgrown bird.

I glanced down at the flash of black markings on Erik's knuckles that his sleeves failed to hide. I looked back into his charcoal eyes and a smile crept across my lips. "When are you going to stop pretending you were merely lost on the mountain for seven years, Bird Brain?"

His face blanched and I yanked my arm out of his grip. I turned before he could say any more and marched into the swirling crowd.

The cackles of the dancers blared in my ears like a tidal wave, so I kept my eyes on the floor as I walked. My hand floated up to my chest, my fingertips gliding along my bare clavicle.

When my blood bond with Grigory had vanished, I tore off my golden Thornebow pendant and shoved it in a drawer in Astrid's room. Now all I could think about was that Thornebow fox sitting amongst Astrid's linens with my old, useless name etched beneath its tail.

I could run to an abandoned house in the most northern part of Ravenwood, hide in the dust of the past, and shut out every man in my life…but that craving at the bottom of my chest could still pull me back.

And Grigory's words, dripping with tainted love, caressed the back of my mind again, "*Fate will always bring you back to me.*"

"Well, look who came back!" said a merry voice.

I snapped my head up to find Endre's smiling face. He shot me a wink. "You here for another dance?"

I forced on a smile and smoothed my voice. "How could I stay away?" I delicately raised my empty goblet. "But first, I need a drink."

Coming soon in the
Lycaster series...

The adventure continues! Follow Annalisa's journey through a
new world of choices, freedom, and love in...
"The Lady of Lycaster"

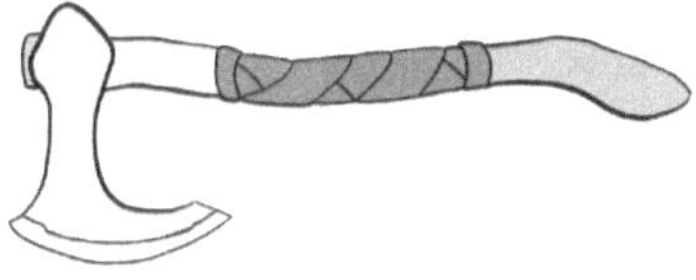

Experience Riyan's war between his mind and his heart and see
the events of *"The Bride of Lycaster"* through his eyes in...
"The Monster of Lycaster"

Serafina

"What if I told Beauty and the Beast, but made Beauty a liar? What if I gave her trauma? What if I made her angry, and bitter, and messy, but she still got her happy ending anyway?"

What started as a fun series of "what if"s ended in a years-long journey of self-discovery and healing—not just for me, but for so many of you wonderful readers out there.

Though the journey was never easy. Sometimes I hated Serafina, sometimes I *was* Serafina, and sometimes I thought she was too difficult of a character to get right and I wanted to give up.

Well, friends, I'm glad I never gave up on her. I am forever going to be proud of my girl who shattered her granite heart and became a sorceress.

Thank you for never giving up on her, either.

And for all you Serafinas out there, you always deserve love. No matter what.

Eternally yours, Perci Jay.

CHARACTER ART BY AMY MARCHANT

Acknowledgements

Firstly, thank you for reading. I left you dangling on that cliffhanger and you still came back to see if Serafina was really going to save him. I am grateful for each and every one of you. I hope you're ready for all else Lycaster has in store.

To my editor, Hina at Faemance: Thank you for being honest with me even when it breaks me a little. Was it painful to rewrite this book again? Yes. Was it necessary? YES. It was an immense challenge to make a story as different as this work, but you had the talent to turn an angsty mess into a tear-jerking wonder that it was always meant to be.

To Erin and Georgie: You read the freshly-written garbage that was the first draft two years ago and still believed in it. We did it, lionesses. Long live Brietta.

To Lauren, Magda, and Krista: Thank you for listening to the plot of this story in restaurant booths, in the car, or on the phone when I started talking and could not stop. Thank you for asking me the tough questions and helping me build Lycaster.

To J.B.: Thank you for dragging me across the finish line and picking me up during the countless emotional breakdowns I had during this process. I'm so grateful I got to publish a sequel by your side. Also, thank you for reminding me to check for typos in my acknowledgements section. Leaving one in would be really embarasing.

To Professor Fraley: Thank you for both terrifying me and inspiring me so much that I could not have modeled an omnipotent sorceress after anyone else.

To Carl: Ten years later and I still love the song. Thank you for composing it for me.

To my brother-in-law, Erik: See? He didn't die!

To BookTok and everyone in the Lycaster discord: Thank you for always lifting my spirits during the rough parts and magnifying my joy during the good. You are the bright spot in my day every day and I am so grateful for you.

To my daughter, T.J.: Please do not read this until you are much older, but thank you for being patient with me while I was always working. You never needed help finding your roar.

To Ryan, my eternity: Thank you for always being there and reminding me to breathe. Thank you for believing in me, my career, and my stories. I love you.

About the Author

Perci Jay was first inspired to write when dealing with those pesky emotions that came hand-in-hand with training bras and boys not texting her back. After 16 years of ideas, Perci composed a dynamic love story full of tragedy, sacrifice, and spicy scenes that make her pray her parents never buy a copy.

When not practicing law or teaching her daughter to smash the patriarchy, Perci is watching "Beauty and the Beast" for the millionth time, debating the finer points of morally grey men with her husband, and running at an excruciatingly slow pace around her neighborhood in the heart of Texas.

www.percijayauthor.com

TikTok: percijay_fantasyauthor   Instagram: percijay_fantasyauthor
Threads: @percijay_author   Pinterest: PerciJay

Discussion Questions

1. How did Serafina's inability to lie affect her relationships with others?

2. Which "Hyton lie" hurt Serafina the most?

3. How was Serafina different from the villains? How was she the same?

4. How was Derrick different from his ancestors?

5. Was Anders Hyton a true villain or was he a produt of his circumstances?

6. Was Adalia more motivated by love or hate?

7. Why did Serafina choose Riyan instead of staying with Derrick?

8.	Could Riyan and his father have reconciled?

9.	What will Annalisa do with her new life?

10.	What will a new Lycaster look like?